STORM FORCE

STORM FORCE

SUSANNAH SANDLIN

Text copyright © 2013 Susannah Sandlin
Originally published as a Kindle Serial March 2013

Published by Montlake Romance
PO Box 400818
Las Vegas, NV 89140

ISBN-13: 9781477807576
ISBN-10: 1477807578
Library of Congress Control Number: 2013904923

Dedication

*To Roger and Isabelle, who've followed every book
and blog post,
every step of the way. You're what makes this
journey worthwhile.*

❁

EPISODE 1

᭟PROLOGUE᭟

The windows on the outside wall bowed slightly, as if taking a deep breath and then releasing it. Texas governor Carl Felderman's first thought was that an earthquake had hit somewhere to the south. It wouldn't be a first—a big earthquake in Mexico City back in the 1980s had caused the sixty-four-story Williams Tower on the west side of Houston to sway.

Then again, the outside air was so damned hot, it was probably an optical illusion, like when a parking lot seems to shimmer from the heated air bouncing off the scorched steel of the parked cars.

No one else in the plush conference room on the fiftieth story of Houston's Zemurray Building seemed to notice, so Carl continued his well-rehearsed spiel. "Gentlemen, I can assure you the State of Texas will provide whatever tax incentives and open access you need to turn the far-northwest side of the city into the country's biggest manufacturing hub. We can even build a fast-access road to Bush Intercontinental Airport so your people can get in and out more easily."

The German CEO of a large biochemical firm leaned forward and propped his elbows on the long, polished conference table. "What about the environmental protesters who have been outside this building every day? Can you guarantee they will not cause us problems? We cannot make this commitment and have our reputation damaged by rabble."

Felderman looked at the balding billionaire, whose sweat beaded on his head despite the cranked-down air-conditioning. In another time or place, he would not like this guy very much. God knew Carl Felderman had no love for the tree huggers who'd been littering the lobby with anti-expansion flyers. If a few coyotes and sand spiders got nudged farther west in order to create thousands of new jobs, well, sorry, coyote. But those were at least people who believed in something beyond the dollar.

He'd long ago accepted that politicians sometimes had to sell their souls for the greater good. Texas needed the cash influx and the jobs. "I can assure you, the environmental groups will be dealt with. In fact..." He trailed off, frowning at the muffled booming sound coming from deep inside the building. Had a transformer blown?

Everything went to hell within seconds, blurring with frantic noise and movement. More booming sounds from above and below propelled everyone around the table to his or her feet. Carl watched with morbid fascination as the windows didn't bow this time but crumpled, the crinkled pattern of broken safety glass seeming to spiderweb outward in slow motion.

"Governor, come this way—we're under attack." A young man he'd never seen before pulled him toward the hallway as white flakes drifted into his eyes, and he had the absurd thought that snow was falling. The hottest August on record in years, and it was snowing inside the fucking Zemurray Building.

"The ceiling's coming down!" a woman screamed, and the room disintegrated into a maelstrom of plaster dust, wiring, and chaos. Even the floor jittered and shook. The young man who'd clamped onto the governor's arm continued to pull him toward the hall, into a stairwell, and down the steps. The stairwell filled with hordes of people from other floors, oddly silent in their determination to descend fifty stories—forty-nine, forty-eight, forty-seven—clattering down step after step after step.

A collective gasp echoed through the stairwell as the lights went out. Everyone froze. A few seconds later, harsh emergency lighting washed the surreal scene in a yellow glow, and the swell of people began descending again, moving faster, eyes on the steps, tongues silent.

Being swept along with the crowd, Carl was unsure but thought he went down two or three steps at a time without actually touching the ground. Still the young man held on to his arm.

Funny, the things one focuses on in a crisis, Carl was to think later. He'd let himself be pulled down the stairs behind a young man he'd never seen, but whose hoodie was on inside out, the seams showing. He'd fixated on that detail, wondering why the kid had been so rushed that he didn't dress properly. He wondered why the kid needed a hood inside the building on a hot day.

What he hadn't thought to wonder—not until he was shoved into the back of a waiting sedan with dark-tinted windows near the emergency exit, his hands bound and a rough blindfold jerked around his head—was who the hell the kid worked for.

❧CHAPTER 1❧

Kell spotted the bird as soon as its wing tips cleared the edge of the cypress stand at the eastern rim of Bayou Cote Blanche. For a moment, he indulged a hope it might be a hawk in search of fish, or a pelican, or a cormorant, or a fucking giant mutant hummingbird.

Anything but an eagle.

"It's her."

Gator raised his spotted head and focused sharp, mismatched eyes on the horizon, barking furiously in his Catahoula hound big-dog voice, usually reserved for alligators and swamp rats.

Kell had been sitting on the porch of his cabin on Cote Blanche since Nik's phone call from New Orleans more than two hours ago, waiting to see who'd arrive first—the man or the bird.

Should've known it would be the freakazoid eagle with the deceptively sweet name of Robin. He'd come to think of her as Razorblade Robin. Nik would have to rent a boat in Jeanerette and navigate the serpentine waterways of Louisiana's Atchafalaya Swamp to get here. Razorblade Robin could just sprout feathers and soar.

The midday sun glinted off the glossy reddish-brown wings of the golden eagle as it swooped over the smooth, murky water of the bayou. It landed with a harsh caw at the end of his dock, spurring Gator to rise to his feet and look up at Kell, asking permission to chase.

"Sorry, buddy. You don't want to mess with that one. She can take you." Hell, she could take both of them.

Kell took a final look at the pile of papers he'd been reading—notes about his team's new assignment. Mostly, he'd been studying the photo on top of the stack. The woman, Emory Chastaine, an environmental activist known for her anti-industry position, had been shot from a distance with a telephoto lens that gave the image a grainy feel. The quality of his generator-powered printer didn't help the photo's clarity. But he could tell she was tall, with an athletic build and shoulder-length blond hair. Dressed in a T-shirt and jeans, she was pretty in an all-American kind of way.

Not his image of a terrorist. Which made her even more dangerous.

Gator sprang off the porch as the eagle strutted down the dock toward them. He approached the bird in a crouch, his growls echoing off the still water. Damn dog never did listen worth a flip. Kell leaned back in his chair to watch the show. With a screech and a blur of feathers seconds before Gator reached her, the eagle morphed into a petite, waifish brunette.

Make that a naked, waifish brunette with a snarky attitude. She arched an eyebrow as Kell's vicious watchdog turned into a slobbering, tail-wagging fool, jumping up and down so vigorously his black-and-white spots seemed to blur. You'd think the hound saw birds turn into people every day.

If Gator went the crotch-sniffing route, Kell might have to die of pure humiliation.

Not like the naked bird-woman came as any big surprise. He reached for the T-shirt he'd thrown across the other porch chair and lobbed it to her as she approached, Gator dancing around her legs. "Put this on."

Robin Ashton, five foot nothing of shape-shifter and the tracker for Kell's new Omega Force team, caught the shirt and used it to wipe the sweat off her face. "It's like a sauna out here. Pretty, though, if you're into the primordial."

She turned to study the bayou, a minor niche in the massive Atchafalaya basin, and Kell made it a point to keep his eyes away from her ass. It wasn't that he wanted to look at it, exactly, but he was a guy, and it was right in front of him.

"Put on the shirt." He paused and gritted his teeth. "Please."

Robin turned back to him with an expression more smirk than smile. "Why? Does nudity make the big bad soldier Jack Kellison uncomfortable?"

"Absolutely." Kell realized his military background—ten years as an Army ranger in active duty, which had involved life with hordes of guys—made him unfit for many things, like dealing with naked female shape-shifters. But he was trying. Sort of.

He pulled a bottle of water from the cooler next to his chair and tossed it to Robin as soon as she'd pulled on the T-shirt. Thank God she hadn't argued about it this time.

He'd spent the past three months with her and the other four members of their new Omega Team, going through the physical and mental torture of Army Ranger School to help bond them as a unit. Afterward, they'd undergone special coursework on profiling and investigation. It had been his brilliant idea. He'd gone through Ranger training ten years ago, and it had been life-changing. The guys in his unit had remained tight because of what they'd survived together.

He figured his new team needed the bonding time. Ninety days ago, he hadn't known things like shape-shifters existed. Ninety days ago, he'd argued that such creatures, if they did exist, had no business being on teams with Rangers who'd spent the last decade building trust through hazardous duty and deprivation.

Ninety days ago, he'd been wrong. The three shifters on the team—the ironically named Robin and a pair of jaguar-shifter brothers—had breezed through the Ranger course, while he and Nik and Gadget, the experienced human badass veterans, starved and suffered from insect bites and pulled muscles.

The whole situation was beyond fucked.

Omega Force was a collective of new human-paranormal special operations units. Kell's had been one of several formed to investigate domestic terrorism cases that needed quick resolutions. Resolutions that might not be strictly obtained "by the book." The first team had come out of Alabama and experienced such success that the program was expanded.

They might or might not be part of Homeland Security. Kell figured they'd never know for sure who truly signed their paychecks. He had a single contact, a former Army colonel and Ranger instructor named Rick Thomas. Kell had picked his two human team members from among his former Ranger command, and the colonel had assigned Robin and the other two shifters.

Their territory encompassed Louisiana and Texas, two states that tended to be short on terrorists but long on garden-variety nutjobs. He could say that; he'd grown up ten miles from here on the edge of the swamp and now lived in Houston, which was nothing but reclaimed swampland with a lot of tall buildings on it.

"What do we know about this new case?" Robin took the other chair and propped her feet on the porch rail. She was flashing a lot of leg, but at least Kell's T-shirt covered the most distracting parts. Her short dark-auburn hair stuck out in spikes. Kind of feather-like.

"Might as well wait until we get everyone together so we don't have to go over it twice. Have any trouble finding the cabin?"

She gave him a calm, maddening look. "Nope. You said ten miles south of Jeanerette, so once I got in the vicinity, your heat signature glowed like neon. Humans are easy." She cocked her head and scanned the water. "He's coming. Boat motor is skipping a little."

Kell ground his teeth. He didn't hear a fucking thing, but he wasn't going to tell her that. These shape-shifters were giving him a complex.

He stared at the bend in the open water that lay to their north and didn't change his expression when the buzzing of a boat engine eventually preceded the small flat-bottomed aluminum skiff churning slowly toward them.

The boat's single occupant, Nikolas Dimitrou, tied off at the end of the dock and jumped to the wooden pier, greeted with much fanfare by Gator. Nik spent as much time at the Cote Blanche cabin as its owner, often with Gator for company. Life was solitary out here, which meant the voices in Nik's head died away and let him sleep more and drink less. At least that's how Kell interpreted it. After being official Ranger buddies since they'd gone through training the first time, he figured he knew Nik better than anyone.

"Hey, you got AC in that cabin yet? This is the hottest, thickest air I've ever tried to breathe." Nik propped his hands on his hips and grinned at Robin. "How long you been here?"

Robin looked over her shoulder and blew Kell a kiss. "So long that Kell got scared he'd lose control and ravage me, so he made me wear a shirt. I'll break through that iron control of his eventually."

Not if he could help it. Kell tossed Nik his last chilled bottle of water.

"Kell's got a soft underbelly; it's just hidden under a thick layer of steel abs." Nik's even white teeth flashed in the tanned face he'd gotten from a combination of sun and his father's Greek heritage. He'd grown up in New Orleans and was as big a Yat as the next guy, but he had the Greek playboy look women loved.

At least until he saw enough of a woman's past and future to ruin any chance of a relationship. Nik was the Omega Team profiler and tactician, along with Kell, and none of the other team members knew for sure whether he was a brilliant reader of body language or an honest-to-God psychic.

He was the real deal, and Kell knew the price he paid for it.

"Computer's charged and set up to Skype with the others. We'll keep things general in case the connection's not as secure as it's supposed to be and work out specifics once we get in place. I have more notes here that were delivered to Jeanerette last night." Kell slowly rose to his feet, lagging behind Nik and Robin as they entered the cabin.

Sharp pain shot through his lower back, into his hip, and down the back of his right leg as he took the first step. The second one came more easily. Three or four, and he could walk without the stiffness that set in after more than a half hour of rest. Of course, if he stood too long, the pain shifted to a different area. It never completely went away.

Robin frowned at him from beside the desk in the one-room-plus-bath cabin. "You're injured. Does the colonel know?"

"Not injured, just a little stiff—nothing big. It's a human thing." Kell exchanged a look with Nik, who'd shoved the industrial-size bottle of ibuprofen behind the generator-powered mini-fridge before Robin could see it.

Kell kept Nik's secrets; Nik kept Kell's. It had been that way for a decade. The compression fracture in his lower back had happened six months ago, in a fall while scrambling out of a village raid in Afghanistan. It was why he was back in the States, why he'd jumped at the chance to lead this new force. He was thirty-two and not ready to hang up his boots, so he needed to prove he still had value. That he could still handle active duty because, frankly, he didn't know how to make a life without it. Didn't remember how to be a civvy.

"Poor old frail humans." Robin walked around the one-room cabin, stopping to examine the sketches tacked to the paneled wall—scenes of the bayou, dripping Spanish moss, cypress forests, birds—and the assortment of carved wooden animals atop the bookshelves full of military history and fictional thrillers.

"You do all this drawing and carving?" Robin picked up a wooden pelican that was one of Kell's best pieces, detailed and delicate.

"Carving's mine. Drawings are by a friend." Kell eased into the office chair behind the wooden desk, which he'd built of reclaimed cypress like everything else here. The art was Nik's work, but if he wanted Robin to know, he'd tell her himself.

Kell opened the Skype connection on his laptop and hooked his computer to the one belonging to Gadget, aka Garrett Foley, the team's intel guy and a Ranger who'd served with Nik and Kell on their last tour. If there was Internet chatter, Gadget could find it.

The image of square black geek glasses filled the screen, wrapped around a prominent nose. Blond hair in a background blur gave the whole thing a fun-house vibe. Kell still treated computers with the suspicion they deserved, but the laptop and cell phone allowed him to hang out in Cote Blanche without being out of touch. He'd been able to cocoon himself here in the month since Ranger School, letting his back recover and popping ibuprofen without an audience.

Kell adjusted the screen so Nik and Robin, sitting behind him, could see and hear. "You got the kitty-cats with you?"

Gadget shifted to the side and a huge face framed by a mane of black hair came into view. "Meow." Archer Logan grinned. "This kitty-cat ate your lunch last course at Ranger camp, old man."

"Ranger School." Kell grimaced. Nothing he hated worse than a smart-ass shape-shifter, although it seemed to come with the territory. But everyone was accounted for. If Archer was there, his brother Adam was nearby, as quiet as Archer was gregarious. Purely muscle, those two, and virtually indestructible, as near as he could tell. They wouldn't be involved in the tactical end of things, but needed to know what was going on.

"Got a call from the colonel yesterday, as you know." Kell leaned back, pulling the sheaf of papers onto his lap and flipping through the notes he'd transcribed after getting the assignment. "You've all heard about the bombing in Houston."

"Told you we'd get that case!" Gadget whooped and high-fived Archer and Adam, or at least that's how Kell interpreted the jostling images on the screen.

"Shut up and sit down, guys. This is bad shit. Seven bombs brought the Zemurray Building down, at least two hundred and fifty dead or unaccounted for, including the governor of Texas. They want us in there by tomorrow."

Everyone sobered.

"How come us and not the Houston PD or Homeland Security?" Nik leaned over Kell's shoulder and scanned the notes written in small, neat script.

"We'll be working alongside them—they just won't know about it because we don't exist." Kell handed him the notes. "Gadget, there's been some online chatter about another strike being planned, so you need to start monitoring the channels I'll be sending you as soon as we finish the call. It's obviously a terrorist attack, but nobody's claimed it so far, although there is a lead."

Robin had been aggravating Gator, but stopped flipping his ears inside out and looked up. "Another bombing is being planned even though no one's claiming the first one? Weird. What kind of lead?"

"Anonymous tip, with enough detail to be deemed credible," Kell said. "Including hints that another bombing by the same people is being planned for Labor Day in New Orleans. That's two weeks away."

Kell leaned in toward the laptop's camera. "Gadget, you and the kitties need to set up base in New Orleans and see what's planned for Labor Day weekend that might make a target. Look for something involving business, manufacturing, expansion, oil. Something with the potential for mass casualties. The info's

pointing to some kind of ecoterrorism. The governor's big industrial expansion meeting could have been the target in Houston."

"You want Robin and me in Houston?" Nik handed the
sheaf of notes to Robin, and Kell's glance rested again on the
photo of Emory Chastaine, all-American girl terrorist.

"The rest of us in Houston," Kell affirmed. "Houston PD's
anonymous rat said the bombing was engineered by this environmental activist group known as the Co-Op. No direct evidence, but Homeland Security is investigating. Trouble is, by
the time the bureaucrats get their heads out of their asses, Labor
Day will be a memory. They can't move fast enough."

Robin had stopped at a page in the notes headed *Co-Op*.
"Says here the director is a woman named Emory Chastaine—
goes by the name Mori. They've been protesting the meetings
to create a new industrial center northwest of Houston, particularly biochemical manufacturing. She's openly accused the
governor of creating a cancer hazard for local citizens as well as
encroaching on native habitats. They've always been outspoken
but peaceful."

Kell nodded. "Unless they've changed tactics. I'll be going
in as a Co-Op volunteer. You and Nik, see what you can find at
the crime scene, and check out the link with the governor. He's
presumed dead, but the body hasn't been found."

Kell looked back at the screen. "We'll work out the rest
of the details on the way to Houston. And remember, this job
doesn't exist. We don't exist. Stay undercover and in touch.
Nobody's a cowboy. Everybody clear?"

"Except for one thing," Nik said as Kell closed the connection. "You're about the least crunchy-earthy guy I know. How
the hell are you gonna pass for a granola grabber?"

He was talking to Kell, but his hooded eyes were focused on Robin, who'd stripped off Kell's T-shirt and was giving Nik an assessing look right back.

Great. On top of everything else, he'd have to come up with a No Sex Within the Omega Force rule. "Robin, don't you have to fly away somewhere?"

She grinned at him, then shimmered back into a golden eagle and squawked at Nik when he opened the door to let her outside.

Kell swore that, before she took flight off the end of the porch, she shook her tail feathers at them.

⚜ CHAPTER 2 ⚜

Mori Chastaine thought she'd be prepared when the phone call came. Not so much.

She'd known Shonna was dead, had been convinced of it deep in her gut where fears hadn't yet been molded into words. Her admin hadn't missed a day of work in almost a year of employment, and if she were going to be late, Shonna would call, text, *and* e-mail to make sure Mori got the message. They'd even joked about her overdeveloped sense of responsibility.

Until yesterday. Everyone in the Co-Op offices had gathered in the cramped conference room, watching the small TV set with sick fascination and a growing sense of dread as the morning dragged on and the news from downtown Houston grew worse.

Nobody said it, but the unspoken thoughts filled the room. Shonna took the Southwest Freeway to work every morning, right past the Zemurray Building. The force of the building collapse had taken down a big chunk of the freeway, always heavy with traffic.

Shonna was never late. No one answered her phone.

Still, when Shonna's husband finally called, Mori hadn't been prepared for the sick feeling that threatened to overwhelm her. His voice was thin and tinny, as if coming through a dense fog. Rescuers had found Shonna's car beneath the rubble of the collapsed section of I-59 nearest the bomb site, he said. It happened so fast Shonna hadn't suffered.

But that was what officials always told family members to make them feel better. One could never truly know another's pain or fear or the fleeting regrets that had to pass through a person's mind in the moments before death.

Standing beside Shonna's desk, Mori flipped through the stack of donations waiting to be processed. Gifts of ten, twenty, fifty dollars from people who couldn't afford to support an environmental action group but who believed in the work they did.

Except it didn't seem so important now. Even the issues she faced with her family seemed to pale beside such violence, although Mori knew her personal problems would resume their proper place of horror soon enough.

Walking into her own office, she slumped in the chair and picked up a wooden carved tree she used as a paperweight, crafted generations ago by one of her ancestors from a piece of live oak uprooted by a hurricane. It symbolized the strength of her people, their ability to draw solace from the earth, the passion that drove her to try and preserve what land they had left.

A passion that—according to her parents, anyway—didn't sink deep enough into her fiber for her to make the sacrifices needed to save them all.

She shouldn't have to bear that burden, damn it.

A tear splashed on the wood worn smooth by years of handling. She wasn't sure if she was grieving for the lives lost in downtown Houston or for her own diminished future if she let herself be bullied into becoming the wife of a man she hated.

"You ready to go downtown?" Taylor Stedman stuck his head in the office door, interrupting Mori's attempts to make sense of the senseless. "Our flyer crew will work harder if they see you there, supporting them."

Mori scrubbed her hands over her eyes, wiping away the tears, and stared at her assistant director. What was he thinking? "Tay, I told you to call in the flyer crews yesterday. Now's not the time to be handing out pamphlets and bad-mouthing the governor. The man might be dead. The executives from the other countries are either dead or wounded. Nobody is talking about building new manufacturing plants anymore."

Tay flinched, and Mori closed her eyes. "I'm sorry. I didn't mean to go off on you. It's just that Shonna…" She took a deep breath. "No flyer crews until further notice, OK?"

"What about the calling campaigns? It might be a good time to shore up our support." Taylor had that pinched, obstinate look Mori had grown to dislike—one he used a lot since she'd beaten him out for the director's job last year.

Co-Op volunteers had been blanketing the area around the Zemurray Building throughout the week as Governor Felderman and industrial leaders from several G-8 nations met to discuss new manufacturing inroads into southeast Texas. Their position was clear, but now wasn't the time to press their point.

"Call the phone crews and tell them to wait for further instructions. We do nothing else until things calm down. All we'd get now is bad publicity."

Mori stood and walked around her desk, not ashamed to use her five-eleven height to intimidate her shorter assistant director. Taylor was a good organizer and had the passion for protecting what was left of the native East Texas–West Louisiana habitat, but the man didn't have a lick of common sense, as Mori's granddad used to say.

"But there are a lot of people out in that area, and it's a good time to remind them what a biochemical plant in their backyard would mean." Taylor got that whine in his voice that annoyed the bejeezus out of her. He was proof that the line between passion and fanaticism was often a fine one. The environmental movement's greatest strength across the board— passionate people—was also its greatest weakness.

"Give it a rest." She raised her voice, not something she did often. The slump of his shoulders told her she'd made her point. "If we go out there now, we look insensitive and lose support, not gain it."

As soon as Taylor sulked his way down the hall to his office, Mori returned to the small conference room. Two of the three Co-Op office volunteers, college students from nearby Rice U, watched the ongoing disaster coverage.

"Anything new?" These kids had been with her when the phone call came about Shonna, and both were failing miserably in their attempts to maintain their cool-dude demeanors.

Brian, an engineering major, looked at her with red-rimmed eyes. "Think there's any way we can help?"

Mori shook her head. "It's too soon. They're still looking for evidence, I imagine. The best way to help is to stay out of their way."

The explosions had turned Houston into a chaotic dough-nut. Business ran at its usual frantic pace around the edges, while everything in the central area near downtown remained at a shocked, fearful standstill. The downtown streets were eerily empty except in the vicinity of the Zemurray Building, where investigators swarmed like ants around a smoke-bombed anthill.

Mori couldn't blame the kids for wanting to help; they were joiners who kept organizations like the Co-Op alive. She'd come to consider this little gentrified house-turned-storefront in Montrose more of a home than the furnished one-bedroom where she slept. She'd poured everything she had into the Co-Op since taking over the directorship, and they'd made progress in small steps, even convincing a couple of the governor's industry-rich backers to consider scaling down expansion.

Feedback screeched through the TV microphones as a middle-aged, stone-faced reporter stopped his ongoing commentary to listen into a headset. "We have a development in the recovery efforts at the Zemurray Building," he said, nodding as the video cut to a barely recognizable pile of rubble. Concrete and rebar had been piled into a mountain beside the tall uprights that at one time had supported an elevated section of roadway and a seventy-story high-rise.

"Sources are saying that a local environmental group known as the Co-Op has been identified as an entity of interest in the investigation. The Co-Op has been actively protesting the industrial expansion policies of Governor Felderman and, specifically, this week's meetings…"

The voice droned on, but Mori blocked it out. Her sense of unreality deepened as she honed in on the image superimposed behind the reporter, the oak leaf in a circle that made up the Co-Op logo. Surely they couldn't be serious. Could anybody really believe they'd work so hard to protect wildlife habitat and then do something that would kill people?

"Mori?" Brian touched her arm, and she startled, looking up and following his gaze to the conference room doorway.

Taylor, so pale his long dark hair looked like a bad dye job, stood next to the anti-Taylor. Tall, tanned, short dark hair just unkempt enough to look as if it might be starting to grow out, strong cheekbones, and eyes a shade of clear blue-green she'd only seen in the Caribbean on her one trip to the Cayman Islands. An Army green T-shirt hinted at the muscles beneath.

She hated to say it of her own people, but this guy looked way too buff and downright *masculine* to be an environmentalist.

He held out a hand for her to shake. "Name's Jack Kelly, and I was hoping to come on as a volunteer at the Co-Op. You're the director, right?"

Mori struggled to focus on his words, glancing back at the TV, where the Co-Op logo had been replaced by the mayor giving yet another press conference. "I'm sorry, Mister...Kelly, was it? This is really not a good time. Maybe you could come back in a couple of weeks?"

Surely to God this nightmare would be over by then, including the ridiculous idea that the Co-Op was involved. Although, for many families, it wouldn't be over for a long time.

A little wrinkle of annoyance briefly appeared between his brows, then smoothed away. Mori knew that look from working with the power brokers. Jack Kelly was used to getting his way. "Call me Kell. I'm sorry for the lousy timing, but if you give me a chance, I promise to make myself useful. I've just come off active Army duty and need something to fill my time. I believe in what you guys do."

Mori rubbed her eyes. She had to find out how the Co-Op had been linked to these bombings, not babysit a struggling soldier. *Be nice. He deserves a break for what he's been through.* But his timing sure sucked.

"OK, of course." Besides, Taylor needed to stay busy, and training a new volunteer would do nicely. "Taylor, can you show Kell around and give him the volunteer spiel? Then I'll—"

Holy cow, when had the Co-Op gotten so damned popular? Two nondescript, somber-faced men wearing somber suits and even more somber expressions had appeared behind Taylor and the new volunteer.

One of the men, a blank-faced brunet, stayed in the background. His companion stepped forward. "Emory Chastaine?"

Jack took a side step so he was facing the newcomers—definitely looked like something a soldier would do. These guys looked more threatening than the soldier volunteer, though.

These guys looked like cops.

She walked toward the man in front, her hand outstretched, ready to greet him despite the dread churning her stomach to acid. "I'm Mori Chastaine. Can I help you?"

Instead of shaking her hand, the guy in the suit thrust a Homeland Security badge in front of her face. "Agent Tim Bradford. We need you to accompany us downtown, please. We have some questions in relation to the Zemurray Building bombing."

Mori swallowed hard, and her gaze met Kell's. He had that look again, the one that said he wasn't getting his way and he didn't like it. Join the crowd, buddy. She turned back to the FBI agent. "Am I under arrest?"

His smile was grim. "Not yet."

☙ CHAPTER 3 ☙

I don't need a fucking bag of cash—she's been detained, not arrested. Find out how long they can hold her without charging her."

Kell ended the call and tossed his cell phone on the scarred dinette table of his apartment, part of a big complex located between Westheimer and San Felipe just inside the 610 Loop. He'd held the lease on the place for more than five years, and it still had the same old furniture he'd taken from his folks' place in Jeanerette when they died in an auto accident. He hadn't been able to make himself move back into their house, where he'd stayed whenever he was home on leave or between tours. So he took Gator, sold everything but the cabin (their "fish camp"), and moved to Houston.

The cabin had survived Audrey, Rita, Ike—any number of lesser hurricanes and tropical storms. He figured any building that stubborn deserved to be kept.

Nik sat at the table nursing a scotch. The city was painful for him, and Kell recognized the tightness of his jaw that gradually disappeared when he stayed outside the city a few days. The man never knew when something he'd touch would bombard him with a story, usually an emotional or traumatic one. The whiskey didn't seem to get him drunk or dull his reaction times or judgment, but it did dull the visions.

"The colonel's trying to give you bail money?" he asked. "I thought they hadn't arrested her."

"Not the colonel, but his aide. It's a precaution, but I don't think it's necessary and it'll take too long. There's no evidence to charge Mori Chastaine with anything. In fact, if Homeland Security wasn't involved, they wouldn't have been able to detain her this long without charging her."

"You think the anonymous caller was the real bomber and was trying to set up the Co-Op for some reason?" Nik took a sip of scotch and rattled the ice around his glass.

Good question. The colonel had told Kell that investigators had found nothing concrete to connect the Co-Op to the bombing except the anonymous phone call and some flyers left around the scene—one was even tacked to a support beam. "Every connection they've found is purely circumstantial. But whoever made that call fingering the Co-Op had some credible information. So the Co-Op is the place to start looking for answers. Either they're involved or someone's out to hose them. Then again, we might be wasting our time."

In fact, it wouldn't surprise him if other Omega Force teams in other states were investigating the same case from other angles. It's what he'd do if he were making the assignments. In case that Labor Day threat was real, he'd spread teams all over the place, exploring every possibility.

Kell opened a new bottle of ibuprofen, poured four into his palm, and knocked them back with orange juice out of the new carton he'd bought at Randalls yesterday. He'd finally escaped the officious Taylor Stedman by late afternoon after learning more about the evils of habitat encroachment than he could ever want to know. Every single hairy spider and East Texas leech and scrubby species of bush was now in his vocabulary. He could be on fucking *Jeopardy*.

He agreed with a lot of what the Co-Op preached, but not if they were willing to kill people. And it hadn't escaped his notice that Taylor didn't seem the least bit concerned that his boss had been hauled off as a potential ecoterrorist.

"Where's Robin staying now that she's here and Gadget and the kittens have taken over her apartment in New Orleans?" Kell sat next to Nik at the table and pulled his tan canvas rucksack toward him, rummaging inside. Gator rose from a dead, snoring sleep in the far corner at the sound of the pack and padded over in hopes of a treat.

"She's at my place." Nik's attempt to sound casual was pathetic.

Kell shot him a sharp look and tried to imagine Razorblade Robin in his friend's downtown warehouse-turned-apartment.

"What?" Nik shrugged. "She relaxes me. I can't get visions off her, and she says such outrageous stuff it makes me laugh. Plus, she goes out flying all night, so I have plenty of privacy. God only knows what she does out there."

Kell arched a brow. "Don't eagles hunt down rats and eat them, tail and all? I bet she has rat-ass breath."

Nik laughed. "I'll not tell her you said that. Why don't you like her?"

Kell shook his head. "I like Robin fine. But a hundred-pound woman who can outdo me on the bench press threatens my manhood, and I'm man enough to admit it." He finally found what he had been looking for in the pack. "Take a look at this."

He set the carved wooden tree on the table between them, and Nik studied it without touching while Kell slipped Gator one of the liver treats he always kept in his pack's front pocket.

"Beautiful work, but it doesn't look like your style." Nik nudged the tree with a finger to see another side of it.

"It isn't. I lifted it off Mori Chastaine's desk on my tour of the Co-Op offices yesterday, after she got hauled off for an overnight stay with the DHS guys. Thought it was worth you trying to get an image. It was the only thing I saw that looked personal."

Nik nodded and pushed his drink aside, drying his palms on the thighs of his camo shorts. He reached out and gently lifted the tree, wrapping his fingers around it. Then both hands. He closed his eyes, and Kell watched in fascination as his friend communed with the tree, or the spirits, or whatever the hell caused the visions.

Opening his eyes, Nik held the tree up to the light. "Weird."

"Weird how?" What was weirder than reading stories off inanimate objects?

"I get stray images with no meaning behind them. I've never had anything read that way before. Usually, it's either an onslaught of history or nothing at all."

Kell's phone chirped, and he read the text. Mori Chastaine would be released at 2:00 p.m. "Gotta head out in a few. Describe the images."

"Forests. Big, empty vistas. Dead cattle." Nik took a sip of scotch. "An old man in a cowboy hat." He set the tree down and shoved it back toward Kell. "Don't ask what it means. I don't have a clue."

Kell picked up the tree and studied it. The carving was old, and it had been cared for. The grooves were worn smooth, and the whole thing shone from handling. It should have a lot of tales to tell.

But it would have to wait. He stuck the tree in his pack so he could slip it back in the Co-Op offices before anyone realized it was gone, and stuffed the bottle of ibuprofen in with it.

"You're gonna eat out the lining of your stomach with that shit." Nik finished off his drink, gave Gator a quick ear rub, and ambled toward the door. "I'm heading over to the bomb site to handle some rubble—see if I can learn anything. Get something else belonging to Mori Chastaine and let me try again tonight."

He paused in the doorway. "I'll do it while Robin's out eating rats."

All law enforcement offices smelled alike, whether a metro police department, an FBI headquarters, or a county sheriff. Entering the first-floor lobby of the FBI field office in northwest Houston, Kell inhaled the same stale-coffee-gun-oil-testosterone aroma he'd grown up with while hanging out in the Iberia Parish Sheriff's Department, where his dad had been a deputy. John Kennedy "Jack" Kellison Sr. always said he had stayed a deputy because he wasn't mean enough to be elected sheriff. When he was a kid, Kell figured his dad was joking. Later, he'd seen what tough SOBs really looked like and figured his gentle, artistic dad was being honest.

After inquiring at the information desk and learning Mori would be out shortly, he leaned against a wall in the back of the waiting area and watched the scurry of activity in and out of one of the country's largest federal field offices. Kell was glad he'd only spent time in Houston between tours. No danger of being recognized or suspected of being anything other than an unemployed veteran with a bad back.

He spotted her long before she saw him. Mori was a head taller than the young Hispanic officer who accompanied her out of the elevator. Kell didn't need Nik's expertise in reading body language to tell she was tense, depressed, and overtired. Her shoulders were rigid but hunched too far forward, and she kept stretching her neck from side to side.

Mori shoved the envelope with her confiscated belongings into her messenger bag and turned with a terse thank-you to the female officer. Her gaze scanned the lobby clockwise, gliding past Kell before suddenly shifting back. Her mouth formed a small, involuntary "O" before clamping shut.

That was his signal. Kell made his way toward her. "See, told you I could make myself useful. I thought you might need a ride home."

Dark circles ringed her eyes and she clutched her purse handle like she was trying to choke it, but she managed a small smile. "Thanks. Your name is Kell, right? Taylor sent you?"

He didn't want to tell her Taylor Stedman seemed to flourish in her absence and had given Kell the impression, without saying so, that he hoped she'd be arrested and detained indefinitely.

"Everyone's worried about you." Tactful, thy name is Jack Kellison—or, for now, Jack Kelly.

Mori laughed. "Sorry, but you aren't that good a liar. Tay probably redecorated the office. He didn't take my desk yet, did he?" She slapped a palm against her forehead. "Sorry, I shouldn't have said that. If you hang around the Co-Op very long, you'll learn I have a bad habit of speaking my mind before I think about how much trouble it's going to cause. I'm not as bitchy as that sounded."

Kell thought she was giving Taylor too much credit. "You just sound like someone who didn't get any sleep last night. Ready to go?"

"More than ready. Oh"—she rested a hand on his arm— "and thank you. I'd left a message for my dad and thought he'd be here to pick me up, but I guess he got delayed or something."

So she had family in town. Kell's gaze met hers as he opened the door and waited for her to go out ahead of him. Her eyes, which crinkled at the edges when she smiled, were almond shaped and a rich brown. Even without makeup, she was smooth skinned and kind of exotic looking, with high cheekbones and full lips.

He'd be damned if he could see anything in that face to indicate she was capable of mass murder. No edge of manic energy, no hard aura of meanness, no pent-up anger. Just fear, which could come from any number of things, including suspicion of terrorism and a night in an interrogation room.

The niggling suspicion he'd had about that anonymous tip grew stronger. While he was investigating Mori Chastaine, he also needed to figure out who might have wanted to frame the Co-Op or Mori herself. Maybe DHS was so desperate to pin it on someone they jumped at the first option.

Ranger training had taught him to trust his gut. He didn't know this woman, but his gut said either she was no killer or she had fooled him so completely that she was very, very lethal.

They walked through the parking lot as he directed her toward the Terminator, a boat of an old powder-blue Oldsmobile that had belonged to his parents for the past two decades.

At the sound of her choked-back laugh, he felt the need to apologize.

"I haven't been in the States much the last ten years." He shrugged and couldn't help but return her grin, which had transformed her from pretty into a wholesome kind of beautiful. Something he didn't need to be thinking about a suspect.

"Therefore, you bought the ugliest thing you could find so you could look like an old lady while you were home?" She laughed, a hearty bray without a trace of self-consciousness. "Sorry, there I go again with my mouth. It's, uh, lovely." She cleared her throat. "Really."

Kell stopped and looked at the Olds. It *was* hideous, with geriatric-blue paint rusted off in spots. Why had he kept it? Probably because it was like the furniture. If he bought his own sofa or drove his own car, it would be admitting he was off duty for good. "I'll have you know it has great family significance."

Mori's chuckle as she slid into the passenger seat said she didn't buy it for a second. He'd outed himself as a commitment-phobe and maybe a mama's boy. Neither of which he could deny.

He pulled out of the parking lot and drove back toward Near Town. She'd wanted to check in at Co-Op headquarters, see how the organization's financial supporters were reacting, and get her car. Meanwhile, he could ply her for information. "Your family lives here in town?"

"West of town, just across the Austin County line." She looked out the window at the endless vista of traffic and concrete.

Which meant farming or ranching, most likely. "What do your folks do?"

She shifted to look at him, the sun glinting off her hair like a halo. Kell looked back at the inching traffic and gave himself a mental shake. Terrorists didn't have halos.

"My turn. Do your folks live in Houston, and are they aware you've stolen their prized vehicle?"

Kell fought to keep the smile from inching its way onto his face. "They died five years ago in a car accident during a tropical storm— back in Jeanerette, Louisiana. You've probably never heard of it."

"I'm sorry about your family. Brothers or sisters?" Mori settled back in her seat and leaned her head against the headrest with her eyes closed.

"No, only me. My turn." Kell thought about how to reapproach the family thing. It seemed to ratchet up her tension level when he'd mentioned them before, pushing her to change the subject.

Mori spoke again before he decided on a tactic. "Did you know there used to be tons of Louisiana black bears around Jeanerette, or north of there?" She still had her eyes closed. "They're endangered now. You ever see one? Oh, and my dad's in finance, but my parents live on the ranch we inherited from my grandfather."

Kell filtered and processed the bears, the finance, the ranch. He wanted to ask about the dad's work—it might provide a motive or connection to the bombing, since there was certainly high finance involved. But he was posing as an environmental nut, so he better play the role.

"I've seen a couple of bears down in the delta when I was growing up. Shame about them." *Shit, that sounded lame.*

"A *shame?*" Mori turned toward him, the beginnings of a frown scrunching her brows together. "They're beautiful animals and running out of space to live. We saved the alligators. We should be able to save those bears. Those are the species the original teddy bear was based on, you know."

Kell felt as if he'd received a gentle scolding from his elementary school teacher. He'd approached this all wrong. The assignment had come up so fast he hadn't been able to do the kind of prep work he needed, so he'd fallen back on the easiest way inside the organization: volunteer. Stupid. He knew the rules: include enough of the truth to make it believable.

"OK, look. Confession time. I'm not an environmentalist, and I'm sorry I lied about that. I'm willing to learn, but I don't know much."

Mori had straightened in her seat and now wore a full-on frown. "So what are you doing here? Are you a cop?"

"Christ. No, nothing like that." *Not technically.* "I really did just get off active duty, and I need something to keep me from sitting around and getting inside my own head. I've driven past the Co-Op before and thought I'd see if you guys needed help."

She was still frowning, so he added the trump card. "I got injured last time out. I don't know anything besides being a Ranger. I need to stay busy."

He'd said it to engender sympathy, which, sure enough, showed on her face. It had come out a lot more truthful than he'd intended, though.

"Rangers are, what, like Marines?"

Kell stared at her, aghast, and had to slam on the brakes to keep from planting the Terminator in the back of a flatbed truck right before the turn into the Co-Op lot.

He was distracted from telling her all the ways Rangers were superior in the Special Ops hierarchy by the news van parked horizontally across two spaces.

"Oh God, I hadn't thought about the press." Mori's fingers tightened on the Terminator's door handle.

Kell eased the car past them, unnoticed. Guess *Eyewitness News* hadn't expected to witness their target's arrival in a senior sedan. "Leave everything to me."

❦CHAPTER 4❧

Mori's birthday had been far from cheerful, but remembering how Jack Kelly had handled the media made her laugh out loud.

"Leave everything to me," Kell had said, and then he'd ordered Mori to crouch on the floorboard while he calmly drove the big, ugly Olds into a tree. Barely hard enough to jostle them, but it got the news crew's attention.

"Get out fast and slip behind the bushes while I keep them busy," he had whispered, and then he'd proceeded to act like a belligerent crazy man, yelling obscenities and charging at the camera crew, claiming they'd distracted him and caused the accident.

And that was only the finale to the zoo of the last twenty-four hours. *Happy birthday to me.*

Mori stood under the hot spray of the shower, her smile fading as she recalled what came next: the piles of messages and e-mails. It wasn't simply Co-Op contributors expressing concern or canceling their pledges. There were calls from complete strangers. Threatening her. Calling her a terrorist. Accusing her of treason, of murder. Telling her to watch her back if she wanted to continue drawing breath.

Kell had insisted on walking her to her car and following her home after the media had finally drifted away.

She turned off the water and wrapped herself in a towel, then wound a second one around her wet hair. A glass of wine and a nice fat fantasy novel might distract her for a while.

The humidity was ridiculous, and a cold, air-conditioned sweat coated her skin in the time it took her to walk the ten steps to the bedroom. She rooted in her dresser for something cool to wear. Even with the AC cranked down to icebox levels, the heat was oppressive. A line of tropical waves off the coast of Africa was marching across the Atlantic and would be one more thing for those along the coast to worry about in another week or so. At least tropical storms offshore would pull some of this awful humidity out of the air.

She chose a pair of loose jogging shorts and a T-shirt, a glass of moscato, and a copy of *Game of Thrones*, which she'd been meaning to read for years. Surely swords and imaginary kingdoms and feast-laden banquet halls would take her mind off her problems.

Only, they didn't. The questions the agents had asked her swirled around in her mind like dancers on a ballroom floor: Where had she been when the bombing took place? Who had she talked to in the last month? Would she turn over her phone records without a warrant?

She'd called her father on the way to the station and left a message, at least hoping he'd recommend an attorney or tell her if she needed one. It wasn't like she was guilty of anything. Despite their problems, she had thought her dad would come through for her. Instead, the only one who'd cared enough to see that she got home after a night in hell was Jack Kelly. Her parents hadn't even called to wish her a happy birthday.

Jack Kelly, who came across as a tightly wound ex-soldier and was probably no more an environmentalist than the governor—well, maybe a little more, but not much. Was he really the wounded vet he claimed to be?

He definitely was in pain, and Mori's guess would be that he'd had a back injury. He moved a little too carefully. And he did have the military look. His dark hair was starting to grow out, showing the least hint of curl, and he had a coiled energy that reminded her of the rattlesnakes she'd come across while growing up on the ranch. Alert, wary, paying attention to everything around him.

The way his muscles moved under that tanned skin had certainly caught *her* attention.

Mori shook her head. There was no point in even going there.

She'd started the same chapter of her book for the fourth time, reading aloud to force herself to concentrate, when a knock at her door startled her enough to overturn her wineglass. *So damned jumpy.* She grabbed a napkin off the kitchen table and dabbed at the wine beaded on the carpet. At least it was white and not a red, or she could kiss that security deposit good-bye.

A second knock and a muffled voice: "Floral delivery."

She peered through the peephole, and sure enough, there was a young guy holding a bunch of flowers. It was the bored look on his face that convinced her he was a flower delivery guy and not a cop or a reporter who'd managed to track her down. Not that she didn't fully expect that the cops, or federal agents, were parked somewhere nearby and watching her every move. Talk about a creepy feeling.

Maybe the flowers were from her parents, at least acknowledging her birthday. The day Mori Chastaine turned twenty-five, her world was supposed to change in ways she didn't want. She had expected the day to be traumatic. She hadn't expected to spend it sitting in a small windowless room on a hard chair after too many cups of coffee, being questioned about a horrific crime.

Maybe they were from Dad, trying to make up for abandoning her today. God forbid Paul Chastaine should apologize for anything. Their recent issues had made her realize her father was not a brave man. He was a decent man, in his own way, but he was weak and would always take the easy route. It was a distressing revelation for her at a time when she needed him so badly.

The delivery boy had started walking away by the time she opened the door. He turned with a smile. "Thank God. You were my last delivery today, and I sure didn't want to have to haul these back to the shop."

She signed for the flowers and dug in her wallet on the counter for a tip, waiting until he was out of sight in the parking lot before turning to look at them.

No way they came from her parents. A dozen perfect red roses in a cut-glass vase was not their style.

Michael Benedict was another matter. It was *exactly* his style—over-the-top, expensive, and with lots of invisible strings attached.

Taking a deep breath, Mori pulled the small florist's envelope from the plastic holder and opened it. Michael had stayed away from her the past couple of months while her parents tried to wear her down about marrying him. But damn it, this was the twenty-first century in the fourth-largest city in America, not the dark ages in a feudal village.

Whatever unholy promises her parents had made to this man when she was born shouldn't bind her to him now. She should have a choice where she spent her life, and with whom.

Did you get my birthday message, Emory? Love, M.

"What the heck?" She took the note back to the sofa and sat down, staring at the card, trying to figure out its meaning.

She'd checked all her office messages—besides, he never tried to contact her there. She dug her cell phone from her purse and scrolled through the call log. Nothing from Michael Benedict or Tex-La Shipping.

What message had she gotten today, except that she never again wanted to start a day sitting in an interrogation room surrounded by grim-faced men and women? Or maybe that *was* the message.

"Oh God. It was him." Her whisper seemed to echo around the small living room. Surely she was wrong. Surely he wouldn't try to set her up for the bombing of the Zemurray Building.

Who was she kidding? It was exactly the kind of thing Michael Benedict would do, to force her hand in marrying him. Knowing her father wouldn't help her and figuring out what might make her desperate enough to turn to him for help.

Fingers trembling, she picked up the phone to call him, then set it down again. She couldn't do it, not yet.

But she could force her parents to talk to her. And pray to God she was wrong.

><+>-O-<+><

The Chastaine Quad-D Ranch was a forty-five-minute drive west of Houston when there was no traffic on the Katy Freeway. Which was exactly never.

By the time she had finally broken loose from the automotive gridlock, Mori had an aching jaw from grinding her teeth and hands sore from gripping the steering wheel of her little hybrid car until it was slick with sweat.

The farther she got from the city, the more she was convinced she was not only blowing the whole idea of Michael framing her out of proportion, but her sanity also might be in question. She could swear that as she stopped and started and stopped and started with the traffic, she'd seen the same golden eagle sitting on fences, perched on power poles, or flying overhead. Eagles were a rare sight in the concrete habitat, and the idea one might be following her was preposterous.

Finally free of the worst traffic, Mori floored it—just in case the eagle *was* tailing her. Who knew what Homeland Security had at its disposal? Mechanical spying eagles might not be outside the realm of possibility.

She rolled down the window and turned off the AC. Now that night had fallen, the temperature had dropped below ninety degrees. Might be a downright nippy eighty-five by midnight.

The turnoff to the Quad-D was hard to find in daylight, near impossible after dark, but Mori had driven this stretch of two-lane blacktop so often her muscles had memorized the turns. She slowed and eased the car onto the gravel road that stretched through a grove of live oaks that met in a dense overhead canopy. During daylight hours, it looked like a grand entrance to an estate, so the simple two-story wooden farmhouse that lay at the end of it always seemed out of place, lifted from another vista.

The upstairs lights were off and her father's SUV was missing, but a light shone in the front living room and she saw a shadow move through the window, followed by a rustling of curtains. Someone was home and knew she was here.

Her mom opened the door before she cleared the front stairs. Celia Chastaine was tall and athletic like her daughter, her blond hair streaked with gray now, but Mori recognized none of her own softness and humor. Celia had named her only child after the school where she'd studied in her one failed attempt at escaping family bonds and striking out on her own. Naming her daughter "Emory" hinted at a sense of irony, if not exactly a sense of humor that Mori had never seen.

"Paul said you'd be here as soon as you got out, to honor your commitment. I thought you'd run away from it. I'm glad you proved me wrong." Celia moved aside so Mori could enter. The ambience of the house wrapped a warmth around Mori that even Celia couldn't completely chill. Her grandfather, Gus Chastaine, had been dead several years, but his sweet, calming influence remained carved into the very walls of the home he'd built. If he'd still been alive, he'd support her. Or at least she thought so.

Regardless, Mori had no intention of marrying Michael Benedict, even if she had officially crossed her deadline of turning twenty-five.

"Why didn't Dad come to pick me up from the FBI offices, or at least send a lawyer?" Mori followed her mother into the living room, where the TV was blaring what looked like some kind of barrel-racing competition. Celia turned it off, and the silence in the room lay heavy.

Her mother sat straight-backed in the overstuffed armchair at the end of the sofa, looking out of place in the homey Texas warmth of the Chastaine family ranch. She'd lived here thirty years and still looked like an interloper. "Paul wanted you to think about the consequences of being so selfish. To think about everything that would be lost if you continue to shirk your duty."

Mori gritted her teeth but only counted to three before she couldn't stand it anymore. "I'm not here to *fulfill my responsibility*, as you say. I know it looks selfish on the surface, but think about it, Mom. All I'm doing if I marry Michael Benedict is delaying the inevitable, so why not live my life? Find a man to spend my life with who—oh, here's a radical thought—I might actually *love*?"

A vision of Jack Kelly's startling blue-green eyes came to her. She didn't love him, of course. He was just the first man she'd met in a long time she was attracted to, and for no rational reason she could come up with, she somehow trusted him. Plus, he was outside this world her parents lived in, which made him automatically—

"You've met someone. I figured as much." Her mother's voice dripped with disgust. "You're sleeping with him, I guess. At least tell me you aren't pregnant. Do I need to remind you the child won't be allowed to live?"

Mori stared at the woman who'd given birth to her and wondered who the hell she was. Wondered if at some time in her youth she'd been just like Mori but had let herself be warped into a soulless monster by circumstances. "I'm not seeing anyone, and I'm certainly not pregnant. If I were, this is the last place I would come."

Her anger brought the details of the room into sharp relief as she got to her feet. The worn, braided rug. Heavy, masculine furniture. Dark, scarred wooden beams on the ceiling. The fireplace it rarely got cold enough to need for warmth. A man's room for the man's world they lived in.

Celia might be willing to live her life on the fringes, but Mori wasn't.

"I'd hoped to talk to Dad, to make sure Michael had nothing to do with whoever told the police the Co-Op was involved in the bombing." She started toward the door. "Because we do good work. Important work. And we do it without hurting anyone. It shouldn't be jeopardized because of a personal vendetta."

She'd pulled open the door, the heat hitting her face like a blast from a steam room. Her mom's voice came from so close behind her it made her jump. She hadn't heard Celia get up, much less cross the room that fast.

"Oh, Michael made that call to the police. We all talked about it weeks ago, Michael and your father and me. It was a warning." Celia's voice was low and heated with its own anger. "If you don't want to see the same thing happen again, you'll change your tune, Little Miss Independent. Michael's been a patient and forgiving man, but he's tired of waiting."

Mori turned and locked gazes with her mother. She knew the shock was visible on her own face, because Celia gave her a cold, satisfied smile before closing the door and shutting her outside.

Michael hadn't just implicated Mori in the bombing. Celia had implied that he had *caused* the bombing, and her parents had known.

The little car bounced along the road beneath the canopy of oaks, but at the end of the drive, instead of turning left toward the freeway to take her back to town, Mori steered the car right, driving in a daze. After a couple of miles, surrounded by open land and occasional clusters of trees, she pulled far enough off the road that she could camouflage her car behind a stand of trees made scrawny by the hot summer and the ongoing drought.

The waning half moon cast a dim light over the scrub-covered land around her. Mori pulled her T-shirt over her head and shimmied out of her track shorts, then her bra and panties, folding them and nestling them beneath the prickly branches of a mesquite bush about ten yards from the car.

She raised her head to pull in a deep lungful of air, felt the ancient blood within her stir, and began to run.

EPISODE 2

⚜CHAPTER 5⚜

Kell pulled the Terminator out of his apartment parking lot promptly at 7:00 a.m., hoping to get to the Co-Op offices early enough to catch Mori alone, without Taylor Stedman as a nosy chaperone. He had plenty of time to plan his strategy as the traffic crawled along Westheimer toward the city.

Homeland Security would be watching the Co-Op offices and Mori herself, but as far as Kell knew, they hadn't obtained a warrant to search the building. He had no doubt they were working on it. So Kell's Plan B was to search every nook, cranny, and pigeonhole of the place before anyone else got to it.

He had devised a Plan A, in case Mori had already arrived. He'd get to know his suspect better, discover her hot buttons (the ones that didn't involve Louisiana black bears), figure out what drove her, earn her trust. He'd chosen his most nonthreatening, all-American clothes this morning, hoping to look less military and more like a regular guy: his LSU T-shirt, jeans, and running shoes instead of boots.

Mori's personal life was a mystery, other than the tidbits she'd dropped on the way back from the FBI offices. She struck him as a loner. No one had come to pick her up when she'd been released. Not her parents. Nobody. Something odd was going on with that. She was pretty. Hell, more than pretty, not that he had any business noticing. She seemed to have a good sense of humor, at least from the glimmers he'd seen in the middle of what had to be monumental stress. Why would a woman like that be so alone? Especially yesterday. When he'd gone home and reread her files, he realized it had been her twenty-fifth birthday.

Something was seriously wrong with the surface picture of Mori Chastaine.

The files compiled on her by the colonel had little information other than that she had lived in Texas all her life, was an only child, and had never been married. No known boyfriends. No close friends, period.

He needed to be her friend. Then he could either stop her or save her.

As he turned on Montrose, he saw he'd have no luck with either Plans A or B. When he eased the Terminator into the Co-Op parking lot, Mori's little hybrid was nowhere to be found, but Taylor's vintage Ford pickup took up two spaces in front of the entrance. Not only because it was that big, but because he'd done a shit job of parking.

Kell didn't like Taylor Stedman, thought he was pursuing his own agenda rather than acting as Mori's second-in-command. The man might not have done anything criminal, but he wasn't loyal to his employer, and loyalty filled up page one of the Jack Kellison Book of Virtues.

Of course, working undercover to gain a woman's trust and then betraying her for the greater good fell into a gray area he didn't want to think about too deeply.

That he was judging Taylor for not being loyal to a suspected terrorist was something Kell didn't want to ruminate on too long, either, because then he'd have to openly admit he was having a hard time thinking Mori could be guilty. And that he didn't want her to be guilty. Or *why* he didn't want her to be guilty.

Horny. That's all he was. Too long in the sexual trough of deprivation and neglect with nothing but a skinny, birdlike, frequently naked eagle-shifter to look at.

No, Kell didn't like Taylor Stedman, but he did like Taylor's ride—a hulking vision of fading black paint with a hint of rust. He stopped for a few seconds to admire it before entering the building. If he were to get rid of the Terminator and replace it, he could totally see himself with something like this, working on it on weekends to fix it up.

The real question wasn't how a jerk like Tay had ended up with such a cool ride, which probably burned gas and oil like nobody's business. The real question was, why was he here so early?

Going into a structure quietly was a Ranger-reinforced habit. He'd spent many hours conducting door-to-door searches in unsafe environments, silent for a couple of very practical reasons.

First, never give an enemy advance warning so he has time to get ready to shoot your nuts off as soon as you're within firing range.

Second, you might stumble across something interesting.

Like the sight of Taylor Stedman sitting at Mori's desk, using a brass letter opener to pick at the lock in a bottom drawer. The weasel-dick was so deep in concentration he didn't notice Kell leaning against the doorjamb, watching him.

"Need help finding something?" Kell crossed his arms as Taylor gasped and jumped to his feet, his face turning a deep shade of late-summer tomato.

"God, didn't your mama teach you not to sneak up on people?" Obviously interpreting Kell's neutral expression as a sign of approval, Taylor took the chair again and resumed his clumsy use of the letter opener. "I want to save the Co-Op, and the only way to do it might be to see what Emory Chastaine is hiding. If we're the ones who expose her, it makes us look good. All our disappearing supporters will come back when they see that the rest of us had nothing to do with her crimes."

Jack nodded, calming his inner urge to shake the man until his teeth rattled out of their sockets. Sure, he'd been planning to do the same thing—but to save people's lives, not to act out a fit of petty jealousy. And he had no doubt Taylor resented every particle of Mori's being. "Find anything?"

"Just this bottom drawer. It's the only one with a lock, so maybe she's hidden something incriminating. You know, some threatening letters or bomb-making supplies."

Taylor Stedman had watched way too much television.

"I doubt she'd be that stupid." More than he could say for Taylor. If Mori had left boxes of wires, explosives, and timers in the drawer of her Office Depot special, locked or not, he'd eat that whole nasty pile of military Meals Ready-to-Eat he'd stashed in his closet five years ago in case of a hurricane.

Taylor shrugged. "Keep an eye out for her while I try to get into this drawer. If you see her car pull in the lot, let me know. Don't want her slipping up on me like you did." He looked up, the sharp angles of his face narrowing. "How *did* you get in here without me hearing you?"

Because the idiot was so intent on his own crime a freight train could have roared past without disturbing him. "Force of habit. You know, from my Army training."

"Right." Tay cocked his head and raised his eyebrows, which made Kell want to throttle him even more. "Did the Army teach you how to pick locks?"

He'd never met a security system he couldn't breach or a lock he couldn't pick, but not for this jerk. That was a solitary activity. "Sorry. I'll play lookout. You break and enter."

He stepped back into the hallway, torn. Some big, macho, asshole part of him wanted to protect Mori, from the cops and from her assistant director. Maybe even from himself. But the stakes were too high to play hunches and trust his gut entirely. He didn't *think* he was so sex starved that he'd ignore evidence against the first woman to attract him in dog years, but then again, it had been a while.

In the end, he didn't have the moral dilemma of whether or not to let Tay break into Mori's desk. A few seconds after he'd stepped within sight of the parking lot, her graphite-gray hybrid pulled into the slot next to the Terminator.

"Mama's home." Kell grinned at Taylor's string of curses and the sound of him running down the hall to his own office. Served the toad right if he'd left something behind to let Mori know she was being backstabbed.

He watched as she sat in the car for almost a minute, her hands resting on the steering wheel, eyes straight ahead, lost in thought. Kell hadn't been able to spend enough time alone with her to get her to open up, but she looked like she needed to talk to someone.

Her body language as she finally exited the car screamed tension. She wore khaki shorts and a loose black tank top, so the slump of her shoulders was visible. Before she pulled the door open, she drew a deep breath and straightened her carriage, as if calling on some inner reserve of strength.

What wasn't visible until she stepped inside the door and saw Kell perched on the corner of the front receptionist's desk were the scrapes and scratches along her shoulders and upper arms. Scabs had formed, but the scratches were fresh enough for the skin around them to still be reddened.

"What got hold of you? And who won? You OK?" Kell rose from the chair and walked toward her, stopping when he realized she'd begun backing away. Shit, he hadn't intended to scare her, and she'd never struck him as skittish. If anything, she'd always seemed too calm for what was going on around her.

He held up his hands. Just an innocent, nonthreatening good old boy from Louisiana. "Sorry, I didn't mean to startle you."

She regrouped, squared her shoulders again, and shook her head. "No, I'm sorry. All this stuff with the bombing has me on edge. I still can't believe they think the Co-Op had anything to do with it. That *I* had anything to do with it. I've never even had a traffic ticket."

He hated to tell her, but that moved her up on the terrorist list, not down. Domestic terrorists—at least the most danger-ous ones—were quiet people with clean records. The ones about which, after some horrific crime had taken place, their neigh-bors would say, *He was always such a quiet man and kept to himself.* Loners. Just like Mori.

"Did someone hurt you?" He watched her face. "How'd your shoulders get scraped up?"

She looked at one shoulder, then the other, and laughed. She had a good laugh. "It looks like I got in a catfight, doesn't it?" She threw her backpack inside the door of her office. "I went running last night, out in the country near my grandfather's ranch. Well, my parents' ranch now. Guess I tangled with some low-hanging mesquite branches. It was really dark out."

Plausible. She looked like an athlete, so he could imagine her running, but not scratching herself up that much without realizing it. Plus, the wounds looked older than something done less than twelve hours ago. A day older than that, maybe. Unfortunately, he'd had a lot of his own injuries for comparison.

"I'm a runner myself." Or he had been before he'd screwed up his back, and he missed the runner's high and the way it relaxed his mind. "Maybe we could go running together one evening—and stay away from the mesquite. Maybe out along Buffalo Bayou."

Kell mentally kicked himself. Where the hell had that come from? He was not here to augment his social life. OK. *Develop* his social life.

When he saw a genuine smile light up Mori's face, though, he was glad he'd suggested it. She was beautiful once all the tension and worry lines lifted from her features, and Kell focused on a light sprinkling of freckles across her nose and cheeks. Sexy as hell.

"I haven't had a running partner since college at Rice. I'd like that. I warn you, though. I'm fast. You'll be eating my dust."

Oh, seriously. Had she challenged him? "You obviously have no idea who you're talking to, little girl. You're on."

Kell struggled to wipe the stupid shit-eating grin off his face. He was acting like a fucking high school boy, not a professional investigating a potential terrorist. He'd gone from looking for an opportunity to search her office to a playdate in the space of a half hour.

Mori cleared her throat. It was a nervous habit, Kell decided. Something she used when she wanted to change the subject, and it was definitely time to change the subject.

"Well, I better get to work since I was late this morning. Has Taylor given you our unlogged receipts to work on?"

No, Tay had been too busy snooping for evidence to use against her. "Nope. But I'm here to give you whatever you need."

They caught glances in the awkward pause, and he realized how his words could be interpreted—and that she realized it, too. A rush of heat flushed his face. Maybe he needed to call the colonel tonight and have himself taken off this case. He was obviously losing his professional judgment.

"Um, well"—Mori looked around the office—"you can go through these last donations we got and log them. Maybe we can get them in the bank before the donors put a stop-payment order on them. You know how to use spreadsheet software?"

God help him, he hated computers. Gadget had pounded the basics into him, but spreadsheets were a nightmare. "Well, I can enter data." And literally nothing more.

"That's all it is. I told our student volunteers to stay home until all this mess is sorted out, so we're shorthanded. I appreciate your help." She pointed to the desk where he'd been sitting earlier, and watched as he started the computer. He was way too aware of her leaning over his shoulder as she showed him how to log donations on the spreadsheet and then write the totals on a bank-deposit form.

Yep, his professional judgment had definitely gone on vacation.

"I'll be in my office if you have questions. If any donors call and say they want to pull their support, send them through to me." Mori rested a hand on his shoulder for a second before turning, disappearing through her office door, and closing it behind her.

Taylor's chair squeaked from down the hallway, and he appeared in front of Kell's desk scant seconds after Mori's door had snicked shut. "She doesn't suspect anything, does she?"

Kell shook his head and raised a finger to his lips. Not because he was afraid Mori would overhear her traitorous associate, but because Kell thought he might have to kill the guy if he started yapping again. "Stay in your office and keep it low-key," he whispered. "I'll be your eyes and ears, and let you know if anything happens."

With a conspiratorial nod, Taylor gave him a thumbs-up and went back down the hall.

For the next hour, Kell played secretary and thought about Taylor Stedman. He wished he could lay blame for the bombing at his Earth Shoe—clad feet. But the same instincts that told him Mori was innocent told him Taylor didn't have the brains or the balls to pull off something like the Zemurray bombing. He was an opportunist who wanted his boss's job and wasn't above capitalizing on her bad luck.

Bad luck, yes, but maybe also bad judgment. The more he thought about Emory Chastaine, the more Kell was convinced that while she wasn't involved in the bombing, *something* didn't add up. She might have gotten those scratches from a low-hanging mesquite branch, but she didn't act like a woman wrongly accused of a horrible crime. She hadn't screamed for an attorney. She hadn't held a press conference expressing outrage over being unjustly accused. If she'd been privately outraged by it, which she should have been if she were innocent, she sure hadn't shown it. She'd seemed hurt, confused, and sad—but never angry.

Had it been Kell in her position, he'd be pissing the fire and brimstone of the righteous and talking to everyone who'd listen. He'd be having fucking press conferences out the wazoo and booking time on talk shows.

He stared at her closed office door with a frown. Mori wasn't acting like a terrorist, but she *was* acting like a woman with a secret.

❧CHAPTER 6☙

Mori paced her office, looking out her window at the traffic maneuvering up and down Montrose Boulevard. She knew what she needed to do, but she hadn't been able to work up the courage.

Her mother's words had kept her awake and prowling around her apartment all night. Celia Chastaine had always been a hard and spiteful woman; Mori knew that better than anyone, except maybe her dad. Celia knew how to phrase the offhand comment to skewer the deepest or how to settle negativity over another's happiness like a thick blanket of soot.

So Mori's first instinct, after she'd calmed down, was to dismiss her mother's insinuations about the bombing as so much more Celia Chastaine drama.

And yet, deep down, it stank of horrifying possibility. Look at what the bombing had accomplished. Even if Carl Felderman's death hadn't left the governor's chair vacant and the halls of power in Austin mired in chaos, any talk of industrial expansion had halted. It might take years to get back to the conference table, if the new biochemical corridor wasn't a dead deal altogether.

If bombing the Zemurray Building could put a stopper on expansion into wildlife areas *and* bring his promised bride to heel, would a few hundred human lives be a worthwhile trade-off for a man like Michael Benedict?

Surely not. Michael was arrogant and stubborn, but she'd never thought of him as deliberately cruel. Yet Mori couldn't shake the idea, which meant she had to talk to him, God help her. And the sooner the better, especially since the birthday deadline had passed. She was getting distracted and careless, not even noticing the scratches on her shoulders when she slid into the tank top this morning. It was the first thing Jack Kelly had seen.

Kell—who had also consumed more than his share of her thoughts during her long, restless night. After her mother's accusation that she'd gotten involved with someone, Mori had indulged in a few daydreams about what it might be like if Kell were more than a volunteer. What if she were the simple woman he thought, meeting him in a casual work environment? What if, after discovering this electric chemistry between them, they could act on it if they wanted? Go on a date? What if she could really get to know him and see if their obvious attraction to each other went anywhere?

What if she could be normal, in other words.

Mori stared at the phone on her desk and took a deep breath. She pulled her keys from her bag and unlocked the bottom desk drawer, frowning at a few scratches around the keyhole. Most of the hanging files contained confidential information on fund-raising prospects she'd been working on to support the Co-Op. But the file in front was personal. If someone were trying to break into the drawer, it was probably her nosy assistant. Taylor did not need to see the contents of that file.

She flipped through it, stopping at the most damning thing—the agreement signed between her parents and Michael Benedict, dated twenty-five years earlier. They'd promised her as his mate, in exchange for a sizable cash "advance." Also in the file: her passport, only used a couple of times in college. She kept it close at hand in case she decided to make a run for it. And, finally, a small case containing a few photos and a business card—the thing she was looking for. Michael's business card. She had his home number in her cell phone contact list, but not his office number.

Mori started to return the folder to the drawer, but thought better of it. What if the authorities got a warrant to search the Co-Op offices? There was nothing here to tie her to the bombing, of course, but she shouldn't have that marriage agreement where anyone could find it and make her explain it. Having Taylor find it would be equally disastrous. He'd probably send it to the *Houston Chronicle* and urge them to write an exposé.

Not that she was being paranoid or anything.

When she was fifteen, she'd found the contract in her dad's study by mistake. Once she'd seen what it was and had a good cry over what it meant, she'd slipped it out of the house and made a copy before returning the original. She should have burned the damned thing instead of copying it, but she'd been too convinced her grandfather, if no one else, wouldn't let it happen.

Then he'd died, and Mori kept her copy of the contract as a reminder of how hard she'd have to fight to hang on to her independence.

She slipped the folder into her bag and relocked the drawer. That contract didn't need to be in her house, either. If she got Michael officially dragged into this investigation, an ugly scenario would grow even worse. Not that the horse's ass didn't deserve it.

She shouldn't think of him as a horse's ass. It was an insult to the horse.

Mori looked at the number on the business card, picked up the handset, and began working the keypad. Before the call had a chance to go through, she slammed the phone back onto its charger. *Stupid, stupid, stupid.* The police were probably monitoring every call out of this office—and her cell phone, too. God, being paranoid was exhausting.

No point in asking to borrow Kell's phone. She didn't want him anywhere near this nightmare. He could never be on Michael Benedict's radar.

She'd have to see Michael in person and make sure she wasn't followed by the cops. Or a mechanical eagle.

Kell was shooting homicidal looks at the computer when she opened her office door, and when he glanced up at her with those amazing eyes, she almost tripped. Those things should be illegal.

"I've gotta go out for a while. You and Tay hold down the fort." She looked down the hallway. Speaking of her second-in-command, he'd been uncharacteristically quiet this morning. "He is here, isn't he?"

A voice wafted down the hall. "I'm here. Just busy doing damage control."

Mori's eyes rolled before she could stop them, earning a grin from Kell. "You have my cell number if anything comes up?"

"Sure, Tay gave me both of your numbers yesterday. You need some company? I'm almost through with these."

Oh no. Taking a guy with her to see Michael? Not happening.

"Thanks, but I need to tend to some personal business. I'll be back in later."

Kell looked like he had more to say, and as much as Mori would rather stay and talk to him, she needed to get this over with. Plus, the more time she was around Jack Kelly, the more she liked him. Which worsened the fact that nothing could ever happen between them, even a real friendship.

The hour's drive to Galveston should have relaxed her, but instead, it gave her sixty uninterrupted minutes of second-guessing. By the time she pulled in to the lot of Tex-La Shipping's Galveston offices, her heartbeat was doing Olympic sprints. Maybe she'd luck out and Michael wouldn't be there.

The office building was, from the front, generic and designed to look vaguely like the Alamo. The company's main headquarters in New Orleans held all the fancy meeting rooms and high-rise views of the river port where most of their business originated. But Michael usually spent August in Galveston, where the sea breezes were cooler than the sweltering sauna of New Orleans, and Mori knew from previous visits that the back side of the three-story adobe building was mostly glass overlooking the water.

When she stepped off the elevator on the third floor where the executive offices were housed, she wasn't surprised to see the man himself leaning over the receptionist's desk, looking relaxed and jovial. He wore a tailored black suit and a patterned tie, and looked exactly like what he was: a filthy-rich businessman at the top of his game.

At least until he turned and saw Mori. Then he looked like a rich, triumphant businessman who'd just scored a record-breaking deal. Mori clenched her fists at her sides. She'd like to slap the lips off his face, just on principle.

"Emory." He smiled and raked an arrogant, possessive gaze across her, from her ponytail, down the length of her black tank top and khaki shorts, and back up again. "We really must do something about your wardrobe."

He turned to the secretary, who'd been studying Mori with naked curiosity. "Bring us some drinks, Tina, and see that we're not disturbed, please."

Not waiting for her, assuming Mori would trot behind him like an obedient puppy, Michael sauntered down the hall to his corner office overlooking the Gulf. She waited a few seconds before following, and squinted as she entered his office. Bright sunlight glinted off the waves below with such fierceness that Mori wished she hadn't left her sunglasses in the car.

At least if she felt the need to drown herself, she wouldn't have far to go. Or felt the desire to drown him, which was more likely.

"I thought I'd be seeing you yesterday." Michael moved past the desk and sat in one of the armchairs clustered around a low coffee table on the far end of the rectangular office.

Mori took the seat opposite him and waited while Tina came in with a tray containing an assortment of sodas, bottled water, whiskey, and iced tea. Michael Benedict was a sweet-tea man during business hours, and Mori hated that she knew such things about him.

She didn't remember a time when Michael hadn't been involved in her life. At every Chastaine family gathering, he'd be hanging around the fringes, always lurking, always a huge presence—literally.

He was the only man who'd ever made Mori feel petite. At six-six, or maybe more, he was broad shouldered and solidly built. All muscle, too. Mori was twenty-five years his junior, but

Michael didn't look fifty. What was it the pop magazines were always saying? Fifty was the new thirty?

Of course, lack of stress would do wonders for one's longevity, and Michael had always gotten his way. Until now.

"Now, Emory, my pet, I assume you're here to work out the financial and practical details of our little arrangement. I assure you, as I've told your folks all along, I'm a generous man, and none of you will ever have to do without. Your daddy doesn't have the intestinal fortitude to thrive in the cutthroat world of finance. He's much more suited to life on the Quad-D, and after we're married, he can retire. Your parents will live very comfortably."

Mori could feel her blood pressure rising, creating a tightness in her chest. The thump of her pulse pounded in her ears. He really thought she'd crawl to him and give in, just like that?

Her fingertips dug into the arms of the distressed-leather chair. "The only arrangements we're making today go like this: you assure me no other people are going to be hurt, in exchange for which I don't turn you in for the bomb-setting bastard you are."

OK, probably not the wisest choice of words. A brief, thunderous flash of rage crossed Michael's face. His tanned complexion took on a reddish hue all the way to his well-groomed coif of dark hair, which was just beginning to silver at the temples. Then the moment passed, and his face settled back into a neutral expression. His brown eyes held both fire and ice, though. He was pissed. Well, good, so was she.

Mori started as an oversize gray-and-black cat jumped on the coffee table between them and settled on its haunches, staring at her with golden eyes ringed in black. The cat's back was to Michael, its tail twitching in nervous sweeps.

Funny-looking animal, although Mori wasn't fond of cats and had never been around many. This one had a small head, and its ears were likewise small and rounded. A spark of recognition jolted through her. This was no domesticated house cat.

"A jaguarundi?" She couldn't take her eyes off the animal, which stared back at her with a hostile show of teeth. "Why would you take one out of its habitat and bring it here?"

The small member of the puma family had been crowded out of its Texas habitat and was believed to be extinct here, but could still be found in Mexico and South America. Plus, these were aggressive, solitary animals unsuited for captivity. That Michael would bring one here as a pet was incomprehensible.

"Very good. Yes, he's a jaguarundi, but Travis here *is* in his native habitat, actually." Michael sipped his tea, an almost delicate gesture for such a large man. "I keep several on retainer."

"On retain—" Mori looked back at the cat, which she swore was laughing at her now. A freaking jaguarundi-shifter. They had to be rare, so why they'd let themselves be answerable to one of her kind was hard to grasp.

Except, they all shared an endgame, didn't they? Survival.

She'd be damned if she'd talk private business in front of one. "If you want to talk to me, you'll ask your pet"—she jerked her head toward the feline, who'd begun to lick his left front paw with nonchalant arrogance but stopped to hiss—"to take his personal grooming elsewhere."

Michael's smile spread slowly and sent chills skittering down Mori's backbone. "As you wish. Travis, take your brother and drive up to Houston. I'd like a complete report on this handsome new volunteer our Mori seems to be on such friendly terms with. So friendly he even picked her up at FBI headquarters yesterday. Name's Jack Kelly, I believe.

"Find out who he is, and who his friends are. Find out where he lives."

❧ CHAPTER 7 ❧

Mori had always known Michael Benedict was a bully. An arrogant jackass who always got his way in the school yard of life, by any means necessary. But until now, she'd never thought him evil, and she'd been wrong. Evil was tanned and wealthy and privileged and thought the world revolved around his wants and needs.

They sat silently, staring at each other, while the shifter went into Michael's private bathroom off his office and changed. In human form, Travis the jaguarundi was a small-boned, slim-hipped man with caramel-colored hair and a nervous habit of tugging on his earlobe. He tugged as he exited the bathroom, tugged when he nodded at Michael, and tugged as he closed the door behind him to go on his nefarious assignment. *Kell. God, Michael already knew about him.*

As soon as the door clicked shut, Mori rounded on Michael, standing so she could tower over him, at least as long as he remained seated. "You do *not* go after my coworkers. They have no part in this." Those cats could tear Kell apart, and he'd never see it coming. If they went after him at work, they'd hurt Taylor as well, or even one of the college kids who happened to drop in at the wrong time.

Michael steepled his fingers—big hands, powerful hands—in front of his face in an infuriatingly calm gesture. "Your mother called me last night after you left the ranch. Did you know that? Said you were fucking some guy and that's what had you digging your heels in. I figure it's the one who picked you up yesterday."

He'd been having her followed. How had she not considered that? She'd been stupid and naive, that's how.

Michael pulled a slip of paper from the pocket of his suit coat. "Your associate Mr. Stedman was most helpful in sharing information with me, thinking me a reporter." He looked up at her. "You really should hire more loyal workers. He said the new volunteer's name is Jack Kelly, just off active duty in Afghanistan. Injured in service to his country. It would be a pity for him to come all the way back to Houston a hero, only to die because of a selfish little girl who refused to do her duty and honor her commitments."

He tossed the paper on the table, crossed his legs, and leaned back in the chair with a rustle of distressed leather, making her feel stupid and childish standing there with her feet in a rigid stance and her hands tightened into fists. God, Michael was threatening Kell. He'd done nothing but try to help her, to look for something to fill his days with meaning while he recuperated.

He'd been battle tested, but not for this kind of battle. This one, he couldn't possibly win.

She had to stay calm. "I haven't been with anyone in a long time, and you know that if your spies are as good as you think.

I barely know the guy; he only showed up three days ago and was nice enough to give me a ride home after *you'd* implicated me in that bombing. I didn't see you rushing to my defense. So leave my coworkers alone."

She'd find time to chew Taylor Stedman a new one later. In fact, when all this blew over, Taylor would be joining the ranks of the unemployed.

Michael gave an exaggerated sigh. "Really, Emory. You should have learned when you went screwing your way through college in some sort of childish rebellion that I don't care who you fuck, or how often. It doesn't change your responsibilities. You've reached the age of twenty-five, and now you're mine until I tire of you. That was the agreement, and I thought my birthday message would make it clear how seriously I take it."

Mori looked at the muted diagonal pattern etched into the thick carpet. The flowers. The note. Her mother's words. It all added up, but she needed to hear him say it. "You implicated the Co-Op in the bombings so I'd run to you for help. I understand that. But I have to know. Did you set the bombs? Kill the governor and all those innocent people?"

Michael's chuckle caused Mori's heart to thud unevenly. "That was a goddamn stroke of brilliance, if I do say so myself." He closed his eyes as if reliving a vacation memory, not congratulating his own genius in killing hundreds of people. "It stopped those industrial meetings, maybe for good. Ended the expansion talks that would have wiped out more habitat. It let me put a plan in place to control the politics in Austin. And it got the attention of my spoiled, stubborn wife-to-be. Win-win-win-win."

Mori sat down hard. "You wanted to get my attention and change politics in Austin, so you killed the governor? Hundreds of people who did nothing wrong? You're insane." Not to mention a megalomaniac. If his gene pool held the future of their people, they deserved to die out. Mori would be doing the world a favor by ending the line.

"What makes you think the governor is dead?" Michael walked to his desk and retrieved an appointment book.

Mori frowned at him. Carl Felderman's body hadn't been found, but neither had dozens of others. Witnesses had seen him in the stairwell at some point before the building collapsed. One man claimed to have seen him leave in a dark sedan, but after Felderman never surfaced, the guy's claim had been dismissed as post bombing hysteria. "What do you mean? If the governor's not dead, where is he?"

Michael returned to his chair and flipped a couple of pages on his calendar. "Let's just say he's been detained while we convince him it's in his best interests to change his environmental policies. You'll be seeing him again soon."

Mori rubbed her temples, which pulsed with the stirrings of a monster headache. She couldn't even think about what his cryptic comments about the governor might mean, except that she was glad the man was alive. She might not like him personally, but she didn't want him dead, especially because of her.

"Labor Day's just over a week away. Did you realize that?" Michael held up his calendar, as if Mori might dispute this earth-shattering revelation.

"Why do I care about Labor Day?" Not only was a tropical storm forming in the central Gulf, but she had a few other problems on her plate—like being suspected of terrorist activities and figuring out a way to avoid becoming a broodmare for Michael Benedict.

He leaned forward, slapped the calendar on the table hard enough to make Tina's tray rattle, and rose to his full, looming height. "You're acting like a spoiled brat, so I figure I should speak in a language you'll understand."

Mori wanted to stand, to move away from him, but she knew he'd still tower over her. Plus, the look on his face scared her. He'd dropped the benevolent, patronizing jerk persona, and his full power shone through the straight line of his mouth and the ice in his eyes.

But she'd be damned if she'd show fear, even though he'd be able to scent it. "And what language might I understand?"

"This. You have forty-eight hours to come to me with an apology and show me the gratitude I deserve for waiting patiently for you until you turned twenty-five instead of taking you at eighteen."

He took a step closer, and Mori tightened her death grip on the arms of the chair. "I have forty-eight hours, or what?"

Michael's gaze never left hers. "Or I put the plan in place to do the same thing in New Orleans on Labor Day that I did in Houston. And then I come and take you, take what's mine. I'm done trying to coax you in like a skittish filly at your granddaddy's ranch. We both know I can take you any time I want, in any way I want, and as roughly as I want. It's your choice as to how this plays out."

He propped a big hand on either arm of Mori's chair and leaned over her, close enough for her to smell the tea on his breath and his minty aftershave. "You won't find being with me unpleasant, Emory. I'm told I'm a very good lover. I can touch you in ways that will make you beg for it, in ways your college boys or your little soldier couldn't imagine."

Michael stood, and once again, Mori felt dwarfed by his size and power. She could never overwhelm him, and they both knew it. She didn't have it in her to kill him, and they both knew that, too. He had enough reach and enough money to find her if she tried to run away.

Which left her one option, her ultimate threat and the only thing she knew he wouldn't want to risk—her life.

To her surprise, her knees didn't quiver when she rose to her feet. Now that it had come to this, an eerie calm washed through her and her voice was strong and steady. "Let me speak in a language *you* will understand, Michael. You will forget about your warped threats for New Orleans. You will call off your jaguarundi thugs and leave my coworkers alone. You will forget whatever it is you're trying to do with the governor. And you will take a nice little cup and jack off in it under a doctor's supervision. If those things happen, I might—*might*—consider having your children and giving you visitation privileges."

Michael's tight smile widened into a grin. "Those are some mighty big demands coming from a woman with nothing to back it up. I'll do those things, or what? You'll try to kill me?"

Clearly, he didn't see her real trump card, so she gave him a cold smile in return. "No, I won't try to kill you, you jackass. I have a lot of more effective options." She rocked back on her heels and stared at the ceiling, pretending to think. "I could find a nice big bottle of sleeping pills and wash them down with a fifth of tequila. Or I could go to the top of the Chase Building and splatter myself all over a downtown sidewalk." She shifted her gaze to the water outside. "Or I could walk into the Gulf of Mexico and just keep on walking."

She looked him in the eye, challenging him. "I'll kill myself before I let you touch me or hurt anyone else. *You* have forty-eight hours to decide."

Mori was on the floor before her brain registered the pain from his fist's impact. By then, he'd wrapped his hands around her neck and jerked her to her feet again, holding her off the ground a few seconds before slinging her away from him. She landed with a hard crash against the sharp corner of the table, the wood chipping into the side of her arm. Tina's tray crashed to the floor, and from her vantage point, Mori watched, dazed, as tea spread over the thick, cream-colored carpet.

The world hung motionless as Mori tried to focus, the blood feeling too heavy as it coursed down her cheek where his ring had cut into her, the rasp of her breath too loud, the clink of ice too brittle as Michael picked up his glass. She heard liquid pouring from a bottle, and the stench of bourbon assaulted her nostrils.

But by God, she'd gotten through to him. Finally. And his fury told her he'd taken her threat seriously. He'd retrieved his whiskey bottle from the floor and taken a drink during business hours.

Mori climbed to her feet and waited for the dizziness to pass. "Forty-eight hours," she whispered. "And I do as I threatened."

Michael's voice was tight with rage. "The timetable's changed. Twenty-four hours and I take you—with or without your consent. I continue with plans for New Orleans. And I'll kill your new boyfriend while you watch."

❦ CHAPTER 8 ❦

Sitting in the outdoor dining area of Niko Niko's, Kell shoved his chair as close to the building as it would go in hopes of soaking up a little air-conditioning. He swiped his hand across the condensation on his water glass and scrubbed his wet palm across his face. What he wouldn't give to be at Cote Blanche. The temperature would still be one step shy of meltdown, but at least he wouldn't be frying from the radiant heat of concrete and steel.

A tropical storm had formed in the lower Gulf, moving at a crawl. Bad thing: slow-moving storms often mushroomed into hurricanes. Good thing: Tropical Storm Geneva had already started sucking a tiny bit of the humidity out of the air. The concrete was still hot enough to bake the soles of his feet through his running shoes, but at least he hadn't sweated all the way through his shirt. Yet.

Kell had propped his cell phone against a votive holder on the table while he demolished a plate of calamari. Finally, the little screen lit to signal an incoming call. About damned time.

He was waiting to hear from Robin, who'd been tailing Mori by air. He was waiting to hear from the colonel, who wanted an update. And he was waiting for Nik to share the results of the past two days spent sniffing around the bomb site, psychically speaking.

He picked up the phone and looked at the screen; Colonel Rick won the jackpot.

Now he had to figure out how to tell the man—who so far hadn't shown any sign of possessing a sense of humor—that not only did he have no leads, but he also might have the hots for the primary suspect. This assignment was shaping up *not* to be his finest hour. "Kellison."

"Where are we?" Colonel Rick Thomas's voice vibrated with the low notes of authority and the high notes of hard-ass.

"We're following up on some leads, sir." Technically true. Nik was bringing some drawings, Robin had put in a lot of flight time, and he...Well, he'd invited the potential terrorist to go on a running date.

"In other words, you've got jack shit."

Kell winced and took a sip of his water. "Pretty much."

An uncomfortable silence swelled over the line. At least Kell found it pretty miserable.

"Here's the thing, Colonel. My gut's telling me the Co-Op had nothing to do with that bombing. Emory Chastaine's got nothing to red-flag her as a terrorist. Obviously, Homeland's watching her every move and hasn't come up with anything, either. The Co-Op has no history of violence; in fact, all their public statements denounce extreme forms of activism. And the assistant director's a dickweed, but he's not smart enough to have pulled off that bombing. Has it occurred to the higher-ups that the terrorist was the one who called in the tip?"

"Of course it has. But even if the bomber is someone with a grudge against the Co-Op or Ms. Chastaine, she's our way in." The colonel paused before continuing. "Have you gotten close enough in the organization—with this Emory Chastaine—to be sure they're clean and that she's a random scapegoat? Sure enough to pull your team off the case?"

Damn it. He was sure Mori wasn't the bomber, but she *was* hiding something and it could involve the bombing. Her response to being wrongly accused was too detached. He might be horny, but he wasn't blind.

"Jack, your silence says more than your words—which haven't told me shit." The colonel's voice barked through the phone so loudly Kell pulled it away from his ear a couple of inches. "Until you can tell me with a hundred percent certainty that Emory Chastaine is innocent, stay on it. Stay on her. Hell, fuck the woman. I saw the file. She's not bad looking. Tell me you haven't been bunking with the Rangers so long you forgot how to sweet-talk a woman between the sheets."

Kell's tongue stuck to the roof of his mouth, and his words came out muffled. "Good idea, sir." He waited to hear a laugh or chuckle—*something*—to indicate the colonel was joking. Right. No sense of humor.

During their months of Ranger School torture and bonding, Robin had called Kell a tight-ass. Actually, "tight-ass puritan" were her exact words, and Kell had blown her off. But she might be right, because the idea of seducing Mori to wheedle secrets out of her offended him to the core.

"Do I need to remind you that it's nine days until Labor Day and there's a fucking storm in the Gulf that's probably going to make landfall somewhere on the central coast?" The colonel was shouting now. Definitely not joking. "We don't have time to jack around."

Kell scowled at Nik, who'd slumped into the chair opposite him and tossed a sketch pad on the table. Kell lifted the corner of the pages and played them like a set of flip cards. There were a good two dozen images drawn in Nik's meticulous pen-and-ink detail. He lifted his eyebrows, and Nik nodded.

"Sir, we do have something to send you. Nik has been able to pull a series of images from around the ruins of the Zemurray Building. Faces, mostly. I'm going to shoot them with my cell and e-mail them to you on your secure account."

"Good." The colonel sounded a little less gruff. "Did he get any other info to go with the images? Memories? Visions? Whatever the hell it is he sees?"

Thanks to the colonel's less-than-subtle voice, Nik had been able to hear him across the table and shook his head.

"No stories. Just faces," Kell said.

The colonel sighed. "It's a long shot, but it beats nothing. I'll run the images through our data bank and see if anything matches. In the meantime, resolve the issue of the Co-Op and Emory Chastaine's involvement. However you need to."

"Got it." Yeah, he had it, all right: a damn headache, plus the muscles in his lower back twitched with spasms, twice worse now than when he'd answered his phone. Kell ended the call and pulled the sketch pad toward him while the waiter delivered his souvlaki and took Nik's order. As soon as the guy had moved on, Kell handed Nik a stuffed grape leaf. "Talk to me."

Nik chewed for a few seconds, scanning the restaurant that was still moderately crowded, even for midafternoon. "I got a lot of images I didn't draw." He rubbed his eyes. "Damn, man. It sucked. I tried not to touch anything personal, but I couldn't avoid getting my hands on stuff accidentally—you know, a shoe, a scarf. I kept thinking if I was any kind of man, any kind of human, I'd go in there and use this ability to help the police identify remains. But I..." He trailed off, shutting down.

They'd talked through this shit before. Nik was afraid if he ever opened up his abilities to be used in an official way, let more than just a very few know about what he could do, it would take over his life. He was afraid he'd end up like his father, putting a bullet in his brain to shut up the noise.

Kell shoved his beer across the table. Nik took it with a nod and upended it, belching when he was done.

"Nice." Kell opened the sketch pad, switched his phone to the camera app, and began taking two shots of each page. "Tell me what's here."

"I figured anything personal belonged to victims, so I focused on the rubble itself, especially around the areas where the bombs were placed. I mean, chances are that whoever's on the top of the terrorist food chain, he didn't plant the bombs personally. But he—or she—might have visited the building. So anytime I got a visual of a face when I touched a piece of rubble, I drew it."

"Good thinking. Maybe we'll luck out and find a match." Kell finished the photos and began the process of e-mailing them to the colonel. "Heard from our feathered friend as to what Mori Chastaine's up to this afternoon?"

Nik's food arrived, and he waited until the waiter left before answering. "Just talked to her. Robin followed Mori to Galveston, where she went into the building housing the offices of"— he flipped through the sketch pad until he found a page with a few lines of writing—"Tex-La Shipping. I did an online search of them, and guess where their main headquarters are?"

Kell groaned. *Damn it, Mori.* "I'm guessing New Orleans."

"You'd be right."

Kell grabbed his cell again and texted a message for Gadget to research Tex-La Shipping—see who owned it and look for connections to the Co-Op, specifically to Mori.

He turned his attention back to Nik. "OK, so Mori went in the building, and then what?"

Nik talked around a mouthful of hummus. "She was still there when Robin left. Couple of guys exited the building, and Robin thought she should follow them instead of waiting. That's all she told me before she went feathery on me and left the pay phone."

Kell looked at the *I'm on it, Boss* text from Gadget and tossed the phone back on the table. "What two guys could be more important than watching our suspect?"

Nik shrugged. "Can't tell you, man. I'm just the messenger. You know Robin's a woman of few words."

She had plenty of words when she wanted to use them. "Damn it, we need to find out what Mori's doing." He hadn't told Nik that he'd undertaken some subtle shift from proving Mori's guilt to proving her innocence. Robin leaving her post was a poor decision, no matter how interesting these two guys proved to be.

"What did the colonel have to say?" Nik ate another bite and pushed his plate away. The skin around his eyes was tight, and his eyes were bloodshot. The bomb site search had been brutal for him.

Well, this would cheer him up. "The colonel says he wants me to seduce Mori Chastaine and get her to make a post-orgasmic terrorist confession."

Nik choked on his drink, simultaneously coughing and laughing. "I think the old man's overestimating your sex appeal, dude."

Glad somebody thought it was funny. The colonel sure hadn't been laughing.

Nik pulled out his wallet and threw some money on the table. "So what are you going to do?"

Kell studied the line of people stretched beyond the pastry counter inside the restaurant and grimaced. "Kellison Seduction Method 101: take the lady some dessert and hope it leads to getting laid and enjoying some pillow talk."

EPISODE 3

❧CHAPTER 9❧

Kell stood in the open doorway of his bedroom closet and surveyed the piss-poor clothing options for his evening assignment. If he dressed up too much for this game of "seduce the terrorist suspect," the whole thing would look as staged as a Shakespearean comedy.

If he wore his normal gear—baggy shorts and a T-shirt— she'd think he was a total loser. Which might not be too far from the truth, considering his goal for the evening was to be a predatory asshole.

After five minutes of indecision, he realized he was acting like a fucking high school girl trying to get ready for prom. *Screw your head on straight, Kellison.* He showered and put on what he'd normally wear for an evening out—a pair of jeans and a plain black T-shirt. It was practically a dress shirt, after all. Had no college logos, Army mottos, or beer icons on the front.

He opened the medicine cabinet in the minuscule bathroom and grabbed the ibuprofen bottle, shaking out four. He thought about it a second, then shook out two more. His back had been bad today for some reason. Probably tension, which annoyed him to no end. Before the injury, stress had gotten his juices flowing, made his limbs itch to move, sharpened his thoughts and perceptiveness. Now, it hurt.

As Kell set the bottle back on the narrow glass shelf, he spotted a box of condoms that had been there since the dawn of time. Shit. Another moral dilemma. As long as he was going to be a jackass, he might as well be a jackass with protection. He slid a foil packet out of the box and stared at it a moment. Might as well be optimistic, too. He pulled out a second packet.

Gator had been hanging tight on his heels ever since he'd gotten home, and Kell almost tripped over him getting out of the bathroom. "What's up with you, big guy? You hungry?" Gator's tail wagged optimistically.

After dumping some dog food into the stainless-steel dish and replenishing the water bowl, Kell flicked on the TV news to make sure there were no new developments in the Zemurray case. A woman was being interviewed, reminiscing about her twenty-seven-year-old son who'd been killed in the explosion. Then a young girl who couldn't be more than twelve, talking about how her mother would never see her and her little brother grow up. Then a man who'd lost an arm, who felt blessed to be alive. And they all wondered why this had happened. Who'd done it, and for what reason?

Kell pressed the OFF button on the remote and sat in silence. He'd needed that reminder. This wasn't about the environment, or business, or politics. It wasn't about whether or not he had to act in ways that went against his own moral code or how much he liked the person he was investigating. This was about people whose lives had been ripped apart for no reason except that they were in the wrong place at the wrong time.

Hell, when he was in the sandbox, he knew there was a chance he'd get blown to hell, but that was what he'd signed up for. These victims had signed up for nothing except doing their jobs and living their lives.

"I still don't think she's guilty," he told Gator, who cocked his head and speared Kell with a sharp look from both his blue eye and his brown one. "But I have to be sure."

He picked up the box of loukoumades he'd gotten at Niko Niko's, gave Gator a parting liver snack, and walked outside into the blast furnace of Houston in August. It was no wonder this place had been considered virtually uninhabitable before some genius came up with the idea of air-conditioning. He set the box of pastries on the passenger seat, but paused on his way around to the driver's side. Two cats, both a mottled gray-black color, sat atop the brick wall that separated the back of Kell's apartment complex from the condos behind it.

He knew everything was supposed to be bigger in Texas, but these cats were freaks. Big, long bodies, little heads, funny-looking round ears. He bet they weighed twenty-five or thirty pounds apiece. "You two should give some extra purrs to whoever took you in because—sorry, guys—you are ug-*lee*."

One of the cats bared its teeth and hissed, which Kell considered his cue to leave. He had enough weirdness in his life, what with teammates who turned into eagles and jaguars, without worrying about one of his neighbors having bizarre taste in pets.

Kell had plugged Mori's address into the GPS in his phone, and it directed him to a small quadplex not far from the Co-Op offices. Her car was parked out front, and as Kell pulled the Terminator into the adjacent space and got out, he automatically scanned the neighborhood. Given enough time, he'd be able to figure out where the DHS guys were basing their surveillance, but it didn't really matter. They were out there somewhere and probably already knew the name of Jack Kelly. Hopefully, they didn't know Jack Kellison.

Mori's door was at the end of the quadplex, on the left. He took a deep breath and knocked. Kell had put the moves on his share of women over the years, but never under orders or with the intent to deceive. Or while Homeland Security agents were somewhere nearby, wires and cameras at the ready. It was fucking creepy.

When Mori didn't answer, he looked back at her car. Everything seemed normal, so he knocked again, harder. "Mori, it's Kell. I brought you a surprise."

A shuffling sounded near the door, then her muffled voice. "Sorry, not tonight, Kell. I'm not feeling well."

Well, shit. That was a scenario he hadn't planned on. He'd imagined her slapping the crap out of him when he put the moves on her. He'd imagined finding her with another guy. He'd imagined her not being at home. He hadn't imagined her refusing to open the door.

"At least open up and take these honey balls from Niko's. I have a Greek friend who insists they're the best." Not that Nik had ever set foot in his father's homeland, but he'd grown up on the cuisine.

"Please, Kell. You need to go home. I'll see you tomorrow."

Something wasn't right; Mori's voice was off somehow. Kell's internal trouble meter sprang to attention, and he heeded it, walking over to Mori's car and peering inside. The interior seats, covered in a dark-gray fabric, held none of the usual assortment of junk he always dumped in the Terminator. All neat and orderly.

He stepped back and looked for any sign of an accident, but no dings or dents marred the metallic surface of the vehicle. He'd have to take her at her word and try again tomorrow night. Gator could eat his weight in honey balls.

The streetlights flickered on, and as Kell turned to go back to the Terminator, he saw a dark smudge on the driver's side door handle of Mori's car. He could either kneel and take a closer look—and possibly rouse the suspicion of the surveillance team—or he could do the smart thing and go home.

To hell with the surveillance team. His instincts told him that smudge was not mud. Kneeling beside the driver's side door, he looked closer at the handle, then used the flashlight app on his cell phone to illuminate it. He didn't need to touch it to know it was blood. And it was fresh.

Damn it, she was going to let him in, or he was going to break in. He didn't want DHS guys coming in behind him and looking at the door, though, so he stood up and leaned against it, swiping his ass across the handle. When he stepped away, the smudge was gone.

He'd just wiped away possible physical evidence in a federal terrorism case using only his ass. What a warrior.

He returned to Mori's door and pounded, not willing to give in this time. "Mori, let me in. I saw the blood on your car door and I'm worried. Show me you're OK, or I'll have to break in."

He waited a few seconds, fingers thrumming impatiently on his thighs, but finally, the deadbolt turned from inside and the door opened an inch or two. One brown eye peered through the crack, the metal door chain stretching across the opening. "I'm fine, Kell. Just not up for company tonight. I'll see you tomorrow at the office."

The door inched closed, but Kell wasn't having it. Something was wrong. He shoved at the door just before she got it closed, hard enough to pop the chain latch and propel Mori back a couple of steps.

"Sorry I broke the chain, but something's—" Kell stopped and stared. Mori's jaw was swollen and discolored, all turquoise, red, and black. Already one hell of a bruise, and it was just starting to form. He'd seen bruises like that before. Hell, he'd had a few.

"Who hit you?" It was a blow from a fist, not an open-handed slap. A big fist, too. A man's fist. He could practically see the damned knuckle marks. "Who is he? Because I'll make damned sure he never does it again."

"You shouldn't be here." Mori turned and walked into the small living room while Kell closed the door and threw the dead bolt. He'd have to buy her another chain latch and put it in. Obviously, she was in danger from somebody—maybe somebody at Tex-La Shipping, but he couldn't admit he knew she'd been there.

Mori sat on the sofa, shoulders slumped, eyes on the floor. Damn it, what was going on with her?

Kell walked into the little kitchen to the right of the front door and opened the freezer. Bingo. Every serious runner kept cold packs on hand for sprains and strains, and Mori had four of them. He pulled out two, turned on the faucet to wet a kitchen towel, and went back into the living room.

"Let me look at your face." He sat next to her on the sofa, reached over, and gently grasped her chin, turning her injured jaw toward him. It might be sexist and about as politically correct as a book of Polish jokes, but it pissed off Kell to see a woman hurt by a man. And that fist had to belong to a man.

Mori remained silent and still wouldn't look at him, but she didn't pull away as he gently washed off the wound. A bloody cut gashed across the jawline nearest her mouth, and he eased the wet towel across it and then pressed on it until the bleeding stopped.

When he turned back with the cold pack, she held out her hand. "I'll do that." She shifted to face him, wincing as her right arm touched the back of the sofa. Another injury. "Kell, I appreciate you being here, but you really need to leave. It's not..." She bit off whatever words she'd planned to say. "You really need to go."

Kell sat back and studied her. "Mori, talk to me. Something big's going down with you, and I don't think it's the boys from Homeland Security. Who hit you?"

"Nobody, I just fell and—"

"Uh-uh. Don't give me that shit." Kell knew better. "I've been around injuries, so let me tell you what I see before you waste time spinning a lie about tripping or falling or running under a killer mesquite branch."

Mori looked at her hands clutched tightly in her lap and didn't answer.

"You were hit with a fist by a right-handed man. I'd say a big man with a lot of physical strength, taller than you by several inches, judging by the point of impact. He was wearing some kind of ring on his right hand."

His gaze slid to her neck. "He tried to choke you, bare-handed, I'd say. Maybe knocked you into something, or you fell on something that injured your right arm."

As he talked, Mori had lifted her gaze and now stared at him, wide-eyed. "How do you know that?"

Kell had hit it on the money; he could see it in her face. "I'm trained in this kind of stuff, don't forget. Rangers don't just go in and shoot people. And I've had my share of being punched in the face. I know what it looks like. Who was it?"

Mori shook her head. "It's safer for you not to know. I'm serious about this, Kell. You need to leave before...before anyone sees you here."

"A boyfriend?" Their intel hadn't mentioned one, but was she the type to stay in an abusive relationship? As much as he felt he'd connected with her, they were still strangers. And even the smartest women sometimes got sucked into a vortex of abuse.

"No. It's...a family issue." Mori leaned against the sofa back and stared at the ceiling.

Maybe her father had hit her, then, which somehow was even worse. Kell settled back on the sofa next to her, their shoulders almost touching. Close enough to be aware of her beside him, to feel her body heat, smell the mixture of blood with her clean, woodsy scent, aware of the shape of the long, toned legs stretched out beside his.

He needed her to talk to him, and not for any official reasons. The seduction game was off the table. She was in trouble, and he wanted to protect her. It was as primal as that. He'd worry about the rest later.

"Family can suck you in until there's nothing left." He knew all about that.

"That's the God's truth." Mori relaxed a fraction, so Kell kept talking.

"I was an only child, and my parents transferred all their hopes and wishes onto me, every damn thing they ever wanted but didn't get. You know, to become the scholarship football player that my dad wasn't quite good enough to be. To get into the college my mom couldn't afford. To settle down in Jeanerette after school, maybe start a business, meet a nice local girl, produce the grandkids my mom wanted."

Mori's voice was barely more than a whisper. "And if you became what they wanted, everything that made you into *you* would wither and die."

"I couldn't do it." His mind conjured visions of his mom's tear-streaked face, his dad's struggle between pride and disappointment, when he'd sat at the dining table and told them he'd enlisted. "I couldn't be what they wanted."

"How did you escape? You ran away from home and joined the Army?" Mori's voice had grown stronger. Maybe if he kept spilling his guts on the living room floor, she'd follow suit eventually.

"That's exactly what I did. Went through combat training at Fort Polk in Louisiana, then Ranger School at Fort Benning in Georgia. I couldn't get shipped out fast enough." His mom's face came to him again. She'd been convinced he'd be killed. And was so disappointed every time he finished a tour and went right back in at the first opportunity. "I hoped eventually they'd be proud that I took my own path, but I don't think they ever were."

They loved him. They feared for his safety. But they never understood why their vision for his life wasn't enough for him. Maybe if they'd lived longer. Maybe.

"Some family stuff you can't run away from," Mori said. "I've never pleased my parents, and it's come to the point where I have to take a stand or give in to what they want for me." She closed her eyes. "I'm so tired of fighting."

Kell hadn't planned to do it, but his arm seemed to move of its own accord, slipping around her shoulders and pulling her against him. She winced a little but didn't pull away, just laid her head on his shoulder. He lowered his chin to rest it on her head and took in the soft brush of her hair against his jaw, her scent of ocean breezes and sunlight and outdoors that surrounded him with warmth.

"Mori, let me help. I know you don't know me from shit, but I can at least listen. It might help to open up. I..." He bit his tongue before *I care about you* came out. "I'm a good listener, for a guy."

She sat up and turned toward him again, her expression more vulnerable than he'd expected. Her guard had dropped, and he saw strength in the line of her lips, intelligence and despair and longing swirling in a storm behind her eyes. "I can't put you in danger, Kell. I won't. You're the kindest, most honest man I've ever met, and in another time or place—or lifetime—I'd want to be with you. But you can't be around me now. You can't get involved in my chaos."

He hadn't been honest with her at all, and the fact that she saw him that way sent a ripple of guilt through him. But the bottom line was this: she wanted to be with him.

Kell shifted until they faced each other, and reached out to smooth a strand of hair from her cheek. She stilled when he touched her, and the moment seemed to pause and hold its breath. He leaned forward slowly, touching his lips to hers, tasting her sweet warmth, feeling the pressure of her mouth as she returned the kiss.

Shit. This might feel right, but it wasn't. He wasn't who she thought he was, and the colonel be damned. He wouldn't make love to this beautiful, damaged woman when she didn't even know his real name.

But she reached up with both hands, slid them around his neck, and pulled him back to her. "God help us both, Kell, but I want you."

≈ CHAPTER 10 ≈

Kell's lips were soft and hesitant at first, but as Mori leaned into the kiss and opened her mouth to his, he responded with a fierce hunger.

She pushed the fear and doubt away. Kell had already been here long enough that if Michael's people were watching, they'd have seen him. She had about twenty hours left before she had to relent to Michael and her family. She'd have to marry him, would have to bear the children who could save their species and hope at least one was a girl. If not, she'd only prolong their existence another generation.

The other option—killing herself—had lost its bite. She had no doubt that if she died at her own hand, Michael would seek revenge against her family. He'd carry through with his threats to New Orleans. He'd go after Kell, whose only crime was being kind. His kindness had been an unexpected gift.

All of those bad things would happen if she killed herself or ran away. If she gave Michael what he wanted—her body, her womb—she might be able to prevent the rest.

If she had twenty hours before giving herself to Michael, she wanted one memory of making love to a man who wanted her, without strings or conditions.

"We shouldn't—" Kell's protest drowned in her kiss, but the hunger with which he claimed her mouth told her exactly what she needed to know.

"We should. Just don't freak out over my arm, OK? It looks worse than it is." Wrapping her fingertips around the hem of her shirt, she pulled it over her head, watching Kell's face. Those beautiful eyes were glazed like those of a man slipping into serious lust mode, devouring her breasts with a look that made her tingle. Finally, he wrenched his gaze to her right arm.

On the skin between her elbow and shoulder, there bloomed a hellish black sunflower from where she'd hit the coffee table in Michael's office. By tomorrow, it would be well on its way to healing, but tonight, it looked nasty and hurt with a dull ache.

No glaze in those eyes now. Kell had gone from lust to possessiveness, from lover to soldier. "Tell me who he is, Mori. I swear I'll make him regret this."

God, if that were only possible. But no matter how good a warrior Kell was, how strong a fighter, how impassioned his determination, he was no match for Michael Benedict. For any of her kind.

"We'll talk later. Not now." She reached out and untucked the hem of his black T-shirt, pushing it up until he finally wrangled out of it himself. He was as beautiful as she'd expected, all hard, smooth muscle and tanned skin.

She slipped a hand to the button of his jeans, and he groaned as she slid her fingers down to cup him.

His breath hitched. "Aw, fuck." He stood up, peeled off the jeans—and oh yeah, he was hard and ready.

"Come here." Kell's voice rasped, lower than normal. Totally sexy. He could make her forget Michael and all his evil crap for a while. One last piece of happiness.

She made a slow show of unzipping her shorts, sliding them down her hips, and letting them fall to the floor before stepping out of them.

He slid his hand to her back, pulling her against him, and slanted his mouth over hers, taking charge, no longer hesitant. She relaxed against him, aware of every place their bodies melded, his hard bulge pressing against the sensitive juncture of her thighs.

Kell was the perfect height for her, and as if reading her thoughts, he backed her against the wall with enough force to jar the picture frame beside them, slid his hands inside her panties, and pulled her hips against his. He rocked in rhythm with the insistent assault of his tongue against hers, and a moan slid from her throat before she knew it was there.

His chest rose and fell with restrained energy as he stepped back a fraction, sliding his hands around her hips and up to palm her breasts, tasting each one, biting just enough to make her catch her breath and arch into him for more.

"Are you sure about this?" He kissed her swollen jaw gently, but of course, with every minute that passed it hurt less, for reasons he couldn't understand and could never know.

"I'm more sure than you know." She thought of another mood-killer. "I'm on the pill and I'm clean, but if you'd feel better with a condom, I'm afraid I don't have any."

He looked around the room and stared at his clothes, probably wondering if he should go and buy some protection. Mori wished she could tell him it was impossible for them to pass diseases between them, but she couldn't.

"Hell. I want to feel you." He pinned her again, but she wriggled away from him, pulling him toward her bedroom. A place Michael had never set foot. A space that belonged to no one but her.

They ditched the underwear and looked at each other for a moment. He was long and ready, and she needed to fill herself with him. Taking his hand, she backed toward the bed and slid to the middle, pulling him with her.

He blinked a couple of times as he hit the mattress. She'd forgotten that he had an injury. "It's your back, isn't it?"

He rolled to his side to face her. "What gave it away?"

She smiled and ran a hand along his cheek. "Sometimes when you stand up, you seem a little stiff, like you have to work off some pain. Is there anything that can be done for it?"

He'd been working his fingers down her side and between her thighs. "Later. My mouth can't talk; it has other things it needs to be doing." He leaned over and sucked one sensitive nipple into his mouth, while his fingers worked their magic inside her. She had to slow him down because when she came, she wanted more than his fingers.

She pulled away. "On your back. Let me take care of you for a change."

With a low chuckle, Kell rolled onto his back, and she crawled between his legs, taking him in her hand. She grinned and he raised an eyebrow in question—until she lowered her mouth and sucked him in.

"Holy shit." He supported himself with his elbows and watched her take one long swipe, then suck him in again. "Wait, wait. Damn."

He slid back and leaned against the headboard, pulling her on top of him. Her fingers etched crescent moons into his shoulders as she eased herself down on him until every inch was inside her. God, he felt so good, like he belonged there.

Their gazes met, and the connection between them took Mori by surprise. Her heart swelled with the joy at having found someone like him, and it swelled in agony that they'd never be together like this again.

Don't think about tomorrow. Enjoy him now. She set up a slow, steady rhythm, her gaze never leaving his, wanting their connection to include minds and hearts as well as bodies. Kell laced his fingers in her hair and pulled her to him, burying his tongue in her mouth even as he rocked with her, inside her.

She pulled back and rode him until he was thrashing and swearing, the sweat standing out on his face, but then her own sensations took over. Rolling her head back, she closed her eyes and focused on the heat building at her core, ready to explode from the power of his thighs and hips. She gasped at a new sensation and looked down to see Kell propped on one elbow, the other arm stretched out to work her clit between his fingers.

"Come for me, Mori. Let it out." He pinched his fingers together, and her world exploded in stars and spasms. It was only after she'd collapsed onto his chest, shuddering as he stroked her back, that she realized he'd turned her into one of those women who screamed incoherent noises when she came. She could do a scene in *Sleepless in Seattle.*

But he was still inside her, still hard, and she wanted him to come as fiercely as she had. She rocked against him, and he groaned. "Your turn." She nipped at his ear. "Tell me what you need."

"Just this." He grinned as he flipped her over and settled between her thighs with a steady, hard rhythm that sent that sweet coil of tension spiraling upward again. She wrapped arms and legs around him, urging him on, and he buried his mouth against her neck, his breath hot and heavy enough to erase the marks left by Michael's hands.

With a groan, he came, his body straining and then shattering. Mori kept her arms around him, stroking his back, running her fingers through his short, thick hair. She would have liked to stay with him like this forever, feeling safe and satisfied and, for just a few more minutes, happy.

Kell rolled over, pulling her with him and wrapping an arm around her. He didn't say anything, so she didn't either. Words would bring back reality, and she wasn't ready for it.

A dog barked in the living room—except Mori didn't have a dog. She sat up, confused.

"Shit. It's my cell phone." Kell rolled to his feet, but the barking stopped before he got halfway to the door. He looked back at her. "Mori, we need to talk. There are things I need to tell you, because that was amazing and I don't want secrets between us."

Damn it. She looked at the floor and nodded. She couldn't reveal her secrets. Whatever his were, she could guarantee they paled in comparison. "Reality sucks."

"Yeah, it does. I—" The barking started again, and Kell disappeared into the living room. His side of the conversation was abrupt, consisting of three "yeahs" and an "on my way."

Mori sighed and padded to the dresser. She pulled out a long T-shirt and slipped it over her head. When Kell reappeared in the bedroom doorway, he'd pulled his jeans back on and was sticking his arms through the sleeves of his T-shirt. "Sorry, a friend's in trouble. I need to deal with it."

"It's OK." She wrapped her arms around him, and he squeezed her tightly, resting his forehead against hers.

"I don't want to leave you here alone. Let me take you to a friend's or to a hotel. Hell, you can come to my place. You need to avoid whoever hurt you, family or not."

For the first time since she'd left Michael's office, Mori wanted to cry. The hours of numb shock had finally been eroded by Kell's gentle concern and his not-so-gentle lovemaking. "No, I'll be safe here. I'm going to sleep a while and then go into the office in the morning. We still have donors to appease." At least if she married Michael, she might be able to keep the Co-Op going. There had to be an upside to all of this.

"How about dinner tomorrow night? We do need to talk." Kell walked into the living room and fished around for a missing shoe, finding it lodged halfway under the sofa.

By tomorrow night, Mori's life sentence in the Prison of Obligation would have started. She didn't want to think about tomorrow night.

But she did have tomorrow, one last day of freedom. "What about lunch instead?"

❧CHAPTER 11❧

Kell pulled in to the covered parking space behind his apartment building and looked up in surprise at being there. He barely remembered leaving Mori's place and didn't remember the drive home at all. His body had brought him home on autopilot while his brain wandered in a moral fog.

What the fuck had he just done? Well, the answer was obvious. He'd turned into a fucking idiot, that's what. Literally. He'd connected emotionally with a woman he was supposed to be investigating. With a woman who thought he was Jack Kelly, unemployed veteran. With a woman who was being abused by some other man who might be using a fake name and misrepresenting himself—just like him.

But he still smelled her, still felt the hot silk of her as she clenched around him, still visualized the look of complete abandon on her face when she came.

He took a deep breath and shook off the Mori afterglow. Nik had been vague on the phone, but insistent. *Come home*, he'd said. *Now. You've been compromised.*

Kell opened his trunk, unlocked a black leather case next to his big duffel bag, and pulled out his clunky Beretta service pistol. After checking its ammo, he stuck it in his waistband under his shirt and pulled out his baby, an M4 rifle that had seen him through a lot. Hopefully, everyone at his complex was out having social lives and wouldn't see their rarely there neighbor trotting around and looking for someone to shoot.

A jolt of pain streaked from his back into his hip when he leaned over to get an extra clip for the pistol. Funny how he hadn't noticed it while he was rolling all over the bed with Mori. Looked like he was going to pay for it now, but he couldn't quite bring himself to regret what happened. Only that he hadn't been honest with her first.

Closing the trunk as quietly as possible, he walked through the apartment courtyard. Weird. His apartment window was dark, and he always left a light on for Gator. The last of the evening's moral quicksand filtered away, and his senses switched to high beam.

Kell stayed in the shadows, skirting the outside of the courtyard, taking the stairs at the far end instead of the elevator nearest his door. Thank God he'd worn his running shoes instead of hard-soled boots. He was able to ease silently around the edges of the balcony, past the stairwell, and within sight of his door.

It was only 10:00 p.m., but the night was still and quiet except for the sound of traffic in the distance. Kell lifted his fingers to his mouth and blew out a half hiss/half whistle, an eagle sound Robin had taught them during training.

An answering, identical call came back immediately from the direction of his apartment. What the fuck was going on?

Kell kept his rifle in position as he inched to his door and reached out to turn the knob. His apartment door swung in on silent hinges before he touched it.

Nik's whisper came out of the darkness. "In. Close the door like nothing's out of the ordinary."

Right. Because this was all so normal. He closed the door behind him and flipped the dead bolt. "Why are we in the dark? Better yet, why are we whispering?"

"Come back to the bedroom. We'll fill you in." Enough light from the courtyard filtered through the curtains for Kell to see Nik's outline as he walked down the short hallway to the bedroom, where a sliver of light shone under the door. Nik waited until Kell caught up, and then they both slipped inside.

Robin lay on his bed crossways, rubbing Gator's belly. Traitorous hound.

As if hearing his master's thoughts, Gator leaped to his feet and bounded to Kell, jumping up and down and talking his Catahoula-speak for "Something exciting happened." Sometimes it meant an alligator had made its way onto the dock at Cote Blanche. Sometimes it meant he'd spotted a cockroach. Kell had learned not to put too much stock in Gator's level of excitement.

"OK, what the fuck's going on?" He scratched behind Gator's ears and motioned for Robin to move. No birds on the bed in his house. Nik took the chair beside his desk.

She patted the mattress beside her. "Join me, and we'll tell you."

Kell sat next to her, reached out for her hand, and jerked her toward him. "Quit screwing around and tell me what's going on."

Robin scooted closer to Kell and sniffed his shoulder, then his neck. She grinned. "Oh, you have been a busy boy. Who was she?"

Nik raised his eyebrows but kept his mouth shut. Like a best buddy should.

"None of your business. Last time I'm asking. What's up?"

"It's about the two guys I followed from Tex-La Shipping today," Robin said, settling back on the pillows and clicking her teeth for Gator to join them, which he was happy to do. Kell needed to have a chat with that dog about who his master was, and appropriate behavior for visitors.

"Yeah, speaking of that, why did you follow them instead of sticking with Mori Chastaine?" Kell had been thinking about Mori's injuries. Whatever happened to her, *whoever* had happened to her, it had been either while she was at Tex-La or shortly afterward. If Robin had stayed in position, she might have been able to stop it.

"These guys were shifters, and they looked like they were moving with a purpose," she said. "I had to make the call, but gut instinct told me to stick with them."

Shifters at Tex-La? It didn't necessarily mean anything. Kell didn't know how many shifters there were in the world. Apparently there were all kinds, and they were relatively abundant. But he respected instinct, and as hard a time as he gave her, he'd learned to respect Robin.

"What were they doing?"

"I can tell you where they were going, but not why."

Kell turned to Nik. "She's playing games. Spill it."

"Robin tracked them first to the Co-Op, then here to your apartment." Nik leaned forward in the chair and propped his elbows on his knees. "They parked around back a few slots down from your space and then shifted."

A tingling sensation stole across Kell's scalp. Those goddamn ugly cats in the parking lot. "Shifted into what?"

"I'm not sure." Robin twisted on the bed till she was sitting cross-legged facing Kell, with Gator between them. "Some kind of feline—a little bigger than your average overweight house cat."

"Black and gray?" Kell asked her. "Funny little round ears?"

Robin straightened. "Where'd you see them?"

Kell rubbed his eyes and thought about the two cats. "They were sitting on top of that brick fence that runs behind the back parking lot. Watched me get in the car when I left tonight. One of them even hissed at me when I told him he was ugly."

A comment that probably wouldn't win him any friends in the cat-shifter club.

Nik got up and paced. "I started to tell you to come to my place, but I knew we needed to get Gator. So the better idea seemed for us to slip in and wait for you here."

"They probably saw you, so you're on their radar, too." A stupid cat could be crouched under a plant in the courtyard with eyes trained on the door.

"Give us some credit, man." Nik took the chair again. "We got an extension ladder and broke in your back window. Figured the cats would be watching the parking lot and the front."

Kell pulled the curtain aside and looked at the small second-story window, which was covered in... "You covered my windows with fucking duct tape? That's...kind of brilliant." He crossed his arms, thinking. "But maybe they aren't even here now. They could have followed me when I left earlier." Had he led them straight to Mori? Or had Mori's appearance at Tex-La somehow led the two shifters straight to him?

"No, they can't fly with the wings of an eagle," Robin said dryly. "Even in a full-tilt run, I don't think they could follow you through city traffic."

"Our guess is they're watching you. Why, I'm not sure. But it had to be prompted by Mori Chastaine's visit to Galveston this afternoon."

At Mori's name, Kell closed his eyes. "What more do we know about Tex-La Shipping? Who owns it?"

"I had Gadget send over a report an hour ago." Nik laid a thin stack of papers on the edge of the bed. "There are about a hundred employees in the Galveston office, but the owner's the most likely connection. Guy named Michael Benedict. He grew up in the Houston area before starting his shipping company in New Orleans. Keeps offices in Galveston, and he is currently in residence. He has a house here in River Oaks, where he lives part of the year, and the rest of the time he stays in New Orleans. Has a house uptown."

The man had money. Neither of those were cheap neighborhoods. "Direct ties to Mori Chastaine or the Co-Op?"

Nik ran his hands through his hair and leaned back. "The only thing Gadget's got so far is that Benedict owns a lot of land west of town in Austin County and part of it butts up against the Quad-D Ranch, which is owned by the Chastaine family."

"It belonged to Mori's grandfather, and her parents live there now." Kell felt as if they were dancing around some big, glaring puzzle piece that would make everything fit together—the bombing, Mori, the shipping tycoon, the shape-shifters. "We're missing the key. Trouble is, how do we find it?"

"I don't know," Nik said. "But you need to move. Pack up whatever you can take without looking suspicious. I rented a car for you in my name, and it's sitting at a lot downtown." He flicked a business card with a key taped to it at Kell, who caught it and saw an address on North Main.

"Let's hang on to the car, but for now, I'm driving the Terminator."

"You can't. It's too risky." Nik's voice rose.

"He has to stay here. He's the bait." Robin got to her feet and stretched. "If Kell disappears, we've lost our connection to Mori and the Co-Op. If he disappears from his apartment but shows up at the Co-Op tomorrow, someone will just follow him again."

Kell gave Robin a rare smile. Smart girl. Eagle. Whatever. "Exactly. I need to maintain as ordinary a routine as I can. Robin, you tail me for a while; you can hide in a tree or something." He ignored her snort. "Nik, I need you in Galveston. Hang out at Tex-La and keep an eye on Michael Benedict. Get a job there if you need to."

Nik nodded. "OK. You want us to stay here tonight?"

Kell thought about it and said words he never thought he'd utter. "You go on home and get an early start in Galveston tomorrow morning. Robin can spend the night with me."

Since he was hiding in plain sight, there was no point in keeping the lights off, so Kell walked Nik to the door while Robin did a quick fly around to spot any stray cat-shifters skulking in the shadows. After a few minutes she landed on the balcony rail and squawked twice for *all clear*.

"Be careful, man." Nik clamped a hand on his shoulder and froze. "Oh fuck, Kell. You didn't." He jerked his hand back and looked at it as if it were burned. "Tell me you were just following the plan. You know, getting laid so you could get information."

Kell looked at him and shrugged, ignoring another squawk from Robin that sounded a lot like laughter. Guess touching his shirt had shown Nik a quick highlight reel of his evening. "I wish it were that simple."

❧ CHAPTER 12 ❧

The Co-Op offices had never been hotter, and it had nothing to do with the hundred-plus temperature outside. Mori got to the office at 9:00, and Kell was already there. She stood at the door, watching him curse at the computer. He looked tired, and when he leaned over to pick up a receipt that had dropped to the floor, his movements were stiff.

Heat rushed across Mori's face at the thought of why his back might be sore. She'd been stupid and selfish. She could have put Kell at greater risk by being with him last night. She hated that she was not the woman he thought—nothing like it. But, oh, she wished she could be.

He looked up and smiled when she opened the door and went inside. The chill of the AC was so delicious she had to stop for a minute, close her eyes, and enjoy the feel of cold air on her skin. When she opened her eyes again, Kell was in front of her.

"Taylor's not here yet. Are we still on for lunch?"

She nodded. Her chance to grasp one last selfish slice of time for herself. "What do you want to do?"

Blue and green were normally cool colors, but his eyes filled with heat. "I have some ideas, but they're probably not appropriate for the office."

The thought made her heart speed up. She reached up to touch his cheek, run her thumb along the strong cheekbone, move toward him for a kiss.

"Well, isn't this an interesting way to start the morning?"

Damn Taylor, and damn her for being careless. She stepped back, not sure how to respond.

Kell took charge. "Don't be jealous, man." He smiled at Taylor, and Mori had to bite her lip to keep from laughing at his cocky, insincere expression. "Guess we'll have to keep it out of the office. At least until lunchtime."

Kell winked at her and went back to the receptionist's desk, ignoring Taylor's wide-eyed gawk.

Right. Work.

"Tay, do you have the last quarterly donor report finished? I wanted to go over it this morning." Mori went into her office and threw her bag on the floor next to her chair.

"Sure, I'll e-mail it to you." Tay stuck his head in her office door. "Also, a reporter called yesterday looking for you and asking questions about our new volunteer. I told him all about our war hero."

Yeah, she knew exactly what he'd told Michael and what had come of it. She'd already decided before Kell showed up last night that she had to give Michael what he wanted in order to keep him from following through on his threats. But being with Kell had erased any lingering doubts. She had no choice. Tonight, she'd tell Michael she was his. At least her body would be his. Her heart would never belong to him, but she doubted he'd care.

About 11:30 a.m., a call from one of the Co-Op's biggest donors kept her on the phone for more than an hour, trying to reassure the man that the million he'd pledged over the next twelve months was not tied up with anything illegal, much less an act of terrorism.

By the time she finally got off the phone, the pledge intact, it was a quarter till one. She grabbed her bag and was relieved to see Kell still at the desk, although he'd shut the computer down and had gotten engrossed in one of the books from the Co-Op's small library. Ironically, the one on extinct and endangered species in the American South and Southwest.

She cleared her throat, and he finally looked up. "Sorry that took so long. Are you starving?"

"No, I've been reading about these species that used to be abundant around here but are extinct, or at least they're thought to be extinct. I guess with a wild animal, it depends on how long it's been since there's been a confirmed sighting?"

She nodded, propping a hip on the edge of the desk. "Like the Louisiana black bear we were talking about. Since they live in the wild, chances are good that somebody's going to report seeing at least one in any given year. But it has been a while. Scientists will go in and confirm as best they can by looking for signs—bear scat or claw marks. If there are no sightings and no signs, eventually they're considered extinct."

Kell turned to a page he'd marked with a sticky note and flipped the book around to face her. "The jaguarundi are interesting. They're thought to be gone from Texas now—mostly, they live in South America. Are you familiar with them? Kind of ugly, I think."

Mori stared at the book, her pulse accelerating. What did Kell know? What was the likelihood that, out of every animal in the book, he'd zeroed in on the jaguarundi? All she could do was play dumb and stay cool.

"Not the prettiest of the wild cats, for sure." She took the book and studied the photo, which looked a hell of a lot like Travis. "I don't know a lot about them. They're in the puma family, a little bigger than a large house cat, I think." And aggressive, territorial, and continuing to exist in Texas only within a shifter population, apparently. She handed the book back to him and gave him what she hoped was a carefree smile. "So, you ready to go? Have any place special in mind for lunch?"

He closed the book and studied it a second before nodding. "You like Tex-Mex? There's a new place over on Kirby I've heard good things about. I thought about Niko Niko's again, but it's noisy and we need to talk."

Talk. Mori didn't want to talk, because what she had to say was one more lie on top of a stack of lies. She had to tell him she couldn't see him anymore. That it would be better if he didn't volunteer at the Co-Op. That she was planning to marry another man.

"Sure, that sounds great. Which car?"

Kell stopped at the door and gave her little hybrid a doubtful look. "I know I'm only a couple of inches taller than you, but I can't see me squishing in that matchbox on wheels."

Mori laughed. "Then the Blue Bombshell it is."

"The Terminator. The car's name is the Terminator."

They were both laughing when he pulled the Terminator into traffic, but silence settled over them within a block. Mori hated this awkwardness. They should have been in the throes of new relationship bliss, but Kell seemed as preoccupied and unsettled as she was.

What an irony it would be if the thing he wanted to tell her was that he didn't want to see her again. She'd been thinking all along this was her decision, as if he didn't have his own life and friends—and, who knew, even a wife somewhere. He didn't wear a ring, but that meant nothing these days, and she'd never thought to ask him.

What a dolt she was, mentally constructing this grand, tragic romance when, really, what they'd had was a one-night stand between two virtual strangers with great chemistry.

"Here we go." Kell wedged the behemoth of a car into a parking spot, and they got out without speaking further. The restaurant was one of those almost-too-cute adobe buildings, landscaped with cactus and palms. Most of the lunch crowd appeared to have cleared out, judging by the sparsely populated parking lot.

Once they were seated and had ordered, Kell reached out and took her hand. He didn't say anything for a few seconds, and Mori held her breath to see what he'd wanted to tell her since last night. She figured this talk could go one of two ways. He could dump her, or she'd be forced to dump him. Either way, it was going to hurt.

"I have to tell you, first, that I don't regret last night. Not for a second." He kept his gaze trained on their twined fingers. "I haven't been with anyone since... I hadn't expected to meet..." He clenched his jaw and looked down, as if searching for the right words. "You were a surprise. *We* were a surprise. So there are some things you need to know about me that... Oh hell."

He sat back in his chair and took a sip of his beer.

Kell had secrets he wanted to tell her? Mori sipped her own beer, watching him. It had never occurred to her that Jack Kelly was anything more or less than what he said.

"You were a surprise to me, too." She thought about their first meeting—only four days ago, but so much raw emotion had been crammed into those days, it seemed like weeks since he'd walked into the Co-Op. What she remembered most about her first encounter with Kell was the way he'd reacted to the

Homeland Security guys, his posture rigid and his back to the wall so they couldn't get behind him. It had looked like the kind of move a well-trained soldier might make on reflex. She realized she'd decided at that moment to trust him.

"I don't think there's anything you could tell me that would change things. I don't regret last night, either, and when you knew something was wrong and bullied your way in"—she looked up at him—"you took care of me. I saw who you were inside. That's what matters."

"Right. But still—"

A commotion at the restaurant's bar, which lay a few feet to their right, drew their attention. "What's going on?" Kell asked their waiter, who'd brought their plates but, like everyone else, was staring at the clump of bar patrons, all talking at once.

"The governor has been found, and he's alive." The waiter set down the plates and poured more water in Mori's glass. "Someone kidnapped him, I think."

Mori had a bad feeling about this and prayed that, whatever Michael had done to Carl Felderman, the governor would come back intact and with his mouth shut.

Kell was leaning so far back in his chair she thought he might tip over. "There's a TV behind the bar. Let's go hear what they're saying."

He was halfway to the commotion before she'd reluctantly risen from her chair. She eased between two of the waitstaff at the end of the bar, and sure enough, there was the old camera hog on-screen with a microphone stuck in front of him, having a press conference.

"Turn it louder!" yelled someone from a table farther back in the restaurant, and the bartender reached up and pushed the button until the familiar drawl of Carl Felderman could probably be heard in Dallas.

Felderman, always a thin stick of a man, looked horrible. Emaciated and pale, he spoke in a voice that sounded strong, but the hand he held up to adjust the microphone shook. Mori had never liked the man, but a deep stab of pity shot through her. Michael had caused this, at least partly because of her.

Mori looked down the length of the bar and finally spotted Kell, staring intently at the screen with his hands on his hips. He'd never mentioned Felderman—had never talked about the bombing at all except in general terms—but she guessed everyone was amazed that he was alive. Except her.

"I'm thankful to God that I've come through this ordeal, and I look forward to getting back to Austin and resuming my duties as governor," he was saying. He pushed away from the table where he was seated, waved feebly at the crowd of reporters, and hobbled away, leaning on the arm of an aide. What had he said earlier?

The camera switched to the news anchor, and people filtered back to their tables or their jobs. Mori looked at Kell, who was still staring at the screen with wide eyes, and she turned to see what he was looking at.

Oh God. "The governor has identified a local environmental activist as being behind his abduction and possibly the bombing of the Zemurray Building," the news anchor was saying. The picture behind him was of the Co-Op offices, with swarms of police cars outside, officers moving in and out the door, goddamned Taylor standing on the stoop running his mouth and pointing at her car in the lot.

And then the background picture changed to one of her. A publicity photo taken a year ago filled up the space behind the newsman's head. "A manhunt is under way, and a reward has been offered for information—"

Kell grabbed her arm and steered her toward the door. His voice was low and tight. "Walk out of here now." He tossed a few bills on their table as they passed it. "When we get to the car, I need you on the floorboard, out of sight. I'm right behind you."

"Kell, I didn't do this." The light as they pushed through the door blinded her, and she stumbled on the sidewalk. Kell grabbed her arm and propelled her forward as fast as they could go without running. "I swear, I had nothing to do with any of this."

He had to believe her. She needed him to believe her. What game was Michael playing this time? One more attempt to force her to come to him for help? Well, it was probably going to work.

Kell opened the passenger door and waited for her to climb in and slither onto the floorboard, then walked around the car and slid into the driver's seat.

"Kell, where are we going?" Was he taking her to the police? They couldn't go back to the Co-Op or to her apartment. She couldn't think of anyplace to go except to Michael, damn it. The Co-Op was ruined; she was ruined. But she'd be damned if she let Kell ruin his life, too.

She sat up and struggled to get back into the seat. "Let me out. You can't get involved in this."

Before she could twist and open the door, he'd cranked the engine and pulled out of the lot. "Get on the fucking floorboard. Now."

His harsh tone startled her so that she swallowed hard and curled as tightly onto the floorboard as her height would allow. Sometimes long legs were not an asset.

"Kell, you have to understand, I didn't—"

"Not now." Once he'd navigated the Terminator onto Kirby, he sped up and blended with traffic. "We'll talk later. Right now, you're on the run. And I'm aiding and abetting."

EPISODE 4

❦ CHAPTER 13 ❦

Somehow, when Kell had slogged through the Ranger School refresher and counterterrorism training with his new Omega Force team, he'd imagined using his skill set to work in tandem with law enforcement, or at least support it from behind the scenes.

Using his know-how to run from the law while aiding a suspected terrorist—and now kidnapper? Not on the agenda.

Yet here he was, driving his parents' ancient behemoth of a car with a silent, panicking woman crouched on his floorboard, his mind ticking through escape routes and assessing options.

He maneuvered the Terminator through the heavy traffic on Kirby and maneuvered onto I-59, headed toward downtown. The jag-shifters had seen the Olds, so his first order of business would be swapping it for the car Nik had rented.

Money fell next on the list—cash, to minimize the trail that would be left by using plastic.

Once those basic needs had been met, he'd figure out what the hell he was doing trashing his career for a woman who, if she hadn't been lying to him outright, had at the very least been lying by omission.

"Can I sit up now?"

He glanced down at a grim-faced Mori, who had folded her long frame into an accordion pleat, trying to squeeze onto the floorboard. He wanted to throttle her and hold her so tightly no one could touch her. And then throttle her again.

Instead, he growled, "Stay."

"Don't talk to me like I'm a golden retriever." She popped her head up and looked out the window before slumping back down. "You need to stop and let me out, Kell. You can't get involved in this."

"It's a little fucking late for that." Damn it, she hadn't asked him to pull the white knight routine, so he needed to quit acting like an asshole—at least until he heard her side of things. First, he had to get them somewhere safe. "Sorry."

He took a sharp right turn a little faster than he should have, causing the Olds's granny tires to squeal and Mori's head to thump on the door of the glove compartment. She rubbed her temple and scowled at him but didn't speak. Smart woman. He needed to think about where to go that wouldn't drag Nik and the rest of his team into the toilet with him if this all flushed south. It was definitely swirling in that direction.

His cell phone vibrated in his jeans pocket, and he maneuvered to pull it out and look at the incoming number. Nik. Kell considered not answering, but his phone shouldn't have been compromised, unless whoever was having him followed had linked Jack Kelly to Jack Kellison. And he needed to warn Nik and Robin to stay away from his apartment and the Co-Op. Thank God he'd decided to send Gator home with Nik last night.

He'd take the risk that the phone was still safe. "Shit creek, man. No paddle."

Nik's words were casual, but his voice was tense. "Where are you?"

"Going for the rental. Is it still in the same place?"

"Yeah." Nik's exasperated huff of air practically puffed its way through the phone. "She with you?"

Kell glanced down at Mori, who'd wrapped her arms around her bent knees and rested her forehead on them. "Affirmative."

"What the hell are you thinking? Tell me you're on your way to turn her in and are getting the rental car to protect yourself."

Kell didn't know what he was going to do beyond getting the new wheels. He wanted to know what was really going on before he took a step as drastic as turning Mori in. His gut told him she was in some kind of trouble the authorities might worsen rather than fix.

One step at a time. "Just stay away from the apartment and the Co-Op—and me. It's complicated."

"Fuck that. You need to go and... Wait a minute."

Robin's voice rose and fell in the background a few seconds before Nik cursed again. When he returned to the phone, he sounded pissed off but calmer. "OK, go to ground and avoid the colonel. Option B as in beta. We'll figure it out from there."

Kell let out a breath of relief and ended the call. They were behind him, and he hoped like hell they wouldn't live to regret it. While going through their counterterrorism training, the team members had privately come up with safeguard options in case one or all of them was compromised. They'd found multiple safe spots that even the Omega Force brass—the colonel and whoever he worked for—didn't know about.

First loyalty was to country. Next, to team. The colonel came in third. Maybe fourth, behind Gator. Kell didn't know where the hell Mori Chastaine fit into that list, except that she shouldn't be on it at all.

Option B was a cheap, utilitarian hotel in extreme far-east suburban Baytown, surrounded by petrochemical plants churning out smoke twenty-four/seven. That would be the next step after the car exchange.

"Who was that? Who knows you're with me?" Mori lifted her head and frowned at him, then unwound those distractingly long legs and levered herself into the passenger seat, her right hand on the door handle.

He watched her out of his peripheral vision. Her eyes scanned the street ahead of them, then locked onto something, her body tensed, her fingers tightened on the handle.

Shit. She was going to make a run for it if that next red light caught them. He obviously didn't have the good sense God gave a duck, or he'd arrest her. Since that wasn't happening, he should let her go, let her run, let her sink or swim in her own mess. Whatever her troubled game was, its players traveled in loftier circles than he did. Governors and millionaire shipping magnates were not the type of terrorist he'd been prepared to go after.

That was his brain doing all the tough talk. His gut remembered the vulnerability she'd shown when he'd touched her, and the open abandon with which she'd given herself to him. She was in trouble, and he had to do something about it.

Damn it. This nobility shit was seriously overrated.

With one eye on the smoke-belching truck in front of him, Kell reached over and flipped open the glove compartment, pulled out his spare pair of handcuffs, and snapped one bracelet around Mori's wrist before she figured out what he was doing. Be prepared, he always figured. *Rangers lead the way.*

"What the hell?" Mori pulled against him harder than he'd expected. In fact, she practically jerked his arm off, but he held on to the other cuff, finally snapping it around the Terminator's gearshift. If she jerked on it that hard again, she'd throw them into reverse and they'd both be shit out of luck.

She stopped struggling and stared at the cuffs. "Why did you do that?"

Kell gritted his teeth and gave her a solid glare. "Because you were getting ready to hop out at the next red light and run like a gazelle on the fucking Serengeti."

She laughed. How dare she laugh?

"I don't see one damn funny thing about this situation."

Mori stopped laughing, but the smile lingered. "I bet you were one absolute asshole as a Marine."

The woman needed an education, and he knew just the man to give it to her. "Ranger."

"Whatever." Mori slumped down in the seat but didn't try to slip the cuff on the gearshift—good thing, since a fender bender that put them in a close encounter with Houston's finest would be counterproductive to an escape.

"Where are we going, anyway? Wrong direction for the FBI or Houston PD."

He glanced at her before snapping his gaze back to the traffic. She was staring out the window, so he couldn't see her expression. How much did he trust her? Right now, not much. "Somewhere we can talk."

She turned to face him. "You aren't turning me in?"

The combination of hope and fear in her voice stabbed his conscience like a knife in the chest. He wanted to protect her, but he couldn't make that promise—not until he knew what kind of shit she was in and how deep. "Not yet."

He pulled into a self-park lot a half block from the rental's location, used the Jack Kelly credit card to pay for a week's parking, and eased the Terminator into a space. "Reach in the glove compartment and find the key to the cuffs. Don't think about running."

Mori huffed. "Or what? You're going to chase me down? Shoot me in the middle of downtown Houston? I mean, what part of *I don't want you involved in this* do you not get?" She dug around in the compartment, fished out a small pair of silver keys on a plain ring, and began fumbling with the cuff. "Just let me get out of this car and walk. Drive away and live your life. It's safer for both of us if you—"

"Who sent the two jaguarundi-shifters after me?"

Mori stopped futzing with the cuff but wouldn't meet his gaze. Just as he'd thought. A normal reaction would have been *What's a shifter, Kell? Jags are extinct, Kell.* Yet Mori was as pale as if she'd seen a fucking Louisiana black bear walking through downtown Houston in the oppressive August heat. She knew about shifters, which raised a whole bunch of new questions.

"How do you know about them? What did they do?" Her voice barely rose above a whisper, and she finally looked up at him. "Did they hurt you?"

"Not yet." He reached over and took the keys from her, quickly unlocking the cuffs. He'd take them with him; he'd never cuffed a woman to a bed with anything more than pleasure in mind, but he had a feeling Mori Chastaine wasn't going to give up her secrets easily.

The shifter comment seemed to have deflated Mori, and her shoulders sagged as she got out of the Olds. She didn't pull away when he wrapped his fingers around her wrist and tugged her to walk alongside him to the trunk, and she didn't raise an eyebrow when he transferred his rifle and the cuffs to a big duffel that still held the clothes he'd taken to Cote Blanche. Mori's slight intake of breath was the only indication she'd seen him slip the Beretta out of the case and into his waistband under his shirt before closing the trunk. He'd have put the rifle with it if he thought he could walk with it stuck down his pants leg.

"Look inconspicuous," he said under his breath, like a six-foot blond Amazon and a guy with a washtub-size duffel bag could be inconspicuous under any circumstances. Especially in a city like Houston, where there were underground air-conditioned tunnels so people wouldn't have to walk outside. "Walk with a purpose, but not like you're in a hurry."

They trekked at a steady clip to the lot where the rental was parked. Kell pulled out the card, found the space number, and detached the key. Escorting Mori to the passenger side of the generic dark-blue Chevy, he unlocked the door, not releasing her wrist until she had slid silently inside. To her credit, she didn't try to run while he walked around to the driver's side and got in. The shifter comment had shaken her big-time. Good.

"I'm stopping to get cash, and then we're going to a hotel where we can talk. There are some things you need to know about me, and there sure as hell are things I need to know about you—and your friends. Like the shifters and Michael Benedict."

Mori's demeanor morphed from worried to petrified before Benedict's name was out of his mouth. *Bingo.* Now he knew who'd hit her. Maybe even who'd sent the shifters after him.

Who, but not why. That big missing puzzle piece still floated out of reach. Why would the millionaire head of an international shipping company be mixed up in something this ugly?

He pulled the rental into traffic and wound his way east toward Baytown. It would take longer going along side streets, but the cops would be watching the freeways and interstates, expecting that to be Mori's logical escape route.

"You got a cell phone?" He glanced over at her, glad to see she wasn't crying. Tears, he couldn't handle. But she appeared to be deep in thought. "Mori? You got a cell phone?"

"What?" She jolted into awareness. "Sure, why?"

"Turn it off. It might have some kind of GPS signal that can be tracked." He thought a moment. "Better yet, leave it on and throw it out the window."

She dug in her bag and pressed the OFF button on the phone. "I'll turn it off."

Great. Now he'd have to make sure she didn't use the damned thing while he wasn't looking, or she'd get them both arrested. Or killed.

He couldn't help but pity her, even through his anger. She might not have realized it yet, but life as she'd known it was over—or maybe she had, from the tilt of her head as she stared out at urban vistas that grew steadily seedier as they traveled east. With the governor fingering her as his kidnapper, it wasn't the Co-Op under fire now, but Mori herself. Unless they could somehow straighten things out, she'd never be able to go home again. Assuming she wasn't in it so deep that things couldn't be straightened out. Then Kell couldn't protect her, or wouldn't. There were lines he wouldn't cross for anyone.

He found a branch of his bank with a drive-through ATM and took out the day's cash-withdrawal limit of $500 using his personal debit card. He stuck the bills in his wallet and tossed it on the console before resuming their twisting, turning route to Baytown. A long, tense, silent hour later, he pulled into the lot of a Super 8 motel tucked within a cluster of truck stops.

"Welcome to paradise." He eased through the lot, dodging potholes, and pulled into a parking space in the back. The door to Room 123 lay directly in front of them.

Thank God they'd made it this far. With the draining of adrenaline came a bone-deep weariness. He hadn't been able to soak his back or apply a heat pack to it for two or three days, and it was catching up with him. A whole bottle of ibuprofen wouldn't faze this kind of ache, and he wondered if Mori would hate him if he handcuffed her to the nightstand while he took a long, hot bath.

Kell reached over to grab his wallet, but it wasn't there, and as he raised his gaze to meet Mori's, he saw his own doubts reflected right back at him. In her hand was his wallet, open to expose his driver's license. His real driver's license.

Judas on a pony, when had he gotten so fucking careless? He reached out for the wallet, and she held on a moment before releasing it with a snap.

"Nice to meet you, John Kennedy Kellison Jr."

❧CHAPTER 14❧

W ho was this guy? Sure, Kell had said they needed to talk, that he had things to tell her, but Mori hadn't figured it was something basic like his freaking *name*. If he was lying about his name, what else had he lied about? And why?

Not that she had a lot of room to point fingers without being the world's biggest hypocrite, but still. At least when they'd had sex, he'd known her name. *There's even more about me, more important things, he doesn't know.*

Yeah, definitely no room to judge. Open-minded, that was her.

Kell stuffed his wallet back in his pocket and jerked the car door open. "Inside."

Open-minded had its limits. "You need to stop barking orders at me in one- or two-syllable words. It might work for your damned Marines, but it doesn't work for me." She knew the difference between a Marine and a Ranger, but he deserved to have his chain yanked and that seemed to do it.

Mori opened her car door in a vain attempt to catch a stray breeze, but stayed inside while he slammed around in the trunk, grumbling under his breath, retrieving that gargantuan duffel bag. Which did look like something a soldier would carry, she'd give him that much.

The trunk slammed shut. "Are you going in, or are we going to have this discussion in the parking lot?" Kell—if he even went by Kell—stood outside her car door, the bag slung over his shoulder. He'd put on a shoulder holster and transferred the gun to it, although she'd seen some kind of rifle or shotgun go into that bag.

"Fine." She'd been thinking all along that, as soon as they stopped, she'd make a run for it. If she went straight to Michael and told him she agreed to their union, there would be no reason for him to go after Kell. Now, curiosity propelled her out of the car and into the hotel room.

It wasn't the Waldorf Astoria, for sure. The choking diesel exhaust hanging in the humidity outside gave way to an assault of floral-scented carpet cleaner trying to mask the taint of stale cigarette smoke. But it was clean. Cool. Two queen-size beds shrouded in dizzying floral spreads completed the ambience.

Mori sat on the edge of the bed nearest the door while Kell closed and locked it, even latching the chain. Then he wedged the straight-backed chair from the desk under the doorknob.

"Paranoid much?"

He barely flicked a glance her way as he hefted the duffel bag and dumped it on the other bed. She couldn't see his face when he straightened up, but his back hurt. His movements, usually fluid and graceful unless he'd been sitting for a while, spoke of sore, stiff muscles. That she knew such a thing meant she'd obviously been watching him way too closely.

He sat on the bed opposite her, perched on the edge of the mattress with legs bent and shoulders tensed like he was ready to sprint on a split second's notice. She sat in much the same position.

Mori fought the giggles—and lost. She laughed so hard that it came out as a snort, which made her laugh even harder. "We are such losers."

Kell's expression traveled the continent from anger to confusion to reluctant half smile. "Pretty much. What gave it away?"

She closed her eyes and took a deep gulp of air to get the silliness under control. At least her outburst had suffocated her anger, and eased his as well. "Look at us. We're both so wrapped up in secrets we can't untangle ourselves, with me ready to run and you ready to chase. And yet..."

And yet her lies had been meant to keep him safe—to keep them both safe.

And yet, even though they'd both thought they were so smart, they'd still ended up hiding in a truck stop paradise.

"And yet here we are," Kell said softly, his blue-green eyes a forty-fathom ocean of feelings she couldn't read, "still together."

Mori nodded, her tongue poised to ask questions. Who was he? Why had he come to the Co-Op using a fake name and pretending to be an environmentalist? And doing a poor job of it, by the way. But the answer came to her.

"Oh my God. You *are* a cop. Or something like that." He'd shown up at the Co-Op only a few minutes before the Homeland Security guys arrived to take her in. He obviously knew when they were going to release her, and had made sure he was there. "You've been playing me all along."

"No, Mori. You don't understand." Kell stood at the same time she did, reaching for her.

She punched him midchest with her closed fist, earning an *oof.* "You came to my apartment and slept with me, knowing you were trying to...to...." To what? Find evidence against her? Seduce her with gentle hands and a hard cock? But wait. Hadn't she made the first moves on him? How screwed up was that?

The heat of shame flushed across her, dulling the effects of the air-conditioning. She pushed past him, knocking away the hand he reached out to stop her. "God, I feel so *stupid*. I'm out of here. Shoot me if you want to."

It was a good solution. All her problems would disappear if she died. Except, Michael would continue to kill. *He might do it anyway, now that he's had a taste that it will work, now that he's gotten control of the governor and the industry plans have fallen apart.*

A foot from freedom, a vise closed around her right ankle, her leg buckled, and she fell to her knees. "Damn it, Kell. Let go of me."

She rolled over and kicked at him, but he was on the floor with her foot tucked under his arm like a football.

His tone was just short of a shout. "Quit squirming and listen, damn it."

She raised her other foot to kick the crap out of him, but lowered it. And the truth hit her like a lightning bolt released by Thor himself. She was being weak by choice. No man— no normal man—could ever physically restrain her. Not with handcuffs and not with a death grip on her ankle. Not if she really wanted to run.

And there was the problem. Part of her didn't want to run. The part that hoped somehow—impossible as it might seem— Kell could help her.

Sensing her change of mood, Kell released her foot and climbed to his feet. He turned his back on her, hobbling to the duffel. He unzipped a pouch, pulled out a bottle, and shook pills out in his hand, swallowing them dry as if he'd done it a lot.

Mori watched him, indecisive. Oh hell, who was she kidding? She needed to hear him out before going to Michael, to know if that one last night of pleasure she'd allowed herself had been real or a setup. "I'm sorry."

Kell raised an eyebrow at her before turning to fill a plastic cup with tap water. "Sit."

"Please."

Kell turned. "What?"

"I am not one of your Rangers that you can bark orders at like a dog. Say, 'Sit, please,' or 'Mori, let's sit down and talk.'"

One edge of his mouth lifted, softening those fierce eyes. "At least you didn't call me a Marine." He crossed his arms over his chest. "Please sit down, Mori, and I'll tell you what I can."

What he could. Which meant not everything. She sat on the bed, crossed her arms in a mimic of his, and jerked her head toward the other bed. "Please sit down, John Kennedy Kellison Jr., and tell me who and what you are. I'm ready."

He sat, wincing.

"What happened to your back?" She wished they were at a place where she could help him—put a hot, wet towel on it, smooth out the tense muscles. But survival took first priority.

He rolled his head from side to side, tendons popping. "Compression fracture in Afghanistan on my last tour."

So the soldier part was true. "Can't it be fixed?"

He cocked his head as if surprised by the question. "There's a surgery that can be done, to fuse some things together. But my mobility would be limited. Or worse."

Kell's gaze had gone distant, his expression troubled.

Clearly a subject he'd given a lot of thought. "You've been weighing the possible worst outcomes against what you can and can't live with, haven't you?" She knew, because she'd been doing the same thing.

His eyes widened slightly before he pulled his stone face back into place. She'd called that one right.

"Here's what I can tell you." In a snap, Jack Kelly the easygoing volunteer disappeared, replaced by a harder, grim-faced version. "You saw my license, so you know my name is Jack Kellison. Kell really is my nickname. The part about me being just off my last Army tour and being injured is also true. The reason I volunteered at the Co-Op is a lie."

Mori nodded. She'd figured that much. "Are you a cop?"

"No." He ran a hand through his short hair, and she tracked the movement. Strong hands, with long fingers, short nails, a couple of scars. Nice hands.

"Then, what? FBI? Homeland Security?" Had to be something like that.

"Let's just say I'm part of a counterterrorism team trying to find out if the caller who fingered you for the bombing was telling the truth."

A chill stole across Mori's shoulders. Suddenly, the air-conditioning seemed to be doing its job too well. Worse than Homeland Security, then. Maybe one of those "secret force" kinds of guys she'd seen in the movies, who she'd always assumed were only fictional. The ones who made up their own rules. "And what did you find?"

Kell stood up and paced between the beds, his hands jammed in his pockets. "Not a damned thing but hunches, but I've learned to trust my hunches. They give me a few details." He stopped and frowned at her.

Mori's mouth felt like an acre of East Texas dust had filled it, and she swallowed hard. "What?" She steeled herself for his answers.

"You're not guilty, for one thing." He walked back around the bed and sat facing her. "At least not of the bombing. And I don't believe for the time it would take a snowball to melt in hell that you had anything to do with Carl Felderman's kidnapping." He paused. "Alleged kidnapping."

Mori couldn't help it. The tears were there before she had time to blink them away, and the tickle of one trailing down her cheek embarrassed her. She should be a stronger woman, the last of her kind. How had she become so damned needy that she turned to mush just hearing someone say he believed her?

She wiped her cheeks impatiently. "You're right. I didn't have anything to do with either one of them." But that wasn't quite true, was it?

"I didn't say you were innocent, either."

Kell's detached scrutiny helped her collect her nerves and bundle them together. There would be time to let them unravel later. "And what have you decided I'm guilty of?"

"Hell if I know." Kell reached across the narrow space between the beds and wrapped his fingers around hers. "Look, you're in trouble. You know a hell of a lot more about this whole bombing—and maybe the threat of a repeat in New Orleans— than you're saying. It's eating you alive from the inside out. Talk to me. Let me help."

Damned tears. She pulled her hand away. "You can't help. I'll only get you killed." She met his gaze, and the worry in his eyes almost unraveled her again. "I don't know what last night meant to you, but it meant a lot to me. Everything. I won't let you be another sacrifice made in the name of my bad choices."

Mori waited for his response, for words to form from the unreadable set of his mouth and clench of his jaw. But a persistent barking from his phone silenced whatever he might have said. He pulled it from his pocket, glanced at the screen, and answered.

"Kell." He looked at his watch. "Got it."

Apparently, he was talking to one of his "team," since he was back to barking himself.

"How many know the situation?" He swiveled to look at his duffel, then the tiny dressing area behind them. "As soon as possible."

He ended the call and turned back to her. "A couple of my team members are on their way. I'd like a shower before they get here."

Well, she'd like a piña colada, but that wasn't happening. "So, take a shower."

"You'll run."

If she had any common sense whatsoever, yes, she certainly would. So far today, common sense had been in short supply. "No, I won't run. I'll stay right here."

Damn, but the man could move fast, and where the hell had those cuffs come from? She could have sworn he'd left them in the granny mobile, but there they were, already snapped onto one of her wrists. Her reflexes had gone on vacation.

"Stop. I will not be cuffed to the bed while you shower. Seriously, Kell." She tugged on the wrist he had already imprisoned, and wondered if now wasn't the time to show him a thing or two about what she really was and how strong she could be.

"Nope." He stood up and pulled her behind him through the barely there dressing room and into the even smaller bathroom. "Sit." He pointed toward the toilet.

Was he insane? "No way. I will not—"

"Suit yourself." With a grunt, he jerked her arm toward the tiny sink and clinked the other cuff around the cold-water faucet handle. It was just big enough that the cuff wouldn't slip off.

"Kell, I mean it. You..." Mori trailed off as Kell grabbed the neck of his T-shirt and tugged it over his head. Heat rushed through her at the memory of that body and how it had felt under her hands—inside her. He unzipped his jeans and reached over the tub, turned on the hot water, and pulled the lever to send the water cascading from the shower in an uneven stream.

"Tell me you're not going to leave me cuffed here to watch you take a shower."

He had to be joking. Surely—

Shucking his jeans and boxers and kicking them aside, he arched an eyebrow, which she barely saw because she was fighting to keep her eyes on his face. "I need heat on my back, and you can watch or not. I don't care."

❦ CHAPTER 15 ❦

Kell reached over and twisted the water control farther into the cold range. He needed the hot spray pounding his lower back, but the rest of his body could feel Mori watching him through the clear plastic shower curtain, and apparently, on some caveman level, he thought it was a real turn-on. How fucked up was that?

"Need help?" Mori sounded like she was laughing again, and he deserved it. He turned to face her, heat running through him as her gaze dropped slowly from his face downward. She even leaned over to get a better view, her face inches from the sheet of clear vinyl. "Looks like you have a problem there, Ranger."

Shit. He turned his back on her, and sure enough, she was laughing—loud. Served him right. He'd gone all macho on her, and she ended up with the last laugh. He hated when that happened.

Why had he dragged her in here and gotten naked? He could have at least cuffed her to the nightstand, or put off his damned shower and popped more ibuprofen.

Except, he couldn't leave her out there alone, for a couple of reasons.

She would run, even if it took chopping off her hand or, more likely, breaking whatever piece of furniture he cuffed her to. She'd find a way. He'd seen it in her eyes and recognized the desperation. He'd seen that same look in the eyes of men he'd led in the sandbox. Men who'd seen so much war and horror, without an end in sight, that they just wanted to run. Didn't even matter where, as long as they were moving.

Whatever shit she was messed up in, whatever he'd stumbled into, it was bad. And hearing the truth from him tonight had pushed her closer to the brink of desperation.

She wanted to trust him; he could see that in her eyes, too. But the fear outweighed it, and he didn't have the time to earn back the trust he'd lost tonight.

The other reason he couldn't leave her locked in the room was that he wanted to be there when Nik and Robin met her. If they got here earlier than expected and found her alone, Nik would be curt but civil, but Razorblade Robin was a wild card. She was volatile; she was strong. And she had a wide predatory streak. Mori would bolt for sure, and someone might get hurt.

Kell was turning into a prune, so he had to face the inevitable. At least the thought of Robin had cooled his hard-on. He reached over, turned off the water, and stuck his arm outside the curtain. "Hand me a towel?"

Through the plastic, he saw a fuzzy Mori cross her arms and cock her head. "Sorry, can't reach it."

Fine, let her look. He jerked the curtain back and exchanged glares as he stepped past her and ripped a towel off the rack over the toilet, knocking another off on her head. "Oops. Sorry."

The cuff jingled as she slapped the towel to the floor, turning to watch him knot the thin white terrycloth around his hips. "I need to pee. And take a shower. Alone."

Kell walked into the bedroom and retrieved the handcuff keys. Unlocking them, he pulled the cuff from Mori's wrist and rubbed where it had left a red mark. Man, he hated what he was about to say. "I'm sorry."

"Sorry is when you do it once. Doesn't work the second time." She stood up. With her in shoes and him in bare feet, they were almost the same height, and he was suddenly aware of how close their bodies were. Two inches to full body contact, and his towel wasn't much camouflage for what that thought was doing to him. Again.

The same awareness flickered across her face, and Kell's gaze dropped to her mouth. Her lips parted on an exhale, and his heart took off at a gallop.

"We can't do this."

"I know." Her voice was almost as rough as his.

Kell took a step back. "I'll give you some privacy." Someone should give him a medal for restraint. "I have an extra T-shirt you can put on after you shower." Mori nodded, and Kell walked out of the bathroom, not turning as the door shut softly behind him and the lock clicked.

He tossed the handcuffs on the dresser, hung the clean T-shirt on the bathroom door handle, and dressed quickly in his camo shorts and black tee. He couldn't find any clean socks in the duffel, so he sniffed out the ones he'd taken off and decided they could live a while longer.

He heard the water turn on and relaxed on the bed nearest the bathroom. How was he going to get Mori to open up and tell him the truth? He knew how to conduct an interrogation, but he cared too much to push her until she was too exhausted or frightened to remain silent. He was way too involved.

He pulled the pillow from beneath his head and doubled it beneath his knees to help relax his back muscles. The shower had been anything but relaxing, but the ibuprofen had finally kicked in, so the spasms had calmed to a twitch. Of course, he might as well not worry about getting called back into active duty. The colonel was going to have his balls for dinner. The man would probably have him castrated and shipped off to Morocco just on principle.

Maybe the whole case wasn't in the crapper yet, though. Kell would try to talk to Mori first, if he had a chance before the others arrived. If she wouldn't talk to him, he'd have to turn her over to Nik and keep his mouth shut if it got uncomfortable for her. Maybe he'd wait outside or pick up something to eat from one of the dozen fast-food chains near the motel. They had to find out the truth now, before this went any further.

Besides, Nik was really good at interrogation, with more patience than Kell and better people skills than Robin. He also could often touch the person being questioned and get mental images that would help him ask such perceptive questions the freaked-out suspect usually answered without thinking.

Labor Day would be here in a week, and they still weren't sure if New Orleans was even a credible threat. He'd talked to Gadget this morning, and he'd been developing threat assessments and floor plans of the convention center and nearby hotels. He'd also found three visiting groups related to energy or industrial expansion. Adam and Archer had been swapping shifts, watching Tex-La's downtown New Orleans headquarters and the company's wharf area along the riverfront. Not much more the NOLA team could do until something broke in Houston.

Kell flicked on the TV and half dozed/half watched the evening news. Tropical Storm Geneva still churned in the middle of the Gulf of Mexico, almost stationary as she gained strength and waited to see which of two slow-moving weather systems would arrive first to steer her toward land. Still could go anywhere.

The water shut off in the bathroom, and he heard Mori open the door, retrieve the T-shirt, and shut it again. Kell sat up, took a deep breath, and prayed for patience. Getting her to open up would test his composure and tact. Neither were among his strengths.

A couple of minutes later, she came out, skin moist and pink from the shower, her shoulder-length hair damp and slightly curled from the humidity. His Ranger shirt looked a hell of a lot better on her than it ever had on him, especially tucked into those jeans that hugged every curve.

He was so fucked.

She threw her old T-shirt on the dresser and turned to face him. "What now?"

Keep it cool, man. "We need to talk. About you, about the bombing, about the governor, about Michael Benedict."

She'd remained stone-faced until Benedict's name was spoken; then she blinked and looked at the door, the other bed, the floor. Everywhere but at Kell.

"I wouldn't know where to start. Plus, it's nothing you can fix. Knowing will only get you—"

He'd expected her to pull out the it's-for-your-own-good card. "Stop trying to protect me. I know how to take care of myself. Did you ever happen to think maybe I could help you? Because from where I'm sitting, you are *way* over your head in this thing, whatever it is."

Mori opened her mouth to speak. Closed it. Kell could practically hear her teeth grinding against each other. She wanted to talk, but someone—Benedict—had her too scared.

He'd try easing her into it.

"How long have you known Michael Benedict?" He leaned back against the flimsy headboard. Relaxed, that was his middle name. Just making conversation.

He could almost hear the thought process going on behind her frown as she decided whether it was safe to answer the question. Finally, she shrugged. "My whole life. He owns the land next to my grandfather's ranch, so I don't remember a time when he wasn't around."

It rang of truth. "He's a lot older than you, though, right? I mean, I've never seen the guy, but you're midtwenties and I figure he can't be that young if he's head of a shipping empire, unless he's some kind of genius." According to Gadget, Benedict was fifty; would be fifty-one next month. He'd sent photos. The man was big, burly, probably considered handsome enough by the ladies. Definitely a power broker.

Mori laughed, and with it, some of the tension drained from her face. Her shoulders relaxed, and she shook her head as she walked over to sit on the other bed. "He's twice my age and used an oil inheritance to start Tex-La, not his own business savvy. That's not to say he's not an evil genius."

Interesting choice of words. Kell kept his tone light. "Like, set-up-the-woman evil or bomb-the-building evil?"

Too far. Mori stood up and paced back to her spot leaning on the dresser, her posture again stiffened. "Just...ruthless, I guess. When he wants something, he goes after it."

Kell sat up. "What is it he wants, Mori? You? Is he the one who hit you?" The bruise on her jaw still shadowed a little. He was surprised it wasn't worse; in fact, it seemed to have healed even since they'd gone into the restaurant at lunchtime, and the marks on her neck had disappeared.

Mori crossed her arms tightly over her chest and traced a line of pattern in the carpet with the toe of her running shoe. *Shit.* He'd gone too fast.

"We just had an argument," she finally said. "No big deal." But she wouldn't look at him.

It was a big fucking deal. He didn't care how much money or power Michael Benedict had—he had no right to hit a woman. And while Mori wasn't expressly defending him, she was making excuses. The beaten, stunned look on her face when he'd come to her apartment and found her hurt had burned itself into his psyche, and he wanted to kill the man who'd done it.

But he stuffed down the feelings. That was a sidetrack to revisit later. "Was Michael the one who implicated you in the bombing?"

Mori scrubbed her palms across her cheeks and let out a whoosh of breath. "Kell, it's more complicated than that. You have to promise to stay away from Michael. I mean it. Away. Completely. You have to let me handle him."

Yeah, because she'd handled him so well when he put a fist to her jaw. "I can't do that, Mori. At the very least, he tampered with a federal investigation, diverting resources spent watching you instead of looking for someone else." Someone like Benedict himself. "I've got to ask again. Was he involved in the bombing?"

Mori pushed herself off the dresser and walked to him, reaching down to stroke her fingers across his jawline. "Kell, I wish things could have been different. I really do. You're a good guy, and I'd almost forgotten there were good guys left in the world."

She leaned over and kissed him, smelling of motel shampoo and sunshine. He slid a hand behind her head and angled to take the kiss deeper, ignoring his raging conscience and focusing on where her left hand was headed as it slid up the inside of his thigh.

She trailed kisses across his cheek until her mouth was poised above his ear. "I'm sorry, Kell."

Focused on the moral dilemma growing inside his shorts, he didn't notice what her right hand had been doing until the click of the cuff around his left wrist.

"What the fuck?" He jerked his left arm away, but she pulled harder, snapping the other cuff around the leg of the nightstand and backing away from him.

"Mori, don't do this." The nightstand proved surprisingly sturdy—he pulled against it until he thought his arm would separate from his shoulder. He only succeeded in cutting his own wrist.

He quit struggling and stared at her. For several long seconds, they simply looked at each other with regret and sadness and, Kell thought, a sense of inevitability.

"Good-bye, Kell. Don't try to find me. Sit tight, and this will all be over in a day or two."

Mori didn't look back as she opened the door, strode out, and closed it behind her.

᠊ᢟ CHAPTER 16 ᢟ᠊

A cross the Super 8 parking lot, through the line of big rigs parked in the lot of the truck stop, over the low hedge separating the brightly lit café from the shadowy lot of the self-storage business next door, Mori walked with purpose.

She circled behind the far row of storage units and leaned against the concrete wall, her heart pounding so hard Kell's T-shirt vibrated. She'd bought some time, but probably not much. She was a bad liar, and Kell knew he was on the right track with his questions. Damn it, why hadn't she run in the parking lot of the Mexican restaurant instead of getting in his car after they'd heard the governor's accusations? Why hadn't she run when they got to the motel?

She'd been careless with Kell's life, hoping he could save her, when, deep down, she knew better. There was only one possible way to fix this, and she prayed it wasn't too late.

Her fingers shook as she retrieved her cell phone and turned it on. She scrolled to his name on her contact list and punched the number marked HOME.

He answered on the second ring. "Mori, I keep underestimating you."

"You win." She hated that her voice shook, but even taking a deep breath didn't stop it. His cool, smug laugh calmed her, reminding her that as much as she hated him, she still held some power. "I'm coming to you now. I'm ready for this to be over."

"Come to my house in town. We'll discuss your conditions over dinner." He paused. "If you're half as smart as you think you are, you'll come alone."

Well, he'd made sure she was totally alone in this world, hadn't he? "Give me an hour. I'm way out on the east side of town."

"I'll send a car. Tell me where you are. It isn't safe, and we wouldn't want any harm to come to you."

God forbid anyone hurt her besides him. "I'll be there in an hour."

She disconnected the call and turned off her cell phone. No point in letting the police try to track her and somehow end up finding Kell. His friends were on the way and would uncuff him. With any luck, they'd talk him into leaving town and forgetting she existed as soon as Michael somehow deflected blame for the bombing and kidnapping onto someone else. The thought made her sad, but she had to be realistic. Even if she were able to get away from Michael and her obligations, she and Kell didn't really know each other. Theirs was simply a physical attraction between two strangers who'd told each other too many lies. It felt more real than that, but it wasn't.

Mori dug in her purse and found her debit card. She slipped around the storage units and waited a few minutes outside the truck stop, watching people come and go, looking for any sign of Kell or his friends. She didn't know who they were, but two military-looking guys would stand out in the Lucky Trucker.

No sign of anyone who didn't look like he'd spent too many hours on long, empty roads with cigarettes and caffeine for company. Mori walked in the store and found an ATM near the cash register of the convenience mart. She knew the police would be monitoring her bank account; she only hoped it hadn't been frozen.

Crap. ACCOUNT ACCESS DENIED flashed across the screen, and the damned machine probably went right through to the police.

She looked at the middle-aged woman behind the checkout counter, who was engrossed in a tabloid. "Could you call a taxi for me?"

Mori's heart sped up as the woman gave her a longer look than was comfortable. Did she recognize her from the photos on TV?

"Sure thing, honey."

Only when the United Cab pulled up in front of the truck stop fifteen minutes later, only after she had her butt planted firmly on the ripped vinyl seat and had given the driver Michael's address in River Oaks, only then did she relax.

Maybe Kell would be safe now. As long as she stayed away from him and kept Michael happy, maybe he'd be safe.

She'd expected to have enough time on the cab ride to pull herself together and prepare for whatever humiliation Michael served up to punish her, but just her luck, she'd get the one driver in Houston who knew all the back roads from Baytown into the city. Too soon, the well-manicured lawns of one of America's wealthiest neighborhoods surrounded her, everything neat and tidy, with working streetlights, a young couple strolling in the rapidly falling dusk. They'd probably wandered over from one of the adjacent neighborhoods to gawk at the $10 million houses.

That was how much Michael had paid for the Italianate estate whose curved driveway the cab pulled into, rolling to a stop in front of the arched, carved double front doors. He'd bragged about it enough.

Soft light shone through the tall windows nestled behind the five stone archways that stretched across the front of the house. Michael walked out and paid the cabdriver without a word, and Mori watched the taxi drive away as if it contained her last hope.

"Good, you're here before my guest." Michael looked like a millionaire shipping magnate relaxing at home after work— dark slacks, tailored white shirt with the collar open, even a flashy gold chain around his neck. A handsome, self-assured, and one hundred arrogant asswipe. Just looking at him made Mori feel like a shabby interloper from the wrong side of town.

"What guest would that be?" She stepped past him onto the polished oak floors of the octagonal foyer, a curved stairway flanked by an ornate wrought-iron banister spiraling up one side. Her running shoes squeaked until she walked onto the round medallion-print rug that filled the center of the floor.

"A business associate, here to sign the final agreement on a new shipping contract out of New Orleans." After closing the door, Michael walked to the foot of the stairs, leaned on the rail, and gave Mori a head-to-toe disapproving look. "It will be your first appearance as my fiancée, although you'll have to hurry to make yourself at least halfway presentable."

"Are you serious? We need to talk about this"—she waved her hands in the air—"arrangement."

Michael took her elbow and pulled her toward the stairway. "And we will. But I need to take this short meeting, and it'll be good experience for you in your new role as my mate."

Mate, my ass. She might have to play the role of wife. She might have to bear his children. But "mate" implied an intimacy that wasn't going to happen.

Mori grabbed the wrought-iron banister to prevent Michael pushing her onto the bottom step. "How are you going to straighten out this legal mess you've created? It'll be hard for me to be your fiancée from federal prison."

Michael grinned. "Don't worry. Once we've *consummated* our arrangement, the governor will recant his statement. In fact, the governor is taking all his direction from me now." He motioned up the stairway. "Top of the stairs, first door on the right. I had some things delivered for you a while back. Wear the navy." His tone turned sarcastic. "There might be dust on it, as stubborn as you've been. Our guest arrives at eight."

"Fine." That statement about the governor sent chills through her, and Mori climbed the stairs without looking back. Obviously, Michael wasn't going to talk until his business appointment was over. He hadn't made any more threats. In fact, her arrival had made him downright jovial. One big, jolly asshole.

She might as well play along for now and put the word *consummate* out of her mind.

Off the landing at the top of the stairs, long hallways stretched left and right, and a boat-size window at the back of the landing looked out on manicured formal gardens circling a fountain. Gas torches lent a soft glow to the whole vista.

Mori paused to look at the gardens, with their rows of neatly trimmed hedges and sections of riotous flowers left unclipped to give the illusion of wild growth. Reflections of the torches seemed to make fire dance in the fountain's blue water.

If she'd given in to Michael six months ago, would all those lives lost in the Zemurray bombing have been saved? How many women would trade places with her, thinking a loveless union was a small price to pay in order to live in such luxury and help her people at the same time? Had she been completely blind and selfish?

And now that Michael had literally gotten away with murder and, if his claims were true, gained control of the governor, would he stop at Texas? Why not Louisiana? Mori could only hope he'd be satisfied with what he had, with her thrown into the bargain.

She took a deep breath and turned the knob of the first door to the right of the landing. The bedroom suite was a confection of cream-and-gold fabrics and dark polished wood. Ceiling medallions, as in the formal room downstairs, were etched with gold leaf. Two windows overlooked the front lawn, and a bathroom full of marble led off to one side. It looked like a professional decorator had been told to "make it look wealthy," without adding a single ounce of personality. The tops of the dresser and chest were bare, the only wall adornment an antique tapestry.

Mori thought of the collection of stuffed animals that filled her little bedroom in Montrose and felt a pang of sadness. If Michael let her bring them here, no telling what she'd have to give up in return.

She looked around for the closet door and opened it to find several items of clothing, all with price tags still attached. Awesome. Only one item was navy blue, and Mori's heart sank as she pulled it out. A silky curve-hugging dress with a deep V in the front that would guarantee she couldn't wear a bra, a sparkly beaded collar that held the whole thing up, and a backless silhouette that dipped almost to the waist. At least it wasn't short. It looked exactly like something that Michael would love and that Mori would normally never wear.

Except tonight. She would force herself to make nice until things were settled.

She only had a half hour before Michael's deadline of 8:00 p.m., so she rifled through the dresser and was horrified, but not surprised, to find a supply of silky panties—bikinis and thongs, of course—and, in another drawer, teddies and negligees.

Maybe Mori's sudden wave of nausea was due to hunger, but she thought not. The idea of Michael touching her the way Kell had touched her...

She shook her head and pulled out the least offensive panties—black, with more than an inch of fabric. Her legs were tan enough to forgo hose.

You can do this. She pulled on the dress and stared at herself in the bathroom's full-length mirror. Thank God she'd thought to bring her backpack when she left the hotel. She dug out a small first aid kit and breathed a sigh of relief when she found two Band-Aids. She flattened them out over her nipples and inspected herself in the mirror again. She wouldn't have Michael mistaking air-conditioning chill for arousal, even if she did have telltale bandage outlines if she pulled her shoulders back far enough.

How could he have thought to buy her a might-as-well-be-naked negligee but not a hairbrush? Huffing, Mori dug hers out of her pack and brushed out the kinks from the hotel shower and the night air. She grinned at herself in the mirror. One thing about tonight she could control. She went to the bed where she'd thrown her jeans and reached in the pocket for a lime-green elastic band, which she used to secure her hair in a ponytail.

She had a feeling small acts of rebellion were all she'd be allowed for a while.

Mori looked at her running shoes, a five-year-old pair of Nikes that had a lot of dust and miles on them. While they'd definitely make a statement, she didn't want to humiliate Michael and risk his anger. The ponytail would annoy him, but the shoes would embarrass him. She'd noticed a few shoeboxes on the floor of the closet, so she opened them and found a pair of silver sandals with low heels she could live with. All the shoes were her size, of course—information probably supplied by her traitorous mother.

At five before eight, she left her sanctuary to return downstairs, practicing the art of keeping a pleasant expression on her face despite the fact that her feet hurt, the house was chilled to the temperature of a freezer, and she was petrified of what Michael might do.

As it turned out, the worst thing he did during the hourlong meeting with George Benoit of New Orleans was tug the elastic band out of her hair as he pulled her alongside him to open the door. She played the dutiful, attentive, smiling fiancée, and Michael the cordial and generous everyman who'd lucked into "this whole shipping thing."

By the time Benoit left, Mori had begun to feel at ease for the first time since walking into the house, and she wished he'd stay longer. An outsider kept both Michael and her on their best behavior. Maybe they needed a full-time in-house referee.

They watched from the doorway as Benoit's taxi pulled out of the drive. Michael's hand strayed from her waist to her butt, squeezing as if testing a ripe tomato for firmness. Mori gritted her teeth and let him squeeze a few seconds before stepping aside and walking back into the big living room, as ornate and passionless as the rest of the house except for the huge fireplace that took up most of the south wall, flanked on either side by floor-to-ceiling windows.

"That went well, don't you think?" Michael followed her into the room, and Mori gasped as he slipped an arm around her waist and deftly twisted her to face him.

"He was nice and seemed to be excited about your business deal."

Mori held her breath to block out Michael's scent of whiskey and aftershave as he pulled her closer and leaned in to kiss her neck. "That dress looks as beautiful on you as I thought it would." He touched his lips to hers, and when she tried to slip away, he pulled her more tightly against him with his left arm.

"Your bruises healed nicely, I see." His big right hand rested across the front of her neck, reminding her of how it had felt to have those hands choking her. She understood the implied threat behind the gesture.

"Michael, please. Let's go slow—"

"You don't think I've earned this?" He slid his hand inside the front of her dress, cupped her bare breast, and laughed as he jerked the bandage away and thumbed her nipple. "You belong to me now. This is what I was promised. This is what your family agreed to."

His kiss was bruising this time, and Mori tasted blood as her lip was crushed against her teeth. God, she couldn't do this. She just couldn't.

"Wait, please." She finally pushed him away, both of them breathing hard for different reasons. "Can't we get used to each other? Just let me stay here a few days and adjust. I will come around, I promise."

She expected an explosion of temper, but Michael looked at the floor and pursed his lips. He turned and walked to the fireplace, then knelt down, pulled a long match from a box sitting on the hearth, and lit the gas flame. The firelight rose high as he turned the knob as far to the right as it would go. Only then did he look at her. "So you need time for it to sink in that you belong to me?"

Mori dragged her gaze away from the fire, so out of place in a Houston living room in August. "Time for me to get used to being...with you. So we can be partners." She belonged to no one but herself.

He nodded slowly. "And tell me this, Emory. When you look into our future as *partners*," he emphasized, "do you see us raising our children together and teaching them about their heritage? Do you see us attending social functions arm in arm? Entertaining guests? Ending our nights in each other's arms, our bodies joined? Because that's what I need in a *partner*."

Mori stifled a shudder and tried to paste in place that pleasant smile she'd been practicing. "I just need a little time to—"

"*Or*"—Michael turned to look at the fire—"do you look into the future and see long nights of sex with a man you find distasteful, raising children you wish had been sired by someone else, gritting your teeth as you sit through endless events with people you don't give a rat's ass about?"

That was exactly what Mori saw in her future. That, and the slow death of her soul and her spirit. The only saving part of it would be the children, because she knew she'd love them, even if they were his.

She sighed. Why pretend when he knew better? "You've won, Michael. I'm here. I've agreed to marry you. What more do you want from me?"

He leaned against the sofa table, arms crossed, and studied her with a dispassion that alarmed her more than his fumbling attempts at seduction. "I want the partner I described, and you might be surprised to hear that I already have a woman in my life who fills that role very well except for the children. Perhaps you'll meet her one day. She picked out the clothes you're wearing."

What? Mori sat on the sofa, weary from fear and from pointless games. "Then why this charade tonight, with the clothes and the 'meet my fiancée' business? Why not become a sperm donor and let's just end all this fighting? That way, I fulfill my obligation as our only full-blooded female of childbearing age, and you get to keep your ideal partner."

Michael paced around the table and went to stand in front of the fire again, his back to her, jabbing into the flames with a fireplace poker as if stabbing it with a knife. "You don't understand, Emory. I spent twenty-five fucking years waiting for you, putting up with your whining, pandering parents, only to have you grow up to be a spoiled, selfish brat."

He turned to face her, and Mori stood, alarmed. She'd seen him angry in his office when he'd hit her, but nothing like this. Rage twisted his handsome features into a cold, grotesque mask. "Michael, I think I should go."

"Sit down and shut up." His voice was low, taut, one timbre short of a growl. "I own you. I bought you when you were born. I've been paying for you since you were in diapers. I've given you enough leash to let you grow up, but now you're mine. Not my partner. My property. I own you, and I don't intend for you to forget it."

The tension crackled in the air, charged and static. Mori was strong, but Michael was stronger, and they both knew it. He pulled a glove of some kind from the table, and Mori watched in confusion as he slipped it on his right hand and retrieved the fireplace poker he'd left in the flames.

"You know what we do with our property on the ranch, don't you, Emory? Your grandfather taught you that."

Mori gasped and turned as soon as Michael lifted the poker.

Not a poker. A branding iron with the letter *B* on the end.

She ran for the door as fast as she could, her heels sliding on the polished floor. She'd made it halfway through the foyer when her bare back exploded in white-hot, searing pain.

The room tilted, righted itself, and tilted again as she dropped to her hands and knees. Her body on fire and her nostrils filled with the smell of her own scorched flesh, Mori heard her screams turn to piteous howls before the world turned black, silent, and painless.

EPISODE 5

✐ CHAPTER 17 ✐

The handcuff keys taunted Kell from atop the dresser, four feet out of reach. Might as well be four miles. God knew he'd tried to span the distance, stretching like Plastic Man until the shoulder above his imprisoned left arm ached as if it had been wrenched from its socket and roughly popped back in place.

He'd gotten the bright idea of using his utility knife to saw off the leg of the nightstand—before he realized it still rested in the pocket of the jeans he'd pulled off for his shower. They, of course, were already stuffed in his duffel.

The damned nightstand was nailed to the wall, as fixed and immovable as a stone monolith.

What a fucking idiot. He couldn't decide who he wanted to dismember first, Mori or himself. No, he knew—probably himself. She'd been on the razor's edge of making a run for it all afternoon, so he had no right to act surprised at anything but his own stupidity. Even that shouldn't have surprised him at this point.

His cell phone barked with Gator's ringtone, and he snatched it off the nightstand, grimacing at the name on the screen. No, he didn't think he'd be talking to Colonel Thomas just yet. The variations on "fucktard" he'd called himself couldn't possibly compare to whatever colorful epithets the colonel would devise as soon as he figured out Kell had gone off task. Seriously off task.

"Kellison, you are a disgrace." He grasped the leg of the nightstand and pulled on it until his biceps bulged and the muscles in his shoulders burned in protest. All he got for his effort was a renewed throbbing in his back and not so much as a hint of splintering wood. He could practically bite through the headboard of the bed, so what was up with the industrial-strength nightstand?

Mr. Neat and Tidy, good soldier that he was, had returned his guns to the duffel and squeezed the bag into the narrow gap between his bed and the wall that separated the main room from the bathroom. It would be accessible without them tripping over it, he'd reasoned, and he hadn't wanted Mori, his fragile flower who'd since proven herself to be a handcuffing vixen, to be freaked out by the firearms.

Yeah, he was both a fucktard *and* a chauvinist.

He pondered his current dilemma. Lying on his back, he stretched his right arm across the queen-size mattress one last time, wishing for either a cheap double bed or Godzilla arms. No way he'd ever reach it.

Not with his hand, anyway, but maybe his foot. Maneuvering around the bed, he wrestled his way onto his stomach, the freakishly bright floral bedspread bunched underneath him in painful lumps. His already-throbbing back taunted him. He was going to pay for this.

Using his elbows, he slid his body toward the wall until his feet touched the wallpapered drywall, then shifted his right leg downward until he finally hooked a foot through one of the duffel's straps. If he could drag it onto the bed without breaking his ankle, he'd shoot off those goddamn cuffs. Of course, the way his luck was going, he'd probably trigger the rifle with his toe and dispatch his own ass to China.

Pain, hot and sharp, shot through his back as he strained to angle his right leg onto the bed with the heavy pack attached to his ankle. And it was working fine—until the duffel turned at an odd angle and got wedged between the bed and the wall, trapping him in a position halfway between a pretzel and a crab. Of all the stupid, fucking—

A keycard slid into the door lock with an electronic whir. Kell groaned and planted his face in the bedspread. Whose bright idea had it been to make sure both he and Nik had keys to the safe places? Oh yeah, that would be him.

He would never live this down. Not in this lifetime or the next. Maybe he'd luck out and Nik would've left Robin in the car.

The gentle whoosh of the door opening, the snap of the safety being released on Nik's gun, the soft footfalls on the carpet inside the door—all were audible to Kell's trained ears, even over the air-conditioning's white-noise roar.

"What the fuck?" Nik's footsteps halted and the dead bolt clicked home. Kell remained facedown and still. If he didn't move, maybe they'd think he was dead and leave.

Something tickled his right ear, and he instinctively jerked his head to the side and opened one eye to see Robin's face about three inches from his. She held up a feather and grinned.

"Let me guess. You were playing Bed Twister and lost?"

"Get my fucking foot out of the duffel bag strap."

Only after she'd extricated his foot and laughed for the week and a half it took him to wrestle himself into an upright position did Kell look up. Nik remained just inside the door, arms crossed, eyebrows bunched, without a trace of humor on his face.

"What the hell have you done?"

Robin danced and twirled to the bed opposite him and sat down with a flounce. "And how'd you get handcuffed to the nightstand?" She was having way too much fun.

"What?" Nik's voice rose half an octave as he walked farther into the room, took a look at the cuffs, and shook his head. "Shit, Kellison. Where're the keys?"

"Dresser." Kell gave Robin his most intimidating stare, but judging by her squawking laughter, it didn't work. "Where'd you get that feather, bird-woman? Out of your ass?"

Instead of shutting her up in righteous indignation, the comment only made Robin laugh harder. There was simply no way of ending this with any self-respect, so he might as well accept it. "Sorry."

Damn, but he was tired of apologizing.

Nik grabbed the keys and tossed them on the bed where Kell could reach them and, blessedly, free himself. Now, if only he'd perfected that disappearing act. He had to settle for what he hoped was an expression that conveyed sincerity, contrition, and good humor. The gritted teeth probably ruined the effect.

Robin snorted a few more times before getting herself under control, but Nik was nowhere in the zip code of amused. "Guess I don't have to ask who nailed you with your own cuffs."

Kell rubbed his back and hobbled to the dressing table for more ibuprofen. He'd taken three times the normal dose already today. Awesome.

No point in responding to Nik's comment; they all knew who'd cuffed him, and he'd only humiliate himself further if he made excuses. "Robin, think you can track where she went? She's been gone about an hour."

"Maybe. You got any ideas on where to start? It's a big old world out there." Robin shifted on the edge of the bed to make room for Nik, who looked like he had a lot to say and was holding his tongue with effort. Had Robin not been here, Kell had no doubt Nik would have chewed up his ass and handed it back to him like so much ground beef.

Kell deserved it, but he desperately needed their backup. "I know it looks like I've gone nuts, and maybe I have. Mori Chastaine isn't guilty. I'm certain of it. But she does know something, and she's our best hope of solving this case."

Nik's doubts were obvious. "And that's the only reason you helped her escape?"

Might as well not lie; his friend knew him inside and out. "Of course not. I want to help her. But that doesn't mean she can't help us, too. She's just scared."

When Kell's phone barked again, Robin picked it up and laughed at the screen. "Poor old colonel. I don't think he really wants to talk to us right now. It would be bad for his health." She set the phone back on the nightstand. "So, where do you think Mori might have gone?"

Kell had been thinking about that. "She knows she can't go back to her apartment or the Co-Op. The DHS guys will be all over both places." He tried to put himself in her position, with fear of the law on one side and fear of Michael Benedict on the other. The way she'd talked about handling the situation with Michael, it sounded as if she had a plan. And knowing that Kell was closing in on the truth, she'd be convinced she needed to move fast. She'd said "a couple of days," but that had been before he let her know how much he'd figured out.

"She'll confront Michael Benedict—maybe at his office or house."

Nik took a deep breath, and the tension eased out of his expression and posture now that he had something to focus on other than Kell's stupidity. "What about her parents? Don't they have a ranch west of Houston?"

Kell shook his head. "My gut says Mori wouldn't go to them for help. She seems to be having some kind of falling-out with her family. They didn't call or pick her up when she was detained by Homeland Security that first day."

Robin turned sideways, leaning against the headboard. "I think she'd go to Benedict's home rather than his office, so I'd nix Galveston. It's almost eight now, and Tex-La would be closed. Does she have a car?"

Kell paused, his anger at Mori slowly shifting to worry. He'd been so pissed off he hadn't considered the danger she could encounter in trying to walk through the eastern 'burbs at night. And if Michael Benedict had hit her before, he'd do it again. Bullies like that weren't onetime abusers.

"No, she left on foot, although she could've gotten a taxi. Her car's at the Co-Op." *Was* at the Co-Op. Kell figured it had been impounded by now. "Sounds like the first place to check out would be Benedict's house in River Oaks. Robin, you know where that is?"

She nodded. "Although the smell of money in that neighborhood might camouflage even the human signatures. Speaking of which, you got anything of hers I could scent that doesn't smell like hotel bodywash? The room reeks of it. Maybe I could check out your car?"

He had something better. "That's her T-shirt on the dresser."

"Did she leave naked?" Nik arched a brow, still without a shred of humor. Kell was going to have some fence-mending to do with his best buddy.

"No, she didn't leave naked." And now it was time for yet another appearance of Kell the Great Apologizer. "I screwed up, and I appreciate you guys going off radar for me. But Mori's being set up by somebody, and our friendly neighborhood millionaire, Michael Benedict, is in it neck-deep and rising fast."

"Apparently, she isn't that interested in your help." Nik's voice bristled with sarcasm. "In case you missed it, the handcuffs were a dead giveaway."

Kell tugged on his running shoes and tied the laces. "Look, you can bitch me up one side and down the other when we get this straightened out. I deserve it. But for now, Robin needs to track Mori, and you and I need to pay a visit to the esteemed governor of Texas and find out why he's going along with this frame job. Is he still in Houston?"

"Yep." Nik puffed out a frustrated breath and tugged his hair back into a short ponytail. "I pulled Archer out of New Orleans and flew him into Houston as soon as the governor showed up alive. He's been tailing Felderman."

Kell frowned. "Tailing him? I thought he was in the hospital. He didn't look too good on the news conference this afternoon. Did they transfer him to a hospital in Austin?"

Robin had been uncharacteristically silent since walking to the dresser to retrieve Mori's shirt, and she looked somber as she rejoined them. She reclaimed her seat next to Nik, the fabric grasped tightly in her hands. Her gaze was fixed on the carpet, her brow furrowed, but she still wasn't talking.

Nik shrugged at Kell's questioning look. They'd often agreed that women—even bird-women—were incomprehensible. "Anyway, Felderman checked himself out of Methodist against doctor's orders late this afternoon. Archer followed him to one of those generic suites hotels off the Beltway, up near the airport."

Kell pondered that information. "Was anyone with him?"

"He was alone, used a fake name, and paid cash for the room."

"Weird." Kell retrieved his wallet from the duffel and stuck it in his pocket. If he'd done that after stopping at the ATM, this afternoon might have gone differently. Or maybe not. "Why would the governor leave the hospital against doctor's orders and hide out in a hotel room outside the city center?"

"I have a bigger question for you to think about." Robin handed Mori's T-shirt to Nik. "A big one."

Nik touched the fabric tentatively at first, then grasped it with both hands and closed his eyes. Finally, he shook his head. "I get nothing from it, not a single image. What's the bigger question?"

Robin's gaze met Kell's, and she'd never looked more troubled. All traces of laughter had disappeared. "Did you have any idea your girl Mori was a shifter?"

❦ CHAPTER 18 ❦

The pain woke her, seeping into her consciousness with increasing insistence until she remembered. The fire. Michael's face twisted in hatred. The brand. The smell of burning flesh. Beginning to shift as blackness fell across her vision like a curtain.

Mori opened heavy eyelids and took in her surroundings—at least the ones visible without moving from her position curled on her side atop a tiny bed that still seemed to take up most of the room. She was naked and shivering with cold except for the hot, burning pain throbbing in the center of her back. She'd wear that "B" the rest of her life; even a shifter couldn't heal a burn without scarring.

Nothing about the room was familiar. Plain white walls. A scuffed-up oak dresser with no mirror but a small TV sitting on top. A ladder-back chair. The twin-size bed. A single floor lamp that cast an elongated shadow across the wooden floor. She angled her head to look up without jostling her back and saw the sloped ceiling. An attic, then.

Moving cautiously to keep her back as immobile as possible, Mori used her left arm to lever herself into a seated position so she could check out the rest of the space. The room was small, maybe ten by ten, with a dormer window through which she could see Michael's gardens, smothered in darkness now except for the decorative lights in the fountain. Through an open doorway, she spotted a toilet and a small dressing table.

Still nighttime, but how long had she been unconscious? Not long enough to have healed much, judging by the pain.

She needed clothes. A shirt would be excruciating against her back, but being naked in Michael Benedict's attic was high on her list of vulnerability-inducing activities. And she was tired of feeling vulnerable. She'd come here prepared to give Michael what he wanted. In order to keep everyone safe, she'd been willing to live a half-life, to do the duty that had been drilled into her since birth.

He'd thrown it back in her face, and had gone too far in doing so.

Mori wasn't accustomed to rage, had spent her life learning to avoid it. So it took her a few moments to identify the chest-tightening sensation, as if her heart and lungs had grown so massive they threatened to explode from the confines of her ribcage. As if the air in the room had grown so thick she couldn't inhale. As if the beast inside her ached to escape, and to kill.

She had to get out of here. She'd find Kell somehow and warn him about Michael, even if it meant revealing the existence of her kind. Once Kell was safely away from them, she'd figure out a way to stop Michael.

She scanned the room, looking for clothes. There were no closets. Mori pulled out each drawer of the smaller dresser in turn, but all were empty.

She noticed a few stairs leading downward in a nook cut into one corner of the room, with a door at the bottom. Easing down them, trying to avoid the creak of old wood, she turned the knob and found it locked. *Damn it, Michael.*

"You might as well come back up the stairs, Emory."

Michael's drawl came from behind her. How had she missed seeing him? Goose bumps dotted Mori's skin as she turned and climbed the four steps back into the room. Looking around in confusion, her gaze finally lit on the TV screen—not a television, but a monitor. Michael's face filled the rectangle in all his arrogant glory.

For the first time, Mori noticed the red dots glowing in the far corner of the ceiling. In all the corners. Cameras.

"You son of a bitch." She walked to the bed and jerked the thin, brown-plaid spread off it, wrapping it around her like an oversize bath towel, letting it hang a little lower in back to keep it from pressing on the burn.

"Might as well not cover it up, sweetheart. I saw it all last night. Who do you think carried you to your new room?"

Mori's heart raced, and her face heated. God, had he raped her while she was unconscious? Planted his precious seed inside her just to prove she had no say in it?

Michael laughed, and his teeth gleamed on the monitor. "I can see what you're thinking, but don't worry. I want you awake when I fuck you. I want you to know who it is that's fucking you, and why. It's time you remember who I am, little girl, and that this isn't about you and your precious feelings."

"I don't want—"

The words fizzled in her throat. He didn't care what she wanted. Probably never had, although he'd at least pretended for a while. She'd kept thinking she could work out a deal with him, hoping he could see the situation from her standpoint and figure out a compromise.

Now, too late, it finally hit her. She'd been thinking of Michael as a powerful man, but still reasonable. He wasn't reasonable, because he'd never had to learn the art of compromise. He was the alpha of the Dire Wolves and fully aware none of the other males could challenge him, much less the females, whose role in traditional Dire society had never been as more than shadows of their mates. Michael held all the cards and always had. To see him as a modern man capable of empathy and reason had been a serious error on her part.

"Very good. You realize it now, don't you, Emory? What you want simply doesn't matter. So sit down, and I'll tell you what your life is going to look like—at least for the next twenty years or so."

Her mind settled into a numb paralysis, incapable of complete thoughts. Only snippets of what-ifs and snatches of things she might have done differently. Thoughts she couldn't articulate, which he wouldn't want to hear even if she could put them into words. Mori shuffled to the bed and sat on the edge, facing the monitor.

"First, forget about trying to escape. The window is unbreakable and bolted shut. The door is reinforced steel. The walls, floor, and ceiling have been soundproofed. Welcome to your new home."

Mori blinked, her gaze shifting to the staircase. How long had he been planning this? Had he planned to keep her this way all along and simply used the marriage as bait? "You can't keep me here forever."

"Not forever. Only until you beg me to come to you and fuck you. And I mean beg. Hands and knees. Naked. Hmm..." He smiled. "Makes a pretty picture."

What was he smoking? He could leave her here for the rest of her life—and Dires had very long lives—and she would never let him touch her. "You're delusional, Michael. Sick and delusional."

Michael laughed. "Oh, you'll beg. You might be able to shift to stay warmer, but you can't do without food forever. If you're stubborn enough to think you'll let yourself starve, I'll strap you down and feed you intravenously, just enough to stay alive, but not enough to rid you of the hunger. And in case you find some other way to try and kill yourself, don't forget the cameras. Your every move will be monitored day and night."

Mori had only thought things couldn't get worse. The room took on a distant quality, remote and detached. The voice coming from numb lips didn't even sound like hers. "What else?"

"Once you've given in and I've fucked you better than you deserve—and you've thanked me for it properly—you can have clothes and regular meals, as long as you continue to cooperate. When you're pregnant, you might be allowed onto the grounds occasionally. With guards, of course. After the child is born, we'll repeat the process until you're no longer of use to me for breeding. Then I don't care what the fuck you do."

The children. She could hate Michael, but she would love her children, and they had to be protected. They'd need her influence in their lives to make sure they grew up to be good and strong, maybe with Gus Chastaine's heart and his gentle wielding of power. He would be horrified to know what kind of man his successor as the Dire alpha had turned out to be. She'd wager he never saw this side of his neighbor.

Her optimism was crushed with Michael's next words. "My real fiancée, Leslie, will be moving in to assume the role of the children's mother. Although human, she knows what we are and why I can't have children with her. You'll never see them after they're weaned, of course. We'll come up with a suitable story about their birth mother."

Mori was on her feet before she realized it, charging toward the nearest corner and shouting at the camera. "You can't do this. My parents—"

"Your parents recently deposited a check for five million dollars. Last I heard, they'd decided to put the Quad-D on the market. They're deeply ashamed that their daughter, who could have been the jewel of the new generation of Dires, has turned out to be such a disappointment. You have no one but me, Emory."

Tears pricked the back of Mori's eyes, but she refused to cry in front of Michael. He'd enjoy it too much.

"But I will allow you one visit."

Mori frowned up at the camera's glowing red eye and turned to face the monitor. Michael had a particularly unpleasant smile on his face, even for him. If he thought she'd want to see either of her parents after they'd literally sold her, he was—

Oh God.

Michael held up a familiar shirt. Kell's olive-green tee with RANGERS stamped across the front. "Recognize this?"

A chill stole across Mori's chest, and she wrapped the bedspread around her more tightly. "Stay away from Jack Kelly. He has no part in it."

Michael sniffed the shirt. "I can still scent him on it even though you were wearing it, which will help me track Mr. *Kellison.* Oh, don't look surprised. A simple call to his apartment manager, claiming to be a potential employer, told me everything I needed to know. Humans are quite careless with their information."

Mori's anger rose again. "There's nothing to know other than that he's a veteran. He's out of work. He's injured. Forget about him."

Michael leaned toward his camera, his face filling the monitor. "Look at you, all filled with righteous indignation. It's the first time today I've seen you look like anything but a scared rabbit. Kellison knows too much, and it's only a matter of time before we find him in whatever hole you two were using as a hideout. The cabdriver won't be hard to find. So I can kill your soldier in front of you or torture him to control you. I haven't decided which."

"Look, Michael, let's talk about this." She'd agree to anything if he'd leave Kell out of it. "Please. We can work something out where nobody gets hurt and you get what you want." She'd get on her damn hands and knees and beg him now if he wanted.

"Too late for talk, Emory." Michael made a show of holding his arm up to his face and looking at his watch. "I have an early meeting in only a few hours. Enjoy the rest of your evening and your day tomorrow. Travis and the rest of my staff will be watching, so behave yourself. Tomorrow night, if you're hungry enough to beg or I have Kellison in hand, we'll talk again."

"But—"

The screen went black.

After a glance at the nearest camera, Mori dragged the ladder-back chair in front of the window and sat, staring out at the part of the gardens illuminated by the fountain. She'd never liked them, and now she realized why. They were beautiful, no denying that, but they reminded Mori of her mother. Like Celia Chastaine, the gardens were elegant but had no life or spark of warmth to them. Even the areas meant to look like wild growth were constrained by hard edges, and should they try to escape their brick and stone prisons, they would be pruned mercilessly.

The irony of the comparison wasn't lost on her. Mori was being pruned.

She let her mind wander and ended up thinking about her grandfather, who'd been the Dire alpha until his death when she was seventeen. Had he known about the agreement between her parents and Michael? She wanted to think not, but he probably had. Gus would have known Michael would be his successor, just as they all had. The entire Dire population that remained—about thirty of them total—had banded together in Texas under the gentle force of Gus's personality.

Her grandfather had known she was the only female Dire at her birth. Maybe he'd hoped she'd grow to love Michael. Or maybe he'd thought another girl would be born in the Dire population, to offer them all a better choice than procreate or perish.

She'd adored Gus Chastaine, that much she knew, and something he'd said more than once came back to her. Vividly, she remembered standing next to a fence, admiring a new stallion he'd bought, black with a snow-white snip on its muzzle. That horse had a mind of its own, full of spit and spirit.

Starlight had kicked or bitten half the hands on the ranch, including Gus, and yet her grandfather had refused to use harsh techniques to break him into submission. "You have to let a wild thing come to you when he wants to and not force him," he'd said. "Force him, and he'll either lose his spirit or he'll bide his time, and then rise up and take you out the first chance he gets."

Those seemed to be her choices now as well. Mori was being forced to submit. She could get on her hands and knees and beg, grasping whatever moments she could out of the next twenty years. Or she could bide her time, think things through, and fight.

She wasn't an alpha. She'd spent her whole life in the Dire structure, where little was expected of the women who'd all grown up in her mother's generation. But thanks to her mother's lack of maternal skills, she'd been on her own enough to know women had options.

She might not be an alpha male, but if she was going to survive, she had to act like one. Fake it till she made it.

Only, how did she do that?

Mori rose from the chair, glared at each of the four cameras in turn, and walked back to the bed. Besides her bedspread-turned-cape, there was a single pillow and a thin sheet. Michael wasn't kidding when he'd said she'd have to shift to stay warm.

A noise at the window caught her attention, and she turned too fast, wincing as the edge of the bedspread touched the raw wound on her back. She didn't see anything at first, but then, there it was again. A rustle. Walking closer to the window, she looked at the sill in disbelief.

Through the glass, outlined by the light of the fountain below, she saw the silhouette of a freaking eagle, its head cocked, staring back at her.

❧CHAPTER 19❧

There was no sign of Archer in the lobby of the King's Crossing Suites when Kell and Nik arrived just before midnight. It was a typical generic suburban suites hotel, filled with furnishings and carpets all dyed a hundred shades of beige.

"Where's our kitten?" Kell studied the few people still wedged into the chairs scattered around the lobby, talking and drinking. It wasn't as if Archer Logan, their jaguar-shifting team member, could easily hide. The man was six foot four of muscle, with shoulder-length waves of black hair and the creepiest green eyes on earth. Women liked that long-haired shit. From what he'd seen, they fell all over the guy.

"My guess would be the bar." Nik angled toward a door leading off the back side of the lobby. The faint sounds of soft rock and clink of glasses met them as they paused in the doorway to give their vision time to adjust to the low lighting.

Sure enough, Archer sat at a back-corner table, flirting with a waitress who stood with one hip cocked provocatively, one finger twirling around her hair. To his credit, as soon as he spotted Kell and Nik winding their way through the tables, Archer seemed to give her the heave-ho. She eyed them with obvious annoyance when she passed them on the way back to the bar.

"Sorry to cramp your style." Kell pulled out a chair and angled it so he could see the entire room. Force of habit.

Archer clamped a hand on his shoulder and almost jarred Kell out of his chair. "Hey, gotta try and keep pace with you, ladies' man. Heard you caught a shifter and didn't even know it."

Kell speared Nik with a you-and-your-big-mouth look, but he didn't have a lot of room to criticize. He'd put them all in jeopardy. "Tell us about Felderman."

The waitress returned, set a beer in front of Kell and a glass of bourbon in front of Nik, and winked at Archer before turning to leave. She added an extra swivel to her hips as she made her way through the tables and back to the bar.

Kell joined the others in watching the show. He wanted to make a wisecrack about tomcats or alley cats or something cruder, but really, it would just set him up for more ridicule.

"OK, then. Felderman." Archer took a sip of his drink. "He hasn't left his room, unless he jumped out the window. I've got a clear view of the elevator from here. He checked into Room 601. Ordered room service an hour ago—steak, rare."

Kell was impressed. "And you know that, how?"

Archer grinned. "Gadget hacked into the hotel's room-charge system. He's sending me text updates. So I also know Felderman hasn't made any phone calls out, but did receive one from a number Gadget traced to"—he punched a button on his phone and looked at the screen—"Travis Milkin. Felderman didn't answer the phone. Name mean anything?"

Kell shook his head. "No, but... What?"

Nik was frowning into space. "That name is familiar." He concentrated a few seconds, then nodded. "I think he's on that payroll list Gadget sent us for Tex-La Shipping, working with Michael Benedict. Security, I think. I remember him because there were two people with that last name."

"Damn it." Kell shoved away his beer. He'd love to drain it, but he had a feeling his long day was about to turn into a long night. "Everything leads back to this guy. Now I really want to talk to Felderman. You ready to meet the esteemed governor of Texas?"

"Hell yeah." Nik took a sip of his bourbon and pushed back his chair, but stopped to pull his cell out of his pocket. The screen was lit with an incoming call. He raised an eyebrow at Kell as he lifted the phone to his ear. "What've you got, Robin?"

Kell strained to hear, but the noise in the bar was too loud. He didn't like the deepening frown on Nik's face, though, and despite his earlier avoidance, he took a swig of beer.

After a lot of non-illuminating grunts and curses, Nik ended the call. "We have one big clusterfuck now."

Not good. "Spill it."

"We need somewhere else to talk, where it's quiet and there are no ears. Wonder if the hotel has a room available?"

Archer reached into the pocket of his dark-green shirt, which looked suspiciously like silk, and held up a keycard. "Already got one, across the hall from Felderman."

"Nice work." Kell hadn't given the kitties—or Robin, either—enough credit. They were smart, and he needed to stop being threatened by them. It was going to take all of them to untangle this monumental pile of chaos.

They didn't talk on the ride to the sixth floor or on the walk down the long corridor. Kell paused outside Felderman's room and listened. The drone of a television seeped through the door, but nothing else. He studied the hallway they'd just traversed. The governor hadn't chosen the room with any quick getaways in mind. The room was at the dead end of the corridor, and the nearest exit lay halfway back to the elevator.

Archer unlocked the door to Room 602, and they followed him inside.

Kell pulled out the chair from behind the small desk and waited till the others were settled. "OK, let's have it."

"You were right—Mori went to Benedict's house in River Oaks. Once Robin had the address, she was able to find a trace of Mori's scent." Nik got up to pace. "The house is a big fortress. Since she was in flight mode, Robin took her time looking at what security setups she could see from outside. The whole place is wired, with cameras all around the grounds."

Kell wasn't surprised. If Benedict was involved in something like the Zemurray bombing, he had every right to be paranoid. Plus, the filthy rich, unlike himself, actually had material things worth protecting.

"Did Robin see Mori?"

Nik sat on the bed nearest Kell and nodded, his expression assessing, cautious.

Kell's adrenaline surged. It was bad news. "Tell me."

Archer moved closer, propping himself against the room's armoire/TV stand.

"As near as Robin can tell, Benedict has Mori locked in a small room in the attic on the back of the house. There's an undersize dormer window that appears to be secured with a steel locking system. Robin judged the window glass was that fiberglass-reinforced hurricane material."

Kell let out a breath he hadn't realized he was holding. This would require an extraction, but it was doable. "Then we should—"

"There's more."

His breath caught again. "Go on."

Nik's gaze was weighted. "Robin was able to hear a little bit of a conversation between Mori and Benedict. The room's wired with cameras, and he apparently can watch her and talk to her via a monitor. He plans to keep her in the room indefinitely as kind of a sex slave, although Robin couldn't hear details. Even with her shifter hearing, she wasn't able to get everything through that glass. He's refusing her clothing or food until she submits to him—although the words Robin heard were a lot cruder than that."

Michael Benedict was going to pay. Kell's thoughts went where they shouldn't, way past proving Benedict guilty of terrorism and all the way to killing the man. Slowly and painfully.

Nik paused and seemed to measure his words, his gaze searching Kell's face. "Was Mori wearing one of your shirts?"

A cold ripple went up Kell's spine. "Yeah, a Ranger T-shirt. Why?"

"Benedict had it, holding it up on the monitor. Robin couldn't hear his words, but whatever he said, it scared Mori. My guess is, he's threatening you as a way of controlling her."

Not happening. Kell propelled himself off the chair and charged toward the door. "Fine. That son of a bitch wants me? He's getting way more than he bargained for."

Archer stepped in Kell's path and planted a baseball-mitt-size hand in the middle of his chest. "Not without a plan."

Nik sighed. "There's one more thing. Mori's injured."

The chill returned to Kell's spine. He knocked Archer's hand away, and turned back to Nik. "How badly?"

"There's a burn on her back Robin says will leave a scar even on a shifter. Worse if infection sets in."

Archer gave a low whistle. "Damn. Yeah, we heal most things fast, but a deep burn is hard to overcome. Could Robin tell what kind of shifter Mori is? Or how she might have been burned?"

"That's a no on the shifter question, but Robin's guessing a pretty large animal. Mori's tall and athletic. But the injury..." Nik shook his head and shifted his gaze back to Kell. "She wasn't just burned, man. Robin says it looked like she was branded—you know, like with a branding iron. B for Benedict."

Kell's breath left him, and if his back hadn't turned into one big stress-filled spasm, he'd have thought he was dreaming. "What kind of sick fuck does something like that?"

"The head of a shifter group," Archer said, his expression grim. He'd moved back to block access to the hotel room door, and Kell gauged his chances were slim of getting around the man without one of them getting hurt. "Chances are if Mori's a shifter, so is Benedict. My guess would be that he's the leader of their clan, or pack, or whatever her species has. The leaders hold all the power; they're all arrogant fucks, but we learn to live with them."

Kell took a step toward Archer, his thoughts focused on getting Mori out of that bastard's house if he had to burn down River Oaks to do it.

"Kellison." Nik's voice was soft. "Rein it in. We charge in there without a plan and we're all fucked. You know that, man. You *know* that."

Kell closed his eyes and took a deep breath. His head had begun to pound in rhythm with his back. Nik was right. He'd get them all killed if he didn't rely on his training. Another mission plan. Another extraction. He'd done it many times before.

He nodded, and hated the look of relief Nik exchanged with Archer. "Sorry. I'm good." And had issued another fucking apology.

"I say we don't go in until daylight." Nik sat back on the bed, apparently convinced Kell had gotten himself under control. "We need to be able to see, since we're dealing with a lot of unknowns."

Kell's mind ticked through what he knew of Benedict. Tomorrow was Friday, a business day, and with any luck, Benedict would go to work to keep his schedule looking normal. If anything else happened to Mori, Robin would let them know.

"Maybe even midmorning." Kell reclaimed his chair at the desk. "It gives us planning time, and if Benedict goes to his office in Galveston, it will minimize our risk in getting Mori out." Then they'd go after the SOB, knowing she was safe—whatever she was.

Kell wished he could chastise himself for not realizing Mori was a shifter, but he'd seen nothing to indicate it. Nothing. And now that he knew, her behavior puzzled him even more.

"Archer, I need an honest answer from you."

The shifter's brows rose, and Kell felt shame that he'd treated both Archer and Adam like obligations rather than partners—even more so than Robin. "What's the question?"

Kell weighed his potential embarrassment against his need to know the truth. Truth won. "If Mori's a shifter, knowing how strong you and Adam and Robin are, she could have taken me out anytime she wanted, right?"

Archer's expression was cautious. "Well, yeah. If she'd really wanted to get away from you—or kill you, for that matter—

she could have. Obviously, she didn't want to. And the fact she hasn't taken Benedict out is what convinces me he's a shifter as well, and probably her alpha."

Which was the conclusion Kell had come to as well. Mori had to know Kell was in over his head. "Why stick with me as long as she did? Why go through all the shit with the hand-cuffs?"

Archer leaned against the wall leading into the entry foyer. "Look, a lot of clans or packs expect women to be docile. Mori's probably spent her whole life having independence drilled out of her. We're also taught not to reveal what we are. So she was into you enough to stay, maybe hope you could help her. When she realized you couldn't, she took off, maybe to protect you and her both."

Kell thought of how many times she'd tried to push him away, saying it was for his own good. She'd gone to Michael Benedict, at least in part, to protect him.

"Let's figure out how to get her out of there." Kell caught Nik and Archer exchanging relieved looks. "I can still function, guys."

He reached behind him and opened the desk drawer, pushed aside the room service menu and Bible, and pulled out a few sheets of hotel stationery and a cheap promotional pen. "Is Benedict still on the property?"

Nik shrugged. "We're assuming so. Robin didn't get a visual, but there are two cars in the garage, including the sedan he's been driving to Galveston."

Kell wrote names on the pad. "Archer, you're our link to Gadget. I need you to go onto the River Oaks estate now, probably on all fours, and assess the security setup, including the roof and access to that attic window." He paused, wondering how high jaguars could jump. "Also, get a guesstimate on how many people he has on staff at the house. Tell us when he leaves, and who's left after he leaves. You want to bring Adam in from New Orleans?"

Adam was Archer's younger brother, born a year later, but close enough in looks to be his twin. He was quiet and reserved, almost shy with people. Content to follow in his gregarious brother's wake. They were almost inseparable.

Archer thought a moment. "No, it would slow us down waiting for him to get here and come into the operation late. Besides, Gadget needs help in New Orleans, just in case we have to change direction fast."

Kell nodded. "Call in or text every piece of information you get so Nik and I can develop the extraction plan and a time-line." He watched Archer Velcro-strap his cell phone around his leg, beneath his pants cuff. It was the same method Robin used to keep her tiny little phone with her when she shifted. "Before you do anything else, see if you can find a way to let Mori know what's going on without being picked up on the cameras or microphones. She needs to act as normal as possible to anyone who's watching, no matter what we're doing outside that window."

"What about Robin?" Archer asked. "Want her following Benedict?"

Kell considered it. While a pair of eagle eyes on Michael would be helpful, they probably needed all hands for the operation. "No, call Robin on the way to River Oaks and tell her to stand by. I want her ready to go inside that attic room as soon as we're able to shut the cameras down. You will get the window open so Robin can reach Mori. Nik and I will take out Benedict's staff."

Archer got up, fished his car keys from his pocket, and handed the hotel room keycard to Kell. "You might need this. Leave it in the room when you're done. I need to change into cat burglar clothes"—he waited for the eye rolls from Kell and Nik—"and then I'm on my way to Casa del Benedict. You going to Nik's place soon?"

Kell and Nik exchanged glances and tacit agreement.

"We have some time before daylight, so we need to pay a little visit first." Kell's voice was grim. "It's time to meet the governor."

☜CHAPTER 20☞

Kell's watch read 2:00 a.m. when he slipped out of his room and across the hall, with Nik waiting in the open door behind him. He scanned the hallway ceilings for security cameras, but if they were there, it wasn't obvious. This hotel was nice enough, but it was the type of place businesspeople stopped overnight because it was convenient to Intercontinental. Customer security didn't rate as high a priority as a bar, room service, and an airport shuttle.

Kneeling in front of the door to Room 601, Kell ran his fingertips along the bottom of the raised pad where customers slid their keycards. He felt the tiny DC port in the middle of the underside. So far so good.

From his pocket, he took a small electronic device that looked like a jerry-rigged cell phone. Gadget had developed it after seeing a similar thing sprung by a hacker at a computer conference the year before, and had sent it with Archer. Two six-inch black wires led from it, ending in a small plug designed to fit in the bottom of keycard locks.

Plugging the device into the lock port, Kell turned on Gadget's gadget and powered it up. After a few seconds, the lock released with a soft whir. He removed the device and nodded at Nik, who pulled out his handgun and held it pointed downward, pressed against his right leg.

The next question was, had the governor used the interior lock as well? Kell turned the door handle and pushed slightly. Their luck held; the door opened with no pesky chain or lever latch.

Standing, Kell pulled the Beretta from its shoulder holster and paused with the door open about a foot, listening. A canned-laugh track sounded softly from the television, but all else was quiet.

Three steps, and he was able to peer around the corner of the entrance foyer into the room itself. Felderman sat on the edge of the king-size bed with his back to the door, facing the window. The curtains had been left open to reveal a smattering of streetlights and the blinking red light of a plane descending toward the runways that lay only a few miles to the north.

On the bed next to the governor lay a gun—a compact Smith & Wesson, from the look of it. Kell stepped aside so Nik could see the setup; then they both raised their weapons.

"Governor?"

At the sound of Kell's voice, Felderman gasped, jumped to his feet, and turned to face them, without so much as a glance at his gun. "Who are you? How'd you get in here?"

While Nik kept his pistol trained on Felderman, Kell reached across the bed and took the governor's handgun. He removed the ammo clip and made sure the chamber was empty before wiping it clean of prints with his shirttail and tossing it back on the bed.

Then he pulled his own weapon and kept the frozen, silent politician in his sights while Nik did a quick search of the room for listening devices or cameras. Benedict would want to keep tabs on his man.

"It's clean, unless he's wired."

Kell nodded. "Who knows you're here, Governor?"

Felderman swallowed hard. "Nobody. Who are you?"

If the governor had left the hospital early to slip away from Benedict's grasp, Kell might get him to talk. He hadn't taken Travis Milkin's call, but Milkin obviously knew where he was, which meant time was limited. "Never mind who we are, Governor. We have questions, and we need quick answers. Sit."

Felderman hesitated, and his gaze shot to the phone on the desk.

Nik reached behind the desk and unplugged the phone, then turned off the television. "The faster you talk, the faster we leave."

Felderman sat in one of two chairs nestled against a small round table in front of the window. Kell sat on the bed in the governor's former spot, facing him. He holstered his weapon, hoping it would help Felderman relax. Besides, Nik had his back.

"I want you to tell us about your kidnapping, Governor." Kell kept his voice low and even. This guy looked as jumpy as Gator when he saw a real alligator.

Felderman's gaunt face developed a tic that jerked the right side of his mouth in irregular spasms. "I've told everything I know. It was that Co-Op woman. Emory Chastaine. She was behind it."

Kell sighed, long and loud and put-upon. "Well, see, that's where we have a problem. I happen to know she *wasn't* behind it, and I'm very curious as to why you'd say she was. Do you know Michael Benedict?"

"Of course I do," Felderman snapped, but however impatient his words were, his body language spoke differently. His hands shook as they clutched at the wooden arm of his chair, and one thin leg began moving in restless jitters. "I know all our Texas major business owners."

Nik walked behind Felderman and rested his hands on the man's shoulders. In an instant, Felderman stilled all his nervous movements, his breath held as if waiting for Nik to choke him. What the hell had Benedict done to the man? Kell had never liked Felderman much as a governor and thought him just another blowhard politician, but this man was a pathetic wreck.

Nik's face bunched in a frown as he massaged Felderman's shoulders in a soothing motion, trying to get a psychic reading.

"Governor, what do you know about the jaguarundi?" Nik asked.

Felderman jerked away from Nik's touch, rose to his feet, and shuffled away until his back hit the wall. "I don't know what you're talking about."

Kell motioned for Nik to take over the questions. Whatever he'd seen, mentioning the jags clearly struck a nerve.

Nik retreated to the other chair and motioned for Felderman to sit down. The governor sat, but his legs were tensed to jump again.

"You were kept in a dark room," Nik said softly. "You were bitten repeatedly by two jaguarundi shape-shifters. You need to tell us their names, what they said to you, and what your agenda is supposed to be now. What is it they want you to do besides implicate Emory Chastaine?"

Felderman slumped in his seat. "You know about sh-shape-shifters?"

"We do," Kell said. "And we've seen those two before, and we know who they work for. What did they want with you?"

"You know who they work for?" Felderman's eyes were wide, bloodshot, and frightened. "They were the only ones I saw. One was named Travis. I don't know the other."

He stood up, starting in one direction toward Nik, then swerving back toward Kell. Panic was taking hold. "They'll kill me if I talk. I have to get out of here. You have to let me leave."

"Governor, we can't help you unless you tell us what the endgame is." Kell nodded at Nik, who moved to take a position in the narrow foyer leading to the door. Felderman didn't look physically capable of making a run for it, but it would be stupid to give him the opportunity. "We know Travis and the other shifter work for Michael Benedict. He's running the show. What we don't know is where you fit in or why Emory Chastaine is involved."

"I don't know about her." Felderman paced halfway toward Nik, then turned and paced back. Back and forth, again and again. "I was told what to say. That she was behind it. That I had seen her." He stopped and looked at Kell. "But I didn't see her. I swear, I don't know why they wanted me to blame it on her."

Kell turned to keep the frantic, pacing man in his sights. "What about Benedict?"

"Oh God, oh God." Benedict ran a shaky hand over his thin hair. "I never saw him, but they talked about him. He'll have them kill me. They bit me, and now I can't . . ."

Kell looked at Nik in question, but he shrugged. "Now you can't, what?"

"I can't control it." Felderman gasped as if struggling for air. "It's going to happen, and I can't…"

Speechless, Kell watched as the governor's face grew rounder with what looked like a painful shifting of bone, his pupils elongating to slits, hair bristling from his cheeks in uneven clumps. Felderman cried out in pain as his shoulders narrowed, and he dropped to his knees. The hands resting on his thighs were half hand, half…black-and-gray paw.

Kell had reached up to unholster his gun when the change started, but froze with his fingers on the snap.

"They turned you into one of them?" This time, it was Nik's voice that shook. "I didn't think it was possible."

Neither did Kell. When Robin and the kitties had schooled them on the ins and outs of shape-shifters, they'd insisted that the old legends of being bitten and turned into new shifters were false, that shifters were born and not made.

Tell that to the governor of Texas. Tears ran freely down Felderman's cheeks, dividing into rivulets around the clumps of fur. "I'm not one of them. I'm a freak. Just a freak. What they call a hybrid. They tell me I won't do this if I calm down. How the hell am I supposed to calm down?" His voice had grown higher and whispery thin.

"Jesus." Kell swallowed hard, trying to sound calm. "What is it they want from you?"

"Everything." Felderman's tone dropped to a whisper. "On every decision, every bill, every law that needs my signature, I will follow Travis's orders, and Travis gets his orders from Benedict."

Kell frowned. So Benedict would be running the state according to his own agenda—at least as far as the governor's power extended. "Or what? What will they do if you don't follow orders?"

Felderman was openly sobbing now. "I have to follow the orders of my hybrid-maker. That's the way it works. Whatever Benedict tells Travis and Travis tells me, I...I can't refuse. I've tried, but it's like my mind loses its ability to control my thoughts."

Holy fuck. Kell wasn't even sure what to ask the man, and the implications were staggering. True, Benedict didn't control the legislature, only the governor himself. But what was to prevent him from doing this on a larger scale? On more lawmakers, or judges, or the fucking president, if he got ambitious or power-hungry enough?

"What happens if Travis dies?" Nik asked. "Then are you free of the compulsion to follow his orders?"

Felderman had calmed a little, and his fur began to recede. "Travis said if he died, I'd die, but I don't know whether that's true or if it was just a way to control me." He got to his feet and took a step toward Nik. "I don't care what it does to me. Will you kill him?"

Nik and Kell exchanged glances.

"We're not in the killing business, Governor," Kell said. They might be forced to kill the guy, but not unless it was self-defense. He was kind of relieved to find he still had some lines he wouldn't cross, and he had to assume they extended to Michael Benedict. Within reason. "What we want is evidence against Benedict. Can you give us that?"

Felderman collapsed into the chair. He'd aged twenty years since the bombing. "They'd never let me testify in a trial; they'd kill me first or compel me to lie. And what if I...change in public? I don't even know how I'm can go back to Austin like this. It just happens."

What a fucking mess. Kell blew out a breath and looked at his watch. It was 3:00 a.m., and they needed to get back to

Nik's and plan the mission. Should they force the governor to go with them? It would keep him out of Benedict's hands, and it would keep the existence of shape-shifters from being sprung on the public in a terrible way. But Kell had found another line he wasn't willing to step over—kidnapping an elected official, even under these circumstances.

"Governor, I don't know what's going to happen." Kell considered his words carefully. "I can't promise you that we can fix this. But if you want to come with us, we'll keep you safe and away from Benedict's people until we figure out what to do."

Felderman scrubbed his palms across his face, which had shifted back to its normal, narrow dimensions. "Who do you work for? Why should I trust you any more than them?"

Kell shook his head. "I'm not at liberty to tell you that. Only that we'll keep you out of sight until we find a solution you can live with."

Felderman's nod was no more than a barely perceptible tilt of the head. "Why not? I can't stay here forever. Word'll get out. It always does."

Faster than he suspected, assuming Milkin's call meant the jag knew Felderman was at this hotel.

"Good." Kell stood up. "We've got a room down the hall. Let us make a few arrangements, and we'll get you out of here within ten minutes."

Felderman's self-assurance was rebounding quickly. He stood and held out his hand for Kell to shake. "Thank you, whoever you are. Anything's better than letting them find me."

"We'll be back in a few." Kell edged past him and followed Nik out the door. They didn't speak until they'd crossed the hallway and were again ensconced in Archer's room.

"I'm betting somebody's already looking for him." Nik crossed his arms and frowned thoughtfully at the door. "Let's take him to one of our safe hotels."

"Agreed." Kell scrolled through the texts and calls that had come in since he'd muted his phone before going into Felderman's room. "The colonel called again—that's three times. And Archer is texting stuff about Benedict's security as he finds it. We've got enough to work out a—"

He halted, frozen, at the sound of breaking glass and a loud pop from the hallway. Or from a room across the hallway.

If there was one thing Kell recognized, it was the sound of a rifle shot.

EPISODE 6

⊰CHAPTER 21⊱

Mori shifted the thin bedspread she'd wrapped around her shoulders, unable to find a position that didn't make her want to scream and claw her way outside her body.

For a while, she'd clutched the spread around her in an attempt to trap enough body heat inside to warm her cold, clammy skin, all the while keeping the rough fabric away from her back. An hour later, she'd be sweating as if baking from the inside. She should be famished after at least fifteen or sixteen hours without food—not that Michael had left her with her watch—but the thought of it sparked waves of nausea.

She'd tried shifting twice for warmth, but hadn't been able to call upon the power and focus it required. Shifting wasn't painful, but it consumed a lot of energy. She'd shift spontaneously if threatened, as when Michael had branded her, but needed to stay in human form to heal.

The inability to shift, plus her erratic body temperature, flashed warning signs that an infection could be setting in already. Who knew if the wound had been cleaned or not? But her guess was that it hadn't. Michael had probably carted her to the attic in her shifted form, dumped her on the bed, and sashayed off to enjoy an evening with his real fiancée.

Sleep would promote healing, but pain and anger and fear had blocked sleep from reach. The blinking red dots in each corner mocked her with the reminder that unknown sets of eyes followed her every move.

She turned her back to the camera nearest the bed and lowered the spread to bare her back more fully. "Michael, if you're listening, I need a doctor. I need antibiotics. You're not going to get your new generation of Dires if I die of infection."

The monitor remained black, the house silent but for the gentle hum of the air-conditioning system. The red light blinked with malevolence, like the Eye of Sauron from atop Mount Doom.

Good Lord, if she were mentally likening her dilemma to the quest of a hobbit in *Lord of the Rings*, maybe the infection had already spread to her brain. After all, she'd spent at least an hour last night staring through the window at a golden eagle.

The big raptor had strutted awkwardly from side to side, its long talons gouged into the wood of the broad sill, its glossy reddish-brown wings sweeping across the glass. Occasionally, it would stop and watch her with sharp golden eyes. A few times, it pecked on the glass with the end of its curved beak, as if trying to break its way inside. Mostly, it looked past her. Around her. Like it was checking out the room and she was blocking its view.

Finally, with a squawk and a flutter of feathers, it had flown away. Mori had remained in the chair pulled up to the window, shivering and sweating in turn. The more time that passed, the more she thought she'd imagined the eagle. She'd thought an eagle had followed her to the ranch on the night of her birthday, after all. Which, even then, had seemed paranoid and stupid.

Maybe her stressed-out brain had conjured up its own avatar for impending madness.

At last, dawn's gray sky ushered in shades of gold and peach to signal the beginning of another day. The first Friday of the rest of her miserable life. Mori shivered and wondered if a hot shower would help the chills that had settled deep in her bones, and maybe wash away the self-pity that created nothing but a sense of helplessness.

Knowing Michael, there was no hot water. She shuffled across the room to the bathroom, the edges of the plaid bedspread dragging on the wooden floor behind her like the train of the world's ugliest wedding dress.

She'd have to keep the water off her back, where she thought even a touch as light as one of her imaginary eagle's feathers would prove unbearable. Unlike the rest of her, that scorched patch of skin between her shoulder blades still felt as if it were blanketed in hot coals.

The contrast of heat and chill left her dizzy after the exertion of walking the eight steps from bed to bathroom. She leaned over the small pedestal sink in the bathroom with a hand clutched to either side of the white porcelain, waiting for the spins to slow down and her vision to clear. She ran some water from the faucet into her cupped palm and drank it, waiting to see if she could keep it down. *Yay, me. I didn't barf.*

When her legs felt more like muscle and bone and less like rubber, Mori turned to examine the small shower that had been installed in the corner. Looking somewhat like a phone booth with clear glass sides, it at least had knobs for both hot and cold water. She opened the door, but as she reached to turn the knob, a red light in the corner over the toilet caught her attention. Another damned camera pointed right at the shower. The idea of showering under the invisible gaze of Michael or creepy, ear-tugging Travis made bile rise in her throat.

She scanned the rest of the room. No other cameras were visible, and since the toilet was underneath it, at least she could pee without feeling eyes were on her.

Screw the shower. It would've been hard to keep her back dry, anyway. Maybe she'd never shower again and then see how Michael liked her after a month or two.

With a sigh, Mori walked back into the bedroom and stopped short. Either madness had finally taken hold or the eagle was back. She still hated Michael, which meant she was sane, and it was daylight now. No way was this an avian figment of her imagination.

It hopped from side to side on the sill, holding something in its mouth. At first, Mori thought it was a leaf or a bit of trash the bird might be using to build a nest—was this even nesting season for raptors? But as she drew nearer to the window, she realized what the bird gripped in its wickedly curved beak was a small sheet of paper. With writing on it. And her name at the top.

Heart pounding, Mori glanced up at the four cameras, each in turn. Only one looked as if its field of view might include the window, and even then, it would be at an oblique angle. Her watchers could see her at the window but not what was outside.

Her heart sped at the thought of help arriving, then slowed just as quickly. Who knew she was here? And what did a freaking *eagle* have to do with it?

Mori resisted the urge to rush to the window and draw the attention of whoever was watching—maybe Michael, checking on his property before going to work. She paced around the room a few times, moving slowly, mindful of not making any sudden turns to further irritate her back.

Finally, on her third pass, she stopped in front of the window as if pausing to look at the world being denied to her, praying that whoever had taken the early-morning Mori watch would think nothing was amiss.

The eagle raised its head to help her better read the note, then remained still as she drew closer. Neat block letters marched across the page, three short lines of black ink on a torn-off piece of what looked like hotel stationery.

MORI—HELP COMING.
AVOID WINDOW.
ACT NORMAL.

A laugh escaped her before she could stop it, and she turned from the window quickly. There was nothing normal about any of this. But...help was coming! She couldn't stop the hope that awoke inside her, drifting like smoke around the hard lump of fear in her heart and rising above it to send her brain humming. It might not be Kell; it could be anyone. At this point, she didn't care, as long as she got out of this room, out of this house.

Her gut told her it was Kell, though. He was the only one who might figure out where she was and might care enough to do something about it. It certainly wasn't her parents, and none of the other Dire males would dare defy Michael.

Her memory had etched Kell's face into her mind, wearing the expression she'd seen just before walking out of the hotel room in Baytown. Begging her to trust him, to not try to handle things alone, to let him save her. Some part of her had known that beautiful, fearless, clueless man was going to come for her. He knew about Michael, or at least had strong suspicions about Michael. He knew just enough to march right into Michael's plans. And no matter how good he was at his job, how smart or well trained, Kell would not be prepared to fight shape-shifters.

Or would he? He'd asked about the jaguarundis—had used the term *shifter*. In the chaos following that conversation, she'd forgotten that detail, and remembering both ramped up her hope for herself and her fear for Kell.

Better she never be rescued than allow him to fall into Michael's hands.

Mori hadn't prayed in a long time. She'd been raised on a peculiar combination of mystical Dire lore and Texas Bible-thumping that never made sense to her. But she prayed now, silently, constantly, like an endless loop of audio streaming out pleas for help. She didn't dare pray for rescue. Only that if Kell came for her, he not be killed or caught.

By the time Mori made another slow walk around the room, the eagle had disappeared. The excitement had turned her chills to heat again, so she loosened the spread around her and returned to the bed. Curling up on her side, facing the window, she could watch for the eagle's return without attracting attention.

Twice, she thought she heard noises from outside, and it took all her willpower to stay in place. As time dragged on, the chills returned, and she pulled the bedspread around her more tightly, moaning as it pressed on her back like the fiery hand of an angry god. Because if he was up there, he must be mighty pissed off.

For what seemed like hours, she lay in a twilight state between a doze and a trance, eyes trained on the window as if Kell himself might come bursting through it in a spray of shattering wood and glass. When something finally did appear at the window, it took a few seconds to register.

It was a rope, dangling from somewhere above.

She dared not move lest whoever watched her on the cameras suspect anything, but her breath caught when a pair of boots lowered into view, followed by long black-clad legs, a tool belt strapped around a narrow waist, and finally, a pair of broad shoulders and a strong-jawed face framed by long black waves of hair. A man with eyes such a brilliant green he had to be wearing colored contact lenses.

He cupped gloved hands around his eyes and peered through the glass, his gaze scanning the room before it finally locked on Mori. He held a finger up to his mouth.

Quiet. She could be quiet, although it wouldn't surprise her if the microphones in the room could pick up her heartbeat. It thumped so hard she could feel streaks of fiery heat reverberate across her back at every beat.

Willing herself to remain still, Mori watched as the man looped the lower end of the rope around his upper thighs and waist, deftly knotting it into a makeshift seat. With both hands free and his boots planted on the outside wall for stability, he felt around the edges of the window, fumbled with his tool belt, and pulled out some type of wrench.

He worked silently, unbolting the steel casing that locked the window into place. Finally, he replaced the wrench with a lever bar and eased the top of the window outward, toward him. The sound of metal scraping metal seemed way too loud, so Mori feigned a coughing fit to cover the noise, ignoring the pain each movement caused.

Finally, the window came free of the frame. Mori sat up fast, dragging the bedspread across her back with enough roughness that the room swirled in gray. She hung her head and clutched the thin mattress on either side of her, willing herself not to faint. Not now. Not when the fresh, warm air had already begun filtering into the room.

"Mori?" The man's whisper was so soft she wasn't sure he'd really spoken until she raised her head and found him watching her intently. "Stay where you are for now. The house isn't secure yet."

She gave a slight nod to show she understood. He grinned, balanced the window on his thighs, and looked upward. Just as slowly as he'd lowered himself into view, someone from above began pulling him up. Soon, all she could see were legs, then boots, then nothing.

The hot air spilling in from the outside smelled like freedom. A plane flew overhead. Birds sang in the gardens below, the gurgling of the fountain like laughter in the background. Mori closed her eyes and let the warmth seep into her. Funny how hope lessened the pain in her back, the promise of help erasing the fatigue and hunger.

At a loud squawk from the window, Mori opened her eyes, no longer surprised to see the eagle sitting in the open frame. It stared at her a moment, then swiveled its head and leaned in a fraction, studying the cameras in the facing corners. Why hadn't Mori realized before—this could well be an eagle-shifter. Maybe Kell hadn't seemed freaked out about the existence of jaguarundi-shifters because he worked with an eagle.

Or was that too far-fetched? How would an Army guy get mixed up with a shape-shifter?

She'd assumed the big dark-haired guy was a member of Kell's team, but if there were shifters involved, she wasn't sure who was rescuing her—or why.

❧CHAPTER 22☙

Nik rattled his bag of chips as he dug the last crumbs out of the bottom. The noise grated on Kell's last nerve. "Where'd Gadget scrounge up this lawn-service van?"

Kell's eyes maintained a sweeping scan of the neighborhood a block from Michael Benedict's house. The clock on the van's dash read 6:58 a.m., and they'd been here for a half hour, hoping anyone who spotted them would assume they were part of the BAYOU LAWN SERVICE crew. Just two green thumbs sitting in their baby-puke-green van and waiting till it was time to clock in and prune some roses.

"He has a cousin who owns the place and didn't mind loaning it out, no questions asked. And if you rattle that bag one more time, I'm gonna hurt you."

He was spared from having to apologize—again—by the buzz of his phone. He'd set the Gator ringtone to silent mode for this operation.

"Window's out." Archer's voice was soft.

"How's Mori?" Yeah, Kell's first question should have been if the kitty had run into complications, or had seen anything else in the security setup they needed to know, or had a visual on Michael Benedict. But they'd already established that Kell's priorities had been screwed six ways to Sunday. "You see her?"

"She's OK. Looks a little unsteady, but she's following direction and knows the house isn't secure yet. Robin's on standby. As soon as the lights on the security cameras go down, she's ready to go in. Also got the make of the front door lock for you—Schnabel."

Good. An easy dead bolt to bump, and he had what he needed to do it.

Kell glanced at the clock. "Give Benedict until eight o'clock to leave. We move as soon as he's out. If he hasn't left by then, we move anyway. Wait for my signal."

He ended the call and stuffed the phone back in his pocket. Talk about a hastily conceived mission plan. He'd had some fucked-up assignments over the years, but none with more unknowns than this one. Human enemies at least had physical limitations. Who knew how many shifters might be inside, what kind they were, or what they could do?

One thing Benedict's people had almost assuredly done— murdered Carl Felderman. The governor had been killed with a single rifle shot to the head, by someone who knew what he was doing. A single-shot kill through an upper-floor hotel window at long range was classic sharpshooter fare. At least, that's what was being reported on the radio. After he and Nik had heard the gun- shot and run a quick check to make sure Felderman couldn't be saved, they'd hustled back to Nik's apartment to plan the mission.

"So?" Nik checked the clip in his weapon for at least the third time. "How's our target?"

Kell knew what his friend was doing, but referring to Mori as a target wasn't going to make him forget that this extraction meant more to him than duty. "Don't sweat it, Nik. I'm not going to fuck up the mission." *Especially this mission.*

"Garage door." Nik straightened in his seat, and Kell leaned forward and grabbed the small binoculars from the dash. The recessed garage doors on the east side of the house slid open slowly, revealing a black Mercedes sedan that backed out the short drive to the side street.

Kell squinted through the binoculars' viewfinder and adjusted the focus until a well-groomed head of dark hair was visible in the driver's seat. "So long, asshole."

"It's Benedict?" Nik reached behind his seat and fished out his gear belt. They'd agreed that packs would be too bulky and tried to anticipate anything they might need. If all else failed, they had combat knives as well as their firearms.

"Himself. And alone." Kell speed-dialed Gadget, who'd been working from New Orleans to identify the estate's security system.

Gadget answered on the first ring. "Are we a go?"

"Yep. Tell me what we know."

Kell heard the clicks of a keyboard as Gadget did his magic. "OK, I was able to procure a schematic from the files of the company that installed the system."

Procure was Gadget-speak for *steal*, but Kell could live with that. He switched the phone to speaker so Nik could hear. "What are we dealing with?"

"Two separate units." More clicks in the background while Gadget talked. "The first is a standard setup that monitors open doors and windows on the first floor only. No motion sensors. All the alarms link to the main power supply, located inside the garage door. Cut the power, and you have thirty seconds to get inside the house and close the door behind you before it switches to battery backup. If a door or window is open at that point, an intruder signal goes straight to the police."

Kell took notes from Gadget's descriptions and sketched the house and location of the power cables. "What about the second system?"

"That one's just for the attic, and it's new—installed about a month ago."

That fucking jerk had been planning Mori's abduction since before the bombing? What kind of hold did Benedict have over her that she'd handcuffed Kell in that hotel room and gone straight to him?

Nik cleared his throat, and Kell mentally slapped himself back into focus. There would be time later to get answers. "What's the setup?"

"There's a central monitoring station on the first floor. The work order describes it as a study on the west side of the house," Gadget said. "Five monitors are installed there, plus a sixth in the attic. The first-floor monitors get feeds from the attic cameras, and the attic monitor gets audio and video from a computer cam in the study. Again, one basic set of lines running into that single computer, and no battery backup on that one. No alarms, either. Benedict must've been pretty sure no one would come to save her."

Cocky bastard. At least it made things easier for Kell's team.

After getting a few more details from Gadget and ending the call, Kell handed his notes to Nik. "Sounds like a pretty basic setup. We'll stay linked with our headsets. Take out the main power cables. Let me know just before you flip the switch, and I'll use that thirty-second window to get inside. It'll look like a power failure. Take out whoever comes to check the fuse box."

He stared at the house, thinking. "Call Archer and tell him to create a distraction on the east side of the house as soon as you get in the garage. Maybe we can draw the staff to that side of the house so I can get to that study and take down the attic security."

"Got it." Nik tossed the notes on the console as Kell cranked the van and moved it to a spot on the side street just out of view of the garage. Thank God for corner lots.

Kell slipped his own belt into place and pulled on a pair of thin, lightweight gloves. No fingerprints at this scene. He wedged a wireless headset into his ear and nodded at Nik, who'd donned his own headset before calling Archer with the plan. It would be important to stay in voice contact from here on. He wished he'd asked Robin to strap a headset to her leg.

They walked to the edge of the property, and Kell slipped behind a broad-leafed palm to wait. The security cameras on this side of the house were trained on the driveway, so if anyone were monitoring them, they wouldn't see Nik's cautious approach to the garage door. Benedict was arrogant enough to not be watching the general monitors, though. Kell would bet his next paycheck all eyes would be on the attic monitors.

Kell waited as Nik slipped a long wire from the side pocket of his cargo pants, leaped like a monkey onto a ledge beside the garage, and threaded the wire through the top of the wide door. The two minutes it took him to hook the wire onto the release catch dangling from the electronic garage door mechanism inside seemed to last a week, but finally, Nik eased himself back to the ground and raised the garage door manually.

He looked back at Kell and nodded.

"Showtime, Kitten," Kell muttered. A few seconds later, a sleek black jaguar—what he'd always called a black cougar or panther until Archer and Adam haughtily corrected him—slinked around the side of the house, looking in windows. Kell had seen the brothers in cat form a lot during their training, but the size still amazed him. This "kitten" easily packed three hundred pounds of muscle and teeth.

A face appeared on the inside of a first-floor window, looking out at Archer. Kell grinned; he could see the guy's mouth drop open even from across the lawn. Shouts followed from within the house.

Archer began his routine, racing in circles around the side lawn, rolling on his back in the grass, and finally, stopping to swipe a tongue the size of a baby blanket across one massive paw. One lick, two licks, three—he'd spotted three people.

Kell nodded. Good odds for success if that was all of them. Now it was showtime for him.

He pushed Mori as far back in his mind as he could get her and skirted the outer edges of the property, ducking from one landscaping feature to the next until he reached the front corner of the house. No more cover remained.

Figuring a man wearing dark clothes in the late-August heat would attract more attention running than walking, Kell said a quick prayer and broke the cover of the azalea stand. He strode up the circular drive to the arched front door and waited, the tools to pop the dead bolt in his right hand. "In position," he whispered.

It seemed like an eon had passed before Nik responded: "Turning the juice off in three...two...one...now."

Kell had knelt in front of the door during Nik's countdown. Now, he inserted a blank Schnabel key into the lockset, pressing and turning while he tapped firmly on the key with the end of a screwdriver. His muscles told him to hurry, to do it fast, but his brain overrode his body's panic response. He finally heard the bolt slide with a click.

Easing the door open, he stepped inside and closed it softly behind him. According to his watch, he'd had four seconds to spare. Not bad for a broken-down soldier. "In," he told the others in a whisper.

He crouched behind a table in a recessed section of an ornate circular foyer to get his bearings. Above his head rose a curved staircase with a wrought-iron banister. To his far left lay what looked like the entrance to a formal dining room. He'd guess the door to the right of the staircase, opening to the west, was either the study or led to the study.

"It's just a fucking power outage. Either that or the AC's working so hard to cool this place that it's flipped a breaker. What d'you make of that cat?"

Kell ducked lower, squinting through a profusion of leaves from a potted plant as two men walked into the foyer from the room on the left. One was about his height, one a bit shorter. The shorter man wore jeans and a T-shirt. Muscle, probably. No surprise there. The tall guy wore a button-front shirt and khakis. Maybe a regular member of the house staff.

"Don't know, but it's gone now, so forget it. Go to the garage and check the breaker." The shorter of the men pointed the taller guy toward the dining area. Kell figured a kitchen must lead off from there, and the garage door probably led into the kitchen. "I'll make sure the monitors in the study have gone to backup."

The taller man laughed. "Yeah right, Travis. You're hoping the chick in the attic will be taking a shower."

"Fuck yeah."

A flash of anger threatened to dash Kell's shaky calm. So the short dude with the brown hair was Travis, one of the jaguarundi-shifters who'd turned the governor into a freak, and maybe even the one who'd killed him. He'd done his jaguarundi research. The cats weren't very big, but he'd learned from Robin that, in a shape-shifter, size was no indicator of strength.

As soon as the tall guy was out of sight and Travis had disappeared through the door to the right, Kell eased out from behind the plant table, wincing at the stab of fire that shot from his back all the way down his right leg. No time to let it warm up. At least one of Benedict's people remained unaccounted for.

He pulled his weapon and eased the slide back, ready to fire. A quick look inside the door revealed no one, so Kell stepped softly into a long rectangular living room. Despite overstuffed furniture made for lounging and a huge fireplace, the room looked anything but lived-in. It was as cold and sterile as the rest of Benedict's palace.

A cold stab of hatred shot through Kell's veins as he passed the fireplace and noticed a long metal rod with a "B" formed on the end. Its rustic craftsmanship clashed with the elegance of the room and the white mantel on which it rested. It was the branding iron, with caked-on ashes at the end that had once been Mori's skin.

Kell promised himself he would kill Michael Benedict or die trying. But not this morning. His first priority was Mori's safety.

Voices wafted from a doorway at the far end of the room. Male. At least two of them. Kell walked softly along the wall, his weapon held in front of him.

He paused outside the open doorway. Definitely two guys talking. If there was a third, he was silent.

"Wish that goddamn woman would do something. She just lies there wrapped up in that bedspread like a mummy." A nasal voice, high in pitch.

"Yeah, but you shoulda seen her last night." Travis—that voice, Kell recognized from the foyer. "Naked as anybody's business. Nice tits and ass. You wait, watching the bitch will be a detail we'll fight over."

Not happening.

Kell stepped into the doorway, glad to see both guys had their backs turned as they hunched over a monitor. He'd focus on Travis and keep the other guy in his sights. "Wrong, Travis."

Both men whirled to stare at him, and for a moment, all three of them were frozen in place. Then chaos erupted as Travis pulled a weapon and Kell fired twice in quick succession.

While Travis dropped, Kell turned the gun on his companion—who'd disappeared. *What the fuck?*

At a scrambling noise behind him, Kell rotated fast, aiming at eye level, and saw nothing.

He scanned the room as Nik's voice sounded in the headset: "Location?"

"Study." Kell glanced at the monitors, and his heart stopped at the sight of Mori curled on her side, her blond hair barely visible from the top of the cocoon in which she'd wrapped herself. He reached behind the computer and jerked out all the wires, not worrying about which one led to which camera. He wanted them all off.

At a hiss from above him, Kell twisted, his gaze locking on that of a jaguarundi atop a bookcase. He raised his gun but never got off a shot. The Beretta hit the floor with a clatter as a blur of sharp claws and gray fur rained hell on his upturned face.

❧CHAPTER 23❧

There was a flurry of noise, then silence. What surely had to be a series of gunshots sounded from below. The cameras in the corners emitted long beeps and went dead in unison, no red lights visible. And the eagle screeched loud enough to be heard in Mexico, hopping from the windowsill onto the bedroom floor with a flutter of broad reddish-brown wings.

Mori sat up, the pain in her back momentarily forgotten as the eagle grew and blurred, leaving in its place the kneeling waif of a girl with spiky auburn hair and huge brown eyes. Well, that answered the question of whether or not the eagle was a shifter. Which meant she'd been tailing Mori all the way back to the night of her birthday.

"You've been following me. Who are you?"

"Name's Robin. Yeah, yeah, I know—stupid name for an eagle-shifter." The girl rose from a crouch to her full height of maybe five feet. Maybe. "What can I say? My parents were hippies with a warped sense of humor."

Mori stood too fast, causing the room to spin. Before she could sink back to the bed, Robin placed a hand on each arm and shifted her around with surprising strength.

"Drop the bedspread and let me look at your back. The cameras are off."

Mori hesitated, not because she was modest, but because she was ashamed. Ashamed for another shifter to see the proof that she'd allowed someone to brand her like a cow, to treat her like property. That she'd walked into it with such naïveté.

She stepped away and turned back to face the girl—no, woman. She just looked like a kid because she barely reached Mori's shoulder. The other person who'd been watching her since her birthday was Jack Kellison.

"Are you with Kell? Is he OK?"

Robin looked up at her with a grin. "You handcuffed him to a nightstand, and wait until you hear what a freaking mess he'd gotten himself into when we found him. I haven't laughed that hard in years. In fact, if we get out of this alive, I owe you a drink for making that big, bossy jerk eat a little crow." She frowned. "I've tasted crow. It's gamey."

Mori relaxed a little. If the eaglet was making fun of Kell, things couldn't be too bad. "Then he's safe?"

"Nothing bruised but his big fat ego." Robin grasped Mori's arms and turned her again. "He and the other guys are taking out the security system, and then…" She pulled down the bedspread that covered Mori's back. "Holy shit. I might have to kill the mofo who did this. Did he not even clean the wound afterward?"

"Don't think so. Just dumped me on the bed and left." Mori eased away from Robin, shuffled back to the bed, and sat, letting the bedspread hang off her back. To hell with modesty, although she could offer Robin some coverage. "You want a sheet?"

Robin shook her head. "I can do better than that."

She walked back to the window, reached outside, and retrieved a plastic grocery bag from the rope. "Archer—he's the guy who took the window out—slipped into your place and brought out a few things. But that back needs a doctor, although what kind of doctor..." Robin cocked her head, giving Mori an assessing look. "What are you?"

Mori's first impulse was to lie, but what difference did secrecy make now, especially with these people who were risking so much to rescue her? "Dire Wolf."

"Dire." Robin frowned a moment as if consulting some inner database, then whistled. "I thought the Dires were, you know, long gone." She mimicked a knife slicing across her throat.

Mori had to smile. She liked the eagle named Robin. "There are only about thirty Dire-shifters left. None of our brothers in the wild exist anymore. They've been extinct a long time, and the shifters aren't far behind."

"So is..." Robin stopped. "Never mind. There'll be time to talk later."

She dug in the plastic bag and brought out a small tube. "This is for burns, but now that I see it up close, I'm afraid to touch it. Better let Nik or Kell take a look first—they know more about injuries. Poor old humans have to deal with that kind of shit all the time, you know?"

Mori took the jeans and chambray shirt Robin handed her, and shook her head, smiling. "You guys couldn't have picked a better shirt. Michael says I look like a Texas ranch hand in it." Which had made it one of her favorites.

"Hope you don't mind my saying it, but from what I've seen, Michael's a total asshole." Robin had slipped into a pair of jeans and slid a T-shirt over her head. She stopped at the sound of Mori's laughter. "What?"

"Nothing." Mori smiled. "You're right. He is a total asshole."

"Is he your alpha?"

Cautiously, Mori nodded. Again, why not tell the truth? Her own family had deserted her, and here, finally, was someone who seemed to be on her side. "Unfortunately, he is our alpha. I've known him my whole life and always thought he was a bully. But he's so much worse than that."

"Hmmmm." Robin sat on the floor with her legs crossed. "What's the Achilles' heel of the Dire Wolves? We have to find a way to take your alpha down." Robin's eyes narrowed. "That going to be a problem for you?"

"God, no." She wanted Michael out of her life, whatever it took. But she had no hope that this fierce little woman and a few Army Rangers could make a difference. "You don't realize how strong he is, and how ruthless."

Robin paused at the sound of a crash from somewhere downstairs, then shrugged. "Look, Mori, you've gotta get past this submissive-little-woman mentality. Strength is more this"—she tapped her temple—"than it is muscle and brute force. Let me ask again: What's the mortal weakness of the Dire Wolves? All shifters have something. For the eagles, it's lead. See, I told you. Now, you tell me. Is it silver, like the legends say?"

Mori shook her head. "Only for the smaller wolves. It doesn't feel good, but it doesn't kill us, because we're so much bigger." She hesitated. Other than damage to the heart, which would kill anything, human or shifter, the only substance guaranteed to kill a Dire was mercury. But could she hand over that knowledge to another species? That was a mortal crime among her people.

"Never mind for now." Robin got up and began to pace. "Think about this, though. Without revealing what you are to the public, it's going to be hard to get Michael Benedict arrested or convicted, or whatever the humans call it. I hate to sound like a bad movie, but a jail's not going to hold him even if we had any evidence against him. Which, by the way, we don't."

"The governor." Mori couldn't believe her best hope for surviving this would come down to Carl Felderman. "If we can get him to tell us—"

Robin cut her off with a quick hand gesture. "He's dead. Felderman told Kell and Nik what happened to him and admitted you had nothing to do with it. Those jaguarundi-shifters turned him into a hybrid, with the plan of controlling him in the governor's office. He made a run for it after his press conference, and they ended up killing him. At least, someone killed him. Again, no proof."

Mori let out a frustrated breath, grabbing the edge of the mattress as another wave of dizziness shot through her. When was this all going to end? She and Felderman had come down on opposite sides of every environmental issue faced by the state, but on some level, she understood where he was coming from and certainly never wanted him dead. And to turn him into a hybrid so he would do Michael's bidding?

"Why would the jaguarundis let Michael use them this way?"

Robin started to answer, but a loud crash of splintering wood echoed through the room, followed by the appearance of a black cat so big he took Mori's breath away. So big he'd been able to knock the steel door out of its wooden frame. Now, he used the door carnage as a ladder instead of going up the stairs.

"Is he supposed to be here?" Mori watched in awe as he gracefully prowled into the room on paws the size of salad plates.

"Yeah, this is Archer, but you can call him Kitten. He likes it." Robin chucked the big cat under its chin, and the damn thing purred. "He's the one who took out the window."

Ah, Mori should have recognized the green eyes. He was too big to be a panther or cougar. Black jaguars were extinct in the wild in North America, but apparently, like the Dires, a shifter population remained. Obviously, Mori had underestimated the variety of Kell's counterterrorist team—*greatly* underestimated it.

Robin scratched behind the cat's ear, but pulled her hand away with a frown. "You have blood on you? Are you injured?"

"No, he's fine." A deep voice preceded another man into the room, a guy with a deep tan, an armful of clothing (which he tossed toward the cat), and an angry expression on his face. "Shift, Archer. The blood is Kell's, and we've gotta get out of here—now."

Kell was injured? Mori jumped to her feet too fast and swayed as the newcomer stepped over and grabbed her arm. He was about Kell's height, a little over six feet, with black hair and liquid eyes so dark they barely qualified as brown.

He pulled his hands away from her as if scalded, eyes wide. "Shit." He took a step back and shook his head as if trying to rid it of bad thoughts.

"What? Who are you? Where's Kell?" Panic rose in Mori's chest. If he'd been killed trying to save her—

"He's downstairs. Let's go." The man gave her a probing look before he turned and ran back down the makeshift ramp and out the door.

The big cat had shifted back into the guy Mori had seen through the window. He pulled on the black clothing he'd worn earlier, but not before Mori saw the blood on his shoulder and chest—a lot of it.

He motioned for Mori to come with him. "Robin, stay and do wipe-downs, then meet us all at Nik's."

Robin had been quiet and serious since finding the blood. She touched Archer's arm and spoke softly. "Is it bad?"

Archer ruffled her hair and smiled. "Nah. He just tangled with a jaguarundi or two. He's tough." He turned to Mori. "You ready? Can you walk, or you need me to carry you?"

Mori blinked. She was almost six feet tall. No man had ever carried her. No man had ever *offered* to carry her. And it wasn't going to happen now. "Just let me go at my own pace, but thanks."

"Here, wear these." He reached in a pocket of his cargo pants and pulled out a pair of gloves. "If you need to hold on to the banister or the wall, you won't leave prints."

God, fingerprints. She looked around her at the bed, the walls, the bathroom sink. She'd touched everything in this room.

"Hey, you heard the man. Wipe-downs are my job," Robin said. "Go find Kell. Seeing you safe will make him feel better. It had to bruise that big ego again to not be the one bashing down the door to rescue you."

Mori nodded and gave Robin a small smile on her way past. In another life, they could've been friends. She didn't dare hope for such a thing now. She might be getting out of Michael's house, but she was probably now a suspect in Carl Felderman's death as well as the bombing and kidnapping. She'd have to disappear someplace remote and obscure. And with her disappearance, the Dires would gradually die off. Despite everything Michael and her parents had done, that was not what she wanted.

The most important thing now was making sure Kell was going to survive whatever the jags had done to him. She followed Archer down the stairs, glad she had the gloves because she needed one hand on the banister and the other on the wall to avoid tumbling down them headfirst. Every step caused the shirt fabric to brush across her back so that by the time they reached the foyer, her every nerve ending sizzled.

She froze on the bottom stair. A smear of blood stretched from the study door on the right—the scene of her branding—to the door on the foyer's left, which led to the dining room, kitchen, and garage.

"Which of Michael's guys are still at the house?" She knew the jags were here if they had fought Kell. Michael also had an estate manager who stayed at the house most of the time.

Archer grasped her elbow, urging her down the last step and toward the dining room. "Let's just say he'll need some new employees. Don't step in the blood."

Mori was sick of death, sick of feeling guilty and afraid and overwhelmed. But all she could focus on now was putting one foot in front of the other. By the time they crossed the dining room and the long, pristine kitchen, Mori was leaning on Archer more than she would have liked.

The garage door was open, and the hot wind hit Mori's back like a slap when they exited the cavernous space and crossed the drive to a lawn-service van in the ugliest shade of green she'd ever seen.

The wind was steady, dry, and tropical, which had to mean the hurricane was on the move again. When they reached the van, the side panel opened, and the serious, dark-eyed man jumped out. Was it Mori's imagination, or did he seem afraid to be near her? This had to be Kell's Greek friend, Nik. Maybe he was just pissed off that she'd gotten his friend in such a mess. She couldn't blame him.

"Up you go." Archer jumped in the back of the van and reached an arm out for Mori to grasp. He pulled her up effortlessly, slammed the panel shut, and headed for the front. Nik, if that's who he was, had already cranked the engine.

Mori turned and her breath caught in her throat. Kell lay on his back, stretched across the van's floor, watching her. Even in the dim interior light, his blue-green eyes were vivid. Deep scratches scoured his right cheek, and his right shoulder looked like raw steak marinated in blood. He was still the most beautiful thing she'd ever seen, and her chest ached to see him hurt.

His smile wasn't wide, but it was genuine as he reached out his hand and grasped hers. "You were right. We're such losers."

ᗷCHAPTER 24ᗱ

K ell had been patient long enough.

On the ride from River Oaks to change vehicles at the lawn-care lot, then on the journey to Nik's downtown loft in his friend's SUV, he'd been content just to look at Mori, to memorize the little laugh lines around her mouth, the slight slant of her brown eyes above the high cheekbones, the way she tightened her jaw when a movement hurt her back, the expressions of longing and regret and gratitude and fear, all warring for dominance on her face when she met his gaze. Their hands never left each other's. She seemed to need his touch as much as he needed hers.

Nik had slipped them into the freight elevator and gotten them to his loft without being seen, and Kell remained quiet while Archer brought in his shifter clan's doctor. The man had first sterilized Mori's back while using a colorful slew of new curse words Kell hoped he could remember and then plied her with antibiotics. Afterward, the cat doctor had used similar curses as he cleaned Kell's scratch marks. Only the shoulder wound was deep, and everything else he stitched up with a deft hand...paw...whatever.

"Will I turn into one of those hybrid freaks?" he'd asked, and both the doctor and Mori assured him at least three deep bites were required for that to happen, and scratches didn't count.

Kell had kept his mouth shut while Razorblade Robin came back from cleanup duty and turned domestic, cooking piles of fajitas and swearing she used goat meat, not rat. He thought it was only a slight improvement.

And he'd remained mute as Nik did his level best to avoid being near Mori. More than once, he caught her giving Nik puzzled looks, to which his friend was oblivious—maybe intentionally so.

There hadn't been much to say as they gathered late on Friday afternoon to eat around the small TV in Nik's central living area—the whole apartment being one gymnasium-size room with cleverly placed partitions.

The local NBC affiliate had three breaking stories its reporters were frantically trying to cover.

Hurricane Geneva, Category 2 and growing, had finally begun to move again, inching at a ponderous pace toward a projected landfall between Morgan City, Louisiana, and Corpus Christi, Texas. Unless something changed, Galveston could be ordered to evacuate as early as Saturday afternoon, and Houston by Monday.

The second story was the ongoing investigation into the murder of Carl Felderman, complete with images of the Co-Op offices, the exterior of Mori's apartment, and then Mori herself.

She watched it with a stony silence Kell could only interpret as fatalistic. They might have gotten her away from Benedict's house, but she didn't think she could be saved. He could see it in her eyes, a remoteness that had been broken only when Robin came back from the cleanup bearing Mori's backpack.

The final story dominating the news concerned three mysterious murders in River Oaks, at the home of millionaire shipper Michael Benedict. One man had been shot, the second stabbed, and the third's throat slashed. Michael had appeared on camera, giving an Oscar-worthy performance expressing his profound sadness over the deaths of his loyal staff members, but Kell recognized fury, and Benedict was furious. The way Kell saw it, Michael Benedict had gotten a free ride so far and had a big payday coming.

The time to talk had finally come, however, and Kell reached for the remote and turned off the TV. Archer and Robin settled in on the love seat; Mori sat cross-legged on the floor to avoid having her back touch anything. Kell had claimed the recliner, and Nik fidgeted and flitted from dining chair to sofa chair to floor and back again.

Gator was so damned happy to see everyone he made periodic tail-wagging rounds, but finally settled next to Kell, conveniently within ear-scratching reach.

"Requesting blackout." Kell looked at each of them in turn, waiting for the nod of agreement, until he reached Mori. "That means whatever is said in this room goes nowhere, not even to our commander, and we lay everything on the table. No lies, no half truths. You agree to this?"

Mori closed her eyes and nodded. He wanted to go to her and tell her it would all work out, that he could both protect her and exonerate her. But until he knew the truth, he couldn't make those promises. And if he had to be a hard-ass to get the truth, then by God it was past time.

"First, has anyone talked to the colonel?"

"He called twice today." Nik had lit on the sofa chair for a while, his right leg jiggling in a nervous tell. According to Robin, Nik had been weird ever since touching Mori when they took her from Benedict's attic. He must have seen something he hadn't expected and hadn't liked. Kell intended to find out what that was—from Nik if he had to, but preferably from Mori.

"How long you think we can keep the colonel on ice?"

Nik shrugged. "His last message was pretty hysterical, and I don't mean funny."

"I'll call him later tonight, then." What the hell he'd tell the man, Kell didn't know. Maybe the truth. See if he could handle it.

"Next, update on the mission today." He filled in his activity, up to the point where the second jaguarundi had parachuted onto his face. Seems Archer had taken down Travis's brother in an extremely one-sided catfight. Nik had been forced to stab the tall guy when he pulled out a weapon of his own.

"The tall guy was the estate manager, I think," Mori said, her first contribution to the conversation. "I met him once before, but don't remember his name."

Gradually, the reports came to a close, and there remained only one ten-ton rhino in the room: Mori and her secrets. Kell looked at her and nodded, and she smiled in return. Her hands were shaking, but her voice remained calm.

"I guess it's my turn, then." She looked at the floor and fiddled with the edge of an area rug. "Only, I'm not sure where to start. Maybe with this." She pulled her backpack from where it had been propped against the side of the love seat and pulled out a folded sheet of paper. She handed it to Archer, who passed it on to Kell without looking at it.

He unfolded the sheet and frowned at what appeared to be a contract. An agreement signed by Michael Benedict and Paul Chastaine regarding the promise of marriage between Emory Elisabeth and—

"Wait. Tell me what this is." He looked up at Mori.

"It's a bill of sale, basically." She raised her chin, almost defiant. "My parents promised me in marriage to Michael Benedict on the day of my christening. The marriage—or at least the formal engagement—was supposed to happen on my twenty-fifth birthday. That was the day after the bombing. Apparently, quite a bit of money was involved."

Only Nik didn't look surprised. Kell struggled to understand.

"But why would your parents sell you to a man twice your age? I mean, even for money. Something's missing here. You're both wolf-shifters, right? Does it have something to do with that?"

"Not just wolf-shifters. Dire Wolves." Mori sighed and went back to playing with the fringe on the rug. "Like the Black Jaguars"—she nodded at Archer—"the Dire Wolves in the wild have long been extinct. All the children born to the people of my parents' generation were males. So we die out unless..." She paused, then took a deep breath. "Unless the only female Dire of childbearing age reproduces and, it is hoped, bears at least one daughter."

"And you're that woman, aren't you?" Robin moved to the floor and sat beside her, taking her hand. "And Michael, as your alpha, thinks he's the one who needs to sire the children."

Mori nodded. "That's been the plan since I was born. I learned about it when I was sixteen, but you know what kids are like at sixteen." Her laugh was bitter. "I thought that nine years until I turned twenty-five was an eternity. I was sure that, by that time, he'd change his mind, or my parents would get me out of it. Or somebody else would have a daughter to carry on the lines. I thought once he knew I didn't want him, he'd give up."

"Only he didn't, did he?" Nik's voice was low and tense, his eyes fixed on Mori from his new perch in the chair next to Kell. "Benedict blew up the fucking Zemurray Building and implicated you to get your attention. More than two hundred people died because he *wanted to get your fucking attention.*"

Mori flinched as if Nik had slapped her.

Kell put a hand on his friend's wrist and shook his head. Throwing blame was going to shut her down just when she'd finally opened up. "To be clear about this, Mori, you didn't know Michael had planned this bombing, did you?"

Her eyes widened. "God, no. I didn't know about it until the night of my birthday—after you'd picked me up at the FBI offices. I got a flower delivery from Michael, with a note asking if I'd received his message." She described her trip to the ranch, where she'd learned the truth, and her trip to Galveston the next day, where Michael had not only admitted to the bombing, but to taking Felderman as well.

"And he hit you," Kell said softly, remembering how vulnerable she'd been that night, how tender and yet desperate.

Mori blushed, as if being hit was something that shamed her, something she'd asked for. Kell didn't know what Dire Wolves were, but he didn't much like them if they took the woman on whose shoulders they'd burdened the continuation of their entire species and then beat the spirit out of her, whether by physical or mental methods. Abuse was abuse.

"Tell us the rest." Kell glanced at Nik. He'd relaxed, the fierce light gone from his eyes, and that more than anything convinced Kell that Mori was being truthful.

She talked for almost an hour, explaining the offers she'd made to Benedict to have his children via artificial insemination, in hopes of keeping the species alive while maintaining her independence. The point at which she'd finally decided she had to give in to Michael was after being with Kell, realizing it might be the only way to prevent Michael from doing the same thing in New Orleans as he'd done in Houston and hurting Kell in the process.

Kell squirmed a little at that, the bandage over his shoulder feeling tight and itchy all of a sudden. He appreciated that not one single member of his team looked at him, because he definitely wanted to thump himself on the head for being an idiot and not seeing what she'd been willing to sacrifice for him.

Mori talked about how Michael had taunted her when she finally went to him, branded her, locked her up, and planned to use her. She managed to talk without emotion, not meeting anyone's eyes, but not hesitating, either. Kell thought she was relieved to be unloading it all.

"The sad thing is," she said, finally looking up at Kell, "I'm not sure it matters. Michael liked the power that controlling Felderman gave him, and he liked that the bombing put an end to the industrial-expansion talks, which would have destroyed more of our habitat. I have a horrible feeling he's going to do it again, no matter what does or doesn't happen with me."

"Have you heard him say anything about New Orleans?" Kell leaned forward, letting out a hiss as the pain in his back from falling on the fucking floor met the pain in his shoulder from being fallen on by the fucking flying cat.

Mori nodded. "Just once—the day I went to Galveston to confront him about the Houston bombing. He said if I didn't give in, he'd do the same thing in New Orleans on Labor Day. I got the feeling he'd already put the plan in place. It didn't feel like a spur-of-the-moment threat."

Kell wasn't surprised. Even if Benedict hadn't planned it earlier, once he had a taste of the power he'd gained by bombing Zemurray and taking Felderman, he would want to try again.

He needed a solo chat with Nik to talk about their next move, but his cell vibrated before he could come up with a way to get rid of everyone else. He looked at the screen, expecting to see Colonel Thomas's name, but it was Gadget.

"Sorry we didn't call you, man. We're back at—"

"We found the bomb site." It wasn't Gadget's interruption that startled Kell, but the gravity of his voice. Gadget was never serious. Ever.

Kell switched the phone to speaker and held it out. "Tell us what you found."

"Well, what Adam found." Gadget cleared his throat and paused as if having trouble getting the words out. "He'd been tailing different employees of Tex-La Shipping, and today his target led him to the headquarters of the World Trade Center on Canal Street."

Nik shuffled through some papers on the table and pulled one from the stack. "The WTC people were planning a kind of meet and greet with new oil interests the state wanted to lure in, right?"

"Yeah, for the day after Labor Day. But then you—wait. Is this on speaker? Take it off speaker, Kell."

Kell shrugged, shut off the phone's speaker mode, and raised it to his ear. "What's up with that?"

Gadget paused. "Adam walked in on two of Benedict's employees arming one of the bombs. He called me about it from the hallway, but they must have overheard him. Kell, Adam's dead. I didn't want Archer to hear it this way."

Kell closed his eyes. *Damn it. Adam should have been working alone.* "I'll take care of it." He leaned back, aware of the others' eyes on him but not meeting anyone's gaze. "What about other bombs?"

"I'm going in tonight, after hours, to cover the building." Gadget's voice cracked. "Damn them. If there's anything left, I'll find it."

Kell ended the call, the silence in the room louder than any conversation. He raised his eyes to look at Archer, who flinched at whatever he saw in Kell's face. Anger. Pity. Sorrow.

The color drained from Archer's face. "It's Adam?"

Kell nodded. "Let's go outside and talk."

"No." Archer's jaw clenched. "Just tell us."

Kell filled them in on the rest of Gadget's report, including Adam's death. Archer propped his elbows on his knees and stared at the floor. When he raised his head again, his eyes had gone a more brilliant green, with elongated pupils. Holy shit. Nik's apartment wasn't set up for a three-hundred-pound cat.

Robin rubbed his arm. "Let me take you to the airport. You want to go to New Orleans?"

"No." Archer looked at Kell. "I'm going to kill Michael Benedict. You with me?"

Kell had just been thinking the same thing, and when he turned, he saw the same resolve on Nik's face.

"Time to plan another mission. This one's full black."

EPISODE 7

⫷CHAPTER 25⫸

Mori wanted to sleep, but the night of talking had left her restless about her future and haunted by her past. In a way, she was relieved to have everything out there. The whole ugly truth, with no more lies. But relief only went so far. Unloading hadn't changed anything; it had only endangered more people.

And then the news about Archer's brother...Logic told Mori she wasn't responsible for what Michael's people had done or the fact that he'd been power-hungry enough to try a hit in New Orleans. But her heart ached to see the funny, full-of-life Archer closing himself off, his eyes dull and empty when Kell finally ordered him to leave. He was in no shape to continue the job, much less go after Michael.

Nik had deposited him at the airport two hours later, where he'd be making the short flight to New Orleans to claim his brother's body and then the long trip to the family's homeplace in Tennessee to say good-bye.

Mori shifted on the bed, careful not to jostle Kell. He'd been restless in his sleep, but had finally settled down a couple of hours ago, his breathing steady.

Nik had insisted that the "walking wounded," as he called them, take his bed while he slept in the recliner. He'd at least meet her gaze now, but still took care not to get too close. She hadn't figured him out, although she couldn't blame him for hating her. She'd dragged Kell into her mess, however inadvertent it had been.

Inadvertent. That was a loaded word, wasn't it? Mori hadn't meant any of this to happen, yet her defiance of Michael had set it in motion. Would he have bombed the Zemurray Building if she'd gone to him before her birthday? If she hadn't spent the last few years openly avoiding him? Would all those people still be alive, all those families intact? Might Kell and his team be off on a less dangerous mission, facing the kind of terrorists they were actually trained to stop?

"You OK?" Kell's voice, slurred with half-finished sleep, startled Mori out of the quicksand of her own what-ifs.

She turned to face him and propped on an elbow. The scratches on his face had scabbed and would probably not scar, unlike his right shoulder. But at least he hadn't bled through the last bandage Nik had used to cover the gouges last night. "My back's healing fast now, which is more than I can say for you, Marine." She kept her voice soft, all too aware that, somewhere beyond the partitions, Nik and Robin might be sleeping. Or listening.

Kell didn't return the humor. "I wasn't talking about your back."

Her smile faded. She wasn't sure her spirit would ever heal, but getting Kell and his friends away from this mess would be a good first step. "I've been thinking about something, and I want you to hear me out."

He arched an eyebrow. "I already don't like it."

She ran a finger along the side of his face, tracing the line of his cheekbone, moving in to brush sensitive fingertips across his lips, feel the scratch of bristly stubble on his strong jawline. She wanted to remember the feel of him, the depth of his eyes, even the little lines that formed on the inner edge of his brows when he frowned—as he was doing now.

"The answer is no."

"I haven't said anything yet."

The frown lines grew deeper. "I know what you're going to say, and it's not happening. You're not going to run from this."

Mori settled onto her side, her hand tracing the indentation of his breastbone. She wanted to touch him as long as she could, both to make herself believe he was really here and alive, and to have that tactile memory to carry with her. "I have to leave, and you know it. You can't arrest Michael without exposing what he is. What I am. Robin. Archer. All of us. The world isn't ready to know about us. The only way I can have any kind of life is to go somewhere no one can find me—not even you, as much as that hurts."

It took him two tries, but Kell finally rolled onto his side, facing Mori. He drew her closer to him. "Listen to me. First, I don't know what the future holds for us, but I'm not letting you walk out of my life." He brushed Mori's hair away from her face and touched his forehead to hers for a moment before pulling back. "Look me in the eye when I say this, and see that I mean it. Michael has to answer for what he's done, and you have to let my team do its job."

He didn't get it. "But—"

"This isn't just about us, Mori, or even about you. It never was. Michael stepped over a line. Hell, he trampled a lot of lines. Whether he set off those bombs to get control over you, or the governor, or the industrial expansion plans, people died. He's gotta pay for that."

A chill ran through her. She'd heard him promise Archer that Michael would pay, but they still thought of this as a regular mission, or job, or whatever they called it in his world. "Kell, you have to be realistic. Robin is shifter strong, but not Dire strong. And as good as you and Nik are, you can't handle Michael Benedict. Do you know anything about Dires?"

She watched his face as his ego flared, then got doused by practicality and curiosity. "Tell me."

"When you think of a big wolf, it's the gray wolf." She slid her hand down his stomach and traced her fingers along the ridge at the top of his hip bone. The soft thud of his heartbeat sped.

"They might weigh a hundred pounds and grow bigger than a German shepherd, right? They're powerful. For a Dire, you can easily double that size and weight. You can't think about him like a regular man, or even a regular shifter. You can't beat him."

"With your help, we could." Kell leaned in and touched his lips to hers. "It's time for you to fight for your life, Mori. Not to run, but to make a stand. And we can help you."

Mori had rested her hand on his side, and under her fingers, the muscles in his lower back spasmed. Kell rolled onto his back again with an involuntary groan, pulling her into the cocoon of his arm, her cheek resting on his undamaged shoulder. It was hard not to believe him when they were here like this, alone. Well, sort of alone. A flicker of hope ignited in her chest.

With her help, maybe they could fight Michael. The beta Dire who'd ascend into Michael's position was a no-nonsense attorney. He'd never go after Michael himself, but he wouldn't step in to help the man, either, especially if it put him in control.

Kell's cell phone vibrated from his pocket, tickling Mori's leg. She moved aside to let him grab it and look at the screen.

"Fuck. It's the colonel."

Last night, after their blackout meeting, or whatever he'd called it, Kell had moved into a far corner of the loft, a space Nik called his office. He'd stayed on the phone with his boss for more than an hour while Nik took Archer to the airport. Robin and Mori had been left to watch hurricane updates and try not to eavesdrop.

At least, Mori had been trying. Robin openly craned her neck and moved from one chair to another in an attempt to hear more.

The first part of the conversation had mostly been talking on Kell's part. "He's cleaning things up for the Colonel," Robin had whispered. "Left out the whole bit about the sex and the handcuffs."

Heat spread across Mori's face, which made Robin cackle. She sounded more like a chicken than an eagle, although Mori didn't share that observation.

The last half of the conversation didn't go so well, she suspected, because most of Kell's end of the call had been filled with "Yes, sirs" and "No, sirs" and "I'm sorry, sirs" and "Won't happen again, sirs."

When he'd finally emerged from the office, his face looked pale and drained of energy.

"Well, that went well." He'd shaken at least four ibuprofen out of the giant bottle on Nik's counter, washed them down with the last of Archer's leftover soda, and collapsed in the recliner with his eyes closed until Nik returned from the airport. Only then had he told them the colonel had ordered them to stay put until morning.

Guess it was officially morning, even though the clock on the bedside table read only 4:35 a.m.

Mori got up and padded into the living room area to give Kell privacy. She was surprised to see Nik sitting at the small dining table with a coffee cup in front of him, writing on some type of pad or tablet. Robin remained curled up on the sofa, wrapped in a blanket so tightly only a few spikes of auburn hair poked out.

"Cups are in the cabinet over the sink. Coffee's next to the fridge." Nik never looked up.

Mori poured herself a cup of coffee and sat across from him. He wasn't writing, as she'd originally thought, but seemed to be drawing on what she could now tell was a sketch pad.

He glanced up, his pen hovering a couple of inches above the paper. "Do I hear Kell talking?"

"The colonel just called." She sipped the coffee, which had a hint of hazelnut and wafted a warm, slightly sweet aroma she found calming. "I wanted to give him some privacy."

Nik stared at her a moment, and she wondered what was behind those wary, assessing eyes. He finally shoved the pad across the table at her. "Look familiar?"

A chill stole across Mori's shoulder blades. The artistry was professional, but it was the subject that startled her. A wolf, its markings detailed and familiar, stood as viewed from the side, its neck arched and head raised, mouth open in a howl. In the middle of its back was a mark, etched in dark, jagged ink—the letter "B."

"It's me," Mori whispered, the moment coming back to her in more detail than she'd remembered thus far. "Right after he did it." No, she might as well call *it* what it was. "When he branded me. Shifting was the last thing I remember before I woke up in that attic feeling like I was still on fire." She looked up at Nik. "How could you know?"

"It's one of the things I saw when I touched you in the attic yesterday." He took a sip of his coffee and grimaced. "Cold." Pushing his chair back, he got up and poured the coffee down the sink, then reached into a lower cabinet and pulled out a bottle of bourbon—Black Jack, the same brand Gus Chastaine used to drink. He poured a generous amount in the coffee cup and returned to the table.

"You're psychic?" Mori looked at the drawing again. Even the unique markings of her wolf's coat, different to every individual, were accurate. "No wonder you hated me as soon as you touched me." She didn't know whether to be embarrassed or relieved.

Nik set the cup on the table with a sigh, and Mori noticed for the first time the dark smudges beneath his eyes. The man didn't look like he'd slept in a month. "I don't hate you. I hate that Kell got in so deep without knowing the truth." He finally looked her in the eye. "I also don't hate you because I saw that his feelings aren't one-sided. You really care about him. But he's my first priority. If it comes down to it and we can save you, good. But Kell comes first."

Mori smiled, earning a look of surprise from Nik. "Good. Because the last thing I want is for him to get hurt because of me." But he already had, hadn't he? "Hurt *again*."

"Then we understand each other."

She nodded. "He's lucky to have you."

Nik looked down into his bourbon-filled coffee cup and pushed it aside. "Goes both ways."

Mori closed the sketch pad and slid it back across the table. They sat in silence until they heard a hiss from the direction of the sofa.

"Touching scene, you two. And noisy. I haven't been able to hear a thing Kell was saying."

Robin had sat up, still cocooned in her blanket, and her faux outrage leached some of the tension from the room. By the time Kell joined them a few seconds later, Mori thought they were all at least giving off the appearance of being relaxed.

"OK, the colonel's got a plan. He's not taking discussion on it, and we've pushed him about as far as we can, so don't even start with me." Kell rummaged in the refrigerator and pulled out a carton of orange juice. He brought the whole carton to the table, taking the chair between Mori and Nik.

Robin joined them, taking the fourth chair. "That doesn't sound good. What's his bright idea?"

Kell took a swig of juice from the carton, earning an eye roll from Robin and a faint smile from Nik. Mori suspected he'd forgone the glass just to get a reaction from them. "Nik, he wants you in New Orleans ASAP, to help Gadget. In case Benedict accelerates his plans, we need to get the trade center offices swept as well as the hotel that's hosting the visitors. You might also be able to touch a few things and find the guys who killed Adam. We don't know if they're human or not."

Nik's dark eyes flashed with anger. "And you and Robin will be doing what? I need to be here."

Kell shook his head. "Colonel wants Robin to take Mori to Cote Blanche today. Again, ASAP. I'll be trying to negotiate with Benedict."

Nik and Robin protested loudly, but Mori couldn't even put her horror into coherent words. This was the most boneheaded plan conceivable. The colonel obviously didn't understand who and what he was dealing with, or he wouldn't consider sending Kell in there alone. It's exactly what Michael wanted. He'd kill Kell without a hint of hesitation—unless it was to torture him first and then kill him.

"Shut it." Kell raised his voice, sounding a whole lot like a soldier all of a sudden. Mori had never thought to ask what his rank had been in the Army, but she'd lay odds he wasn't a private.

"Consider these direct orders—from the colonel and from me. Nik, I need you on the next plane out. Gadget can use your particular skills. I don't need to remind you what happened at Zemurray. We can't have a repeat in New Orleans, and you might be able to touch the stuff Adam uncovered and find us someone to question."

Mori waited for Nik to argue, but instead, he closed his eyes and nodded. "Understood."

Kell turned to Robin. "Mori needs to be off Benedict's grid, and Cote Blanche is isolated."

"Wait a damn minute." Mori had finally had enough. "I don't know what Cote Blanche is, but I do know this. You can't approach Michael alone, Kell. You won't live long enough to negotiate where you'll sit, much less anything to do with the bombing."

The blue-green eyes she'd always found so rich and deep had turned hard as brilliant marble. "Cote Blanche is my family's cabin in Louisiana, out in the middle of nowhere. And the plan's not up for discussion."

"I'm not one of your team members, so you can't—" Mori stopped as a pain shot through her right ankle, then another. Robin was kicking her.

"Kell's right." Robin's voice held its usual chipper tone, but with more than a trace of sarcasm. "We'll go to the cabin in Louisiana—where there's no electricity, by the way, and where no one can reach us, including Kell, except by boat. And never mind that there's a hurricane headed for us. No problem. Let's get the women out of the way."

Kell's eyes had grown narrower and narrower as Robin talked. When she finally stopped, he leaned toward her and spoke through clenched teeth. "Are you finished with your bullshit, or do you have any useful input?"

"Oh, go fuck yourself." Robin slumped back in her chair and scowled at Kell as he turned to Nik with instructions for Gadget.

"C'mon, Mori. We need to see if we can scrounge up some food to take with us on our holiday in the swamp." Robin shoved back her chair and walked into the kitchen, so Mori followed.

Kell paused to watch them a moment, suspicion causing those little frown lines to make a reappearance.

"Want us to take Gator with us?" Robin asked, pouncing on a jar of peanut butter and handing it to Mori.

Relief relaxed Kell's features. "Yeah, thanks."

As soon as he began talking to Nik again, Mori turned to Robin in outrage. She, of all of them, should understand what Kell would be up against in meeting a shifter one-on-one. Before she could say anything, however, Robin held a finger to her lips. She leaned toward Mori as she handed over a box of raisins.

Her whisper was barely enough for Mori to hear and too soft for the humans to pick up on. "Don't worry. We're not following orders. Goes against my upbringing."

❧CHAPTER 26❧

Thank God Robin had finally unruffled her feathers and agreed to take Mori to Cote Blanche without a fight. Actually, she'd come around faster than he'd expected. Maybe she was finally catching on to this business of following orders.

Kell had returned to Nik's little corner "office," a nook set apart by bookshelves, and had spent the last frustrating hour trying to line up someone in Jeanerette willing to rent him a couple of boats in a hurricane—one for Robin and Mori, and one for himself when he came in after his meeting with Benedict.

Kell's usual marina operator had laughed and said Kell obviously had been gone from Louisiana too long if he thought coming to Iberia Parish was a good idea right now. And fucking stupid to boot if he thought anyone would let him take their boat into the wilds of western St. Mary's Parish before that storm came ashore.

The "fucking stupid" part was probably right. Kell agreed that going alone to confront Benedict would not be on his top ten list of things to do on a Saturday two days before a hurricane was expected to make landfall.

Maybe the weather would work in their favor. He'd pointed out to the colonel that if Benedict knew Kell's real name, it wouldn't take much to dig into his background and discover where he'd grown up. A little more digging around in Jeanerette—very little—and he'd know about Cote Blanche. Kell might have been an only child, but there were Kellisons scattered all over Iberia and St. Mary's Parishes.

No doubt Benedict could get that information, the colonel had conceded. But the man wasn't an idiot, and only an idiot would travel to a wooden cabin in a South Louisiana swamp when a hurricane was chewing up the landscape. Assuming the cabin didn't come down on their heads, it should provide a safe haven for at least two or three days. By the time Geneva had blown through, Michael Benedict would be contained.

At least, that was the plan. The way Colonel Rick Thomas saw it, Benedict had backed himself into a corner. He figured the man had a strong self-preservation instinct and a lot to lose—enough to recognize that he needed a way out of this colossal fuckup that wouldn't land him in jail, expose his kind to the public, destroy his business, or get him killed. Colonel Thomas had pulled some strings in higher places than Kell could even imagine, and had devised the escape hatch Benedict needed.

Now, Kell just had to convince Benedict to take it.

Having exhausted all the boat rental listings for Iberia Parish, Kell went to his last resort—family. Scrolling through his contact list, he found his cousin Trey's number, took a deep breath, and hit CALL.

Trey Kellison was the son Kell's parents had wanted. He'd gone off to university in Lafayette, majored in horticulture, come home to Jeanerette, and opened a feed 'n' seed that now had two satellite stores. He also married his high school girl-friend, fathered three kids to carry on the Kellison name, and went to Mass on Sundays. Trey was three years younger than Kell and always managed to make him feel like a screwed-up perpetual adolescent.

If the shrimp boots fit.

"Jack? What's wrong?" Trey sounded half-asleep, and Kell winced as he looked at his watch. The cousins didn't talk often, and for Kell to call at 6:00 a.m. on a Saturday, no wonder Trey assumed it was an emergency.

Except, it sort of was an emergency.

Less than five minutes and only a sketchy explanation later, Trey had agreed to take Mori and Robin to the cabin this after-noon, and to take Kell out later tonight or tomorrow morning, depending on the weather. The readiness with which his cousin agreed without asking a lot of details, and the fact that Trey sounded surprised Kell would even think he might *not* agree, pricked at Kell's conscience. He really needed to stop selling people short. Let people help him. Maybe he'd get that whole asking-for-help thing down by the time he hit forty.

Next, he called Gulf State Auto Rentals and left directions on where they could pick up the sedan he'd driven to Baytown. Robin and Mori could take Nik's SUV to Cote Blanche, and Kell would drive Archer's truck. Once he got his weapons together, they'd be set.

Except for one final call.

He stopped on his way to the living area and watched Mori and Robin laying waste to Nik's food supply, stuffing every-thing in plastic bags to take with them. They were whisper-ing furiously to each other, laughing occasionally despite the palpable tension. The only reason they'd be whispering was if they were talking about him or hatching some kind of scheme he wouldn't like. Maybe both.

"What are you two up to?" Mori jumped, and even Razor-blade Robin looked startled. Whatever they were discussing, it had consumed their full attention.

Robin recovered quickly, her face settling into its usual smirk. "I was telling Mori about your cabin. We were thinking maybe we'd paint the walls while we were stuck there during the storm. Girls love to redecorate, you know."

"We were debating colors." Mori took up the lie, and the light in her eyes almost made him smile. Almost. "Do you like pink? I'm thinking a pale-pink, glossy paint would look great with all that wood on the inside. Or maybe an icy green, to tie in with the green of the swamp."

"Oh, definitely pink," Robin said, pointing at Kell. "That's a little-pink-house kind of dude if ever I met one."

Right. If they'd been talking about interior decoration when he walked in, he'd eat his fucking watch.

"Fine, lie to me. Whatever the hell you're planning, let me just say this. Don't do it. And that's an order."

Robin saluted. "No problem, Sergeant First Class Kellison, sir."

Kell shook his head. If he could put the eagle-shifter in lockdown until this was over, he'd do it in a heartbeat, and Mori alongside her. But he had to focus on Benedict and not wonder what these suddenly fast friends were plotting.

"Mori, I need Benedict's phone numbers." No surprise that the Tex-La founder had unlisted info, and he didn't want to use her phone and slap Benedict in the face with the fact that she was with Kell and not him.

She frowned and stared at him, pausing with a can of soup halfway into a bag. "If you use my phone, he can track us here to Nik's apartment, right?"

He laughed, and it sounded bitter, even to him. "At this point, it doesn't matter."

He hadn't told the colonel this, but if Benedict rejected the offer to bail him out of this mess, Kell would see him dead. One way or another, he was determined that Michael Benedict's days of tracking Mori were about to come to an end.

Hesitant, Mori retrieved her cell phone from her backpack, still propped against the sofa, and turned it on. Kell looked at the leather pack, thinking about last night's meeting, about her expression when she'd handed over that contract.

She'd found it when she was a teenager. What would it be like to know your parents had sold you, bargained away your future? Even if their intent had been a noble one in the long run—to ensure the survival of their people—it had to feel like a betrayal.

Mori had been alone a long time, ignoring an unwanted future that was barreling up behind her like an oncoming freight train, until, finally, she couldn't outrun or ignore it any longer.

It was a truly fucked-up situation. Kell's own family issues paled beside hers. If anything, he'd been loved too much. He'd felt smothered but never devalued, much less betrayed. Mori thought of herself as weak, but he thought she might be one of the strongest people he'd ever met.

"Let me give you his home number and his private office number." She scrolled through her contact list and read out the numbers as Kell entered them into his phone. He hoped he'd never need them after today.

He called the home number first, and a woman answered. He took a deep breath and began the first part of the script, as the colonel had given it to him.

"I'm Jack Kellison, and I'm—"

"I know who you are. Hold on." The woman sounded like a true queen bitch, cold and arrogant. A perfect match for Benedict, in other words. Maybe the real fiancée.

Benedict's voice was anything but cold. Clipped words, voice just short of a growl. The man was mad as hell. "Where is she?"

Mori's location was definitely not on the script. "I've been authorized to make you an offer to end this situation—a generous one." And more than the bastard deserved. "Where can we meet?"

Kell could virtually hear Benedict shifting gears, and when he spoke again, his voice conveyed nothing but good humor and reasonableness. Anyone who could change emotional direction that thoroughly and that quickly was either an extremely good actor or an extremely crazy fuck.

Kell suspected the latter.

"I'd love to meet with you, Mr. Kellison." Benedict paused. "Or should I say Sergeant Kellison?"

So he'd done his homework. No surprise there. "Whatever you prefer, Mr. Benedict. Should I come to your house?"

Out of his peripheral vision, he saw Mori vigorously shaking her head, but at least Robin had reached up and clapped a hand over her mouth to keep her quiet.

"No, I was about to leave for my office in Galveston. The island will be under mandatory evacuation by midafternoon, and I want to retrieve some files in case Geneva proves as deadly as Ike."

Kell had been deployed when Hurricane Ike hit in 2008, but the storm had torn up everything from Central Louisiana to Corpus Christi, with Galveston almost at ground zero.

"Fine. Galveston it is." Kell glanced at his watch. Traffic headed toward the coast should be nonexistent. Coming back would be another matter. "Say in an hour?"

"I look forward to it."

Yeah, Kell just bet he did. Ending the call, he saw Mori and Robin standing side by side, frowning at him. But this wasn't up for discussion. "You need help getting the food to the car? You got everything Gator needs?"

Gator had been pacing restlessly between the library and the kitchen, sensing the way dogs do that something was afoot and fearful he'd be left out. Upon hearing his name, he stood and cocked his head at Kell, ears alert. "Sorry, big guy." Kell scratched his spotted, floppy ears. "You have to keep an eye on things at the cabin."

At the word *cabin*, Gator got his tail mojo going. God, Kell loved that goofy dog.

"We've got everything." Robin hefted a box of food and supplies almost as big as she was. "I'm just gonna take this to the car. Meet you down there in five, Mori?"

"I'll be there." Mori spoke to Robin, but her gaze was fixed on Kell. The door clicked shut behind Robin, and he was alone with her for the first time since the hotel in Baytown.

"I know I can't talk you out of this, but please be careful. Don't turn your back on him. Don't believe anything he tells you." She slid her arms around his waist and kissed him, her lips soft and warm. He gave himself over to the moment, trying to convey in the movement of his lips and tongue everything she'd come to mean to him.

Did he love her? Kell didn't know the answer to that question. It was too soon. Theirs was a foxhole relationship, born amid danger from a common enemy. He knew only that he never wanted to say good-bye to her. Even when he'd just been a fake volunteer at the Co-Op, he hadn't wanted to say good-bye.

A salty tear hit his tongue, and he stepped back, using his thumbs to wipe away the tears that streamed down her cheeks. "I'll be at Cote Blanche tonight—tomorrow if the weather's too crappy for me to get there after dark. You gonna be OK?"

Her eyes were still glassy with tears, but she laughed. "Kell, Robin and I are both shifters. I think we can handle a little wind."

Yeah, she had a point. While he was learning to ask for help, he'd have to develop a taste for pride. If he was going to have a relationship with a woman who could throw him the length of a football field—and he had little doubt Mori could do that if provoked enough—he was going to have to swallow a lot of it.

❦ CHAPTER 27 ❧

Kell nailed the traffic situation. He cruised down I-45 South toward Galveston with six lanes all to himself, while the northbound lanes bulged, bumper-to-bumper, with people hoping to get out of Galveston and the coastal communities before the evacuation order became mandatory. Then it would really get crowded.

At the noon hurricane-hunter update, if the NOAA forecasters felt more confident that Geneva wouldn't take an eleventh-hour swerve to the east or west before landfall, they'd make the evacuation mandatory. Riding out the storm would be a dicier option then, especially after Ike had proven how destructive even a Category 2 hurricane could be. If Geneva strengthened to a Cat 3 or higher, Houston itself might be cleared out, all 2.1 million residents. Talk about hell on wheels.

Even in that case, Kell suspected he wouldn't suffer. No sane person would evacuate from one swampy, vulnerable spot to another. The roads into South Louisiana should be deserted.

The water had already begun chopping into whitecaps by the time Kell crossed the bridge onto Galveston Island, exiting the freeway at its termination point and cutting down to Seawall Boulevard. Little traffic was moving on the island as near as Kell could see, and even a glance down the historic Strand as he passed revealed unusually empty streets and sidewalks.

Benedict's dark-blue Lexus was parked near the back entrance of the three-story faux-adobe Tex-La building, and Kell parked Archer's pickup two spaces down. Across the boulevard, he could see past the building's edge to where the waves crashed against the rocky seawall, a steady, dry wind blowing off the Gulf. The air smelled tropical, with an almost palpable gathering of energy not yet released.

Definitely a storm coming.

Kell did a mental check of his weapons. The Beretta was secured in a shoulder holster. He expected whoever Benedict had for security to take that one. He'd tucked his personal weapon, a Smith & Wesson, into an ankle holster that hugged tight to his skin and rested on the inside of his leg. Not as handy from a quick-draw standpoint, but easy to miss in a halfhearted pat-down.

He had two combat knives on him: one strapped to his other leg, one stashed in his right pocket. The 75th Ranger Regiment didn't carry knives as standard issue, but he'd found them useful in close situations.

He hoped like hell he didn't need any of those weapons today, but the colonel's plan made a couple of assumptions Kell didn't think were true. First, he viewed Michael Benedict as a rational businessman who'd made some extremely bad errors in judgment. Second, he thought the prospect of making a clean start would outweigh shape-shifter politics.

The colonel hadn't seen Mori's bruises or the letter branded into her back. He hadn't seen that contract or heard her tell her story. Kell didn't think Benedict regretted a single choice he'd made. He only regretted that they hadn't all succeeded.

Kell would do as he was told, however. He'd make the colonel's offer. If Benedict rejected it, well, Kell was as prepared as he could be for whatever happened afterward. Mori might prove to be right; he could be badly overmatched in a fight. But if he died today, at least he was doing something he believed in, fighting for *someone* he believed in. Bullies and tyrants couldn't be beaten unless someone was willing to try.

The glass back door into Tex-La Shipping was unlocked. Sandbags sat to either side of it, burlap-wrapped beacons of hope that whatever this storm brought to shore, it would do it somewhere else and only send a little water over the seawall.

The lobby was empty, and even with soft-soled shoes, Kell's footfalls echoed. No sign of security. From his visits to Tex-La, Nik had told him Benedict's offices took up most of the third floor, so Kell found a stairwell and climbed. No point in having an elevator bell announce his arrival. The building's oppressive silence was eerie.

On the third-floor landing, Kell paused and regrouped, letting his mind flip through the mantra of his training. Breathing regulated. Muscles ready to move. Thoughts focused and sharp. Hands loose, fingers relaxed.

He grasped the metal knob and pulled open the door into a narrow hallway. Its lush carpet, a greenish-blue print in a subtle pattern of swirls and curlicues, sank under the weight of his steps, absorbing the sounds. A central lobby area sat empty, but as soon as he stepped in front of the reception desk, a voice boomed from down the hall to his left.

"That you, Kellison? Last door on the right."

As he crossed the length of the hallway, Kell expected one of Benedict's security staff to block his way and search him. If he forgot for one wrong instant that Benedict and any of his employees could be shifters—sharper hearing, keener sense of smell, greater physical power—he could pay for it with his life.

He paused in the doorway of the oversize corner office at the end of the hall. The windows showed a turbulent sea and, in the far distance, a looming mass of clouds. The outer bands of the storm would be here before long.

A small seating area had been placed to the left, but Kell's focus riveted on the big oak desk and the man lounging behind it, his hands clasped behind his head, a big smile on his face— and a simmering of rage behind his brown eyes. There had been no sign of any security, so either they were hiding until needed or Benedict had underestimated Kell. If so, he'd regret it. He might not be as strong as the shifter, but he could guarantee he was more stubborn.

"I meet the competition for Emory's affections at last." Benedict stood up, and Kell was glad Mori had warned him about how big the guy was. At six foot one, with a muscular frame, Kell hadn't found many guys that dwarfed him. Michael Benedict made him feel like a scrawny teenager, but since they both knew it, there was no point in getting his jockstrap in a bunch.

Benedict didn't offer to shake hands, robbing Kell of the chance to refuse him. He pointed to the chair facing his desk, an expensive-looking armchair of tufted beige leather. "Have a seat, after you rid yourself of the gun, please. I'm curious to hear about this *generous offer* of yours." He stressed the words as if they were a joke, and Kell suspected that's exactly how he'd treat the colonel's proposal.

Kell paused, recalling the colonel's admonition to be cordial, serious, and not insulting. Undersell the fuckup Benedict had made of things. Be Mr. Cooperation.

He unsnapped the Beretta holster, emptied the gun of ammo, and laid it on the table. He stuck the clip in his left pocket and mentally took a deep breath as he settled into the chair. Time to start an all-star performance.

"I think you'd agree that the events since the Zemurray bombing have unfolded in a way that'll be hard to untangle."

Benedict leaned back in his chair, steepling his fingers in front of his chin. "Maybe. Although that unfortunate tragedy did have some positive outcomes."

Kell's vision washed red, but again he took a mental step back. "Possibly. The industrial expansion plans are down the drain, so your goal of protecting the native habitat was a success. But the loss of lives was a big price to pay." *A damn big price.*

At the mention of habitat, Benedict's expression changed from cheerful arrogance to wariness. "I suppose."

Interesting. Benedict seemed genuinely surprised they understood the environmental benefits. Did he really think Mori would keep his secrets after what he'd done to her?

Kell continued. "Another upside for you—you found a way to potentially control environmental policy from the governor's office, although the thing with Felderman and the jaguarundis didn't work out very well. Clever piece of work to use them to make a controllable hybrid, by the way. Kept your hands clean."

As Kell talked, Benedict slowly leaned forward, propping his elbows on the smooth, polished wood of his desk. His arrogant smile had left the building. "I have no idea what you're talking about."

"Course not. I have a tendency to ramble." Kell smiled and leaned back in his chair, mimicking Benedict's earlier posture. "Then there was the whole screwup in New Orleans. The bombs have been cleared, by the way, and we're a step away from identifying the Tex-La employees who planted them." Or they would be as soon as Nik did his psychic vision act. Benedict said nothing, so Kell pretended to examine his cuff and kept talking. "Here's the way I see it, Mr. Benedict. More important, here's the way the people I work for see it."

Benedict had gone perfectly still, and it was fucking creepy. Not so much as a muscle twitch while several seconds ticked by. Finally, he broke the silence. "And who *do* you work for, exactly?"

"People in very high places, Mr. Benedict, and here's how they see your situation." Kell ticked off offenses on his fingers. "You have committed one act of terrorism and have plotted a second. Very serious federal crimes, by the way. You have directly or indirectly cost more than two hundred lives, including that of the governor of Texas. A capital murder charge in each case, and Texas does love its death penalty.

"You fabricated a report to Homeland Security, resulting in wasted dollars and man-hours investigating a false lead." Kell looked Benedict in the eye. "You've committed two incidents of kidnapping and torture, and a possible case could be made for engaging in human trafficking by your purchase of an infant twenty-five years ago. An exchange, by the way, for which you arrogantly signed a written contract that is currently on its way to Washington."

OK, so he might have been exaggerating. The contract was on its way to Iberia Parish, Louisiana.

Were the stakes lower, Kell might have laughed at the range of emotions that ran over Benedict's face as he talked.

From shock to outrage, back to shock, then all the way to fury. With this guy, it always ended in anger.

"I think our mutual friend Emory has been talking too much, which doesn't speak well for the future of either one of you." Benedict's hands lay on his desk, his clenched fists the size of small hams.

Kell had one more piece of info to share. "I should add that I know you're the alpha of the Dire Wolves. I know what started this whole fiasco. I know what you'd planned to do before we took Mori out of that ice-cold palace in River Oaks you call a home."

Benedict raised an eyebrow at Kell's blunt words. "That little bitch has a lot to answer for. Did she also tell you that revealing our existence to humans, especially human authorities, is a mortal crime?"

Before Kell could answer, Benedict stood up and began to pace back and forth behind the desk. Kell crossed his legs and kept his hand within easy reach of the Smith & Wesson.

Benedict didn't notice. "You're seeing only one side of this situation, Sergeant Kellison. The only thing—the only person—who has a chance of keeping our species alive for another generation is Emory Chastaine. Did she ask for that burden? Of course not. Believe me, I wish it had fallen to anyone but Gus Chastaine's spoiled little granddaughter, but the responsibility is hers nonetheless."

Kell knew he was going off script and warned himself to stay calm. But Benedict was so full of shit it should have been running from his eye sockets. "Mori is more than willing to do her part in continuing the species."

On some possessive, asshole level, the idea of Mori carrying another man's child made him want to shoot something, but he understood why she needed to do it.

"She's even offered to have *your* children, as the Dire Wolves' alpha," Kell said. "It's your refusal to compromise that's brought us to this state of fuckery. So don't blow off my offer before you've heard it."

Benedict stopped pacing and stared out the window at the roiling gray Gulf. "And what is this offer?"

"A way out. Obviously, we realize you can't be brought to trial without revealing the existence of your people. No one wants that." Kell got to the part that really ate at him. "Walk away from this obsession, keep your hands clean, and the people above me will make it disappear. You won't be tied to it, Mori and the Co-Op will be cleared, and everyone goes on with their lives."

As Kell talked, Benedict turned to look at him with naked surprise. "Who do you work for?"

"It doesn't matter." Like Kell even knew. Who had enough power to make an offer like that? Not a semi-retired Army colonel from Georgia. "The stipulation is that your comings and goings are monitored for the rest of your life, with a zero tolerance for anything remotely illegal. You'll have no contact with Mori Chastaine without her permission, although whatever arrangement you mutually agree on regarding children is up to the two of you."

"That is quite an offer." Benedict turned back to the window. "It's also the biggest bunch of bullshit I've ever heard. Do you think for one minute"—he turned back to Kell and slammed his office chair against the desk hard enough to send a Texas-shaped paperweight tumbling off the end—"that I would agree to let human bureaucrats dictate where I go and who I fuck and what business plans I make? Or that I'd let that selfish little girl dictate whether or how our entire species continues?"

Kell slipped the Smith & Wesson out of its holster as he uncrossed his legs and stood. He needed to stem Benedict's growing agitation before this got any uglier. The man was as coiled as that storm sitting two hundred miles offshore, gathering fury.

"Just think about it, Benedict." A last appeal to reason. "It's a good deal for everyone. Especially you."

Benedict rounded the edge of the desk faster than Kell would have imagined possible, but by the time his hands closed around Kell's neck, the Smith & Wesson was pressed into his gut.

The big man grinned and stepped back, throwing his hands in the air. "How much do you know about Dire Wolves, Sergeant Kellison?"

Kell aimed the gun slowly and deliberately, bracing his right wrist with his left hand. "Enough to know that even the biggest wolf's heart can't survive a close-range shot with a large-caliber weapon."

"Unfortunately, that's true." Benedict knelt and tied his shoelace, looking up as he spoke.

Kell tracked his movement with the gun, but wasn't prepared when Benedict lunged forward with a head butt to Kell's groin. He had the dizzying sensation of flying in reverse before they hit the floor. The gun clattered across the hardwood, out of reach.

Holy fuck. This was definitely not on the script.

Benedict rose off him and stepped back, motioning for Kell to get to his feet. Kell struggled upright, reaching for the combat knife in his right pocket as he stood. He'd just touched it with his fingertips when Benedict spun him around and locked a meaty arm across his throat from behind, pressing his windpipe until the room turned gray.

"Looks like our Emory forgot to mention something, the careless bitch. A human and a Dire going one-on-one in a fight?" Benedict sounded downright cheerful again as he leaned in to whisper in Kell's ear while his arm continued to squeeze. "Human's never going to win that one. Oh, and I discovered something very interesting about you in my background check, Kellison."

"Yeah, what's that?" The rasp of Kell's lungs trying to suck in air through his crushed trachea sounded deafening from inside his head. Choking out those few words hurt like hell.

"You've had a little back problem, as I understand it. I might be able to help."

The arm across his throat disappeared. Kell gulped in a few huge, desperate lungfuls of air before Benedict grabbed his shoulders and slammed him, back first, into the desk at the perfect angle.

The sharp corner of the desk corner dug into Kell's lower back with a sickening crack. Again, the room grew gray, but Kell fought it off. He had to stay conscious if he had any hope of surviving.

Benedict released Kell's shoulders, and he slid to the floor, coming to rest on his side. The pain shooting in all directions from his lower back was his friend, he kept reminding himself. The pain was the only thing keeping him conscious.

"Did that help? Maybe we should try it again." Benedict stood over Kell, looking down with arrogant mirth. "Or better still, maybe we should get Mori here. See what kind of deals *she's* offering. I bet she'd fuck me in front of you if I'd agree to let you go, don't you agree?"

While Benedict talked, Kell worked his fingers slowly to his right pocket and clenched them around the hilt of the knife.

Praying Benedict was too intent on his taunting to notice, he slid the weapon out slowly and gathered up all the energy he could muster for one final surge.

With a feral snarl worthy of a wolf, Kell lunged upward with the knife, aiming for Benedict's femoral artery. If he missed and stabbed the son of a bitch in the balls, so be it.

But the knife hit true, slicing through Benedict's trouser leg like it was butter, digging into his thigh until its hilt hit skin. The bleeding was instant and heavy.

The toe of Benedict's shoe smashed into Kell's gut, sending him sliding several feet across the floor, robbing him of air again. The room grayed. The gray deepened.

The last thing Kell witnessed before it all went black was Benedict falling and, in his place, the biggest goddamn wolf he'd ever seen.

⚡CHAPTER 28⚡

The closer she and Robin got to Galveston, the more Mori fidgeted and imagined what they might find. Kell dead and Michael unharmed. Both of them dead. Kell maimed or injured so badly he couldn't recover.

She couldn't forget what he'd told her at the hotel in Baytown about his back injury. He'd put up with the pain because he wasn't willing to risk paralysis, and she'd gotten the impression he feared being incapacitated more than being killed.

"This interstate is surreal." She was driving Nik's SUV, since Robin had said she didn't like Houston traffic. But with the cars all headed in the opposite direction, that excuse didn't quite ring true. This vehicle was big, however, and Mori suspected her petite new friend couldn't reach the gas pedal.

Besides, driving gave her something to focus on other than what might be happening in Galveston. Gator, pacing back and forth in the backseat with an occasional high-pitched whine, seemed to pick up her mood.

"Coming back's going to be a bitch." Robin pointed to the northbound lanes, which were at a standstill.

"I've been thinking about that. We can take the ferry if it's still running, skip the interstate altogether."

Robin turned sideways in her seat, eyes wide. "I love ferries. We use them a lot in New Orleans to cross the river. I didn't know Houston had any."

Mori smiled. "Not Houston, but Galveston. There's a ferry that runs back and forth between the eastern tip of the island to the Bolivar Peninsula. Then it's an easy drive from there into Louisiana." She'd taken that trip a lot, looking for the deserted stretches of narrow beach to shift and run along, or letting her wolf explore the miles of wildlife refuge near Cameron, just over the Louisiana state line.

There would be no stopping to frolic today. She had a bad feeling about what they might find, but at least she and Robin had been of one mind. It had been hard to let Kell bark out orders and make plans, knowing they had no intention of following them. But she thought one of her grandfather's old sayings applied here: it was easier to ask for forgiveness than permission.

On that, she and Robin had agreed instantly last night. "He always says because I'm small, I can't help him, even though he knows I'm physically stronger than him," she'd said while packing food. "Jack Kellison, in case you haven't figured it out yet, is a stubborn, misogynistic oaf. Thought I'd save you some time by telling you. You'd have figured it out eventually."

Robin had whispered the entire time they loaded pantry items into bags for the trip. She'd talked strategy, asked questions about Michael, and assured Mori that they'd help Kell whether he asked for it or not. "I've gotten kinda attached to the bossy old goat, so we're going to save him from himself. That's why I'm following him to Galveston. I don't have to ask why you want to help him. It's all over your face whenever you look at him. Kind of makes me want to hurl."

Mori didn't know how to respond to that, so she just shrugged.

By the time they'd finished loading the SUV and driven out of downtown Houston, Kell had a thirty-minute head start. Thirty minutes alone with Michael was plenty of time for things to fall apart.

Because of the dearth of traffic on the southbound interstate, the drive to Galveston went quickly, according to the time on the dashboard clock. According to the tension building in Mori's gut, it had taken way too long. Finally, she reached Seawall Boulevard.

Robin craned her neck to see out the windows on Mori's side. "Man, look at those waves. I'd have trouble flying in this shit already, and the storm's still pretty far offshore."

Mori had ridden out both Rita and Ike at the Quad-D. Michael had been there, of course. Hovering. Possessive. Now, it was easy to look back and see how obsessed he'd become with her as she grew older. At the time, it was just Michael being Michael.

Nothing looked amiss at the Tex-La building. Mori drove into the back lot and spotted Michael's sedan and a shiny black pickup. "Is that Archer's truck?"

"Yep." Robin hopped out as soon as Mori pulled into the space between the vehicles, and was halfway to the back door before she climbed out.

Damn, but the little eagle was fast.

Mori said a few calming words to an agitated Gator before locking him inside the vehicle, leaving the windows open enough to get him some air, and making sure his water bowl was open and within reach. With any luck, they wouldn't be here long.

Robin waited for her at the door. "Think there's an alarm on it?"

Michael was too arrogant to think anyone might break in, and she'd bet he hadn't brought in extra security on a Saturday, either. He wouldn't consider Kell enough of a threat to warrant the expense.

"My guess would be that it's not even locked." Mori reached out and grasped the handle, pulling it open. "See? After you."

She followed Robin inside, shivering as the air-conditioning enveloped her. After the dry, hot air outside, it felt like walking into a meat locker. "Third floor," Mori said. "Elevator or stairs?"

"Better do stairs. It's quieter." They found the stairwell and started to climb. Halfway between the second and third floors, a crash sounded from somewhere above them.

"Gotta be Michael's office." Mori took the remaining stairs two at a time, with Robin close behind. "It's to the left when we get to the top."

"Don't rush in." Robin stayed her hand as Mori reached for the hallway door handle. "We have to go slow, make sure we don't stumble in and make things worse."

Slow sounded like the worst idea in the world. Mori's sense of foreboding had grown with every mile as they grew closer to Galveston. She'd written it off as paranoia and fear for Kell. But even a paranoiac was right sometimes.

Robin was the one with the military training, however, and Mori respected that. She hoped she'd get a chance to kick back at Kell's cabin and learn more about how an eagle-shifter got tied up with this quasi-military bunch of guys. Between her and that hope, however, stood whatever situation lay at the end of this floor.

"Shit." Robin looked up at her as soon as they stepped into the hallway. A strong reek of blood wafted from the other end of the corridor.

"Michael's office." Mori mouthed the words, and Robin nodded. As they crept closer to the office door, their decision not to bring weapons struck Mori as foolish. They'd agreed that since they'd both need to shift if forced to fight, their weapons could just as easily end up in the hands of Michael or one of his thugs. Still, Mori would have felt better walking in that office with something lethal.

They stopped outside the office door for a second, exchanging glances that said everything and nothing. Robin's plan had been to stick her head in, see if Kell was in trouble, and if not, try to slip out unseen. They'd drive on to Louisiana, and he'd be none the wiser. If Kell or Michael saw her, she'd improvise.

Unless Kell was in real trouble, Mori had reluctantly agreed to stay out of sight.

The door stood open, so they could see the portion of the office visible from the hallway. Michael's big desk sat empty, but the blood scent was definitely coming from this room. Mori could tell some of it was human blood—but some of it wasn't.

She nodded at Robin, who stepped forward and cautiously peered around the doorjamb into the long rectangle of the office. Then she stepped in fully, her sudden flare of agitation scraping across Mori's skin like sandpaper. Robin was ready to shift.

Mori pushed past her into the office. Her heart stopped at the sight of the enormous wolf, Michael's wolf, standing over Kell.

God, what if he was already dead? What if they were too late?

"Michael." Her hands shook, but she managed to keep her voice strong, commanding his wolf to listen. She'd never used her own wolf to hurt or to fight. That was about to change.

Slowly, Michael's wolf raised his massive head and bared his teeth. Mori had seen him in wolf form, of course, but never in the confines of an office. He was almost six feet long from nose to tail and almost waist-high on an average human. He dominated the room.

While the wolf focused on Mori, Robin circled the office behind him, trying to get a look at Kell. She nodded, and Mori breathed again. He was still alive.

She wanted to keep the wolf's focus on her. "Your fight is with me, Michael. Not with him. We'll go back to Houston and work it out."

She didn't mean a word of that nonsense, and the wolf's snarl said he knew it. The good news was she'd spotted the source of the wolf blood she'd scented. A deep wound in the right haunch bled freely. Her guess would be that, somehow, Kell had gotten a knife at just the right spot to nick an artery. Michael would have to shift back to human form to heal.

For the longest time, none of them moved. Mori feared if she did anything sudden—or anything at all—Michael's wolf would take a bite out of Kell. She had no idea how badly he was hurt, but he hadn't moved since she and Robin had arrived.

Behind the wolf, Robin had already shifted, her eagle stepping daintily out of the clothes left crumpled on the floor. But she hadn't squawked or otherwise moved. She simply watched the wolf and Kell with sharp, intelligent eyes.

Kell started the train in motion, and then it rolled downhill fast. He groaned back into consciousness and tried to roll onto his back, only to find himself trapped between the front legs of the wolf. He turned his head from side to side, paused for a second at the sight of Mori, then reached up and tried to jab his thumbs in Michael's eyes. All the while, he'd been thrusting his legs in different positions, trying to leverage himself away from the snapping teeth of Michael's wolf.

He wasn't fast enough, and there was another momentary pause as the wolf's powerful jaws clamped down on Kell's left hand, causing him to cry out. Michael's wolf had bitten, broken skin. Was it the first bite? The second?

The horrifying idea that Michael might try to turn Kell into a hybrid jolted Mori out of her trance.

She shuddered through her own shift, her released wolf finally raising her head in a howl as Robin's eagle began an awkward flying assault on Michael. A heavy, hooked claw caught in his ear and distracted him enough for Kell to claw his way across the hardwood and out of snapping distance.

Good, that cleared the path for Mori.

She crept closer, her wolf tracking Robin's movements. She couldn't attack until Robin was clear. But Michael caught the eagle first, his jaws snapping down on her wing and slinging her back and forth like the world's biggest dog with the world's oddest chew toy. Finally, he slung her hard to the right and released her with enough force to send her through one of the big windows in a shattering of glass, followed by silence.

Mori was only marginally aware of the hot air rushing in through the broken glass, or the sudden tang of sea air, or what might have become of Robin. All her wolf saw was an injured dominant that needed killing. She leaped without hesitation, knocking Michael to his side and following him down. Her teeth closed over his throat with a satisfying snap, his pulse thudding against her lips. She bit down enough to break skin and shook her muzzle, dragging his head back and forth.

Dire ritual dictated that when a new dominant attempted to wrest control from the alpha, there always came this moment. It was the old alpha's one chance to relinquish control without fighting to the death. All Michael's wolf had to do was relax his muscles and give one short whine.

Mori waited, feeling his pulse race against her tongue. But instead of relaxing his muscles, he tightened them. He wanted to fight it out? Then fight they would.

They exploded in a tangle of limbs and teeth and fur. She had no idea what she was biting—only that if it wasn't attached to her, it was fair game. They rolled into the edge of the desk, and Michael's wolf took advantage of her cracking her skull against the wood to back away and regroup.

Not happening.

She charged again, drawing blood from a bite to his neck. Pain shot through her left shoulder as he made heavy contact. The injured haunch was her target, and they rolled back and forth across the floor, knocking furniture aside and ignoring the glass from the broken window. Always, she tried to twist herself into biting range of the injured haunch.

"Mori, hold him still so I can get off a shot!"

The noise came to her, but the bloodlust was greater. The weakness lay in the bloody hind limb. She had to reach it, had to tear it open.

"Mori! Hold him still!"

The noise filtered through again; only, this time, she recognized it. Kell's voice. Kell wanted to kill the dominant, but that was her job. He was hers.

She pivoted again, at last finding what she sought. Her teeth sank into the ragged, bleeding wound, and her ears filled with the howl of the alpha before the world exploded around her in five sharp pops and the sting of a bullet.

EPISODE 8

⚛CHAPTER 29⚛

Kell managed to roll himself toward the spot where his weapon had fallen and then pushed himself into a seated position against the wall. He aimed, pulled back, and aimed again, glad the wolf had mangled his left hand instead of his shooting hand. Still, he hesitated.

The two wolves had similar markings, but the male wolf was slightly larger, maybe a hand taller and broader across the shoulders. His muzzle was a silvery gray, whereas when Mori had shifted, in the brief moment he saw her, he thought her wolf's muzzle was black. But they were a constantly moving tangle of teeth and blood and fur.

He shouted for Mori to stop moving so he could get a clean shot, but she was beyond hearing. If he waited until he was totally in the clear, Benedict might kill her.

Finally, after his second shout, Mori's wolf paused briefly before resuming her attack. In that moment, Kell took his best shot. For agonizing seconds, he wasn't sure if he'd hit the right wolf—not until Benedict shifted back to his human form, unconscious, his neck and chest a bloody battlefield.

Mori's wolf watched the transformation before leaping to place her teeth over his throat. She started to bite down, but hesitated.

Shit, is she going to kill him?

Kell had a split-second moral conflict. He wanted Benedict dead. All the way into Galveston this morning, he'd sensed that one of them—either Benedict or himself—would not survive the day.

But if Mori killed him now, it wouldn't be self-defense. Not with Benedict unconscious.

"Mori, stop."

The massive wolf looked up at him, her teeth still locked on Benedict's neck. She hadn't bitten down, but she hadn't let go, either. Her eyes were a deep-goldenrod yellow, and blood covered patches of her silver-and-sable coat, tinged with touches of gold. He couldn't tell how much of the blood was hers, but figured most of that coating her black muzzle was Benedict's.

He also didn't know how much of Mori remained inside the wolf. In his head, he'd known she was a shifter, but it was an abstract sort of knowledge. Things had been moving so quickly that he'd never taken the time to think about what that truly meant, about how much of her was inside when the wolf was dominant.

But he had to figure out something fast because the wolf had shifted her gaze from him back down to Benedict, and her muzzle was wrinkling like Gator's when he cornered a lizard in the cabin. Only, the teeth of a Dire Wolf were a hell of a lot longer than those of a Catahoula hound.

Kell tried to stand—hell, even to roll to his knees—but after being still for a few minutes, the pain of movement was blinding. As the adrenaline drained, he realized that, if nothing else, he'd managed to get his back good and truly fucked this time. He cursed and settled back against the wall, closing his eyes and waiting for the pain to ease before he could try again, all the while hoping Mori wouldn't tear out Benedict's throat in the meantime.

At the sound of a high-pitched whine, he opened his eyes and found her wolf focused on him again, her head raised and away from Benedict for the first time since he'd fired his weapon. Was it his imagination, or did she look concerned? This might be his last chance to get through to her.

"Mori, listen to me. Do not kill him. Don't."

The wolf looked down again, and Kell banged the gun on the floor to get her attention.

"This is not who you are, Mori. He deserves it, but not like this. You won't be able to live with it."

She looked at him a moment longer before hanging her head with another high whine. Then she ran from the office, her paws slipping on the bloody hardwood floor for a few steps before she gained purchase and disappeared into the hallway.

Damn it.

Gritting his teeth against the spears of pain that gouged into his back with every movement, Kell half rolled, half pushed himself closer to Benedict's body until he could set a couple of fingers against his neck. A rapid thump from his carotid pulsed against Kell's fingertips. The son of a bitch was alive, which meant he'd heal. Who knew how long it would be before he regained consciousness?

Kell understood Mori's impulse. He was tempted to dig that other combat knife out of its sheath and carve out the SOB's heart or put the gun to his temple and scatter his brains across Seawall Boulevard. Who would know? Moreover, who would care?

He would. Apparently, he'd found another line he couldn't cross. Instead of contemplating Benedict's murder, he needed to find Robin. He needed to stop Mori from running away and starting this whole cycle again.

Walking. That had to be his first priority. Slipping the gun into his pocket, Kell crawled to the edge of the desk. He reached up and clutched the same corner Benedict had slammed him into, what, an hour earlier? Two hours? Time had become muddy and abstract.

His swollen left hand slid off the desk, slick with blood, unable to hang on. He suspected at least one finger had been broken in the grip of the wolf's massive jaws. He reached up with his right hand instead, grasped the beveled edge of the desk, and finally pulled himself to his knees.

So far so good. Sweat broke out on his forehead from the exertion, and a bead trickled down the side of his face. He'd fought through pain before, and he could do it again. Only, the nausea had never been this bad. The more he moved, the more stomach-churning waves washed over him.

Pressing his lips together tightly, he slid his left leg forward until his knee bent at a ninety-degree angle, then shifted his weight onto it. His thigh muscles burned in protest at having to do all the lifting, but they responded. It seemed as if the process took an hour, but eventually he managed some pathetic, hunched-over version of standing.

"Did that slobbering, four-legged fuckwad bleed all over my clothes?"

Oh, thank God. If Robin's mouth still works, she's fine.

Kell turned like an arthritic eighty-year-old, shifting his entire body around to keep his back rigid. She stood in the doorway, naked as the proverbial jaybird—or eagle—and righteously pissed, with one hand propped on her hip, the other clutched tightly against her stomach.

Kell blinked. "You OK?"

"Hello, do I *look* OK? My fucking arm is broken, thanks to this overgrown"—she stomped on Michael's bare back to get to her clothes—"wildebeest of a wolf. How Mori turned out so normal is beyond me."

She snatched up her jeans but couldn't put them on one-handed.

Oh shit. Has it come to this? "Need me to help you put on your pants?" He couldn't quite imagine how that scenario would work, but he felt the need to offer and prayed she had a better idea.

"If you come anywhere near my ass, I'll cut off your—" She spun around. "Where's Mori?"

Hell if he knew. She could have driven halfway to Houston in the time it had taken him to stand up. "See if you can find her while I try to wipe down the office. We need to get out of here before Benedict wakes up and we have to do this all over again. She ran out when I shot him."

He thought about the blood on her wolf's coat. "She might be hurt."

"I saw her shift for just a second before I got slung half-way to Mexico through a flipping window." Robin picked up a shard of glass and lobbed it at Michael's head. She stomped on his back again before heading toward the hallway with her clothes and shoes, stopping to pick up Mori's stuff. "Her wolf was beautiful."

Yeah, it was. And she was still Mori. She'd known him, and she'd listened to him.

Kell hobbled around the room, using Benedict's shirt to wipe down the surfaces of anything they'd touched. The psycho wouldn't call the police, but there was no point in taking chances. Even with most of the island evacuated, someone might have reported gunfire.

"You ready?" Robin returned a few minutes later, fully dressed, and Kell saw Mori leaning against the wall of the hallway, her gaze fixed on the floor. Smears of blood crossed one cheek and the side of her neck, but it was drying. And she hadn't run away.

Kell nodded, but a spasm hit his back when he turned to scan the room one last time and make sure nothing had been left behind. A sharp gasp escaped before he could stop it. Damn it, he didn't have time for this.

"Here." Mori edged around Robin to enter the office, grabbed his hand, and pulled his right arm around her shoulders. "Put some of your weight on me."

She could pick him up and carry him, and they both knew it. But at least she was letting him save face.

They made slow progress down the hallway, trailing behind Robin. There was no reason to be quiet now, so they took the elevator. Good thing, because Kell wasn't sure he'd make it down two flights of stairs—at least not on his feet.

Twice, Kell tried to make eye contact with Mori, but she wouldn't look at him. She stared straight ahead or at the floor. They needed to figure out their next move, but in order to do that, she needed to talk to him.

"Are you hurt?"

"I'm fine." Eyes straight ahead. No emotion.

"Are you pissed off that I asked you not to kill him?"

"No. You were right."

Kell huffed and pulled his arm away from her, wavering a few seconds while his legs decided whether they were going to hold his weight or collapse. He stayed upright. "Then fucking talk to me already." Robin had been silent on the elevator ride and was almost to the back door into the parking lot when she stopped abruptly and turned. "Listen, you two." She waited a second, her eyes blazing. "Well, are you listening?"

Kell crossed his arms over his chest, stretching his back muscles in all the wrong ways, but he'd be damned if he'd let them see it. *Damned women.* "What?"

Robin pointed a finger at Mori. "She's embarrassed because you saw her consider eating Michael's throat out like a bowl of spaghetti. She thinks you'll see her as a monster now, and for some insane reason, she cares what you think."

She shifted the finger to Kell. "And you're too damn dense to see it."

Finger back to Mori. "He doesn't think less of you. He thinks you're beautiful. He likes your wolf."

Finger back to Kell. "Tell her you like the wolf, asshole."

Kell started to protest that Robin was full of shit, but he slid his gaze to Mori and realized his team member was right—about both of them. Mori met his glance with a fraction of a smile.

He reached out and scraped a fleck of blood off her cheek. One of his bullets had fragmented, and some of the cuts looked like they'd come from shrapnel. "I do like your wolf. Benedict would have killed me if you hadn't gone after him."

She shook her head. "I wanted to kill him. If you hadn't stopped me, I would have."

"Believe me, I considered taking him out myself, right before Robin came in."

She looked up at him and must have seen the truth in his face, because her shoulders visibly relaxed.

"Hallelujah. Let's get the hell out of here." Robin threw her good arm up in the air, turned, and barreled through the door. She held it open while Mori helped Kell through.

The clouds had moved ashore while they were inside, the wind strong and steady from the south, rain spitting in fits and starts. Spotting them from the front seat of Nik's SUV, Gator began howling.

"Here's what we're going to do." Robin held out her hand. "Give me the keys to Archer's truck."

"Who made you boss?" Kell frowned at her, then chastised himself. *Damn it.* If they'd followed his orders earlier today, he'd be the one lying on the floor in the Tex-La building, only he'd be dead instead of unconscious. "OK, sorry. What's your idea?"

Robin arched a brow at him and grinned.

Insufferable eagle.

"I need to see someone who can set my arm—one of my people's healers." She looked out at the water, which was the same gray color as the deepening sky. "You guys go on to the cabin. I'll stay here and keep an eye on Benedict. He doesn't know me, so it'll be easier."

"What do you think?" Kell turned to Mori. See? He was getting better at this delegating-and-asking-for-input thing.

"Makes sense. I told Robin earlier we should take the Bolivar ferry and drive into Louisiana that way instead of going back to Houston in all that traffic." She turned to Robin. "Since you're being blunt, so will I. Can you reach the gas pedal of Archer's truck?"

Kell bit his bottom lip and looked at a tree behind Robin's head. He could imagine the outraged expression she probably wore, but if he saw it, he'd laugh. If he'd asked that question, she would have had his balls in her talons before he could take a breath, but she seemed to be ignoring Mori. He held out the keys, still avoiding her face.

"Don't worry about it." Robin grabbed the truck keys from Kell, handed the SUV keys to Mori, and walked away. "I'll call you."

"Want me to drive?" Kell asked Mori, but when he looked back at her, she was already halfway to the driver's side door. "Guess that's a no."

He grabbed his duffel from the back of Archer's truck, hobbled to the SUV, and, after a couple of false starts, managed to get in the passenger seat, ass first. "I hope the ferry's still running."

"So do I, and I hope it's running fast." Mori's voice sounded high-pitched and jittery. He looked at her, then followed her gaze to the upper floor of the Tex-La building. Silhouetted in the window of what had to be a third-floor back office, looking out at them, was Michael Benedict.

☙CHAPTER 30☙

Mori white-knuckled the SUV eastward along Seawall Boulevard. The traffic was almost nonexistent, although a few hardy, foolish souls remained on Stewart Beach, playing in the high waves, even trying to surf. Most of the restaurants and businesses had nailed plywood over their windows or were in the process of doing so.

She turned north on Ferry Road, praying to whoever might be listening that they weren't too late. The state would shut down the ferry system once the water got too rough. And she and Kell needed to move fast. Michael would come after both of them now. Before today, Kell had been an irritation, a means Michael could use to control Mori. Now, he was an enemy.

But Michael would be expecting them to ride out the storm in Houston, not ferry across Galveston Bay and drive the length of the narrow, isolated Bolivar Peninsula into Louisiana. He was already conscious, obviously, but those wounds would take a while to heal, even for a Dire of his strength. He was arrogant enough to wait, thinking they'd be cowering in fear.

"There's a ferry at the terminal, but no line of cars waiting to get on it." Kell leaned forward to get a better look through the rain-spattered windshield. He tried to hide it, but Mori saw the slight wince of pain even such a small movement gave him. They needed to get wherever they were going and let him take the strain off his back. In that sense, the hurricane might turn out to be a blessing. It should halt everything for at least a couple of days. They could mend, and they could plan.

One car, a small red sedan, was stopped in front of them at the gated entrance ramp onto the ferry, its driver talking to a Texas DOT worker wearing a yellow slicker. A second guy approached and signaled for Mori to roll down her window.

His round face was weather-beaten and reddened from being pummeled by the hard spits of rain. "We got the weather service and state DOT on the line now, seeing if it's safe to make one more crossing. Ferry captain will have to make the final call, though. Any reason you folks can't drive north to Houston and travel that way?"

Mori's mind raced through the communities she knew along the peninsula. "My grandparents are in the Gilchrist area, and I need to get them out while there's still time. It'll take too long to backtrack to Houston, and you know what happened during Ike."

Gilchrist had been utterly destroyed, that's what happened, with only a single house left standing and most of the residents who'd stayed to ride it out swept into the sea. Mori knew the community was mostly gone, but there were always a few stubborn residents who'd refuse to give up on their narrow strip of paradise.

The DOT guy's gaze scanned Mori's face, then he bent over to look in at Kell. "If you don't mind me saying so, ma'am, both of you look like you need a doctor more than you need to get to Bolivar. We're still more'n twenty-four hours out from landfall, but that wind's gonna start pushing water over the coastal road when high tide comes in, if not before."

Kell leaned over, wedging his blood-covered left hand between the seat and the center console, out of sight. "Sir, her grandparents are disabled, and we really need to get them out. Do you at least know anyone out that way who could get word to them if we can't cross? Make sure they have food and water if their house survives the storm surge?"

Mori nodded. "They haven't had phone service since Ike." She feigned a worried look and added, "Please?"

"Jiminy Christmas. OK, wait a minute." The guy got on his walkie-talkie and walked a few yards away, waving his hands in the air as he talked. Mori heard the words "grandparents" and "Gilchrist" and "Ike." Her hope swelled when he walked to the small car in front and talked to his coworker.

Mori didn't dare speak or look around at Kell. The tenser they looked, the better. And her tension level was off the charts.

Finally, the guy gave them a thumbs-up, and Mori released a breath as he approached the window again. "Captain says he'll do it, but it's going to be rough. It'll be our last run, and then we're shuttin' down till the storm blows through, so you'll have to take your grandparents out on the road north into Beaumont. You folks be careful."

Mori thanked the transportation worker and raised the SUV window, then used her left arm to wipe the water off the vehicle's interior. Nik already disliked her; letting mold set up inside his SUV wouldn't improve his opinion.

She finally looked over at Kell. "Good acting job."

He smiled. "Hey, you got it started. I wouldn't have even thought about the endangered-grandparent story. What made you think of it?"

"I've been on the peninsula a lot. There are lots of wildlife refuges and protected lands along there. I like to go over and..." She paused, not sure how to explain.

"Let your wolf run free?" Kell rested his head against the back of the seat as the gate onto the ferry opened. "Makes sense."

Mori drove the SUV onto the ferry ramp and followed a rain-soaked worker's directions, parking the car in the middle of the ferry on the opposite side from the red sedan that had been in front of them. The ferry was a broad blue-and-white ship that could park three rows of cars along either side of the tall central staircase that led up to an observation area. Today, it parked one car on each side.

Mori thought the ferry would sit at the terminal a few minutes longer and see if other vehicles arrived, but the captain wasted no time. The ship hitched like a hiccup underneath them in less than a minute, and they began moving. She glanced over to see how Kell was doing, but his eyes were closed.

It gave her a chance to look at the left hand now resting on his thigh. Most of the blood had dried, but the oval of holes in the shape of Michael's bite still oozed, and the pinkie finger was crooked. Definitely broken. Maybe the ring finger, too. Both were so swollen it was impossible to tell for sure, and underneath the blood, the skin was turning purple.

The roiling waves of the Gulf swelled toward Galveston Bay through the narrow gap between the eastern end of the island and the western point of the peninsula. The crossing usually took about twenty minutes, but Mori figured the ferry captain would be hauling ass to get to Bolivar and back while he could still navigate.

The ferry took a sickening dip to the port side, leaving the SUV leaning at a precarious angle, driver's side down. Then it righted briefly before tilting in the other direction. The SUV was heavy and solid, but it swayed with each blast of wind coming off the open water.

Kell groaned. "I'm gonna heave if this lasts too long. How far is it across?"

He did look kind of green.

"Less than three miles. Think you'd feel better up on the observation deck?"

"Are you insane? If I'm gonna drown, I'm going down strapped to this seat."

Mori laughed, but it was more bitter than amused. "Wouldn't it be ironic if we survived Michael, only to die in a ferry accident?"

He turned his head to look at her, not smiling. "We're going to get through this." His voice was soft. "When we get to Cote Blanche, we can relax for a couple of days and figure out how to handle Benedict."

Mori liked the sound of "we." Maybe he'd finally stop trying to do this by himself. "So you've finally accepted you can't take him down on your own?"

Now it was his turn to sound bitter. "Oh yeah. That point was made loud and clear today. I realized something else, too. It's not just that Benedict's strong or that he's an alpha. Oh, holy shit!" Kell grabbed the door handle as another swell hit them broadside, then tilted them in the opposite direction seconds later. A cascade of water shot over the side of the ferry and doused the window next to Kell. Mori started feeling queasy herself.

Finally, the ferry righted itself again, and Mori let out a tense breath. The Bolivar terminal was finally in sight. *Keep talking. Don't look at the water.*

"What do you mean, it's not just that he's an alpha?" In her world, alphas were like the president—or, in Michael's case, a malevolent dictator.

"I mean—fuck!" A dip to starboard, and another wall of water hit the passenger-side window next to Kell's head, hard enough to rock the SUV. He closed his eyes again and swallowed hard. "I mean that Michael's not only an alpha. He's a sociopath. You realize that, don't you?"

Mori frowned as a lightbulb went off in her head. In all the angst over Michael, all the fear, all the anger, she'd always been thinking of him as her alpha. She'd considered him only in terms of the Dire culture, not as an individual.

What if Kell were right?

"Tell me what—ow!" The ferry took a final lurch to the left just before settling into one of the three Bolivar terminal slips, cracking Mori's head against the SUV window.

Now wasn't the time to talk. She gripped the steering wheel with both hands and carefully steered the SUV off the unsteady ferry, rolling down her window at a DOT guy who approached just before they reached the gated exit.

"You folks need to get off the peninsula as soon as you can. Evacuation's mandatory now." He shouted against the gusts that buffeted the hood of his navy windbreaker.

Kell leaned over and shouted, "Just the peninsula evacuated? What about Galveston?"

"Galveston and Houston, too. Houston's recommended, not mandatory, but it's gonna get bad. Highway Eighty-Seven's still open for now, but cut north first chance you get. Water's going to start coming over the road in places. Be careful."

Mori nodded and drove on, passing quickly through the settled area near the ferry and onto the isolated stretch of highway that hugged the Gulf side of the peninsula. Angry waves crashed into the rocky seawall until the road shifted farther into the center of the narrow peninsula and took them away from the shoreline. Hurricane-proof houses had sprung back up along the highway in spots—or as hurricane-proof as technology could make them, standing high on deeply embedded stilts that would theoretically keep them high and dry when the storm surge arrived.

Mostly, though, the land was flat and desolate, with not even a tree to break the bands of wind and rain moving ashore with more intensity. Neither Mori nor Kell tried to talk. She was focused on keeping the SUV on the highway, and the few times she wrenched her gaze from the road to glance at Kell, his eyes were closed. She hoped he could sleep. Relaxing the muscles along his spine would help his back, and sleep would help him forget the injury to his hand. She had a feeling he hadn't even begun to feel the pain of that one yet, as it had been masked by adrenaline.

At Johnson Bayou, the houses visible from the highway became more numerous, but most looked empty. All had plywood covering their windows. People were either socked inside or gone. Just past Crystal Beach, the highway jogged back toward the Gulf.

Mori watched the looming clouds with worry. It was only 1:00 p.m. but looked more like dusk. When they finally reached

Gilchrist and the bridge spanning Rollover Pass, Mori saw she'd been right. A few hardy souls had rebuilt, but not many.

She drove slowly along the coastal highway, gasping each time a wave sent water rushing up the narrow shoreline and onto the road.

"Damn." Kell shifted in his seat and looked to the right. "Big one coming in. Hold on to the wheel."

This time the water came ashore with enough force that it still had energy to spend as it washed over the road. The SUV tires left the asphalt, and gritting her teeth, Mori steered into the turn as it swept them sideways.

They ended up with the SUV's nose on the left shoulder of the highway, but since they were the only fools on the road, no damage had been done. She backed the SUV into position and moved forward again, driving slowly, holding her breath at each rush of water that crossed the highway around their tires.

A half hour later, they reached the eastern end of the peninsula and turned north, running from the weather now instead of crossing through it.

"That was hairy. Nice job."

Mori glanced at Kell, who looked as relieved as she felt. "I hoped you were getting some sleep." Last night hadn't been exactly restful for either of them.

"And miss that? I just didn't want to distract you. Want me to drive a while?" She must have looked skeptical. "C'mon, let me drive. It won't make my back any worse. Might even help me relax."

She nodded and pulled off to buy gas and change drivers. Once the power got knocked out, they'd have to rely on whatever gas they had, so it made sense to top off the tank as often as was practical. Plus, they still had long stretches of isolated roads to cover before reaching I-10 and what she hoped would be a faster drive into Central Louisiana.

Once they'd settled back into the drive and were able to go faster, Mori's thoughts returned to Michael. "Tell me what you meant earlier about Michael being a sociopath. Do you mean that literally, or do you just mean he's screwed up in general?"

Kell glanced at her, then back at the road. "I meant it literally. Remember the old Charles Manson case? Jim Jones and the Kool-Aid?"

Mori laughed at the idea of Michael having revival meetings and passing out doses of poison or collecting a tribe of naive groupies. "I don't see the connection."

Kell turned up the wiper speed as another round of heavy rain set in, and remained silent for a couple of minutes, squinting as he struggled to see the edges of the highway.

"He has the classic signs you look for in a sociopathic personality," he finally said, settling back as the rain slacked and lifting his fingers off the steering wheel as he talked. "First, he can be really charming and engaging, right?"

Mori thought back to the meeting between Michael and his business associate that night at River Oaks, and then of his banter with his secretary. "When he wants to be, definitely. There's something about him that makes you want to believe him and like him."

"Right," Kell said. "Two, he's good-looking, and sociopaths are usually people that others find attractive. Third, he'll do anything to get what he wants, without hesitation. Fourth, he doesn't have regrets. He doesn't regret that bombing, or branding you, or getting Adam killed.

"I realized that when I was talking to him at the office." He snorted. "You know, before it all went to hell and back. I think he honestly believes himself to be in the right and justified in whatever he does to get what he wants."

Mori closed her eyes and settled back against the headrest. "Me, in other words."

"Sure, he wants you, but not just you for yourself. He isn't obsessed with Mori Chastaine the woman. He's obsessed with the person who can help him get what he wants—not the chance to save the Dires, but to win, to be the hero of the Dires. In his mind, anything he does to you, or anyone around you, is justified."

Mori thought about Michael's presence as she was growing up, waiting patiently for his promised mate to reach maturity, and the violent direction he'd taken when he realized she wasn't willing to meet him on his terms. If he'd only wanted to save the Dires, as an alpha should, he wouldn't have objected to her offer of artificial insemination. He'd still be fulfilling his role as alpha. He could marry his human partner. The children would be theirs to raise together, in whatever way they agreed. *That* was how a true alpha should behave. It's how Gus Chastaine would have behaved.

"I can't believe I never realized this." She turned to look at Kell. "He's not being an alpha at all. He's just...nuts."

"Exactly. All along, we've been thinking about him in the wrong way." Kell shook his head. "I knew the colonel's plan wasn't going to work. He offered to let Benedict walk away from this whole mess without criminal charges. Benedict didn't even consider accepting. A sane man—even a sane criminal— would have jumped at that offer, unless he cared more about winning than living or unless he thought he was invincible."

Invincible. That was Michael's thinking, in a nutshell. But the biggest question remained: How the hell were they going to stop him?

❧CHAPTER 31❧

The eastbound I-10 had been almost deserted from Beaumont, across western Louisiana, and into Lafayette. There, Kell left the interstate and began winding his way south again toward Jeanerette.

Then the roadblocks began. Time after time, at parish line after parish line, Kell rolled down the window and, shouting to be heard over the rain that was coming in steady squalls now less than an hour apart, lied to another member of the Louisiana State Police about why he was traveling into the storm zone instead of evacuating.

Though she didn't say it aloud, Kell knew Mori would be happier if they'd stopped at a hotel in Lafayette or New Iberia, or even Jeanerette itself. Her shoulders had settled into a tense, rigid posture, and he wasn't sure she realized that, for the past hour, she'd been holding on to the door handle as if it were a lifeline.

But his gut told him Cote Blanche was where he needed to go, logic be damned. Yeah, it was closer to the coast. It was more isolated. They had no way to get help. If the cabin got wrecked, they could be literally dead in the water.

Maybe the old cabin lured him because he knew it so well, the way he knew the road from Lafayette down to Jeanerette, his muscle memory keeping him on course in the dark as he steered through the twists and turns of narrow roads.

Maybe it was because when you got in trouble, or when you got hurt, or you weren't sure where else to go, you went to whatever place your heart considered home. And no matter how long he lived in Houston and how much he loved it, the bayou was home.

When they got to Jeanerette, he stopped long enough to buy more gas and call his cousin Trey to make sure he was still willing to grant this boneheaded favor.

He answered on the first ring, and his voice was tight. "This is a big storm, Kell, a slow-moving Cat Three. You sure you don't want to stay here with us? We're stocked up and riding it out."

Kell heard Trey's kids in the background, laughing and shrieking like all kids did in close quarters, and felt a stab of guilt at dragging his cousin away in this kind of weather. But he couldn't let go of the call of Cote Blanche. In the backseat, Gator, who'd slept through most of the drive, smelled home. He'd begun pacing and whining as soon as they hit Iberia Parish.

"I really need to get out there. Just let me borrow one of your boats. There's no point in you going down there and risking getting stuck."

"Well..." Trey hesitated, and Kell knew it had been the right offer. It made Kell feel better, too. Trey needed to be home with his family. "OK. Drive straight to the landing, and I'll have the boat ready. The quicker you get where you're going, the better."

Once out of town, Kell wound his way toward the small bayou that ran along the back of Trey's property. It fed into a byzantine network of lakes and bayous that eventually led to Cote Blanche Bay and the Gulf of Mexico. They wouldn't be going quite that far.

He skirted the road around Trey's home and drove to the boathouse and dock. A light shone through the window, and as he stopped the SUV, Kell could see movement inside.

He turned to Mori, who'd been mostly silent since they hit the state line. If he had to define her mood, he'd use the word *thoughtful*. She had seemed truly surprised at the idea that Michael Benedict might be mentally ill instead of just a bully alpha wolf. Kell was no expert, but he figured mental illness didn't play favorites with species. They all had their bullies and their evil, and even their sociopaths.

"You ready to meet the family?" He took her hand and squeezed it. "We're almost there. We'll get to the cabin, dry off, and eat some of the best nonperishable food this side of heaven."

There it was—the light he'd been missing in her eyes. And the smile.

"Well, how can I pass up that offer?" She opened the door and gasped as a gust of wind blew rain in her face. "Hey, that feels pretty good."

She stood in the rain outside the SUV, tilting her chin up to the dark sky and scrubbing off any traces of dried blood that remained. The minor shrapnel wounds to her face and neck had already healed.

At the smell of fresh air and damp earth, Gator scrambled between the seats and took an excited lick along the side of Kell's face before leaping into the rain with Mori.

Kell stifled a groan as he heaved himself out of the vehicle, carefully shifting his weight to a standing position and waiting until the spasms settled. His back muscles were tighter than a well-tuned guitar string. A good thing in a guitar, but not so good in a person who needed to steer a boat through two hours of bayou in the dark, never mind the hurricane.

He followed Mori's lead and let the rain wash off as much grime and blood as possible. There was nothing to be done about his hand or the jaguarundi scratches that still trailed down his left cheek.

Which Trey noticed right away, observant Kellison that he was.

"What got ahold of you, man?" He pulled Kell into a bear hug before introducing himself to Mori.

She kind of looked like a drowned rat, but an awfully sexy one. Trey noticed that, too, if the nod and lift of his eyebrows behind Mori's back were any indication. He might be married, but he wasn't blind.

Trey was the nickname for Dwight Eisenhower Kellison III, named after their grandfather, who'd seen fit to name all his sons after dead presidents. The family resemblance could be seen in the blue-green eyes and dark hair. Trey was skinny, though—always had been.

But he'd never been afraid of work, and he'd been busy. The larger of the two boats bumping against the slips had been stocked. Kell spotted two or three gas cans, lanterns in sealed plastic bags to keep them dry, a couple of coolers strapped shut with duct tape, a stack of blue tarps, and two large boxes wrapped in plastic that, if Kell had to guess, probably contained food.

Trey helped them unload the SUV, taking the duffel, Mori's backpack, and the supplies she and Robin had packed and stashing those on the boat as well. It was a big load.

"You got plywood at the cabin?" Trey handed Kell the keys. "Got all the tools you need?"

Kell nodded. "I'll shore everything up as soon as it's daylight." And while thank-yous were as awkward as apologies, it had to be said. "Thanks for all this. Not just for the boat, but for not asking questions."

"No problem." Trey looked at him with the Kellison eyes, and Kell tried to remember why he'd wanted to leave here so badly in the first place. "That's what we do, you know?"

Yeah, that's what they did. They were simple people who worked hard, earned an honest living, and didn't give a fuck about politics or position or being the biggest, baddest Ranger on the block. Somewhere, Kell had gotten lost.

He nodded, not trusting himself to keep from blubbering like a girl, especially when the only girl in the boathouse was watching.

"Should Gator stay here?" Mori walked up beside him and touched his arm. "I'm afraid if he gets off the boat on the trip down, we won't be able to find him again."

Gator had sniffed his way around the boathouse and had finally come to rest next to Kell. Man, he hated to leave his dog. But Mori was right. A long, dark ride through a turbulent bayou was no place for him.

"The kids'll love to have him," Trey said, pulling a leash from a hook on the wall and attaching it to Gator's collar. The Catahoula danced around like it was walk time. "The cat will have to live with it. Take care of the boat, man—and yourself."

Kell watched them leave, then turned to Mori. "You ready for another travel adventure?"

She hopped on the boat, strapped on one of the Day-Glo orange life jackets, and handed the other to him. "Let's do it."

Kell said a prayer of thanks for Trey as he navigated the *Belle Teche* out of its slip and into the bayou. The water was choppy, and the rain came in at a slant, but the boat had a sturdy portable cover on it, and he was able to steer from the back in relative dryness.

He flipped on the two spotlights attached to the front of the boat and made his way down a stretch of water he'd crossed hundreds, if not thousands, of times, beginning when he was a kid. Traveling by water was a way of life around here, and it felt natural, even in the storm.

The lights had trouble cutting through the rain that kept coming down in sheets, so he barely saw a downed log in the water in time to throttle back and ease around it. Close call.

Mori had been perched on one of the boxes of supplies, but now she was making her way to Kell. "How about I hang in the front and keep a lookout for stuff that's fallen in the water?" She had to shout for him to hear her. "I'll signal if you need to change course."

Good idea, but she was going to be drenched. "Cover up with one of the tarps."

She nodded and grabbed a folded tarp on her way to the prow, almost losing her balance as she left the flimsy sanctuary of the canvas cover.

Mori wedged herself into a stable spot at the front and tried to unfold the tarp, but a gust of wind caught it and blew it away. When she looked back at Kell with a shrug and a laugh, a surge of joy raced through him. He had no right to feel such joy. They were in a blinding rainstorm, in a dark bayou, on the run from a murderous shape-shifter, and if his new back injury didn't end his career, the broken fingers probably would.

But watching Mori's wet hair whipping around her head like the serpents of Medusa as she hung over the front of the boat, her face alive and excited to be living in the moment, he felt an inexplicable happiness. He didn't know what the future held for them—too many obstacles still remained. But she made him happy. For now, that was enough.

Between Mori's hand signals, Kell's knowledge of every bend of the bayou, and her willingness to hang over the side of the boat, using a pole to move the flotons and shifting water lilies aside, they finally rounded the bend to the cabin on Cote Blanche Bayou just before midnight—assuming Kell's watch was as waterproof as it claimed.

They arrived at the cabin during a lull in the weather. Only a light rain fell as they silently unloaded the boat and set all the supplies at the end of the short dock. Once the boat was empty, Kell took down the poles that held the canvas cover, unhooked the spotlights from the prow, and handed the lights and their battery packs to Mori before levering himself back up to the dock. He wanted to prevent those poles from becoming projectiles when the real storm arrived, and they needed the battery-powered spotlights to get settled.

"I'll secure the boat against the side of the cabin in the morning, but it'll be OK out here tonight." He gritted his teeth as he squatted to tether the boat securely to the dock, and gritted them more when he stood up. Damn, but he hoped that first aid kit had some kind of sports cream in it and that his industrial-size bottle of ibuprofen had stayed dry.

Another squall line moved in as Kell set up one light on the dock and the other on the cabin's porch. After unlocking the door, he started up a couple of fluorescent lanterns to light the interior.

In sync, they worked through the wind and rain to move the supplies into the cabin, and Kell breathed a sigh of relief when they finally shut the door behind them.

Mori had stopped just inside, dripping on the little braided rug he kept as a doormat. He tried to read her expression as she looked around, but couldn't.

"I know it isn't much." He tried to imagine it as she might see it and ended up somewhere between rustic and primitive. "We used it as a weekend fishing camp when I was a kid. I don't think it was ever meant as a place to actually live—at least not until I sold my parents' place in Jeanerette and began staying out here."

What had he been thinking? There was no electricity. The water was iffy. There were no people within thirty miles, even in good weather. And this wasn't good weather.

She grinned at him. "I think it's cool. It's just...you." She waved her hands around, looking for the right words. "It's not pretentious or trying to be something it's not. It's...Jack Kellison, if he were a cabin."

Uh-huh. Well, Jack Kellison the non-cabin was tired and wet. His back hurt like nails had been driven into it, and his left hand throbbed and was so swollen it probably weighed about twenty pounds.

He lifted it and studied the black, misshapen fingers and the puncture wounds from Benedict's teeth.

"Hey." Mori's voice was soft as she walked toward him. "Let's dry off and put on clothes that aren't soaked full of bayou rain, and then I'll take care of that. You have a first aid kit?"

"Yeah." He reached out with his functioning hand and pulled her toward him. "Thank you." Somehow, saying it to her was easier. When she stepped closer and pressed her lips to his, that strange joy crept over him again. He must have been losing his mind. That was the only explanation.

She stepped back. "I'll get changed. There's a bathroom, at least?"

Kell laughed. "Yeah, the one modern amenity." Well, not all that modern, but functional.

She grabbed her backpack from inside the door and went into the small room set off in one corner. Kell hobbled to his desk and saw his MP3 player where he'd left it the day after the Zemurray bombing, just before the orders from the colonel had arrived. It seemed like a lifetime ago.

He stuck in the earbuds and pressed the PLAY button, not remembering what he'd been listening to. Anything would beat the eerie wildcat whistle of wind moaning around the edge of the cabin. They'd be hearing enough of that in the next day or so.

Slaid Cleaves's voice erased the sound of the wind, but Kell froze as the lyrics to "Borderline" sank in with a different meaning than they'd had the last time he heard the song. The message of its chorus rang true: "When love is stronger than fear, no line is uncrossable. No sin is too great."

A chill stole across Kell's shoulders, and he turned off the music.

He'd told himself in Galveston that murder was a line he couldn't cross. He'd even taken comfort in it, congratulating himself for his moral uprightness. But he'd been wrong. Those surprising moments of joy tonight—when it had come down to just him and Mori and the storm raging around them—had drilled themselves deep into his heart.

And he knew now that if pushed hard enough, there was no line he wouldn't cross to protect that feeling. Not one.

❦ CHAPTER 32 ❦

Mori folded the towel she'd used to dry off, and hung it over the rack. She turned around, studying the tiny bathroom. A square shower stall not much bigger than a phone booth. A low toilet. An undersize pedestal sink with a mirror above it and a wire rack beside it holding guy stuff.

She smiled as she fingered the shaving cream and razor. She wasn't surprised that he used an old-fashioned stainless steel razor instead of one that ran on batteries. Kell had a simplicity about him that Mori loved. Not simple as in stupid or resistant to change—well, maybe a little resistant to change—but simple as in real. He was what he was, and you could take it or not.

He'd shown her what a good man looked like and, by comparison to Michael, what a bad man looked like. They had to make plans to deal with Michael once and for all. It probably meant killing him, and maybe Kell was right that it wasn't her nature to commit murder. Maybe he was right that she'd find it hard to live with herself if she killed her alpha. But she was the only one strong enough to do it. She'd fought against him now, wolf to wolf, and knew she could stand up to him.

Maybe he was stronger physically, but he wasn't as moti-
vated. Greed and plain old crazy didn't propel a person to act
the way love did—love for her people, who deserved better than
Michael to lead them, and love for Jack Kellison.

She stared at her reflection in the mirror, half expecting to
see a different Mori looking back at her after that self-revelation.
But she still had the same hair. Same eyes. Same annoying freckles scattered across her nose.

Kell's voice had begun a steady drone in the main room of
the cabin, so she smoothed down the T-shirt she'd pulled on
with the khaki shorts and went to join him.

He sat at his desk with his cell phone stuck to his ear, the computer open to a satellite image of Hurricane Geneva. Mori looked
over his shoulder at the projected landfall track and groaned
when she saw it was supposed to hit just east of Galveston, on the
western end of the Bolivar Peninsula. Galveston might be spared
the worst of it if it kept to that path, but if it moved into Galveston Bay, Houston would be hit hard. And God help everything
between Houston and Baton Rouge, including Cote Blanche.

Kell ended his call and plugged the charger into his laptop.
"Don't know how long we'll have cell service and Internet. The
storm's sped up and is going to make landfall early tomorrow
morning. See where it's going?"

"Yeah, it'll be bad for Houston if it goes in the bay."

"Storms always take a last-second curve to the north right
before landfall, plus maybe it'll lose some strength before it goes
ashore. They seem to do that a lot."

She sat on the edge of the bed, a double with an old patchwork
quilt and a rough oak headboard. "Were you talking to Robin?"

Kell rolled his head from side to side, and Mori could hear the
tendons pop. "Yeah. She followed Benedict back to River Oaks

and hung around for a while, but he seems to be staying put. She had to leave so the doctor could set her broken arm—wing."

Mori laughed. Poor guy was trying. "Who told you about us—about shifters and other things that are supposed to be fairy-tale monsters?"

"The colonel. He'd started a mixed-species Omega Force team in Alabama, and it seemed to be working, so he pulled in some people he thought could deal with it to form new teams. Nik and I both served a couple of tours under him, and we brought in Gadget."

"How'd he find Robin and the big cats?" She liked the kind of work they did and the way they'd all blended their skills to get her out of Michael's house. It was impressive.

Kell stood up and flexed his back, not able to keep the wince of pain from showing in his eyes. "I think they were rec- ommended by their respective alphas, or whatever it's called in their worlds. But I have to be honest. I've spent a lot of my time with them feeling threatened, which I now realize was stupid. They're good people...birds...cats...whatever."

Mori watched him move around the desk, walking to keep his back from getting stiff and freezing up. She'd seen him do the same thing back at the Co-Op. "What can I do to help your back? Massage?"

He stopped and grinned. "I don't think it would help my back, but it would do wonders for my spirit. No, what I wish I could have is a hot shower, but we need to conserve the clean water supply in case we run out of drinking water."

A strong gust of wind hit the side of the cabin, rattling the windows and giving Mori an idea.

"Why do we need to use the water supply?"

Kell frowned at her. "What?"

She walked to the cabin door and pulled it open. The warm rain was falling at a slant from the south, and with the door open, the lanterns sent out a shaft of light that illuminated the dock perfectly. She pulled her T-shirt off and turned to look at Kell.

His gaze dropped to her breasts for a few seconds, his smile growing wider, then he looked back up. "Are you thinking what I think you're thinking?"

She couldn't believe she was being this brazen, but it felt right. She unbuttoned her shorts and shimmied out of them, as well as her panties, with deliberate slowness.

"Uh..." Kell's lips parted slightly, and she recognized the "guy glaze" in his eyes, that moment when all the blood rushed south and the brain ceased proper functioning.

"See you in the shower." She laughed and ran out the door, relishing the feel of the rain as it pounded into her skin. Better than a shower massager. She turned back and saw that Kell had ditched his shirt and was fumbling with his belt, not an easy task with that mangled left hand.

Brilliant, Mori. They deserved some time to enjoy each other. Reality would come crashing back soon enough. She'd tend to his wounds, the wind would force them inside, and they'd have to talk about the nightmare named Michael. But they had right now. She turned her back to the cabin and waited for his touch, knowing he'd be moving up behind her at any moment. Imagining the water running over his long muscles and taut skin, her growing anticipation revved up her heart rate and sent her own blood supply south.

When his hands slipped around her from behind and cupped her breasts, she shivered. He slid his right hand down and pressed between her thighs with...

She looked down and laughed. "You brought soap?"

She tried to turn and face him, but he held her in place with his left arm while his right hand used a bar of Ivory—probably the one she'd seen next to the bathroom sink—in a way that wasn't the least bit pure.

He said something, but between the wind and the rain and the fingers he slid inside her, she couldn't understand the words. He reached around with his left hand and took the soap while his right hand continued to stroke her inside and his thumb kept a steady motion on her clit.

Again, she tried to turn, but he held her in place. His mouth worried at her neck, sucking hard on the sensitive skin beneath her ear and nipping it with his teeth, all while his left hand circled her nipples with the bar of soap.

Finally, she couldn't help but give herself over to it. She threw her head back and let the rain pound her face while the pressure inside her built, Kell's hands working her until the heat between her thighs exploded and she felt her knees sag. Her cries were absorbed into the storm, drowned out by the wind.

Finally, he let her turn and tugged her against him, letting her feel the hard heat of him as he pressed against her belly. She wanted to pull him down to the dock, to feel him inside her as it rained bullets on their skin, and she knew he'd do it without a second thought.

But she wasn't going to risk making his back worse. And he might have temporarily forgotten his broken fingers, but they'd remind him soon enough. She'd had her hurricane orgasm. Now it was time to play Nurse Mori.

Edging around Kell, she grabbed his right wrist and pulled him along the dock toward the cabin, the soap falling to the wood and falling between the planks. He protested, shouting what might have been "Wait," until she let go of his arm and made a dash for the cabin door.

He hobbled up a few seconds behind her and followed her inside. "Hey, what's the big idea? I thought—oh shit."

His breath hitched as she squeezed his cock, just enough to get his attention.

"You don't need to think. Just stand there." She waggled a finger at him in one of Robin's favorite moves. "Perfectly still."

She went into the bathroom and dried herself off quickly, then pulled another towel from the shelf and returned to the main room. He hadn't moved. Except, maybe his breathing had grown a little unsteady. *That* she planned to make worse.

She unfolded the towel and walked behind him, loving the way the skin under his shoulder blades rippled as she rubbed the terry cloth across his back. She gave proper attention to that fine ass and grinned at his hissed breath when she reached between his legs from behind and stroked.

"Just had to make sure nothing else needed drying down there." She ran the towel down one muscular thigh and calf, then the other.

"You might need to check again." Kell's voice sounded strained.

"Oh, don't worry, I'll be very thorough. I think you need to lie down for the rest, though." Mori walked to the bed and pulled the pillows from beneath the quilt. She'd leave the quilt in place since, despite her best efforts, they were both still half-soaked.

He followed her, his mouth finding hers as soon as she turned around. His lips were insistent and possessive, his tongue mimicking what she wished he could do with his body. But not tonight.

She pulled away, trying to catch her breath.

"I think I still need a little drying off." His lips traced her jawline, leaving only when she pressed on his chest and pushed him toward the bed.

"Then assume the position, Marine."

He smiled and settled back on the bed, not quite able to hide the relief on his face as his back muscles finally caught a break. She started by using the towel to massage his feet, only learning he was ticklish when he almost kicked her in the head.

He was still chuckling as she smoothed the towel up one calf, then the other, but the laugh turned to a satisfied groan when she reached his thighs. She finally tossed the towel aside and wriggled her shoulders between his legs, forcing his thighs apart.

And then she feasted, each lick, each stroke of her tongue, trying to convey how much she wanted him and how much pleasure she wanted to give him. It could never be enough to make the pain he'd already suffered worthwhile, but it was all she had to give him now.

As she took him into her mouth—or at least as far as she could—he began a gentle thrusting movement. She lifted her head and used her sternest tone. "That isn't a prescribed activity for the privates, Private. Keep the hips on the bed."

"You're a sadist," Kell mumbled, then gasped as she began to do the work for him. He grabbed a fistful of her hair, but didn't force her to take him deeper than she could.

He pulsed against her lips and shuddered as he came. She gave him one final lick in exchange for one final groan, then took the towel and cleaned them both up.

"C'mere." Kell's words slurred a little, and the smile he gave her when she climbed up beside him and nestled in the crook of his arm was lazy and satisfied. Their one time together, he'd been called away before they had time to just lie in each other's arms, holding and being held.

She leaned over and kissed him. "Nurse Mori has a few things left to minister to."

"Oh no." He laughed and tried to grab her as she slipped away from him. "I'm not sure I could live through more, although I'm game to try."

She slipped back into her T-shirt and panties and brought him a pair of loose jogging pants from his duffel, easing them over his feet and up his legs. It was warm in the cabin now, but it would cool down soon enough. "Hips up." When he raised his hips, she tugged the pants up and patted his belly. "You follow orders pretty well."

"Don't get used to it." She glanced up to see if she'd pushed him too far with the order bit, but those clear blue-green eyes were far from serious.

She lifted his left hand and studied the swollen fingers. She wasn't sure if it would be worse to wrap them or leave them. Finally, she decided to leave them. "Think there's any cold packs in Trey's ice chests? You need something for this swelling."

"Not yet. Come here and settle down. Let's just stay like this for a while." She wedged herself back into the cradle of his arm and rested her head on his shoulder. His heart kept up a steady, gentle rhythm beneath her hand, gradually slowing as his breath grew deeper. Finally, for the first time in at least a couple of rough days, he slept.

Mori thought about getting one of the sheets she'd seen folded on a corner shelf to cover them up, but her own muscles had grown lax and comfortable, plus the cabin was still a bit toasty.

She closed her eyes, lulled by the rain and the rhythm of Kell's breathing, occasionally jolted from a half doze by an eerie shriek of wind. Funny how that wind could sound like a human cry, or the yowl of a wildcat, or a moan worthy of a ghost in a bad B-movie.

Once, just before she drifted off, Mori even thought it sounded like the howl of a wolf.

EPISODE 9

❧ CHAPTER 33 ☙

It was technically daytime when Kell stirred, although most of the light in the cabin still came from the fluorescent lanterns they'd left on last night. He'd been dreaming of his mom. She'd been ironing one of his uniforms, crying because he was leaving again. He'd reached to comfort her but instead had clamped his hand onto the hot iron.

Only, when he awoke, the burning didn't stop.

Mori still nestled in the crook of his left arm. Kell lifted his head and tried to look over her to see his hand without waking her. But those brown eyes popped open before he'd gotten a glimpse of even one mangled finger.

She sat up so he could pull his arm back, then they both studied the hand. It looked even worse than last night. The swollen, purple fingers had taken on an angry reddish hue, and they felt as if they were covered in hot coals.

"I don't like this," Mori said, turning the hand over to study his palm. "You bring those antibiotics with you?"

"In the duffel." He hadn't thought to take one since early yesterday, before going to the disastrous meeting in Galveston.

Mori went to retrieve the pills and a bottle of water. He watched the way her hips swayed as she walked, even in rumpled khaki shorts. Her total comfort with her body and her sensuality was a serious turn-on, and he was glad to note that his pain level hadn't entirely slaughtered his libido.

She smiled. "Get your mind out of the gutter, Kellison—at least until you've taken these." She piled up the pillows so he could lean against them and then handed him the antibiotics, a glass of water, the huge ibuprofen bottle, and a protein bar. "May I present you with our finest room service gourmet breakfast? It's guaranteed to keep all those pills from eating a hole in your stomach."

Yeah, it was the same gourmet breakfast he ate most mornings.

"What about you?" Kell asked.

She held up another protein bar as she crawled back onto the bed, settling next to him. "I'm good."

"Yes, you are." He leaned into her for a kiss—soft, warm, and sweet. He ignored the tightening in his balls; they could be ready for action all they wanted, but his back and hand had other ideas. He kissed her again, with deep regret.

They ate in silence, the wind moaning and crying like a living thing, which in a way it was. The storm had a life span and a force that had to play itself out. So far, the little cabin hadn't moved. The cypress pilings it had been built on went deep and had been repeatedly reinforced over the years.

But if he felt the floor so much as vibrate beneath them, it would be time to put on the orange life jackets lying on the floor inside the door.

"You think this is the worst of it?"

Mori settled next to him, her right shoulder touching his left. He rested his mangled hand on her thigh, palm side up. Maybe the heat from her body would ease some of the pain—or at least he told himself so.

"Probably not."

If the storm had taken a last-minute curve to the north and weakened offshore, which had been his prediction (and he trusted his own forecasts more than the so-called professionals), the maelstrom raging outside was probably Geneva's leading half.

"We should have a lull if the eye goes over, then the second half will be the worst of it." Just to be safe, he reminded her where the life jackets were. "If we end up going in the water, best thing to do out here is find a cypress knee and hold on— those things are indestructible. Find a tall one, because the water levels will go way up."

Kell could tell from Mori's expression that she had more on her mind than hurricane survival. She leaned forward, resting her elbows on her bent knees, her gaze distant, her jaw tight.

The wide neck of her T-shirt had slid down in the back, and the edge of the "B" between her shoulder blades stood out, a shiny, pink new scar that looked as if it had been applied to her smooth skin with a single brushstroke. Another day and it would be healed, while Kell kept adding injury upon injury: jaguarundi scratches, broken fingers, wolf bites, and the ever-present back pain that two encounters with unfriendly shifters had worsened.

"I have to go after Michael."

He could barely hear Mori's words over the wind and rain beating on the south side of the cabin.

"We both do. This isn't your fight to fight alone." It never had been, really. Not after Benedict had ordered that first bomb to be planted.

Mori twisted to look at him. "I'm the only one who can fight him, Kell. I know you don't like to hear that, but—"

He held up a hand. "Wait. You're wrong." Well, she was right; he didn't like to hear it, but he realized it was true. "I agree. You're the only one with the physical strength to take him on."

Mori raised an eyebrow. "Who are you and what did you do with Jack Kellison?"

Yeah, he probably deserved that. "I've had to re evaluate some of my former statements in light of recent events."

The eyebrow rose farther.

Kell chuckled. "OK, after Michael beat the crap out of me without breaking a sweat and you pretty much tore his face off, I'm eating my words. Happy?"

"Yep." She leaned back again. "So you agree that, as soon as the storm blows through, I'm going back to Houston to end this, one way or another."

"Absolutely not. I said *we* will be going after Benedict, and I meant it. You have the physical strength, but I have the experience planning operations. What were you going to do—knock on his front door and bite him?"

She looked sheepish. "Well, I hadn't gotten that far, but I hope I'd be a little more subtle than that. Although…" She paused, wrinkling her brow and tilting her head in a way that sent too much blood rushing south again, forcing him to have another conversation with his balls. He jammed his left pinkie against his thigh, which took care of the problem. Hard to focus on sex when it felt like a gator was gnawing its way up his arm from fingertip to elbow.

"But what?"

Mori glanced at him with a frown. "Your voice sounds funny. What's wrong?" Nothing. He'd just put himself in agonizing pain to teach his cock a lesson. Probably not his sharpest move. "I'm fine. What were you saying?"

"I hate to admit it, too, but I think you're right. It's going to take both of us." She frowned at his left hand, which he was holding aloft in the hope that all the blood would drain to his elbow and lead to numbness.

"I mean, what you guys did in getting me out of Michael's house was amazing—all the planning and coordination that went into it." Mori shook her head. "If we put your strategic skills and my physical strength together, I really think we can beat him. For the first time, I believe it."

Her excitement was contagious, and he couldn't help but smile. Sure, he'd like to be the big bad Ranger and go charging in to neutralize the enemy and save the damsel in distress. But that wasn't even in the same zip code as reality.

"But I do need to be able to back you up, which means I need to know Benedict's weaknesses. If we can't figure a way out of this peacefully..." He trailed off, remembering his vow last night to see Benedict dead.

"You and I both know that won't happen." Mori's voice was hard and determined. "I've pretended he was a reasonable man for long enough, and look where that got us. So let's not even pretend we're going in there to negotiate with him. Do you honestly think there's any way to end this other than killing him?"

Kell thumped his head against the rough wood of the headboard he'd never quite gotten around to finishing and polishing. It went against everything he believed in to go into a mission like this, with not even an option for a peaceful resolution, but he'd already tried going that route, hadn't he?

"No, I came to the same conclusion last night." Besides, even if they went in trying to talk to Benedict, the man had already proven he'd gravitate toward violence in the end. "And we need to hit him as soon as we can get back to Houston, before he can make the next move himself."

Mori walked to the desk and picked up his cell phone, punching the power button and shaking her head. "No service. I wish we knew what was going on in Houston, but Robin probably can't get back to watching him until the storm passes. With the winds this high, no way she could fly."

She set the phone back down and started pacing at the foot of the bed. Even with a case of bedhead from sleeping with wet hair, she was distracting enough for Kell to raise his left hand in front of his face as a reminder to stay focused.

A loud thump from the front of the house stopped her, and they both looked at the door.

"Probably a tree branch," Kell said. Loose and dead tree limbs became projectiles during hurricanes. "Or Trey's boat bumping the dock. With this wind, the water has to be rough. The storm got bad earlier than I expected. I've waited too late to move it."

No further sounds followed other than wind and rain, so Mori resumed pacing.

"Dire Wolves are hard to kill but not impossible." She crossed her arms as she walked. "A close-range shot directly to the heart would usually do it, but to be sure, the heart needs to be cut out."

Kell nodded. *Gruesome, but effective.* He couldn't imagine what kind of Dire laws she was breaking by telling a human how to kill one of them, especially their alpha. "What about a head shot?"

"Only if it's within close enough range to take off the whole top of the head. Otherwise, you just end up with a brain-damaged Dire, and Michael's already crazy enough. Beheading would work, too." Mori scrubbed her fingers through her hair. "I can't believe I'm even saying this."

Another loud thump came from out front, but this one definitely sounded like Trey's boat hitting the dock. Kell had a feeling he was going to owe his cousin some serious boat repairs.

He opened his mouth to comfort Mori, to tell her they were just talking theoretically. But what could he say, really? This was information he needed, and she knew it. "What about silver bullets?"

She stopped pacing and smiled at him. "No, that's were-wolves."

He started to ask if werewolves were real, too, but decided he didn't want to know the answer. There were limits to how much weirdness a man could accept in any given year—or life-time.

"Most shifters do have something they react violently to, though," Mori said, coming back to sit on the bed. "Ours is mercury, which is why, back in my grandparents' day, Dires couldn't get their cavities filled. There were lots of toothless old wolves. These days, we can't eat wild-caught fish or seafood, especially tuna."

Not that helpful. "Great, you can hold Benedict down while I pour canned tuna down his throat."

Kell didn't know what kind of connections the colonel had, but he could probably get his hands on mercury without too much trouble. Except, then Kell would have to tell him what he planned to do with it. The colonel probably wasn't ready to sanction murder; however much he and Mori wanted to think of their plans in terms of the greater good, what they were plotting was plain old homicide.

Which is why he didn't want Nik and Robin and Archer in on it. It was one thing to flush his own career, but another to let them flush theirs out of loyalty to him. And they'd do it, every one of them.

"Tomorrow, then, or maybe even tonight, we can—"

Mori hesitated at another noise from outside. It was more of a crash than a thud, although Kell couldn't think of anything he'd left on the porch that would make such a sound.

"I'm going to see if I can tell what's going on with Trey's boat." Kell got up and walked to the door, gritting his teeth as pain shot through his right hip and the back of his leg. As long as he was lying relatively still, he'd been able to ignore it.

Mori sat on the edge of the bed. "If you decide to go out on the dock, let me tie a line around you so you don't get blown into the bayou without a way for me to pull you back."

Kell looked over his shoulder at her and laughed. "I wouldn't have thought of it, but it's a good idea. You can reel me in like a fish if I go flying off the dock."

He opened the front door, taking an instinctive step back as the slashing rain hit his face and chest. At least the combat pants were water-repellent.

"Can you see anything?" Mori walked up behind him and peered over his shoulder. "The boat looks OK."

It did, but the water level had gone up at least a foot. If it rose too far before the storm's eye passed over, they'd have water in the house by the time the second swell of the storm surge moved inland.

There was no point in worrying about that yet, but they'd need to get perishables off the floor.

"Might as well wait an—"

Kell froze as he turned back, seeing the outside of the door for the first time.

"What's wrong?" Mori walked around him and gasped.

The bar of soap they'd dropped on the dock last night had been skewered to the door with a long, serrated knife. Kell grabbed the handle with his right hand and worked the knife out of the wood.

"It's him." Mori pulled Kell back into the room and slammed the door, looking around frantically. "How could he be here?"

Kell didn't know how, but that bar of soap told him one thing. Benedict had been watching them last night. He'd either followed them or else made a lucky guess as to where they were headed and found a boat more easily than Kell had.

"Where do you think he is now?" Mori's face had turned the color of milk.

Kell didn't have time to answer. He didn't have time to theorize that maybe Benedict had left his calling card and was waiting until the storm passed to make his next move. He didn't have to time to think how enraged Benedict would be if he'd seen them on the dock last night.

He barely had time to register the front door being kicked in, or Mori's screams, or the bear of a man barreling toward him with a bellow of rage and arms as strong as a Louisiana cypress.

❦ CHAPTER 34 ❧

Before the splintered door swung all the way inside, half of it
crashing to the floor, Michael had gone straight at Kell with
the power of a locomotive. Mori didn't wait to see whether Kell
was conscious after his head cracked into the footboard of the
bed. She focused on calling her wolf, and the wolf came with a
painful, violent shudder.

Her shoulder hit the desk chair as she dropped to her knees,
which were rapidly replaced by paws. Her fastest shift yet.

She raised her head, watching for a split second as Michael,
screaming in rage, spittle flying from his mouth, beat Kell's
head against the wooden footboard a second time.

Before he could crush Kell's skull, Mori gathered the
power in her wolf's back legs and launched, landing on
Michael's back. She dug into the nape of his neck with her
teeth, biting hard, shaking her head. She tasted blood, and
she wanted more.

But not yet. She leaped to the side when Michael reacted as
she'd expected, releasing Kell and grabbing for her.

When he caught only empty air, he too shifted—but not as fast as she had. They stared at each other, wolf to wolf. She waited for him to come after her, but instead, he backed up. What was he doing? Mori's wolf didn't react fast enough when Michael spun and sank his teeth into Kell's calf. Kell was unconscious, so he couldn't fight back. And that was the second bite.

There couldn't be a third, or Kell would be a hybrid if he survived, compelled to do whatever Michael dictated. Mori couldn't let that happen.

She threw the full weight of her wolf into a shoulder tackle, and they tumbled away from Kell, crashing into the desk. One of the fluorescent lanterns fell on Michael's head, and he responded with a snarl, his gaze again coming to rest on the unconscious man.

Mori had to draw him away from the cabin. Kell hadn't even been willing to have back surgery because it carried the risk that he'd lose control over part of his life. He'd rather die than become Michael's property and become no more than a puppet. She had to protect him, and she had to win.

With a soft growl, she backed toward the door, willing him to follow her. He looked at her, over his bleeding shoulder at Kell, then back at her again. Slowly, with a heavy thud of paws, Michael followed her.

The rain fell in hard, heavy drops, and the wind blew it in sheets. Visibility was all but nonexistent. The water seemed to be rising fast, which had to mean the storm had gotten to shore and was pushing in the sea ahead of it.

Wolves were powerful on land, but not on water—at least not for distances or in this kind of weather—and certainly not steering a boat. Mori needed her hands.

While Michael's wolf watched from the porch of the cabin, she turned and raced toward the end of the dock, leaping into the *Belle Teche*. She landed on a middle seat, her paws scrabbling against the wet fiberglass until she found purchase. Then she ran toward the back of the boat, willing herself to shift.

By the time she reached the motor and ripped off the cover, she had hands.

Again, Michael's reaction was slower, which told Mori she'd hurt him with her bite to the neck today—and, with any luck, he had remaining pain from the fight yesterday in Galveston. He'd lost a lot of blood from Kell's knife wound.

He shifted as he loped along the dock, but before he reached the end, she'd managed to propel the boat away from the cabin, using her hands to try and bail the standing water out of the boat's bottom.

Michael glanced back at the far side of the porch, where a second boat had been tied up, not visible from the front door. So that's how he'd gotten here. All those bumps and thuds hadn't been Trey's boat, but Michael's. How had they let him slip up on them? Follow them?

A chill stole across Mori's scalp when she took another look at the boat. She recognized the distinctive blue markings on the side—she'd seen that vessel last night in the boathouse alongside the *Belle Teche*.

The only way Michael could have found them out here was through someone who both knew they were here and knew the place well enough to give directions. Which meant Trey Kellison, who didn't seem the type to have given up that information easily. If Michael had hurt Trey or one of his family members, Kell would never forgive himself.

But first, they had to survive.

Mori steered the *Teche* farther along the bayou, forced to go slowly so she could squint through the rain that blended water and shore into one gray blur. Finally, she reached the bend that would take her out of sight of the cabin. She looked back and tamped the motor down, scanning the dock for Michael. She wasn't even sure she could see the dock anymore. The water was rising fast, and the smooth water of the bayou roiled and rolled.

The roar of a second motor finally reached her, and she strained to see, scrubbing the rain out of her eyes and putting the *Teche* back in motion. By the time she saw Michael, his boat had rounded the corner, headed straight for her.

The smaller boat was lighter and faster, and Mori hadn't had much experience in boating—not like Michael, who took his yacht on the regattas that ran from Galveston to South Padre. He was outmaneuvering her, and she wasn't sure what to do about it, except to keep going.

Michael tried to pull the small boat alongside the *Teche* and got close enough for Mori to read *Belle Bleu* on the hull before she jerked the tiller to the side and bumped the *Bleu* hard enough for Michael to lose his balance.

She sped up, weaving the *Teche* from side to side to make it harder for Michael to pull alongside again. But he obviously was tracking her movement and compensated for it. When she next cut left, the prows of the boats collided with a crack of fiberglass, crunch of glass, and roar of motors with no place left to go. Both motors died, and their sudden silence made the roar of the rain and wind seem even louder.

Mori found herself on her ass in the bottom of the boat, sitting in several inches of water. She scrambled up to see Michael climbing aboard the *Teche*.

"Time to go home, Mori!" Michael shouted with enough force for the cords to stand out in his neck, but Mori could barely hear him over the storm. Behind him, the tops of bald cypresses and water tupelos bent horizontally with the wind, and Mori had to grasp the side of the boat to stay upright.

Michael used the benches along the side of the boat to pull himself toward her, while Mori backed up as far as she could. Panic threatened to overtake her, and she shifted without meaning to, her wolf's feet underwater to the first joint. But with the lower center of gravity, she handled the wind better on all fours.

Michael laughed and shifted as well, pacing through the water toward her.

Damn it, she would not go out whimpering and waiting for him to kill her. She ran toward him, propelling herself out of the water and pushing him backward with her momentum.

Water was in her ears, her eyes, her mouth—but also fur and blood.

A massive paw caught her on the muzzle and pushed her head under the water in the bottom of the boat. Mori stilled, unable to breathe, and felt the sharp bite of Michael's teeth on her throat.

Once he had her pinned, he allowed her to lift her muzzle from the water. They were frozen in this position for what seemed like forever, although Mori knew it couldn't have been more than seconds.

The stupid, stupid man still thought he could get what he wanted. He was giving her the chance to submit, wolf to wolf, in exchange for her life. A few days ago, she would have, thinking she could at least keep Kell safe.

Now she knew Kell's only hope was for her not just to survive but to win. And sometimes, to win, the good guys had to stop playing by the rules.

She willed her muscles to relax and whined to indicate her submission. Slowly, Michael's wolf relinquished his hold on her neck. They stared at each other, rain dripping off his face onto hers, half of her head still pinned underwater.

Mori raised her head and licked the muzzle of Michael's wolf in another sign of submission and obedience—and then bit as hard as she could. She locked her jaws and held on as he tried to shake her off, unable to reach her with his own teeth.

Blood poured into her mouth, and she relished it, keeping her jaws clamped as Michael's wolf tried to roll, then shake.

Finally, he slammed himself against the side of the boat hard enough that she lost her grip and tumbled overboard, hitting the water on her back and going under.

Mori's first instinct was panic, and she used her legs to bring herself to the surface. Dires were big animals with heavy muscle, which made them poor swimmers. But while Michael had more experience with boats, Mori had been on her college swim team, her long arms and legs well suited to moving her through water.

She'd sink when she shifted, so she tried to steel herself for that and focused, but nothing happened. Her wolf's legs kept pumping, telling her survival instincts they had to keep moving.

She thought of Kell, lying on the floor of that cabin, unconscious, with the water rising so fast it could be coming into the cabin at any minute. The thought was enough to force her legs to stop struggling to keep her afloat, and she let herself go under.

The shift seemed agonizing and slow, and by the time it was done, Mori's burning lungs felt as if they would burst. She'd like to know where Michael was—and whether or not he'd shifted before she resurfaced—but she couldn't wait.

She swept her arms to the side and kicked upward, trying to come up for air as close as she could to the dark shadow of the boat visible from below.

With a gasp, she surfaced face-first, struggling even then to get a deep breath of air with the rough water and the blinding rain. The only consolation was that Michael couldn't see any better than she could in this mess.

Something grabbed her ankle, and she barely had a chance to suck in a lungful of air and rain before she went under again.

Beneath the water, the world was eerily silent. The rain pelted the surface above her with muffled beats, but the wind-driven currents remained silent. Visibility was poor, but not so poor that she couldn't see the big hand clutching her ankle.

Using the last of her energy, Mori twisted in an imitation of an alligator death roll while kicking at Michael's head with her free foot. The spin did it. He let her go, and she swam not for the shore but for open water.

Normally the water of the bayou, which came off one of many branches of the Atchafalaya River, flowed south, toward the Gulf. But with the hurricane pushing the water ashore ahead of it, the bayou—and she along with it—pushed north, away from the cabin.

She let it carry her along, keeping her focus on breathing, on staying afloat. So far, she hadn't seen Michael behind her, although he'd proven himself adept at sneaking up on her today.

To her right, a portion of the bayou branched off, and she followed the swell of water into an area of mixed water and land, the swamp grasses growing up in clumps. It looked like a dead end, but maybe it would give her a place to catch her breath and hide from Michael.

Here, unlike on the main branch of the bayou, she saw the cypress knees Kell had talked about, sticking out of the swirling, muddy water like skeletal fingers next to the huge trees they helped nourish and support.

Shoulder and thigh muscles burning from the work of keeping herself above water, Mori made her way to the most solid-looking of the knees, sheltered from the main part of the inlet and tucked a bit out of sight of the main swell of Bayou Cote Blanche.

There wasn't enough unbroken waterway to swim back there, so she pulled herself along using some of the flotons—literally "floating land" covered in grasses—Kell had shown her last night. They looked solid enough to step on, but there were no guarantees. One step in the wrong spot, and a person would sink right through and straight into the water.

Finally, Mori pulled herself to the cypress knee she'd been working toward. She wrapped her arms around it, taking comfort from the smooth, wet wood and thankful for a couple of knotty areas she'd found below to rest her feet on.

There was still no sign of Michael, and given her first chance to indulge in speculation since opening the door of the cabin and finding Michael's macabre calling card, Mori's mind went back to Kell. Would Michael give up on her and go back to the cabin? Whether or not he thought she was dead, would he try to finish turning Kell into a hybrid, just out of spite?

He would. Mori had to get back to the cabin.

A swirl of water rose over her mouth and nose, and she scrambled higher onto the cypress knee. The water had risen at least an inch in just the minute she'd been there. At some point, and soon, her wooden sanctuary would be underwater, and again, she'd have to swim for it.

Back to Kell.

❧CHAPTER 35❧

Two of the earth's biggest dust bunnies stared at Kell from beneath the bed. Or was it three bunnies? And why was a high school drum corps pounding out a dissonant rhythm in his head?

Groaning, Kell rolled onto his back and struggled to hang on to his cookies until the wave of nausea subsided. Above him, two beams spanned the ceiling of the cabin where he knew good and well there was only one. He closed his eyes. Maybe if he slept a while longer, he'd wake up from the world's most realistic dream.

Except that the vision his mind conjured up—a snarling, shouting Michael Benedict, bursting into the cabin and knocking him to kingdom come and back—was no vision. He remembered his skull cracking against the footboard of the bed, but nothing after that.

Where the hell is Mori?

Kell sat up too fast and had to grab the desk chair to keep from fainting or throwing up from the nausea spins—or both.

When the Tilt-A-Whirl sensation eased, he rolled to his knees and pulled himself onto the bed with his right hand.

Funny how his left hand didn't seem to hurt as badly now that jackhammers were going off in his skull and his back was in full spasm mode.

He'd closed his eyes and almost faded out again when the banging of the front door startled him back to awareness. That big son of a bitch had broken his grandfather's cypress door. Part of it lay in splinters on the floor, while the rest swung open and shut on worthless hinges with every gust of wind.

The rain still blew horizontally from the south, which meant either the eye of the hurricane hadn't arrived yet or he'd slept through it.

There would be time to have a concussion later, or there wouldn't. For now, Mori was out there somewhere with that sociopathic jackass, and Kell had to find her.

He stood up and congratulated himself on staying upright—at least until he staggered to the desk and upchucked the remains of his protein bar in the trash can.

From his new vantage point, leaning over with his face resting on the desk within easy puking distance of the trash, he could see the dock—or, rather, the expanse of water where the dock used to be. The storm surge hadn't brought brackish floodwater into the cabin yet, but another foot, and he'd be in a wading pool. There was no sign of Trey's boat. Had they taken it, or had it become untethered in the rising water? Could wolves swim? Of the questions he'd asked Mori, that one hadn't occurred to him. Dogs could swim, but not all of them liked it or were good at it.

No time to worry about that now. Kell took a deep breath and stood upright again, getting his legs under him before walking slowly to the door. No fast movements because his head might explode. No sudden turns because his back might give way. He'd never felt more pathetic and useless. How could he help Mori if it took his every ounce of strength just to walk across the room?

Her voice came to him, and the look on her face when they'd talked this morning about going after Benedict together. They'd agreed she was physically stronger than him, even if he were at a hundred percent, but he had the ability to think strategically and to plan.

Benedict was strong and smart—he'd give the son of a bitch that much. But he also ran on emotion, usually anger. Emotional people made bad decisions, and Kell would bet emotional Dire Wolves did as well.

He could find them if he was smart, thorough, and dispassionate. This was just another mission. The target, Michael Benedict, was on the move, with an unknown destination. His choices were limited, however, especially in this weather, and Kell knew the terrain.

Mori might be with him, and she might not. His target had to be Benedict.

First, he needed to be able to maneuver the best he could, given his injuries. Pretending they weren't there hadn't worked out so well for him. The time for being stubborn and stupid was done.

Turning slowly, he made his way to the corner of the sleeping area and moved the fluorescent lantern off the top of a trunk that served as a bedside table.

The old leather trunk was one of the few things Kell had of his grandfather's. He'd found it in the attic of his parents' house after they died, and moved it out to Cote Blanche when he put the place in Jeanerette on the market.

Pulling open the lid with his right hand, he stared at the item on top. He'd been such a fucking dickhead. He'd been given a back brace when he was sent home from his last tour, and had he ever worn it? Hell no. Mr. Macho had seen it as a sign of weakness. He was a Ranger, a man's man. He could tough it through the pain. That's what Rangers trained for— persevering through adverse conditions, never giving up.

They *hadn't* been trained to be stupid, prideful idiots. No, he'd learned that all by himself.

He fitted the brace around his waist and cinched it good and tight. The effect was immediate, with the muscles surrounding his spine no longer straining to support his upper body without help.

Next, a weapons check. Kell dug in his duffel and pulled out the lightweight black muscle shirt that went with the combat pants. They'd been made of some high-tech fabric that didn't absorb water, so they were perfect for working in these conditions.

He pulled out the rifle and looked from it to the rising water. There was no point in taking it. He made sure it was ready to fire and stashed it on the ledge above the front door. He'd know it was there if he needed it.

Kell's head felt like it had been stuffed with cotton and nails, but he forced himself to keep moving. He took the Beretta and strapped on the shoulder holster. At the apartment in Houston, he had a specially fitted holster that nestled the gun at the back of his neck, at his collar line, but wishing for it didn't accomplish anything. He'd have to keep the Beretta as dry as he could and hope like hell it fired if he needed it.

His knives had been lost in the Galveston fiasco, so Kell returned to the trunk. He seemed to remember some of his granddad's old hunting knives being stashed there.

He pulled out a box of letters and mementos he'd always meant to go through, but hadn't found the time or the right frame of mind: a few photographs, mostly of relatives he didn't recognize anymore; a big folded piece of burlap that had been used for God only knew what; an old, rusty thermometer from the 1930s, about a foot long and sporting a big red logo for Lucky Strike cigarettes; and below that, the knives.

One, a pocketknife, had a cracked handle and was so worn Benedict would be able to kill Kell before he ever got the damned thing open. The other was a jewel—long, with a serrated edge and a good grip. It had been well cared for, and even had an aroma of ancient oil. His grandfather had probably used it to skin gators back when such things were legal. Now, a thirty-day gator season was all the swampers had, and Kell thought it was plenty. Not to sound like one of Mori's tree-hugging friends, but people had almost killed off the gators, and they were as much a part of life in the bayou as the cormorants and egrets.

Kell took the burlap, wrapped it around the knife blade, and looked around for something to carry it in. He'd left his own backpack at Nik's, but Mori's sat inside the door next to the life jackets.

He opened it, took out her wallet and phone, and set them on the desk, along with an assortment of pens and a couple of small notebooks. And that damned contract promising her to Benedict—it went on the desk, too.

Before sliding the knife into the pack, he unwrapped it again and used it to cut a big square out of one of the tarps.

This, he used to wrap the Beretta's barrel and grip, leaving only the trigger exposed. Might work, might not.

He placed the knife back in the pack and looked around for anything else that might prove useful.

A pole in one corner caught his eye—he'd brought it in off Trey's boat when he removed the cover. Brilliant. If he could swim to the nearest bank without losing everything, it would be the perfect tool to use in navigating flotons, to test their solidity.

He took one last look around, mentally ticking through everything he saw and gauging its worth. A tarp would keep the rain out of his eyes, but would be cumbersome to carry and impossible to swim with. Foodstuffs were useless; he didn't plan to be out there that long. The life jacket would be helpful in the storm, but too bulky with the other stuff he needed to carry.

His gaze passed over the old Lucky Strike memento, then returned to it. He stuffed it in the bag with the knife.

Slipping his arms through the straps of the backpack, he adjusted the fit to make it snug and secured the bottom strap around his waist. He reached up and loosened the pack's flap enough to stick his right hand inside, and positioned the knife handle so he could make a quick draw if he needed to.

Taking a deep breath, Kell stepped onto the porch of Cote Blanche and squinted through the gray gloom. His watch said it was noon, but it looked more like dusk. The dark, swaying outlines of the trees along the bayou were vague shadows. Nearly unrecognizable as they were, if he hadn't known them so well, they might have been giants dancing in the storm.

The water seemed to have crested in the last few minutes, which he hoped meant the eye of the hurricane was drawing close. The dock remained passable.

A gust of wind caught the backpack and almost blew him off the porch. He was too top-heavy. Kell descended to a crouch, moving his center of gravity lower, and splashed his way to the end of the dock, ignoring the protests from his back.

He knelt at the end and looked around. Nothing within his limited field of vision looked out of place, so he scanned what he could see of the shoreline, which wasn't much. The water ran down his face in streams and hit him like a slap when he faced south, into the wind.

He couldn't see much, but he knew this bayou. The bank on the south side looked closer, but the water between the cabin and the north bank was normally more shallow and less likely to be clogged with tangled underbrush invisible from the surface. He doubted the storm surge would change that.

Plus, the north side usually had more flotons. In a boat, they were a nuisance. On foot, they would help him navigate.

Kell wedged the aluminum pole into the backpack and took a few seconds to get centered, to transport himself mentally back to his training. One of the tests to even be admitted to Ranger School was a series of water-combat survival exercises, including a distance swim wearing full combat gear, and that shit was a lot heavier than what he carried now. The exercises were the easy part, designed to weed out who would and wouldn't get into the program. Then they got to the really fun stuff. The final sixteen days of Ranger School had been spent in Florida, testing swamp-survival skills under extreme conditions and low rations.

So Kell had done this before. The hurricane added an extra twist, but he could do it.

"Rangers lead the way," he announced to the wind, then took a deep breath and jumped in feetfirst. He let himself drop to the bottom, adjusting to the pressure of the water and the weight of the wet pack before launching himself back toward the surface.

Although he hadn't thought about it when deciding which way to swim, heading for the north bank meant the wind and rain slashed at his back, helping to move him along.

He swam in steady strokes, cursing every time his swollen left hand hit the water. Splash, *shit*, splash, *shit*. When the bank was clearly within view, he pushed on for a few more strokes before lowering his feet. Normally, from this spot, the water would hit him midcalf. Now, it lapped just beneath his armpits.

Can Mori swim? He pushed the thought aside and struggled to the bank. Benedict was his target. Benedict had to be his focus.

He pulled the pole free of the backpack and used it as a walking stick, placing it on the muddy bayou bottom and pushing himself out of the water and onto the bank. The land was solid there—at least by Atchafalaya Swamp standards—running in a narrow, tree-filled ridge that, on summer days, was full of birds and the lazy rustle of Spanish moss.

Most of the moss was gone, and the trees were denuded of leaves. Probably blown halfway to Lafayette by now. A lot of limbs littered the ground, but the wind levels had dropped, and Kell no longer worried about being hit by projectiles.

The eye must have finally been moving ashore. The rain slackened and, within seconds, stopped.

Kell looked at the sky, where there was an impossible bank of clouds to his north and, moving overhead, a clear patch of blue sky so rich and clear it didn't seem real. The eyewall and eye of Geneva.

He might have an hour, maybe two, before the back half of the storm slammed them with even more force. It all depended on how big the eye was and how fast it was moving now that it was over land.

It was time to move.

Kell got to his feet and used the pole to test the land around him, making sure he didn't wander off solid ground and onto a floton. It wasn't infallible, and twice, he ended up stepping onto what he thought was solid earth and sinking waist deep. Then the pole became a lever to get himself unstuck.

He froze at the sound of a nearby splash and crouched low, peering through the grass. It was too big a splash for a fish, unless it was a gator gar or catfish, and the alligators would be chilling on the bottom of the bayou until the storm passed.

Not a fish or gator, but something bigger and nastier.

Swimming across the span of bayou toward the dock was Michael Benedict.

Target identified. Game on.

❧ CHAPTER 36 ❧

The storm surge had finally dislodged Mori from her cypress knee perch, and she'd had to swim back to the main channel of the bayou. Finally, she struggled onto solid land and scrambled beneath a massive water oak, curling herself between the roots that twisted through the shallow, landlike arteries.

She'd give a lot for clothes right now, or at least one of those electric-blue tarps sitting back in the cabin. But she rested in the shelter of the tree to catch her breath and make a plan.

For the first time in what seemed like hours, Mori thought the water levels had dropped a little—or at least weren't getting higher. The wind seemed to be dying, and the rain, still heavy, wasn't hard enough to pelt her skin. At the height of the storm, it had stung like she imagined buckshot must feel.

She had to get back to Kell, had to see if he'd regained consciousness, had to make sure the water levels hadn't flooded the cabin while he was out cold. He'd been lying facedown last time she saw him. It wouldn't take much to drown.

She had to make sure Michael wouldn't return to the cabin and finish the job he'd started by biting Kell.

The first step would be to get back within eyesight of the cabin. She looked out at the water, which had calmed considerably, and realized she could see farther than even a few minutes ago. The rain was softening.

This must be the storm's eye, then.

She could move more easily, and if she could, so could Michael.

Mori stood up and decided to shift. She could move with more stealth on land as her wolf, and she would try to stay on land until she got the cabin within view. Her senses would also be sharper. If Michael was out there, she wanted to surprise him for a change, not the other way around.

The shifts hurt more each time, and drained more energy from her. She'd done it too often, too fast, and it was taking a toll. Once the shift had been completed and her bones and muscles and tendons had reshaped themselves unhappily once more, she moved away from her shelter at the base of the tree.

The air smelled of mud, and fish popped to the surface of water at an unfamiliar depth. Dead fish littered the waters of the bayous after a storm surge flooded in—or at least Mori remembered reading that somewhere. The fish couldn't get enough oxygen with all the influx of storm water.

But the dead and dying fish would feed the gators and the birds, so it all evened out. Too bad Michael couldn't accidentally ingest a few mercury-riddled catfish. It didn't take much at all. Actually, one big, whiskered mudcat would do the job.

Mori slowly picked her way along the soggy ground, a paw occasionally sliding through what looked like a solid patch of grass-covered earth and reaching water underneath. Flotons had made her way into the inlet easier, but now that she was walking, they posed a hazard.

Another paw slipped through, and she found her front legs tangled in the mass of grass and underbrush. Her wolf wanted to run, but she forced herself to remain still, then back up the way she'd come. One front paw finally pulled free and then the other.

She had to move even slower, lowering only one foot to the ground to test her weight. If it held, then she could attempt the second foot. At this rate, she'd never get back to the cabin. Still, she pushed on. The last shift had exhausted her, and she didn't know how many she had left in her before her energy failed and she was stuck in whatever form she happened to be in at the time.

She reached the bend in the bayou that would lead her back to the cabin. Mori was about to try and shift one last time, to swim the wide expanse of water to the dock. But then she scented them.

The stronger of the two was Michael, but farther away, she could sense Kell. They were out there somewhere.

Looking around, her sharp eyes assessing any movement, she nosed along the bank. She hadn't realized before because of the dark last night and the storm this morning, but the land jutted out a bit south of the cabin and offered a shorter swim. Kell would know that.

Still, Michael's scent was strongest. It was a human scent, so he wasn't in wolf form.

His trail ended at the water's edge, within sight of the dock, although not at the land's closest point. She saw him, finally, his head bobbing above the smooth water. He reached the dock, and maybe it was her imagination, but he held on to the dock mooring for a few seconds before hefting himself up.

Maybe he was as freaking tired as she was. She knew he had more injuries, and fatigue would slow his healing. This might be her only chance.

Still, she'd scented Kell on the bank, and it had to be recent—the heavy rains would have washed away anything from before the hurricane. She'd keep an eye on the cabin but check on Kell first.

Nose to the ground, she snuffled and inched her way along the bank, careful to stay behind trees and in the taller grasses as much as possible.

She stopped to sniff an aluminum pole with Kell's scent all over it. He'd used it—and recently. A patch of burlap, too.

At the sound of a splash, she cautiously lifted her head above the line of thick grass and looked toward the cabin. Michael had gone inside, apparently, as there was no sign of him. Then movement in the water caught her eye, and she ran to the waterline.

Kell was swimming to the cabin and had almost reached the dock.

Mori's wolf opened her mouth to howl, to warn Kell. But then she snapped her jaws shut. She'd also be warning Michael. Kell's best advantage would be surprise.

She said a prayer of thanks as she lowered herself onto her side and willed her body to shift one final time, hoping the prone position would make it easier. She was thankful Kell was not only alive but strong enough to swim and not injured so badly he couldn't think. He had to have seen Michael going into the cabin, and he was going after him.

The shift happened even slower than before, and Mori knew she'd reached her absolute limit. She lay on the wet ground, her lungs sucking at the thick, moist air for oxygen, waiting for her muscles to stop screaming at the repeated abuse.

She rolled to her knees and crawled down the slight embankment toward the water. This time, she welcomed the floton when she splashed through it. The longer she could stay camouflaged, the better.

Mori made her way parallel to the bank, staying hidden while Kell hefted himself to the dock. He flexed his left hand as he crouched low and shrugged out of what looked like her backpack. He pulled a long knife from it—along with something else she couldn't make out—and crept along the dock toward the cabin.

Time to get moving. Once she was slightly behind the cabin, Mori launched herself into the water, swimming with as little splash and noise as she could.

She glided to the edge of the porch, then reached up and used her fingertips to pull herself high enough to peer over the edge. Kell's feet disappeared through the doorway. At the sound of shouts and a loud crash, she dropped back into the water and swam for the end of the dock as fast as she could, no longer worrying about stealth.

She finally reached the rope ladder and pulled herself onto the dock. The adrenaline pumping through her body like wildfire, she ran the length of the dock and reached the porch as a loud blast sounded from inside the door.

She paused outside, trying to look through the broken parts of the door to see who'd done the shooting.

"Missed the heart, you little shit." Michael's voice rasped with anger or pain—Mori couldn't tell which.

She heard two clicks, and then Kell's handgun hit the floor.

"Now you can meet me like a man." Michael came within Mori's view. His chest was coated in blood, so if the bullet had missed his heart, it might have nicked a lung.

"And there you are." His gaze landed on Mori, heavy as an anvil. "Just in time to see your lover turn into an obedient little pet. One more bite, and even a bitch like you won't touch him."

Mori pushed her way through the door, glancing at Kell. He was breathing heavily, but she didn't see any blood on him. In his right hand, he clutched the long knife he'd pulled from her backpack. She couldn't see what was in his left hand, but she doubted, given his injuries, it was any kind of weapon that required much dexterity.

"Michael, you can still end this and go back to your life, back to your fiancée." Mori circled the room until she stood facing Kell. Michael couldn't go after both of them at once, and she wanted him coming for her. Mori doubted she could shift again, but maybe he couldn't, either.

Kell was staring at her and frowning. She caught his gaze, and he tilted his head slightly toward the door. Did he really think she'd leave him here? But when she glanced toward the door, she saw something barely visible on the shelf above it. It looked like a wooden box—or the handle of the rifle she'd seen in Kell's duffel back in Houston, when he had ditched his parents' blue Terminator and set this train in motion.

The only problem was, Mori had never handled a rifle. She had, however, used a shotgun back at the ranch. When they'd go riding, it was a requirement in case of rattlesnakes.

She dipped her head in a slow nod to show him she understood, and slowly began sidestepping closer to the door. It wasn't a very tall door; Michael had had to stoop a little to come through it. She should be able to reach the rifle without standing on anything.

"Planning on running away, Mori? Leaving your little human here to his fate? Probably not a bad idea."

"Like you'd let me walk away, right?" Mori took another step toward the door. "Because even if you turn Kell hybrid, if I walk away, you lose. So maybe I will walk out on the porch, take a swim. I'm a better swimmer than you, you know? Actually, it's becoming pretty clear I'm better than you at a lot of things."

Michael's attention was riveted to her now, and his face turned an ugly shade of beet red. Kell took the opportunity, running at Michael and burying the long knife hilt deep in Michael's bloody chest. Michael struck out as Kell gritted his teeth and tried to twist the blade of the knife under the rib cage to get at Michael's black heart.

With a feral sound between a roar and a howl, Michael backhanded Kell, who hit the far wall hard enough to jar a handful of the carved wooden pieces and unframed drawings off a shelf several feet away.

Mori didn't wait to see whether Kell was OK. She raced the remaining steps to the door and pulled the rifle down, fumbling as she managed to chamber a shot and aim it.

The movement caught Michael's attention, and he turned to face her, holding his hands out to his sides. Empty hands. "You think you can kill me face-to-face, little girl? With me unarmed? Go ahead, then. I don't think you have it in you."

Mori swallowed hard, her fingers shaking as she wrapped her right index finger around the trigger. "I will kill you," she whispered. "I swear I will."

Michael laughed and turned away from her to face Kell. "She can't do it, Sergeant. Sorry. Your only hope just turned out to be what I said she was all along—a spoiled, useless little girl."

"Not so useless." Kell's voice was surprisingly calm and steady. It had to be his training kicking in, because Mori was anything but calm and steady. Still, she tracked Michael's movement within the rifle's sight. "You still need her."

"Don't go any closer to him." Even to herself, Mori sounded shrill and scared.

Michael shook his head at her. "Stop pretending to be what you aren't, Emory. Your only value is as a broodmare, so you might as well accept it. And I'll have a new employee. I think a man with military ties would be useful, don't you? One who has to do anything I say?"

He stood only a couple of feet in front of Kell now, and Mori tensed. One more move, and she had to pull the trigger. If he took another step, she might miss and hit Kell instead. Why couldn't she shoot him?

The moment seemed frozen, until one motion set off everything at once. Michael made another step, and Mori gritted her teeth and pulled the trigger. The blast was deafening, echoing around the small cabin. Kell shouted something and reached out with his left hand to press it against Michael's neck.

Michael's eyes widened, and he stepped back, looking down in confusion. Mori was confused, too. She saw a bullet lodged in the wood a few inches past Michael's head. Her shot had missed. Fingers shaking, she managed to chamber another round and aim the rifle again.

"You told him?" Michael turned to her, his face a pasty mask of shock. "You betrayed us? With him?"

Michael coughed up a clotted red mass of blood and fell heavily to his knees. With one long, shuddering breath, he collapsed. Mori waited for him to move, to reach out with some new horror, to shift—to breathe. He wasn't breathing.

"Holy fuck." Kell closed his eyes and slid down the wall, letting something clatter from his left hand onto the floor. Nothing but a rusty old piece of metal with a cigarette ad painted on it in faded red and white.

Mori looked closer, leaning down to pick it up. Not just a piece of metal, but half of an old thermometer.

"Oh my God. Mercury." Mori looked back at Michael, now just a man—a very human looking, very dead man—with the business end of a thermometer sticking out of his throat.

She couldn't quite process that it was over, but her muscles told her the truth of it. She walked to the wall and slumped to the floor next to Kell, staring at the dead king of the Dire Wolves.

"Just tell me one thing." Kell sounded bone weary, but his eyes were lively pools of blue-green fire when he shifted his head to look at her.

She hoped it wasn't about how they'd explain all this, because she didn't have a clue. "What is it?"

Kell reached out with his right hand and grasped hers. "Please tell me the new alpha of the Dires isn't a sociopath."

❧ EPILOGUE ☙

That is one scary couple of women."

Garret Foley, aka Gadget, sat on the porch of Cote Blanche early Labor Day morning. On the dock, tossing a dirty yellow tennis ball back and forth while Gator bounded between them, stood Mori and Robin, just a wolf and an eagle enjoying a game of ball with a hound dog.

Kell needed a drink.

"You don't know the half of it, man." Nik emerged from the cabin with a glass of whiskey and handed chilled beer bottles to Kell and Gadget. "And by the way, the room service ends here unless you start tipping better."

"Yeah, yeah, whatever." Kell raised the bottle in salute and took a long drink. "Happy Labor Day."

Only, it wasn't happy for all of them. Archer remained in Tennessee and didn't know when he'd return. Losing Adam had sapped his spirit, and Kell knew firsthand that mourning didn't operate on a time clock. However long it took, they'd give it to him.

Not that he'd be going on any missions himself for a while.

"When's the surgery?" Nik watched the drama unfold on the dock as Robin pushed Mori in the water, then dove after her. After a few seconds of whining and pacing, Gator jumped in as well.

"Next week. Back in Houston." He didn't know when he'd made the decision to have the spinal fusion, but he thought it was sometime between getting his head bashed against the footboard and pulling the back brace out of the trunk. The decision had come long before he got his fingers rebroken and set, before he made sure that Trey and his family were OK and that Michael had merely eavesdropped on them and stolen the boat, and before the colonel had chewed him a new asshole to go along with his previous three or four.

He turned to Nik. "Can you tell me if the surgery's going to be successful?" At the frown on Nik's face, he retreated. "Never mind. Not fair of me to ask you that."

"I'd tell you if I knew, but I'm not getting any visions on that subject."

"What about me?" Gadget balanced his chair on its back legs, finally setting aside the cell phone that seemed attached to the end of his fingers. "Can you tell when I'm going to find a woman?" He watched Mori and Robin climb out of the water, their clothes dripping. "Maybe one like that?"

Knowing those two, they'd be naked within the hour.

Kell shook his head. "Man, you aren't ready for one like that."

"And I can't see that far into the future," Nik said. "You know, because it's *so* far from happening."

"Funny." But Gadget grinned.

Kell's phone rang from inside the cabin, and Gadget levered himself out of the rocker. "I'll get it. Probably the colonel wanting to yell some more. My turn to get reamed. You two have had your time in the hot seat."

Nik watched Robin and Mori sitting at the end of the dock, their legs dangling over the side, Gator sitting between them. "You two staying together?"

Kell glanced at him but couldn't read his expression. "I figure you already know the answer to that."

"It's not going to be easy."

"I know." He didn't know, really. After the colonel had spun some magic, everything had been tied up all nice and tidy. Michael Benedict, the millionaire shipping magnate, had been living a secret life, it seemed. He had masterminded the Zemurray bombing to kill off the business competition, then mysteriously died in a freak boating accident near Lake Charles after Hurricane Geneva made landfall. Nik had arrived in time to dump the body.

The media ate it up.

The colonel made a lot of noise about protocol and unacceptable behavior, but Kell figured he was just glad to have the whole thing go away, case closed. No one was alive to contradict the story except Mori's parents, and he didn't think they'd be talking.

The new Dire alpha was a hotshot lawyer with a busy career, a human wife, and no interest in Mori other than as a possible means of extending their species, however she wanted to do it.

So his woman, his mate, his whatever-she-turned-out-to-be, would have another man's children. Kell thought he was OK with that, but he couldn't be sure until he was faced with a toddler who could bodily throw his stepdaddy through a plateglass window. Nik was probably right. Not easy at all, but worth it.

"So is that what's been eating at you since you got here?" Nik had been drinking even more than usual and talking less. At first, Kell thought it was because he didn't like being around Mori—he knew his friend blamed her for dragging him into Dire politics. It had been his choice, though, and he had no regrets. In some ways, things were better. He had finally accepted that his active duty to the Rangers was done. But he'd also learned that he could be just as valuable as part of Omega Force.

Nik shook his head. "I don't know what's wrong. I've been having dreams—bad ones. Like something's going to happen that's"—he shrugged—"catastrophic, maybe."

Kell studied his friend's profile. He looked as exhausted as the rest of them, but haunted, too. And Nik wasn't one to exaggerate. If he thought something bad was coming, it probably was.

Gadget came back out with the phone. "It's the colonel, all right. But he wants you."

Kell took the phone. "Colonel?"

The man was never much for small talk. "When's that surgery of yours?"

Mori and Robin walked down the dock toward them, clearly listening.

"Next week. Probably a month of rehab after that."

The silence on the line was ominous. "Put Dimitrou on the phone."

Kell raised his eyebrows and handed the phone to Nik, who looked a little ill. And worried. He pushed the button on the side of the phone to put it on speaker.

"What's up, Colonel?"

"We've got a job. Kellison's strictly strategy on this one, so you're leading the team. Get to DC yesterday. Kellison, get Archer Logan back on the job and wait for instructions."

The call ended as abruptly as it had begun.

"That man needs a sedative." Robin jerked her wet T-shirt over her head and shimmied out of her shorts. Kell shook his head at Gadget's audible gasp. "And I need a swim. Sounds like vacation is over."

⊰AUTHOR BIOGRAPHY⊱

Susannah Sandlin is a native of Winfield, Alabama, and has worked as a writer and editor in educational publishing in Alabama, Illinois, Texas, California, and Louisiana. She currently lives in Auburn, Alabama, with two rescue dogs named after professional wrestlers (it was a phase). She has a no-longer-secret passion for Cajun and French-Canadian music and reality TV, and is on the hunt for a long-haul ice road trucker who also saves nuisance gators. Susannah is also the author of the Penton Legacy paranormal romance series: *Redemption*, *Absolution*, and *Omega*.

Kindle *Serials*

This book was originally released in episodes as a Kindle Serial. Kindle Serials launched in 2012 as a new way to experience serialized books. Kindle Serials allow readers to enjoy the story as the author creates it, purchasing once and receiving all existing episodes immediately, followed by future episodes as they are published. To find out more about Kindle Serials and to see the current selection of Serials titles, visit www.amazon.com/kindleserials.